THE STONING

In Cobb, a small town in the Australian outback, the local schoolteacher is found stoned to death.

On the town's northern outskirts, the large new immigration detention centre is viewed by the locals with suspicion. Tensions are high: between whites and Aboriginals, between immigrants at the refugee detention centre and the townies.

Still mourning the recent death of his father, Detective Sergeant Giorgios 'George' Manolis returns to his childhood hometown to investigate. He soon realises that the place where he grew up has changed. Cobb once thrived, but is now poor and derelict. As Manolis negotiates the simmering anger of a community destroyed by alcohol and drugs, the ghosts of his past flicker to life.

PETER PAPATHANASIOU

THE STONING

Complete and Unabridged

AURORA
Leicester

First published in 2021 by
MacLehose Press
An imprint of Quercus Editions Limited

First Aurora Edition
published 2021
by arrangement with
Quercus Editions Limited
An Hachette UK company

This book is a work of fiction. Names, characters, organisations, places and events are either the product of the author's imagination or are used fictitiously. Any resemblance to actual persons, living or dead, events or particular places is entirely coincidental.

A catalogue record for this book is available from the British Library.

ISBN 978–1–78782–789–9

Published by
Ulverscroft Limited
Anstey, Leicestershire

Printed and bound in Great Britain by
TJ Books Ltd., Padstow, Cornwall

This book is printed on acid-free paper

For my children, with love and gratitude

She was being pushed now, her body folded in on itself, crammed into a shopping trolley with a wonky wheel, her face crosshatched by the hard wire frame. Shreds of her skirt hung beneath the trolley, together with hanks of her sandy-blonde hair. Sweaty and matted, they left a light trail of droplets that quickly evaporated on the warm bitumen.

With each passing metre, her body sank lower, limp, taking the shape of the metal frame. A pair of white headlights appeared at the end of the next street. In response, the trolley was stopped in the middle of the road. Then it sped up, going twice as fast, until it reached the gutter, its wheels sticking, unable to climb the high concrete. The ute revved its eight cylinders, a deep mechanical growl echoing across the night. It closed in, swerving only at the last minute before thundering away.

Once up the nearest footpath ramp, the trolley was returned to normal speed, passing Saint Matthew's and the adjoining cemetery with its faded headstones and waist-high grass. The tinderbox trees drooped along Glenmore Road, heavy with excess oil. Their glassy green leaves hung like safety matches in the hot night air, scratching precariously against each other. A pale-blue mist of eucalyptus obscured the stars above, a new moon cloaking the land in darkness.

The trolley was pushed further. Its home was normally at the northern end of town, at the Cobb Friendly Grocer. Not that it had been there in months; these

1

were free-range trolleys, available to transport beer or trash or people. Its hard plastic wheels clunked along each corrugated square in the footpath, jolting and sending a light shockwave through her body at regular intervals.

The trolley was paused again before accelerating, rattling, shaking, picking up even more speed as its swivel wheels flicked erratically, left and right, left and right. They were soon passing the ex-services club, the cenotaph and the war memorial, inscribed with the names of those who fought and died, the unassuming digger with his slouch hat and gun.

The final destination was downhill, a gentle roll to the eastern end of King Street. The oval was there, peaceful and quiet. Footy in the winter, cricket in summer. The dilapidated wooden grandstand was where teenagers conceived children and spread diseases.

The trolley was eased up on the final approach before being released, left to its own momentum as the earth fell away. It floated forwards and rotated sideways before it ran aground and tipped over at the end of the concrete footpath leading to the oval. She fell hard, landing on her face, twisting her neck, a mess of arms and legs and yellow hair. Her thin cotton skirt lifted around her waist, exposing pale thighs.

The crash startled a mob of kangaroos feeding on the grass. They had loped into town at dusk, thick tails skipping across the hot asphalt. The roos sought relief from the dry, yellow plains that surrounded the town, going in search of the slightly less yellow grass of the sportsground. Both were home to nests of brown snakes by day, drawn to the heat of a constant sun. The local base hospital never had enough antivenom.

Grabbed by her hair, tensed tight like twine, she was dragged across the grass, her skirt tearing, briefs around her knees. As if sensing something unusual was happening, the roos scattered, hopping this way and that. They were hungry, thirsty and, as a consequence, aggressive. They had overcome their fear of humans but remained feral; they lashed out at passers-by, dogs and dog walkers and drunks, boxing claws and firing kicks. But not tonight.

The sound of a second car approaching interrupted proceedings. The lack of a fast-revving engine indicated either a lost out-of-towner or a local police vehicle on routine patrol. Flashing blue lights confirmed the latter, but the knee-high grass obscured the oval and its occupants saw nothing more than a discarded shopping trolley on its side, wheels static. The car kept going, the neon blue disappearing, and the night again falling dark and silent.

Heavy footsteps were soon around her ears, hands on her hair pulling backwards, dragging her limp body further east. They were leaving the oval, heading for the copse of gum trees behind the scoreboard. Dry sheets of sharp bark clawed at her skin, leaving dark-red whiplashes across her milky white back. The next sound was of her spine crunching against one of the thick trunks as she was moved into position and fixed with a thick roll of gaffer tape around her shoulders, breasts, wrists, torso, thighs, ankles.

She was left there for some time — several minutes. Ample opportunity for her to be found had it not been such a late hour or desolate part of town. She hung there, strung like a puppet. Something began to crawl up her leg.

The wind picked up. It blew the crusty hair from her

eyes and rippled the long green curtains of leaves on the hunched willows beside the creek bed. Running parallel to the oval, the creek hadn't held moisture in years.

A darkened hand touched her face, caressed it gently. Then the blade of a long machete knife, shiny and cold, pressed against her cheek, its diamond-sharp point trailing down to her neck.

Stepping away, the silhouette disappeared into the darkness. When it reappeared it came at speed, its arm cocked back before extending and releasing.

The first stone flew through the air, caved in her forehead and smashed the frontal bone.

1

Old Ida Jones was on her way to steal her morning paper from the bundle left outside the newsagent. She carried her own penknife that she wielded with precision to cut the plastic packing strip and claim her daily prize. A sharpened cricket stump doubled as a walking stick and protection from local wildlife, human or otherwise.

She used the stump to poke the body at first, in case someone was playing an elaborate prank. The cloud of blowflies around the head suggested differently, but Ida's eyesight was failing and experience had taught her to be suspicious of everything in Cobb, always to second guess. Inert bodies lying on park benches or under trees at first light were not an uncommon sight. But those bodies moaned or snored, their brains addled with booze and drugs, and they weren't taped to a tree and caked in black blood.

Of course, Ida recognised the face, even with all those wounds, and knew the woman's identity immediately. In such a tiny flyspeck of a town, it was impossible for her not to.

Ida walked home as fast as her arthritic legs and cricket stump would allow her. She dialled Sergeant Bill Fyfe's direct number on her landline, blurted her horror, hung up, consulted her address book and kept dialling.

★   ★   ★

'Christ,' was all Fyfe said as he rolled out of bed, sleep deprivation whittled under his eyes. His wife grunted and went back to sleep.

Fyfe worked fast. When old Ida knew something, the whole town knew it, word spreading like an infection.

He dressed and rang the station as he exited by the rear flyscreen door, rusted, half off its hinges. He wasn't sure if anyone would answer. His team often wasn't there.

The cop shop phone rang out. Fyfe swore and tried a second time. Turning left into Eyre Street, he was just about to hang up and try the two-way. Mobiles had variable reception in Cobb. But then Sparrow answered.

'The hell's going on there?'

The constable coughed. 'Sorry, boss. Ol' Geoff was here again.'

'Not more bloody stolen chickens . . .'

'Yair. You know how he goes on.'

'Well, enough faffing about, son. Is anyone else there?'

'Nah. The old coot's gone now.'

'I meant us. *Police.*'

'Nah, just me.'

'Lock up, then. Meet me in five at the Crapp. Bring the gear.'

'What gear? Me boots? We kickin' the footy around?'

There was a pause.

'We got a body.'

The sports oval came into view. Fyfe parked at a drunken angle and as close to the log fencing as possible. Stepping out of the car, he moved his sunglasses onto his bald head and surveyed the scene. Aside

6

from a laughing kookaburra high in the branches, the Alfred Crapp Reserve appeared empty. Fyfe saw the overturned shopping trolley and shallow trench in the long grass leading to the oval. Careful to avoid the fresh trail, he followed it to the large gum. He had to shoo away a big mob of roos that had gathered around the tree, sniffing at the ground. They were reluctant to leave, as if protective of the body. A long Bowie knife was stabbed into the trunk about a metre off the ground, a twisted roll of tape by its base. Bloodied stones were scattered everywhere, ranging in size from tangerines to cantaloupes. A foul smell hung in the air like a presence.

Fyfe wiped his dry mouth. He approached with trepidation, fear rising in his throat like nausea. Steeling himself, he warily lifted her chin.

'Oh, Molly. Fuck.'

The scene was just as Ida had described. Those were the details she was now circulating through Cobb, one gruesome phone call at a time. Fyfe stepped back from the body, from the gobbets of flesh littering the ground. Sighing, he withdrew the tobacco tin from his breast pocket and began to chew.

Sparrow arrived, hands on hips, unlit smoke in mouth. He saw Fyfe's face, now heart-attack red. 'Jesus,' the young constable said, 'what's with all the rocks everywhere? Was she — ?'

'Hey! Didn't you hear me earlier, son? You got rocks *in your head*, son? I said no faffing about. Get on with it. We ain't got all day here.'

'Alright, alright, keep yer pants on. Did you ID the body?'

'I already know who it is.'

Sparrow unzipped his black duffel bag and began

7

removing equipment.

Fyfe took notes. 'Ambulance?' he asked.

'An hour or so.'

'An hour . . . ? Christ. Photos, fast.'

Sparrow snapped like a paparazzo while Fyfe continued to chew, spit and scribble. He regularly looked over his shoulder to scan the perimeter of the oval. His ears pricked whenever he heard a noise, but it was invariably the same cackling kookaburra, mocking his efforts from up high.

Without warning, Sparrow gagged.

Fyfe looked up from his sketch to see the young constable bent over, coughing. 'You OK?'

Sparrow spat, nodded, spat again. 'It's the sight, not the smell. Medieval shit.'

'Biblical, actually.'

'Boss, you don't reckon . . . ?'

'Look, probably. But not now. Reckon later. You finished?'

'Yair.' Sparrow closed the camera and walked away, spitting.

'Good, get the baggies.'

The constable retrieved two garbage bags and handed one to his sergeant. After snapping on bright-purple rubber gloves, they picked up all the rocks and tape. Fyfe had to wrestle the tree for the knife.

'Right, got it all?' he breathed. 'Let's get the f — '

The sound of voices cut Fyfe off. They were approaching from the north and getting louder, closer. He gestured at Sparrow to go deal with them.

Sparrow trotted off, weaving his way through the gums like his ancestors had, moving silently across the fallen bark to the space where the creek refused to run. Fyfe looked around for a place to sit; finding none, he eased himself, aching, onto the dry ground. Sucking thoughtfully on a long blade of grass, he watched a flock of mynas roam the oval, introduced pests looking for trouble, flexing their feathered muscle. Above, sulphur-crested cockatoos spiralled high on the morning's thermals with barely a flick of their wings. The sun was impossibly white now, its early yellow glow intensified until it lost all colour, the mercury rising a degree a minute.

Sparrow reappeared. 'Just a coupla teenagers.'

'Wait here.' Fyfe stood, knees cracking. 'I'll grab the tarp from my car. Cancel the ambo.'

He retrieved the big blue sheet. He'd only just rinsed it clean the previous day, using it to transport drunks found by the roadside.

Fyfe and Sparrow cut her down carefully and slid the plastic tarp under her body. They lifted it with zero effort, her slim frame about the same weight as the tarp. When she was in place in the back of Fyfe's four-wheel drive, Sparrow returned for the shopping trolley.

'See you at the station,' Fyfe said, turning his steering wheel in the direction of the hospital. 'Lock the doors. Don't do anythin' yet, ya hear? Nuthin'. Wait till I get there.'

Sparrow nodded. 'I'll inform her next of kin, though.'

'Yeah, do that. But only that.'

'OK.' Sparrow waited a beat, then added, 'There's gonna be trouble, eh . . .'

'Yeah, I know.'

Fyfe drove to Cobb Base Hospital and parked in the discreet spot reserved for drop-offs. After he rang the buzzer it was some time before the heavy double doors swung open. An orderly, an Aboriginal elder, stepped forward, tugging on his matted grey beard, pushing a gurney. He coughed into his hand and flicked a cigarette butt over Fyfe's shoulder.

Words weren't needed. Both men knew the drill. Fyfe led the orderly to his car, and together they loaded the tarp onto the gurney. The elder handed Fyfe a clipboard and pen and lit another smoke to wait for the paperwork. The sergeant's handwriting was illegible, but the orderly cared little. He tossed the clipboard onto the tarp with no regard and wheeled the gurney back inside.

Fyfe went home to shower. The water around his feet turned a murky brown. He shaved and changed into a fresh shirt. He drank strong black instant, the bitter brew burning his mouth. Persistent grinding had worn down his teeth to nubs. His wife was still snoring.

The streets were deserted as he drove to the station just after lunch. It was a calm that felt distinctly uneasy, knife edged. Sparrow was right. With word spreading and the temperature rising, trouble lay ahead.

Fyfe took to his office with the blinds drawn and air conditioner on full bore. He received a brief call on his direct line, barked into the mouthpiece and hung up. He passed the afternoon playing solitaire and drinking whisky anaesthetic. Out front, an answering machine with a dry bureaucratic voice screened all other calls. In the tearoom, Sparrow detailed the morning's grisly find to Constable Kerr, and they began comparing theories.

The afternoon slipped by without incident. Fyfe fell asleep in his weathered office chair, as per schedule. Sparrow informed the next of kin, filed a report, stored

10

the evidence in the dedicated room and rejoined Kerr in the tearoom. They chewed long black strips of emu jerky and discussed the relative merits of stun guns versus pepper spray. Both items were on the station's wish list alongside a new dartboard, riot gear, danger money and access to mental health services.

It was a second direct call to Fyfe's office at dusk that woke both the sergeant from his slumber and the station from its hibernation. He emerged from his office caked in sweat, shirt hanging loose, fly undone, and with a steely look in his eyes.

'That was the brown house,' he told his crew. 'They're reporting two security vehicles and a dumpster on fire.'

★ ★ ★

The area outside the immigration detention centre was cordoned off. The police arrived in minutes, sirens blaring, but could only watch the metal twist and burn as they stood comparing notes with the security guards. Fyfe rested his heavy frame against the bullbar of his car while the facility manager, Frank Onions, leaned against the fender.

'I reckon the bastards from town tried to light the building,' Onions said. 'They reckon someone inside is guilty.'

Fyfe wiped his mouth with a big hand. 'Yeah? How'd you reckon?'

'C'mon, Bill. Don't play dumb. Look. The bin's parked right near the wall. There's all sorts of flammable material on the other side. And those are the two nearest cars. All someone needed to do was run up and toss in a match.'

'Well, it's certainly one theory,' Fyfe exhaled.

'Bugger off. It's obvious.'

'We're cops, Frank. We don't deal in obvious.'

'Well you should. That's your problem.'

The dumpster crackled and woofed in the flames, the inside glowing like a smelter. The stench of burning plastic and rubber intensified as separate objects melted and congealed into one. The fumes hit the back of Fyfe's throat, coating and clinging and popping acid hot against his tongue.

'Thank Christ there's a northerly blowing,' Onions said.

'Religious intervention, eh,' Fyfe said. 'Good ol' God.'

Onions looked at him with cement-grey eyes. 'The fire meant we had to evacuate the entire block. They're crammed in like sardines now because someone decided it must have been a detainee.'

'Lucky for you the hopper was only half-full.'

'Lucky *for you*, you mean,' said Onions, voice thick. 'It's bushfire season.'

'It's always bushfire season 'round here.'

'You want the whole town to go up?'

Fyfe whacked the bonnet with a callused palm. 'Jesus Christ, Frank. How many times have we come out here in recent memory cos one of your detainees decided to burn down this hellhole in protest?'

'Those were different.'

'My arse they were. It's usually bins and mattresses. Then it's makeshift weapons with whatever they can get their hands on, rocks and sticks and branches. The last time we came out here, Kerr copped a bottle in the head. She had concussion, was seeing double. You forget that?'

12

Onions let out a laugh. 'Get your hand off it, Bill. This here tonight is clearly different and *clearly* an outside job. It's the townsfolk getting revenge for what they think happened today.'

Fyfe gave his poker face. 'What happened today? Dunno what you're talkin' about.'

'Please. Everyone knows.' A pause. 'You hear that?'

They listened.

'Hear what?' Fyfe asked.

'Listen. From inside.'

Another pause. 'I hear nothin',' Fyfe said.

'Exactly. Silence. We've been out here an hour now, and there hasn't been a peep from inside the centre. That's cos the detainees are all scared to death after what happened last night.'

'Why, what happened last night?' Fyfe asked. 'Nightmares, sleepwalking? More rapes by your goon guards in the women's dunnies? Or was there just more bedwetting to avoid running the gauntlet to the loos?'

Onions waved a hand in dismissal. 'Pah. That's kindergarten compared to being effectively decapitated with rocks.'

'Mate, if this 'ere fire was an outside job done by someone in the town, then what happened last night to that poor woman was a bloody inside job done by someone from the centre.'

The low rumble of a diesel engine announced the arrival of the Rural Fire Service: a single truck with two overworked volunteers from the nearest town. The firies were father and son, shared their first and last names. On this particular night their role was limited to dousing a smouldering black wreck with a low-pressure hose. Brilliant sparks and orange-yellow

13

embers floated gently overhead, coating the crowd in a glowing red dust.

Onions looked across at Fyfe, met his gaze.

'I've had enough. Expect a call from the city.'

2

The phone call woke George Manolis at dawn, on a Sunday no less. He lay with his head buried in the pillow, hearing Detective Inspector Porter describe a small town with a big problem. Manolis yawned, scratched the sleep out of his eyes and numbly said 'uh-huh' a few times, before ending the conversation with a noncommittal grunt. Reluctantly, he got out of bed.

Manolis showered, long and hot. He'd been craving a day off. That Sunday was supposed to be his first in three weeks after working a junkie-on-junkie homicide. So much for the break that Paul Bloody Porter had promised him.

Manolis shaved four days' worth of silver stubble, ran hands through his hair, now more salt than pepper. Examining his forty-year-old face in the bathroom mirror, he inspected his angular jaw, most recent wrinkles and deep-brown eyes, slightly bloodshot. His best years were behind him, but he remained ruggedly handsome. Selecting a charcoal-grey suit and crisp white shirt from his wardrobe, he stood before the wall mirror.

'There,' he said. 'Ready.'

In the kitchen, he boiled a shot of strong Greek coffee, dark and viscous like mapping ink. He sipped it thoughtfully. Smoking a cigarette, he opened his phone, examined a map of his upcoming route, viewed photos of his destination, checked the region's weather forecast. He was frustrated he couldn't access

15

more, but Porter had made it clear that some information was classified.

Manolis checked his messages, hoping for something from his wife. There was nothing. He was not at peace with their recent separation and suffering as a result. He still loved Emily deeply and missed her terribly.

'You'll be fine,' he told himself in Greek. '*Ola kala . . .*'

Manolis spoke to himself often, a carryover from childhood, from having no siblings and keeping his own company. Speaking in Greek was another remnant; it calmed him to hear his first language. But it embarrassed him when he was caught talking to himself, to have people think he was crazy.

He avoided the news, radio and TV and otherwise. It was all bad anyway, doom and gloom. Instead, sipping his coffee, smoking his smoke, he stood before the fridge door and the glossy images of his toddler son. These were the latest photos Emily had sent, and he gazed upon them as if taking in nourishment, gathering strength. He spoke to them, said all the things he could no longer say in person each day. There were no photos of his wife; it hurt too much to look at her image. Next to his son were photos of his elderly parents. He avoided conversation with them altogether; Con had recently died, which had left Manolis feeling bereft and his mother despairing.

Manolis turned away. Packing a bag with precision and efficiency, he pocketed his badge and closed his apartment door behind him with a muted click.

★ ★ ★

The roads were quiet as he left the sleeping city, the sky cloudy and overcast. Manolis drove slowly, waiting until the engine oil warmed through. Buying the restored Chrysler Valiant had been a decision of the heart, not the head: it was the same make and model that Con had once driven. The car was a connection to his past, to when Manolis was young and innocent, and petrol was leaded and affordable. The colour was almost identical too, gold-tan exterior, brown interior. It had real bumper bars, not crumple zones. It had locally sourced metal parts, not foreign-made plastic. No airbags. Emily hadn't approved of the purchase, thought it was impractical and unsuitable for a new parent. But Manolis figured that was fair since he didn't approve of her new partner, a tradesman with questionable ethics, who now put his son to bed every night.

The city limits fell behind, and the road and sky opened up ahead. Manolis felt the torque in his fingertips, humming, tiny sparks of electricity that trickled up his arms and neck to elicit the slightest smile. He planted his foot, was pressed back into his seat. This was his first opportunity to take the car for a good run beyond the central metropolis. Subjecting the Val to the tight streets, traffic and constant stopping was a cruelty, like running a thoroughbred racehorse through an equestrian event.

He stopped midmorning to refuel: eighty litres of premium unleaded for a hundred and twenty dollars, and a six-dollar cheese salad sandwich paid for with street-blackened coins. He choked on every tasteless morsel.

Back behind the wheel, he concentrated on the long empty road. The Val's eight cylinders pulled him along the outback road effortlessly, accelerating with ease. A hazard soon tested its brakes, the object appearing as a large round lump on the road, sitting across the white lines. Manolis thought it was a rock or misshapen cardboard box, but as he drew closer he saw it moving, and far too leisurely for its own good. He swerved with some urgency to avoid it before pulling up with a short screech.

The hairy-nosed wombat was about a metre in length and smelled oily, a strong combination of musk and digested grass. It was also predictably heavy but stayed calm as Manolis carried it to the roadside and checked its fur for blood or injuries.

'There you go, mate,' he said. 'Safely across.'

The stout creature let out a hearty grunt, which he took as appreciation. Manolis watched it claw the dirt with its dozer-like paws, then disappear into the scrub. He continued on his way.

As he drove further inland, he watched the signal bars on his phone disappear one by one. The trees, once lush, became empty hatstands, the earth drier and yellower before a sudden change to cattle-dog brown.

Finally, the outskirts of Cobb appeared. It was a town of several dozen streets spread over an area of six kilometres and accessible by only two roads at opposite ends of the compass. Manolis approached along the southern route with the noonday sun in his eyes. Crosses and floral wreaths littered the roadside, slowing his final approach. A big yellow sign said: *No gambling, No grog, No humbug.* Next to it, a fire-danger sign had the needle on red, in the 'extreme' region; only black remained, for 'catastrophic'.

Cobb's main street was deserted. Discarded

newspapers, plastic bags, hollowed-out cartons of booze. Manolis decelerated, scanning the street and shopfronts. He muttered to himself, voicing his disappointment. He drove past a church, then another. Most of the houses were flying Australian flags in their front yards, all at half-mast. In such a small community, Manolis imagined this was out of respect for the murder victim. He lingered outside a takeaway, the motor idling, eyeballing the grimy glass window with faded photos of enlarged hamburgers, pizzas and hot chips. He couldn't work out if the business had ceased to trade or was simply closed. He was about to engage the handbrake and investigate when a red light appeared on his dashboard. The petrol tank was nearing empty. He passed two more churches and even more mournful flags before pulling into the first servo he found.

Heat billowed from the thirsty Val's bonnet, the air shimmering before Manolis's eyes. A group of kids mosquitoed around the petrol station toilets. They were instantly curious about the stranger and his shiny machine and gave both their undivided attention. They wore sleeveless footy jumpers and basketball singlets or no shirt at all. One had a bike. They smoked cigarettes, ignoring signs that said not to.

'Nice car, mister!' Wolf-whistles added their approval.

Manolis smiled and got out of his vehicle. The heat hit him like a blast of dragon's breath. There was only one working bowser, and the cost per litre was outrageous, more expensive than he'd ever seen in the city. He filled up listening to the tick-tock of cooling metal beneath the stove-hot bonnet. Entering the shop, he eyed the empty shelves as he waited for the proprietor to appear. He called out, looked down the aisles, but after five minutes just left cash on the counter and walked out.

In his absence, Manolis's car had been modified. The Val's antenna was bent at a painful angle, the circular hood ornament absent, souvenired. He looked up to see the kids laughing and slapping each other on the back.

'Shit car, mister!'

'We made it better for you!'

'Get an Aussie car, a Commodore or Falcon, a real donk with some chrome spillin' out the front!'

Manolis wanted to hurl a stream of abuse at the disrespectful youths, tell them those cars were tin cans beside his Val. He thought to collar the punks, drag their skinny arses in for vandalism. But taking charge of the case himself would mean filling in paperwork, preparing a brief, and so on. And he hadn't been sent here to do that.

Filling his lungs, Manolis strode over to the kids. Identifying himself as a policeman did little to garner their attention. It was only when he mentioned he was a 'detective from the city' that he ended their fun.

'Now, gentlemen, I want your names and addresses,' he said calmly. He pulled a notepad from his pocket and began scratching away with a supermarket biro.

The boys answered one after the other, stony-faced, no tone.

'Thank you, gentlemen,' Manolis finally said. 'Have a nice day.'

Reefing the steering wheel clockwise, he drove on.

The wooden cop shop came into view. As Manolis pulled up, a strange rattling sound came from beneath the bonnet. That wasn't there before, he thought. Surely it wasn't the kids at the servo as well?

20

He reminded himself to get it looked at on his return to the city.

Manolis sat, watched, waited. The station was as lifeless as the town. Porter had never said anything about this. Manolis checked his phone — no reception. Approaching the station door, he bashed twice, called out. He peered through the window, obscured by metallic mesh security grilles. Seeing nothing, he crunched back to the street and gathered his thoughts under a brutal sky of boundless blue.

'What in God's name am I doing here . . . ?' he asked himself. Cobb had certainly laid out the welcome mat.

Behind him, the sound of a deadbolt lock being opened. He swung around to see a hard face scowling at him.

'You Manolis?'

'Yes. Hi.'

The face softened, a thin arm extended. 'Constable Andrew Smith, but everyone calls me Sparrow. Come in.'

Sparrow was a callow stripling who spoke with an easy, laid-back drawl. He had skin the colour of dark ale, which made a striking contrast against his powder-blue shirt. He wore pressed navy shorts, long white socks and sensible black shoes.

Manolis was surprised to find more blowflies inside the cop shop than out on the street.

'Welcome to Cobb,' Sparrow said. 'Boss told me to expect you.'

'Is that Fyfe? Where's he?'

'Up at the brown house, trying to sort out the — '

'Wait, he's *where* . . . ?'

'The brown house,' said Sparrow. 'You'll hear

21

people call it that around Cobb. It's the new immigration detention centre at the northern end of town. You're here about the homicide on Friday night, yair?'

3

Sparrow showed Manolis the tearoom with its plastic garden furniture and curling linoleum floor. A faded green sofa was against the window. Using the ratty remains of a sponge, Sparrow mopped at the base of an incontinent urn. He offered weak black coffee in a chipped mug and an assortment of dried meats made from Australian native animals. Manolis declined both. Along with flavoursome olive oil, decent coffee was an eternal struggle for him whenever he left his house or office. There, he had his own equipment and blend, thick lumps of chocolatey Greek coffee brewed black and strong in a briki pot. It was heady stuff, left unfiltered with a delicate foam on top and an undrinkable sludge at the bottom. He knew that rural Australia would be a battle, one he would surely lose.

The cops looked at each other across a collapsible table. Manolis sensed a hint of alcohol in the air. Sparrow's left eyelid drooped slightly.

'Here,' said Manolis, 'take this first.' He tore a page from his notepad.

Sparrow studied it. 'I know these kids. They're good kids.'

'I don't think good kids go around vandalising cars,' Manolis said.

Sparrow regarded him with suspicion.

'It was my car. It's outside if you want to see what they did.'

'That's OK,' Sparrow said, pocketing the note, 'I

believe you. Leave it with me, I'll take care of it.'

'Thanks. I've always found that independence is best in police cases.'

Sparrow shot him a salty smile. He leaned forward to speak.

'To be honest with you, mate, we really appreciate you comin' out, but we got the other situation under complete control. I dunno why they sent you.'

Manolis had expected resistance. He came prepared.

'They sent me because this town is out of control,' he said firmly. 'They sent me because you've got members of the public assaulting detainees in parks and trying to burn down a government facility and vandalising cars. That's why they sent me.'

Sparrow glared at him with vacant eyes. It was some time before he spoke again. 'Yair, well, fair enough,' was all he said.

Manolis let his face soften. 'Our superiors want this case solved yesterday. It's a critical time for the public perception of refugees, and they want to avoid negative press.'

'Ah, so your appointment is political. It was the same when the brown house first opened. All politics.'

The lines returned to Manolis's face. 'Forget politics. That's got nothing to do with me. I'm just here to do my job, to solve a crime.' He eyed the station, looked around. 'So where's your boss, where's Sergeant Fyfe?'

Sparrow checked his wristwatch. 'Actually, Sarge would've probably left the brown house by now.'

Manolis smelled his fingers, metallic from coins. 'Is anyone else here?'

'Nah. Bastards left me on me own.'

'Where's the investigation up to? Take me to the

crime scene. Did you know the victim? Has the coroner seen the body? Can I read their report?'

Sparrow stared straight through his city colleague, his eyes glassy and unfocused. A fly buzzed lazily against the window.

'Where's your evidence locker?' Manolis continued. 'What did you recover from the scene? Any witnesses? What about suspects? Leads? Have you spoken with the media . . . ?'

The country cop kept staring. Finally, he leaned forward in his stackable chair and helped himself to a strip of crocodile. Tore a piece. Chewed.

'Well,' he said, mouth full, 'you've asked a fair bit there, mate. And we've only just met. Tell you what, let's go to the pub.'

It wasn't a request. It was an initiation. Manolis was loath to go; there was a murderer at large. Reluctantly, he agreed.

They walked past the empty drunk tank on the way out. Manolis gestured at it, surprised.

'There's never enough divvy vans and drunk tanks,' Sparrow said. 'Most days, it'd be easier to just lock up the sober people.'

He secured the station using three different locks and strode to his patrol car, a white Ford sedan with a red bonnet, no hubcaps and the biggest roo bar Manolis had ever seen.

'We'll take my car,' Manolis said.

Sparrow's sunglasses caught the glare like popping flashbulbs. 'Suit yerself. North please, driver. We're going to the top pub.'

Situated at the top end of town, the so-called top pub was appropriately named and easily distinguishable from the bottom pub, at the southern end of town, near the Aboriginal community.

'Top pub whitefellas, bottom pub blackfellas,' was how Sparrow explained it. 'Put simply.'

He also admitted he was technically in the wrong place, but that most of his people considered him 'a sell-out anyway'.

They made small talk on the way. Sparrow explained the town's two stale pubs were the epicentres of trouble most nights of the week, which kept the cops sufficiently occupied.

'Good distraction for a murder,' he added.

He asked if Manolis had seen the Aboriginal settlement on Cobb's southern outskirts. He had. Sparrow said he grew up there. Manolis recalled a shantytown, all aluminium sheeting and milk crates, old tyres and mattresses for walls, clumps of clothes. Bodies were strewn across the land, the soles of dusty feet, people and dogs sleeping under whatever had shade. Seeing the Valiant, a group of Aboriginal kids had stopped kicking around a battered Australian Rules football between two groups, and stood eyeing it roll by.

'Yair,' Sparrow said. 'That's me mob.'

'How's your mob with the police in this town, they get along?'

'Not really,' Sparrow sighed. 'Far from it, in fact. Pigs will always be pigs, but hopefully a black cop in town changes that. That's what I'm tryin' to do.'

'You always wanted to be a policeman?'

Sparrow shrugged. 'Tried to be a tradie once, a chippie. Couldn't get past the hazing. What about you, why'd you choose to become one of the bad guys?'

Manolis rubbed his jaw in thought. 'Dunno,' he finally said. 'I just never imagined doing anything else. You remember when you were a kid and the adults

26

asked what you wanted to be when you grew up and all the boys said policemen or firemen or astronauts? I guess I never grew out of that phase.'

Sparrow smiled warmly, perhaps remembering his own childhood.

'I like that story,' he said with a chuckle. 'Much better than saying you were trying to avoid being shot with a nail gun.'

4

It was a short ride to the pub, past the post office, memorial hall, two overgrown tennis courts without nets, and a dozen more limp Australian flags. Parking outside the pub, Manolis saw a long queue of people standing under the shade of the street's only tree.

'What are they doing?' he asked.

'Watch,' said Sparrow.

Manolis saw a clapped-out hatchback appear at the end of the street and drive towards them at low speed. It picked up the first man in the queue and drove him fifty metres up the road to the drive-thru bottle shop. It waited until he made his purchase, then returned him to the starting point and picked up the second in line, repeating the process. The first man staggered off into the scrub, slab of beer under his arm, song in his heart.

'That's the rules, the drive-thru only serves cars,' Sparrow said, smiling. 'We coppers can't do anything about it. And not that we'd want to, it'd only cause more trouble. Whitefella who owns the hatchback charges a fee. Smart, eh? Name's Trev, he's run off his feet every second Thursday when the dole payments come in, one client after another, nonstop all bloody day. Trev's a bloody millionaire. C'mon, it's your shout.'

'Aren't you on duty?'

Sparrow snorted a laugh of disbelief. Still chuckling, he entered the top pub.

Inside, the air conditioner was doing battle with the

smell of sweaty men, cigarette smoke and free-flowing beer. Sergeant Fyfe was propping up the bar. He had a fresh pint in his hand and was holding court with two fellow barflies and the publican, all dressed in footy shorts and singlets, bare feet. Manolis felt decidedly overdressed.

'Well fuck me without a kiss,' Fyfe said. 'You must be the city mouse.' His voice was wet and sluggish with booze.

'Hello,' Manolis said, offering his hand. 'Detective Sergeant George Manolis.'

Fyfe crushed Manolis's fingers and palm in a show of cop strength. Fyfe's red scabrous face and spider veins made him look like he'd been marinated in beer and left in the sun to dry. The dead glare in his dark grey eyes said this was a man who'd seen many horrors.

'Nice clobber, mate.'

'You look like you've come straight from a catwalk.'

The 'flies laughed, full and hearty, guts quivering, mouths agape, rotten teeth, shrivelled heads. Beneath their amusement, Manolis sensed a hostility. Indeed, it was almost tactile.

He acknowledged the barflies with a polite nod. Eyes were looking at him for an unnervingly long time, much longer than they would anywhere in the city.

'So you're the white knight,' said the publican.

His hair was albino, his skin paler than snow. Manolis wondered how that was even possible in country Australia.

'Come to save us from ourselves, eh?' the publican continued. 'Bless ya, son. Reckon that deserves a drink. What's yer poison?'

Manolis was about to mention 'duty' but then reconsidered. When in Rome. He eyed the bar. It had a selection of nearly full liquor bottles, all weighed down with a thick coating of outback dust. The bar itself had four taps, all the same beer, full strength, lager, domestic. The walls and ceiling were covered with a selection of second-hand bras, jocks, footy jumpers, X-rays, business cards, photos and yet more Australian flags.

'Whisky,' Manolis said. 'A double.'

His order seemed to silence the room. The publican looked at him crookedly. He wiped his nose, his odour yeasty. 'Sure you don't want a beer, mate?'

'No thanks.'

'Sure? It's good 'n' cold.'

'Don't drink beer. It bloats me. But I'll have one for young Sparrow here . . . ?'

Sparrow nodded blankly, as if he'd just seen something horrific, an abomination. He took his schooner and astonishment and went to sit in the corner while Manolis corralled Fyfe at the bar and pressed him for details about the investigation. Fyfe was elusive. Manolis pressed harder.

'Look, mate, honestly, right now, we're in mourning,' Fyfe said. 'Cobb's a small place.'

'I know it's small,' Manolis said. 'Small and insular. It's why I got seconded here from Major Crimes.'

'I think that had more to do with what went down last night at the brown house than anything else.'

'It does. But it doesn't sound like it was an isolated event.'

Fyfe sucked on his beer like a vacuum cleaner. 'It wasn't,' he said through a frothy moustache. 'That place was supposed to turn this town around. Jobs, they said. Economy, they said. Arse, I say. The jobs they brought in pay minimum wage — part-time cleaners and untrained security thugs.'

Manolis took a very deliberate sip of his room-temperature whisky. It tasted stale and sour, an oily texture, and lingered on his tongue like an old coat. Perhaps he should've listened to the publican and bought a cold beer. He regretted ordering a double. Twice the pain.

'Molly was a good woman, you know,' Fyfe continued. 'Real good.'

'Good lay, ya mean . . . ' said a 'fly with a wry smile.

'Town bike,' muttered another. Laughter ensued.

'Oi!' Fyfe said. 'Shaddup, you lot.'

Manolis waited for the chortling to stop before he spoke again. 'Molly?'

'Salt of the earth,' said Fyfe. 'She taught our kids.'

'She was a schoolteacher?'

'Yep. She didn't deserve to go out like that.'

'No-one ever does.'

'I'm pissed off deluxe. Those animals.'

'Who?'

Fyfe's glare seemed to bore right through Manolis. 'The scum who did this,' he said flatly. 'Who else did ya think I meant?'

Manolis didn't reply, drank his whisky fitfully. 'I need to see the body and crime scene.'

'Sure, mate. But not today. Tomorrow.'

'Who found the victim? Can you take me to them? Why not today?'

Fyfe drained his pint halfway with a rapid, throaty glug. 'Son, it's Sunday. You can't hassle people on a Sunday. That's the Lord's Day.'

'Sergeant,' said Manolis, pulling on his earlobe, 'are

31

you saying the day of the week takes precedence over the course of a murder investigation?'

'Thass right, city mouse,' Fyfe said combatively, puffing out his chest. 'This ain't the city round 'ere. Round 'ere, Sunday still means something. It's a day of worship. It's a day of rest. Rest and rehydration.' He drained the other half of his beer and caught the publican's eye.

'Well, I didn't drive all this way to sit and watch you drink,' Manolis said.

'Frankly,' Fyfe said, 'I couldn't think of anything more compelling.' He proceeded to wrap his fingers around a freshly poured glass and sauntered back to the 'flies, who slapped his back hard and clinked pints, beer sloshing.

Manolis watched them laugh and drink and smoke and sway. He leaned against the bar and downed the rest of his whisky in a single gulp. It avoided the taste.

The publican reappeared.'Let 'em be. Like Bill said, we're all hurtin'. Molly was dear to us all. Him especially.'

Manolis spun around. 'What's that supposed to mean? Was he close to the woman?'

'We're all close. It's a small town. Bill just sees himself as a shepherd. A wolf took one of his flock.'

'He's got to be professional, though.'

'He will be, when he's sober. Today, don't consider him a cop. He's only human. Poor bastard nearly died last year himself.'

'Oh?'

The publican rested his weight against the bar. 'This one mad fella slashed Bill's wrist with a broken bottle, severed an artery. Bill needed three pints of blood and a pint of whisky to keep from passing out.'

32

Manolis slid his empty glass across the bar. 'Thanks,' he lied.

'No worries. Around here, the pub's where you go when you're doing it tough and need a pat on the back. I'm Turps, by the way.'

Manolis shook hands, introduced himself. 'Nice place,' he said.

'It's a shithole,' Turps said. 'But at least it's an honest business. Not like that bloody brown house.'

Sparrow walked over with his empty schooner, lace stuck to the inside like spider webs. 'C'mon,' he told Manolis. 'I'll take you to where you're stayin', let you settle in. Thanks, Turps.'

'See you boys later.'

Sparrow instructed Manolis to drive west, the afternoon sun in their eyes.

'Why'd you take me there?' Manolis asked. 'Fyfe didn't want a bar of me.'

'It was only meant to be a friendly g'day, an intro. We'll talk more tomorrow.' Sparrow scanned the empty streets through the dirty windscreen. 'Hopefully it's quiet out there tonight. No trouble.'

'Why? What've you heard?'

'Just chatter.' He paused. 'Talk of reprisal attacks, people vowing revenge for what the brown house did to Molly.'

'That implies knowledge of the perpetrator.'

'Assumptions are enough. Makes life simpler.'

Manolis kept driving. After some time, he asked, 'Her name was Molly?'

'Yair, Molly Abbott. Taught at the primary school. Well liked, popular. Early forties, widowed.'

Manolis's heart sank a few inches. Being separated from a loved one was unfortunate, heartbreaking. But

33

at least they were alive. To be widowed so young was tragic.

His detective brain swiftly clicked into gear. There would be no ex-husband to chase up. An obvious lead was gone.

'Did she have a boyfriend?' Manolis asked tentatively.

'Don't think so,' Sparrow said. 'But I know there's this one bloke in town, he's been lusting after her for a while.'

'Lusting? Who's this?'

Sparrow took a moment to respond, then seemed to choose his words delicately.

'Name's Joe. Relatively harmless bloke. Ever since Molly's husband died, he's been courting her without success. Even made a scene at the top pub one night.'

'What kind of scene?'

'Nothin' major. He'd had a few, made a pass at her. She slapped him, humiliated him in front of his mates. Bruised his ego. Not the first woman who's slapped Joe at the pub neither . . .'

Manolis smiled to himself. 'That's all good to know.'

'I doubt he could do this, though. He's a pest, but no predator.'

'Track him down.'

'Mm, OK.'

'And have you any idea who might've seen her last?'

'Not yet.'

They left the town behind. Vast brown plains soon stretched in every direction. Manolis gunned the accelerator, the pistons singing. The road heading west wasn't on any map he had seen. He thought it strange not to be staying in Cobb itself, close to the action. He would've been happy enough to flop in

34

someone's granny flat or spare room, or even on a bunk at the station. His eyes squinted, darted, tried to work out where the hell they were going. Sparrow said nothing; he stared straight ahead from behind impenetrable black sunglasses while his fingers drummed a high-powered rhythm on his thigh. Manolis wondered whether they were heading to a farm or a property with a long rambling homestead overlooking bushland. Or maybe a slab hut made of timber and bark where early settlers once lived, drovers and woodcutters and shearers. He was so distracted that he nearly missed the crooked wooden archway announcing their arrival in Olde Cobbe Towne.

'Holy shit,' Manolis said.

'Yair,' said Sparrow. 'Ever since the brown house opened, there's not many cots available in town. This was Sarge's idea. It's away from the worst trouble.'

They parked outside a demountable office building with an Australian flag in the window. As they entered, Manolis got tangled in the multicoloured plastic strip curtains hung across the doorway; he hadn't seen curtains like that since he was a kid.

Sparrow called out. A groan came from a back room, followed by cursing. A chair was shunted, another groan, heavy, slow footsteps.

The proprietor shambled out under a cloud of broken sleep. At first he had his head down, patting his comb-over to ensure it remained in place. When he finally looked up and stood erect, he appeared imposing, tall and broad, matching Manolis's six feet. The proprietor wore a navy-blue shearer's singlet and a pair of old tennis shorts. An overgrown moustache obscured his mouth, a hairless patch of skin on his arm appearing white. Rubbing his cheeks, he passed a

35

pair of deep-set eyes over Sparrow and then Manolis.

'Well, I'll be a monkey's . . . '

After this half-sentence, the proprietor's voice turned to dust in his throat. Stepping out from behind the counter, he approached Manolis with wide eyes and wide arms. His moustache was quivering. Manolis backed away a step but was powerless to stop the embrace that clamped around his chest and squeezed his heart till it hurt.

'Ma! Ma, quick, come see!' the man called over his shoulder. He turned back to Manolis. 'I thought I might've died in my sleep, or that I saw a ghost,' he whispered. 'You look just like your father.'

Manolis glared straight at Sparrow, whose confused expression showed he'd heard what the proprietor said.

'I grew up here,' Manolis said. 'Here in Cobb, I mean. It's the reason they sent me. And I think I knew Molly.'

5

The four of them now sat behind the office demountable, around a large wooden picnic table, faded and
splintering from relentless sun. Made of flimsy green
corrugated plastic, the pergola roof offered nominal
shade, though it seemed only to intensify the blistering
heat. Blowflies were everywhere, slow and disorien-
tated in the late afternoon swelter. There wasn't a
breath of wind.

As proprietors and hosts, Rex and Vera Boyd had
insisted their guests stay for dinner. On seeing Manolis, Vera had hugged him tightly, and he had kissed
her on both cheeks in the Mediterranean way. Standing at the head of the table, she was now spooning
out generous helpings of rich beef stew. It was a meal
totally at odds with the weather.

'Wait till you try Ma's lamb curry,' Rex said. 'If I
was on death row, it'd be my last meal.'

Vera chuckled, her bosom and stomach quivering
with delight beneath the gold crucifix around her neck.
Her wrinkled face folded into what Manolis supposed
was a smile. He ate hungrily, dipping a square hunk
of damper into the dense brown sauce. The flavour
was intense and glossy with the subtle sweetness of
apple. He avoided the chunks of meat as much as he
avoided the topic of being vegetarian.

With the snap of a well-practised wrist and the flick
of a long hunting knife, Rex opened a series of beer
bottles with four little gasps. They were longneck bottles without labels, his special home brew. He poured

thick beer into four enormous stein glasses and forced one onto Manolis. Rex took his guest's refusals of the beer as a mortal blow. Fortunately, Sparrow came to the rescue of the unwanted stein.

'The meat's from the slaughterhouse,' Vera said proudly. 'That's why it tastes so bloody good, aye.' She wielded a flyswatter with laser precision, every few seconds claiming another marble-sized victim.

They talked about the past and present, but mainly the past. Manolis remembered the town as thriving and home to nearly five thousand people.

'It's about half that now — permanent residents, I mean,' Rex said. 'People have left and no-one's come in to replace them.'

Manolis said he vaguely remembered the couple who'd run the tourist park for years and lived in the cabin behind the office. Rex described how he used to visit the milk bar run by Manolis's father in the centre of town. In close-knit country communities like Cobb, the local Greek café had been a meeting point. It welcomed everyone, irrespective of creed or colour, espousing the Greek virtue of *filoxenia* — 'generosity of spirit'.

'I used to take the kids for a milkshake after school,' Rex said. 'Your dad Con made the most delicious shakes, he used real vanilla pods. We'd never seen anything like it.' He added that Con was one of the most generous people he'd ever met, often letting customers eat for free if they couldn't afford their bill.

Manolis smiled. 'I don't seem to remember your children. How many, boys or girls?'

'One of each,' Rex said. 'They were a few years older than you. I remember you clearing tables, restocking napkins, sweeping up, emptying bins.'

38

'We hoped our kids might one day run this place,' Vera said.

'Did they leave town too?' Manolis asked.

The dinner party went unexpectedly quiet. Sparrow played with his cutlery. Vera wiped her mouth with a paper serviette. Rex finally cleared his throat and said, 'Karen died when she was sixteen. Blood clot on the brain. And Patrick had a heart attack.'

Manolis stopped chewing. 'I'm so sorry. I had no idea.'

Vera wiped her eyes, swatted.

'Not your fault, son,' Rex said, quaffing his ale. 'God works in mysterious ways. I'll always have the memory of vanilla shakes. Seeing you today transported me back to better times.'

Manolis's lips curled into a soft smile as the image blossomed in his mind. The tall soda glasses with long straws, the shiny silver mixing cups with condensation on the outside, cold from the fresh full-cream milk of fat country cows.

Sparrow swallowed his mouthful, placed his glass on the table. 'Patrick and Molly got married,' he said.

Manolis turned to his hosts, saw their eyes turn down. They seemed almost embarrassed. Misfortune had stalked them: their kids, and now their daughter-in-law.

'They were high school sweethearts,' Vera said slowly.

'We loved her like a daughter,' Rex said. 'Especially since her own parents had passed.'

Manolis extended further sympathies. He couldn't remember a boy named Patrick Boyd at all.

Vera tossed her empty tin plate on the table, making it rattle. A slammed fork followed. 'What happened to our kids was nothing compared to poor Molly. The mere thought makes me sick. Imagine if her parents were still alive. The grief.'

Vera crossed herself; Rex followed suit. 'Perhaps it's better that Graham and Edith are no longer with us,' he said.

'Their daughter's joined them in heaven,' Vera said, voice bright. 'She's with God now, in the comfort of the Lord.' Her lilting tone contrasted with the hard lines on her face.

'What's happened to Cobb recently would make Graham turn in his grave,' Rex added. 'He served ten years as an alderman, you know.'

'On the town council alongside Pa,' Vera added proudly.

'You were a councillor?' Manolis asked. 'Like, a politician?'

Rex laughed. 'Local government is hardly big-time politics. I mean, I could do it in my spare time. But yes, I guess you could've called me that.'

'And you gave it up?'

'Like for most politicians, it was forced retirement.' Rex paused. 'I lost an election. Game over.'

'Graham fought in the war, too,' Vera said.

'Victoria Cross,' Sparrow said.

'Quiet, you,' Rex scowled. He ran a sweaty hand across his gauze of hair, reining in the loose strands. 'But my bloody oath, he did. He was a brave soldier. Corporal Graham Abbott stared down the yellow peril in the jungle, killed six of the squinty-eyed bastards and saved his whole platoon. He was an Australian hero.'

Sparrow sarcastically mouthed the word 'hero'. Manolis sensed an unspoken tension in the air, as if

40

he'd just walked in on a long-term feud. Sparrow took another draught of homebrew and returned to studying the dustbowl in the middle distance.

'Graham fought to keep people like that out of this country,' Rex said. 'Turn in his grave.'

Manolis pushed his plate away. He wasn't full but could suddenly eat no more. 'That was absolutely delicious, Mrs Boyd. Thank you.'

'But your plate's still got all that meat on it,' she said bluntly.

'Yes, but I couldn't eat another bite.'

She looked at him with zero expression. Her next fly swat had extra venom.

'So you became a copper in the city, eh?' Rex said. 'Good onya, son. Protector of the people, your ol' man would be proud as punch. And they say the only way out of Cobb is in a wooden box. Reminds me of that old cop show on TV, the actor, what's-his-name . . . Greek bloke, bald head, sucked a lollipop . . .'

'Kojak,' Vera said.

The show was before Manolis's time, from the 1970s, but even he had heard of Greek-American actor Telly Savalas, who played Lieutenant Theo Kojak.

'That's it, Kojak,' Rex said, smiling. 'I remember watching that show, your dad probably does too. By the way, you never told me, how's your old man doing these days? And your mum?'

Manolis's mind drifted. Eventually, he let his shoulders slump a little and spoke.

'Mum's well, but Dad passed away,' he said heavily. 'It was recently, only a few months ago.'

His admission was met with a sincere chorus of condolences. Vera was moved enough to stand and embrace him tightly, her ample bosom momentarily

41

restricting his air. Everyone, it seemed, was grieving.

'Oh,' Rex said. 'I'm genuinely saddened and sorry to hear that. I just assumed he was alive and well.'

'You poor boy,' Vera intoned. 'We're so, so sorry. We didn't realise you were in a period of mourning.'

That was certainly how Manolis's mother Maria had approached it, donning all black and refusing to leave the house for forty days. By necessity, her son's life was more practical.

'Having work to go to has been good,' Manolis said. 'Distracts me, keeps me busy.'

'From the sounds of it, he lived a full life,' Rex said.

'He did. His body just couldn't go any further, it was his time. And to be perfectly honest with you, it was a bit of a relief. Mum's lonely and heartbroken, but she's no spring chicken either, and couldn't keep caring for him.'

Towards the end, Manolis had dreaded visiting his parents' house. His father, emaciated and weak, was effectively bound to his battered armchair. Meanwhile, Maria laboured to maintain her impeccable standards of cleanliness and hygiene, and somehow satisfy her husband's many rules and demands. Steeped in cultural expectations, Greek women engaged in a game of competitive hardship as a means of gaining prestige in their gossip-hungry communities. When Con finally died, Maria — as with all Greek widows in black — made her husband a saint.

'I think returning to Cobb may be just what I need,' Manolis said.

'Your soul,' Vera said.

'Reckon so,' agreed Rex. 'And you say you think you knew Molly?'

'Might have. I seem to remember the name. I think

42

she was in the class above me at school.'

Vera tut-tutted. 'Poor girl. Such a tragic life. Still, you reap what you sow.'

'Ma.' Rex glared at his wife.

'How'd you mean?' Manolis said.

'Do not be deceived,' Vera said. 'God is not mocked, for whatever one sows, that will he also reap. For the one who sows to his own flesh will from the flesh reap corruption, but the one who sows to the Spirit will from the Spirit reap eternal life.'

'Galatians,' said Sparrow.

'I'm Orthodox,' Manolis said hesitantly.

'That's good,' Vera said. 'Still Christian, yep. We were at church this morning, but I couldn't tell you the last time I saw Molly there. She was like a daughter to us, once upon a time. Somewhere along the way, she strayed from the righteous path and drifted away from the flock.'

'Ma —'

'Oh hush, Pa. The detective probably wants to know these things.'

Manolis nodded. Sparrow freshened his stein. Rex grunted softly.

'I'm not one for gossip.' Rex exhaled. 'And besides, her body's barely cold, her spirit can still hear us.'

'Molly was never quite the same after Patrick died,' Vera said. 'And frankly, neither was I. But really, she should've known better.'

'She was probably just profoundly lonely,' Manolis said.

'From what I heard, the kids at school absolutely adored her,' Rex said. 'And those kids need a good teacher in this town.'

'Specially the black kids,' said Sparrow.

43

'Teachers, doctors, cops, it's hard to attract any professionals to Cobb,' Rex breathed. 'Drunks and druggies seem to like the place, fairly flock to it, really thrive here. You couldn't get any more committed or professional-grade scum than you do in Cobb, and we're only producing more by the day. So, despite her flaws, Molly was needed.'

A long-dormant memory shunted itself to the front of Manolis's mind. It was of Molly standing on stage at a school assembly, being applauded, the dux of her year. She'd been a bright student, full of promise and potential. Inevitably the reality of living in Cobb had caught up with her.

Manolis retrieved the notebook and biro from his pocket. 'Sorry to ask, but when did your son die?'

Vera sat back in her chair and considered the burnt-orange sky. Her eyes were soon glistening. 'Four years ago this April. I'll never forget the day. We'd just returned from protesting.'

'Protesting?' Manolis asked, writing.

'The brown house,' Rex said. 'It was around the time they first mentioned plans for it to be built.'

Vera nodded lightly and fixed her gaze on a small patch of dirt near Manolis's brogues. 'That place has absolutely gutted this town,' she said coldly.

She described how the detention centre had been 'foisted' upon them, and that the information they were given was 'bloody lies'.

'We used to get out and enjoy the town,' Rex said. 'Not anymore.'

'Look, I'll be the first to admit we've had a few more bookings,' Vera said. 'So the money's been good, yep. But it's still a pittance compared to the trouble that comes with it. The security guards, interpreters,

44

cleaners come and go every few weeks, so they don't give a hoot what they do to the place.'

'They come for the money and a good time, but that's about it,' Rex said. 'We're like a paid vacation for them.'

'My back's broken from cleaning their mess, and poor Pa has to fix all sorts of damage to the cabins,' Vera said. 'They're animals. And don't even get me started on the boat people.'

'Dangerous to our nation,' Rex grumbled. 'To Australian unity.'

'We're under attack,' Vera said. 'Look around you, look at the town, there's no Aussie faces anymore.'

'We've already got terrorists here,' Rex added. 'Right here, in Cobb. We're living among the enemy, and they're runnin' up a tab on our dime.'

Vera looked up at Manolis. 'I bet you my bottom dollar those troublemakers are mixed up in this.'

He stared at her blankly for a while. 'How . . . so?' he asked gradually. 'Did Molly have anything to do with the asylum seekers?'

'I wouldn't be surprised,' Vera said.

'You're not sure, then?'

'Not really, no,' Rex said. 'We'd drifted apart in recent times. She loved our Patrick dearly, so I think we became a painful reminder.'

'And do you have anything to do with the asylum seekers yourselves?'

'No way,' Vera hissed. 'Not a chance.' Her voice was as soft as cotton, her words as sharp as glass.

'Look, I couldn't give a brass razoo what they do in their countries,' Rex said. 'Just don't bring that kind of behaviour here. It's un-Australian.'

'What behaviour is that?' Manolis said.

45

'Bloody hell it's hot,' Sparrow said.

'They've got everything you could possibly imagine in the brown house,' Rex said. 'The joint's totally refurbished, they spent millions. There's air conditioning, flat-screen TVs, cable, gym equipment, prescription medicines —'

'Meanwhile, we sit and roast in old caravans, watching static and drinking snake oil,' Vera said.

'Hot,' Sparrow said.

'They come out here and demand all these freedoms,' Rex said. 'It's a bit much, don't you think?'

'They're your evildoers, Detective,' Vera said. 'Focus your energies there. That's what *they* do, isn't it? Torment women? Stone women?'

Her face and mood darkened. It was an energy that permeated the air and blackened Manolis's thoughts like a squid with its ink.

Rex shook his head. 'Multiculturalism is the greatest failed experiment.'

'I just hope no-one tries to stone me,' Vera said, half-speaking and half-cringing. 'But I know that God will help us through this difficult time.'

'Oh, I'm sure he will,' Sparrow said with a smile.

'My heart breaks for the women especially, the way the men treat them in those cultures,' Vera added. 'Bring 'em to justice, Detective.'

Manolis pretended to check his watch before forcing a yawn. 'I'm sorry, it's been a long day. And you've both been very hospitable — thank you again for the delicious meal.'

Rex apologised, stood. 'We do go on. Let me show you to your cabin. It's a pleasure to have you stay with us.'

'Thank you,' Manolis said. 'I'm happy to be here

46

too.'

Vera hugged him with a warmth he wasn't expecting. 'Sorry again for your loss, love. Lamb curry next time.'

'Can't wait,' he said with a sigh.

6

The three men strolled at a leisurely pace in the disappearing light, their bellies straining with beef and beer. Manolis swung his arms lethargically as if they were full of warm oil. The tourist park's main street was disturbingly quiet.

Rex walked tall, back straight. He took great pleasure in describing his pride and joy, which he had built from the ground up. But he admitted it had seen better days; it had fallen on hard times and out of memory.

'No-one holidays in the outback anymore,' he grumbled. 'People want exotic destinations, international locations. No-one drives, they all fly.'

In the middle of the park, an old broken bike and rusted shopping trolley lay on their sides in an empty, above-ground pool with a collapsed wall. At the picnic area, a dilapidated brick barbecue was overrun with stinging fire ants. Behind the cabins, a crumbling boardwalk offered panoramic views of the detention centre to the north. The long grey buildings sat like lumps of featureless plasticine behind high-wire fencing, their walls coated in dull paint, their windows small and prison-like.

Inspired by the town's history, the tourist park's cabins were from the Wild West. The men walked past the general store, the chemist, pub, bakery, bank and saddlery. The barber shop had a pole with a helix of red and white stripes. There was a hand-operated iron-frame mangle outside the Chinese laundry. Manolis touched it, felt its latent heat accumulated during

48

the day, and smudged the gritty oxide residue on his fingers.

Sparrow made a clinking sound at each step, like he was wearing spurs, striding down Main Street looking for trouble and a draw. He had bottle caps in his pockets.

Rex spoke a little about each cabin, its history, and the long-term residents who lived in the adjoining caravan park. They were a combination of retired pensioners and leathered bikies.

'Right then, Kojak, here's your cabin,' Rex said.

Manolis looked up. 'Of course.'

The large five-pointed star and faux WANTED poster indicated they'd arrived at the sheriff's office. A knee-high garden statue of bushranger Ned Kelly stood beside the entrance, tin shotgun extended. Rex unlocked the sliding glass door, wiggled it to make it glide properly, and showed them inside. The cabin was a main room with kitchenette, bar fridge and formica table, a bedroom with metal-frame bed and polyester quilt, and a small ensuite with a cracked vanity mirror. The quilt cover was pockmarked with the signatures of forgotten cigarettes. The air hung thick and heavy.

'I'll turn on your gas and electricity now,' Rex said. 'And we've stocked your fridge and cupboards with the staples. Any questions, give us a hoy.'

'I will,' Manolis said. 'And thanks again.'

They shook hands. Sparrow hung back on the verandah as Rex disappeared up the road. Manolis watched him, leaning against the doorframe.

'So now you know what you're up against,' Sparrow said.

'What *we're* up against,' Manolis said.

'Bloody loonies. Why is it you reckon all whitefellas

49

think they're under siege?'

Manolis exhaled. 'Probably because they are,' he said in a defeated tone. 'Always have been. I reckon it's got to do with the brutality they faced trying to tame a wild land. They arrived from lovely green England, most of them dragged here in chains.'

Sparrow eyed the heavens, black skies exploding with white star showers. 'Multiculturalism is a failure,' he mimicked. 'What horseshit. It's our gross neglect of Aboriginal people which is a fucken failure. Whitefellas treated us like flora and fauna when they first arrived, and for a long time since. And do you reckon Captain Cook adopted blackfella values when he rocked up with the First Fleet?'

Manolis smiled nervously, a wave of heat washing up his neck. It was the shame that much of White Australia carried around Aboriginal people: that of invasion, rape, genocide.

Sparrow looked at Manolis head to toe, his eyes turning dark. ''Course, the tension round here may also have to do with the murder of Jimmy Dingo.'

Manolis stopped smiling. 'Sorry?'

'You don't remember? Ha, course you don't . . . you're white.'

Manolis frowned. 'No, I don't remember. What murder, what happened?'

'It was yonks ago, decades. People say it changed the town, 'specially the elders.'

'And he was murdered?'

Sparrow sighed. 'So it goes. Jimmy was this blackfella, young, fit, best bloody footballer this town had seen in fifty years, prime of his life. He was killed by a whitefella who got off scot-free. The whitefella was a clever bastard and made it look like a tribal punishment by stabbing Jimmy in the thigh. Doin' that meant he could pin it on us blackfellas. We knew we didn't do it, but the cops wouldn't listen.'

'Another reason, perhaps, why you signed up for the bad guys?'

Sparrow smiled white teeth. 'If you hang around long enough, you'll notice whitefellas round 'ere never wanna hear ol' Jimmy's name. It's a dirty word. But we blackfellas, mate, we never forget it.'

Manolis imagined that outback towns had all manner of cold cases, but Cobb especially. As a kid, he remembered adults often disappearing without a trace; he hadn't thought much of it at the time. People had just walked out of town, often swaggies, travelling by foot from farm to farm, town to town, whichever way the wind blew. Viewing the situation as an adult, he saw it was conceivable some might've been murdered, and the perpetrators never brought to justice.

He decided to change the subject, return to the case. 'Did you ever hear of any trouble in Molly and Patrick's marriage? Violence, infidelity, anything?'

Sparrow appeared to cast his mind back. 'Nope. At least, nothin' reported.'

'What about rumours?'

Sparrow swished his shaggy hair. No rumours.

'OK,' Manolis said with a sigh.

'What are you thinkin'?'

'Not much. Just looking for an angle.'

Sparrow half-closed his eyelids. 'It's not too late if you want out.'

'It was never early enough.'

The two men went silent a while, listening to the night, to the singsong of unseen cicadas. Manolis pointed out the lack of mosquitoes, which was a welcome surprise.

51

'Too hot for mozzies, mate,' Sparrow said. 'There's nuthin' to 'em. In this heat, they'd go up like lit matches.'

There was a long pause, insects chirping. 'So what now?' Manolis finally said.

Sparrow retrieved a cigarette, made it glow. 'Shower, sleep. We'll regroup in the morning.'

Manolis checked his watch. 'What time?'

'Nine. Come by the station.'

'Want a lift back?'

'Nah, I'll walk.'

'All that way?'

'Yair. Clears my head. My people have walked much longer distances over many thousands of years. And besides, it's a nice evening.'

Manolis looked to the sky, the twinkling galaxy. 'Certainly is. I haven't seen this many stars in a long time.'

'Not since you were a kid, eh?'

'Well, no. I mean yeah, probably. What I'm trying to say is that this is just a regular night for you, right?'

Sparrow didn't respond. He stepped from the verandah, landed on the dirt without a sound. Bending down, he removed his shoes and socks and let the earth's warmth seep into the soles of his broad feet. He stretched his arms out wide, as if striking a Christ pose. For a moment, Manolis expected him to ascend into the night sky.

'Catch ya tomorrow,' Sparrow said without looking back.

'See you.'

Manolis watched as the young constable dissolved into the distance like a tracker following prey.

7

Manolis checked his phone; it had reception again, albeit a single bar. Who could he call, who should he call? His wife? His mum? Paul Bloody Porter . . . ?

At that moment, the thought of more conversation tired him. What few close friends he once had had drifted, left the high-rises, been absorbed into a new world of their own families and children and sprawling suburban life. Manolis had hoped to join them, out there amid the glorious madness of overgrown backyards, broken lawnmowers and sticky play equipment. Instead, he now felt more like a bachelor than ever.

He re-pocketed the phone. Reaching into his other pocket, he extracted a stout pouch of rich tobacco and a delicate envelope of wafer-thin papers.

Taking his time, savouring the ritual, he prepared his nightly cigarette. He arranged the golden tobacco meticulously, rolled the paper methodically. He was trying to cut down and ultimately give up. It was a habit inherited from his father, who had smoked for decades until his lungs and liver turned into ash and soot. Manolis inhaled deeply, felt the coolness crawl through his veins. Silver smoke rose and climbed over his shoulder, a distinct nebula forming above his head.

'*Signomi, Baba. Mono ena.*'

Con had been a heavy smoker since his teens, and a major carnivore throughout adulthood. He developed diabetes in his fifties and needed a bypass in his sixties. Manolis thought about that a lot — it had turned him into a vegetarian and often made him extinguish his cigarette early, as he did this evening in a deep Soreno glass ashtray. Con had always hated that his son smoked, which forced Manolis to hide his cigarettes. He still felt a twinge of guilt every time he lit up, and now needed to ask his father for forgiveness.

Manolis fetched his Val and parked it beside the sheriff's office, where a marshal might otherwise have tied his trusty horse. He checked the cupboards, failed to locate olive oil, found only instant coffee, and sighed lightly. As he stood under the shower for nearly twenty minutes, the cold water tore away his layers of dry sweat and dead skin and returned his body to life. The bedsheets smelled like bleach and were as rough and hot as burlap. He flung the top sheet onto the linoleum floor and opened all the windows and doors. The overhead fan spun so fast it stood still.

Sleep came effortlessly, against the backdrop of chirruping cicadas. Having pondered his own issues over a cigarette, Manolis often liked to think about a case in the haunted moments before sleep; he did so in the hope that something might come to him on either side of consciousness that cracked an investigation wide open. He claimed to have once solved a homicide after taking an afternoon nap and dreaming the location of the key piece of evidence. On other occasions, he'd dreamed the faces of perpetrators and where bodies were buried. It wasn't some divine gift — it was just the spillover from a dedicated mind. Ruminating on a case also had the recent bonus of preventing Manolis from thinking about his wife. He especially missed her warmth beside him in bed. As his head found shape in a flat pillow leaking feathers, he tried to picture Molly's face being pummelled with stones, but in the end saw only black. The investigation was still too new, and his weariness too great.

★ ★ ★

A loud clatter woke Manolis after an indeterminate period of time. It interrupted his dream, recurring, of an antiseptic hospital ward, and his dying father. He sat bolt upright in bed, sticky-mouthed, in a damp pool of his own sweat, listening.

Was the commotion inside or outside?

More banging, noisy and metallic, too close for comfort, the main room. His breath was quick and shallow. He reached instinctively for the gun under his mattress and stepped forward into the darkness, barrel first. While he scanned the room with tired eyes, sweeping with his revolver, the dark space was still unfamiliar, a collection of vague black outlines. His movements were calculated, careful and, most importantly, silent, honed over years of training and experience apprehending and eradicating the dregs of society.

Another crash, this time to his right. The tiny front room, murky and claustrophobic, suddenly felt the size of a galaxy, peeling off into the distance. Manolis heard the dull thump of blood in his ears. Steadying his breathing, he stretched out his left arm, feeling the fake wood on the wall, fumbling. The light switch was there, somewhere. It slipped through his sweaty fingers twice before he finally got a grip and flicked it down. He held his breath at the same time, acutely aware that this was the very moment when he was most likely to discharge his weapon.

The room's gaudy green and brown interior came

55

alive in the sickly white fluorescent light. Manolis's retinas worked hard to readjust. The culprit was less startled, blessed with extraordinary night vision. It was a brushtail possum, taking inventory in the cupboards, reorganising pots and crockery to its liking. The marsupial yawned, appearing unperturbed by the gun barrel pointed squarely at its plump little body.

Manolis lowered his weapon and his eyelids. He shambled over to the animal, who was now examining him distrustfully with black saucer eyes.

'Hey, little fella. You're hungry, and probably wondering what this stranger is doing in your pantry. Sorry about that, I had no choice. Here . . . '

Manolis tore open a packet of saltines, cracked a few into bite-sized pieces on the countertop and stood back. The possum sniffed the air intently before scampering forward and commencing the dry feast, flaunting a short-haired tail with a white tip and flickering its whiskers. The possum's demeanour of cheeky cuteness left Manolis fascinated and delighted. A city high-rise did not offer such pleasant surprises.

'I probably shouldn't do this cos you'll only be back for more. But a midnight snack is one of life's great pleasures.'

The possum ignored his host and kept munching on the jagged white square in its claw.

'Wanna be mates? Just don't trash the joint and we'll be sweet.'

With no more crackers to eat, the possum turned its attention to Manolis's revolver, which he'd absently left on the counter. Its sharp claws were surprisingly nimble across the grip, flirting with the trigger. With a swift clap of his hands, Manolis put an end to the possum's inquisitiveness and reclaimed the weapon.

56

The marsupial sniffed the air a final time and ran out the nearest window. Manolis sighed, switched off the light and lay back in bed.

A second disturbance, much louder than the first, woke him some time later. It was in the near distance — a series of loud bangs. Out of habit, his instant thought was of an illicit drug lab exploding. There was one every week in the city, usually meth-amphetamines, often a single big explosion that shook the immediate area, not several that echoed into the night. These bangs sounded more like kids letting off fireworks, or a car backfiring.

Manolis sat silent for a moment, listening, in case there were more. Then he exhaled, lay back into his pillow and rolled over.

The third disruption was more like the first: closer to home. Manolis's initial reaction was to wipe the dry drool from the side of his mouth and regret not closing the window. Bloody housemate, he thought. Raiding the cupboard again.

Then he heard it. Not just a bang. An explosion.

The bed shook.

And the unmistakable smell of smoke filled the air.

8

Manolis's immediate thought was the immigration detention centre. Another arson attempt, another revenge attack. But then he realised the crackling of the flames was too loud, and the smell of smoke couldn't have travelled that quickly.

The fire was close.

'*Gamoto . . .*'

This time, he needed no light switch to see. A harsh glare eddied through the outline of the door, illuminating the room. Manolis felt the heat, considered his escape route. There was only one door, glowing hot-plate red. And the windows were built for possums, not people.

He snatched his gun and the first piece of clothing he could find, a shirt. Folding it tight across his hand, he reached tentatively for the doorhandle. The surging heat penetrated the cloth and seared a doubt in Manolis's brain. What if there really was no escape? The wooden cabin was no more than a hollow box of kindling. A city coroner had once told him that being burned alive was the most painful way to die. The process took several minutes and involved damage to millions of individual nerve endings. Manolis gave a fleeting thought to his furry flatmate and hoped that he — or she — was safe.

With one swift motion, Manolis flung the door open, expecting to see the room ablaze. But it was only glowing, a warm iridescent orange, reflecting a fire that was in fact external, on the cabin's right side.

For a second Manolis thought it was the Chinese laundry and tried to recall if he'd seen any occupants. Until he remembered where he'd parked his car.

Manolis could make out only the trunk of his Val. The rest of its body and bonnet were obscured by a raging fireball. It spewed a thick black column of smoke that spiralled into the night. He was forced back, a hand over his nose and mouth, coughing, his lungs burned by the slew of freshly liberated chemicals. The smell of petrol choked the air, burning alongside everything else that was flammable — vinyl, foam, metal. The petrol tank hadn't ignited. Unless a tank ruptured and air rushed in, which Manolis had seen in accidents, its contents didn't usually explode. But tyres did: brand-new radials, one by one, like rifle shots, *bang-bang, bang-bang*. The car's windows shattered. With a southerly blowing the flames away from the sheriff's office, the Chinese laundry was now safe from their fiery reach. Its darkened windows suggested it was unoccupied, or that the tenants were very heavy sleepers.

Standing in his briefs, Manolis fought hard to suck oxygen into his lungs, to force sulphur out. As his breathing returned to normal, he half-closed his eyes, placed his hands on his hips and resigned himself to his fate, to watching his love burn. He returned briefly to the cabin to check in case there was an extinguisher. There wasn't. The fire continued its work.

'*Sto kalo … ah sto thialo … gamo to kerato sou . . .*'

Manolis heard himself muttering, sounding like his father when he'd been frustrated, at a loss. Returning to Cobb made Manolis remember his dad doing it when he didn't approve of a customer, so that they wouldn't understand him. At the time young Manolis found this disturbing, as if his father was going mad, and felt on edge around him. Now, when Manolis caught himself doing it, he was equally disturbed.

Rex arrived in his Y-fronts, breathing like an old bike pump. He carried a kerosene lamp in one hand, its light appearing greasy. Seeing him, Manolis stopped his muttering.

'Bugger me,' Rex said. 'You OK, sport?'

Manolis gnawed on a thumbnail. 'Got an extinguisher?'

'Back at the office but it's for small grease fires, not the gates of hell.'

Manolis exhaled. 'That's OK. Let it burn.'

A small crowd of residents soon appeared, shadows in darkness, milling around in case it was something worth seeing. When they realised it was just another burning vehicle, they began to leave, disappointed. Manolis asked if anyone had seen anything suspicious. They told him no or ignored him altogether.

'Maybe it's the uniform,' he said, looking down at his red underpants.

'Nah,' Rex said. 'You could just as well be wearing the Queen's jewels. Even if they saw something, they'd still say bugger all.'

'Why's that?'

He shrugged. 'People are more scared now than ever. Can't blame 'em, really. There's a killer out there.'

'What about you? You scared?'

Rex laughed. 'Me? Nah, mate. The Lord could take me now and I wouldn't give a toss. I've lived, loved, lost. Not much more left to do. Drink?'

At a safe distance from the flames, the men sat on two milk crates. Alternating swigs from Rex's hipflask, they watched the Australian sedan reduce to ash. As it reached the rear of the vehicle, the fire made the fuel tank go up with a flash and a woof. Manolis talked about his history with the car, and with the model. How it was the first new car his father had bought in the city. It was the car in which Con had taught Manolis to drive after much frustration and argument. Manolis would later steal the keys and cruise the streets with his dropkick mates, trying to intimidate local boys and impress local girls. Rex listened attentively, his face tiger-striped by the flickering flames. Patrick had once done the same, he said. Pestered his dad to teach him to drive, then run off with the keys.

Rex understood the significance of the moment — a man was witnessing part of himself die. Both men smiled nostalgically, drank.

Finally, Rex asked, 'So, no chance it was a mechanical fault?'

The thought had crossed Manolis's mind. There was clearly a firebug at large in town, perhaps linked to the stoning of Molly Abbott. At the same time, the Val's eight-cylinder engine, with its spaghetti mess of hoses, was a recipe for disaster. The car's wiring was so complex that it came with its own consciousness. A pinhole in any one of the fuel-injection lines was all that was needed for Carmageddon. There was also the accumulation of heat after driving so far in such temperatures, along with that strange rattling sound he'd heard from beneath the bonnet. A fault was certainly possible; he was no professional mechanic. But probable . . . ?

The local police arrived just as the wreck began to smoulder, a single car with no siren or flashing lights. Rex had called them when he heard the first explosions.

'If this had been the brown house, they'd have come in a flash,' he grumbled.

Manolis expected Sparrow to emerge from the driver's side. He felt decidedly underdressed when he saw a ponytail bobbing in his direction. She strode confidently and introduced herself as Constable Kate Kerr. She was wearing a navy-blue singlet top tucked into her shorts and had thongs on her feet. Manolis judged her a few years younger than him, perhaps mid-thirties — much older than Sparrow, who was mid-twenties. She was long-limbed, her legs a rich golden brown, her posture soldier-like, arms taut with dense, corded muscle. She already knew who Manolis was.

'Thanks for coming out,' he said warmly.

'It's my job,' she said, arms folded. 'Want me to summon the firies? They could be a while, an hour at least.' Her tone was curt, the lines in her face like warrior paint.

Manolis considered the steaming mess, the hour of night. 'Let 'em sleep.'

'Good. You OK, Rexy?'

Rex held up his flask in cheers. 'Couldn't be better, love.' He smiled. 'How's ya mum?'

Her face softened, arms falling by her sides. 'She doesn't even know who I am anymore,' she said with a sigh.

'Bloody dementia,' Rex said. 'Cruel way to go. You die twice.'

Manolis caught Kerr's eye. 'Constable, may I speak with you privately?'

Rex overheard. 'Don't mind me. I'm off to bed anyway, Ma will be wondering where I am. Sorry again about your car, Kojak. This bloody town. You can borrow my truck while you're here. I barely use it, got nowhere to go anymore.'

Manolis thanked him for his kind offer. Rex shuffled back to his cabin, dragging his right leg. Manolis hoped Kerr would sit on the vacated milk crate, but she stayed standing beneath the moth-encrusted light of the verandah. She re-crossed her arms.

Her facial lines reappeared. 'Detective, it's late. Can't we do this another time? I need to get home.'

Manolis checked his watch — a quarter to four. The sun was still hours away. 'Have you been up all night?'

'Don't act like you care. You don't even want to be here.'

She's been briefed, thought Manolis.

'Who told you that? I was born in Cobb, you know?'

'I know. So was I.'

Manolis didn't remember her. 'Your name isn't familiar.'

'Well, I don't remember your family either,' Kerr snapped. 'You left, remember. Not me.'

'And your civic loyalty is to be admired, Constable. Really it is. But all I wanted to ask you about was the deceased.'

She cocked her head to one side. 'Hasn't anyone briefed you? What about your boss in the city?'

'He has, but very little. And I suspect I'm only here because he saw the place of birth on my employment record.'

'You're coming to the station in the morning, right?'

Manolis nodded. 'I am.'

'So what do you want to know now? In two minutes. It's late.'

'I want to know what your theory is.'

Kerr arched her overgrown eyebrows, no time or inclination to pluck. 'Why are you interested in what I think? It's just a theory.'

'Well, you're a local cop who obviously knows the town, the people. I don't. At least, not like you.'

It was a concession she seemed to welcome hearing.

'Did you know Molly Abbott?' Manolis continued. 'I understand she was a schoolteacher. Have you any suspects in mind?'

Kerr shrugged her exposed shoulders. 'Maybe once. But the town's changed, even I don't recognise it anymore.'

Manolis paused. 'You mean, because of the brown house?'

'If you mean the *immigration detention centre*, then yes. I don't use that other name.'

'Oh, I'm sorry. I was told that's what people call it around here.'

'They do. But I don't.' She exhaled her frustration. 'There's just so many new faces around town now. It's possible to have secrets.'

'You mean compared to before?'

She sighed, as if pining for a simpler time. 'We were just a quiet little town. Not much happened. Unfortunately, that was also why people left — they went looking for adventure and opportunity and excitement. People like you. People once knew everything about everyone around here. Do you remember that?'

Manolis didn't, he'd been too young. 'I do,' he lied.

Kerr tugged at her ponytail. 'We had issues, of course. There's always been tensions between the blacks and whites. But we were still two communities with a common home. We were like siblings fighting.

64

The detention centre changed all that. Like some strange cousin moving into our bedroom.'

Manolis wiped his sweaty cheeks. 'Changed it how?'

'Well, for a start there's all the transients — guards, cleaners, cooks, interpreters.'

'You have much to do with them?'

'We're banned from entering the centre unless we're called, which happens rarely. They handle incidents in-house. They run that joint like their own little country.'

'Like an embassy.'

She nodded. 'It's all very secretive, very hush-hush. Reports are written up on absolutely everything that happens. Incident reports, they call them. Any disturbance, no matter how big or small, is classified and categorised, and fed into the massive bureaucracy that maintains the detention machine.'

Manolis was familiar with the excruciating minutia of report writing. But the overall intention of the detention policy was clear to him. Stifle the flow of people with red tape and wire fences so that gradually their wills would erode, and they would just . . . give up. It was the inexorable crushing of the refugee spirit through the regime of detention and the trap of bureaucracy. The world would reabsorb these problems. It was both the compassionate and cost-effective thing to do.

'Whistleblowers can be sent to jail,' Kerr said. 'They're too scared to speak out.'

More fear, thought Manolis.

Kerr explained that an overseas company had been contracted to manage the centre. Worth billions, they were involved in military logistics, traffic management, hospitals and prisons.

'Prisons, eh?' Manolis said.

'You could argue they operate from a prison model,' Kerr said. 'They're printing their own money and making a killing.'

Where governments saw problems, others saw opportunities. Money wasn't lost, it was made.

'It costs millions to be so remote, so gloriously isolated,' Kerr said.

Manolis wondered if he would see the day when the police force was privatised, when he would work for a faceless global conglomerate instead of a plodding, corrupt bureaucracy.

'So the detainees feel like prisoners?' he asked.

'Well, it makes a difference that they can come and go,' Kerr said.

'Come and go?'

'The centre is only low security. At night there's a curfew, but the detainees are able to move around town as they please during the day. It's supposed to help them assimilate.'

'Assimilate? They move around?'

This was another detail that central office had neglected to communicate. Manolis looked north to the detention centre, to the dim orange lights in the distance, illuminating the perimeter. His mission was at a stroke more complex.

'Not that there's been much movement this weekend,' Kerr said. 'The place has gone into lockdown.'

'Like a country, shoring up its borders.'

'Most of the town's residents haven't been fifty clicks outside of Cobb their whole lives. We get zero holiday makers, and there's very few newcomers. That all changed when the detention centre opened for business.'

'So your theory is that Molly's murder is the work of an outsider?'

Kerr fixed him with a long, unblinking gaze. Her words were precise:

'No local did this.'

She said goodnight and flip-flopped back to her car, slamming the door and driving away at high speed.

The night fell quiet. No sign of the possum, who Manolis hoped had sought shelter in a tall eucalypt. He took one last look at his Valiant, now a charred, empty shell. He muttered a final few Greek curses, went inside and collapsed into bed.

★ ★ ★

Manolis overslept. It was a combination of sheer exhaustion and the lack of background noise. He was more used to hydraulic garbage trucks, snarling traffic and raised inner-city voices, not idyllic nature and unfamiliar silence. He woke to the gentle babble of sweet birdsong. The laughter of kookaburras and warbling of magpies flooded the pleasure centre of his brain and transported him back decades. For a brief moment, he heard his mother yelling from another room, imploring him to get up or he'd be late for school. He smiled softly.

Manolis showered and dressed: shirt and trousers, no jacket or tie. He smoked his morning cigarette calmly and methodically down to his fingers, really made it count. He quaffed a mug of instant, avoiding the taste. Talked to himself, outlined his day, summoned his energy and willed his confidence.

Stepping onto the verandah, he was hit by a wall of heat. The sun was barely up and already the air was beginning to cook. The new light revealed the extent of the devastation, the wreck of the Val still smoking, the air acrid. It was hard to look at and made him queasy. He kicked around in the ashes in case there was something of value or interest. He found neither. Just charcoal and dust and bitter disappointment.

It was only as he walked to the office that he saw it, sitting in the gutter outside the Chinese laundry, shining like a beacon in the morning sun.

'Why you glorious little fucker . . .'

An empty box of firelighters.

9

Manolis drove to the police station in Rex's battered old pickup truck. It was unlicensed and unroadworthy. The gears crunched, the brakes felt spongy from lack of use and none of the dashboard instruments worked. The cabin promptly filled with exhaust fumes — just as well there was no windscreen. The truck also emitted a strange, unnerving sound from under the chassis every time Manolis touched the brakes, like a copper pipe being rolled along a concrete floor.

On the drive to town, he must have counted a hundred kangaroos. Most of them stood staring by the roadside, others in the middle of the road. He pressed the horn but it wasn't working and emitted a dull whirr that seemed only to attract more roos the closer he got to town. It was an eerie feeling, zigzagging through such a large colony of ruggedly built roos.

When he wasn't dodging wildlife, Manolis contemplated the crumpled box of firelighters on the seat beside him. His fingers tensed on the steering wheel.

With the exception of a few more sombre-looking roos, Cobb's main street was as deserted as it had been the previous day. Shops remained closed, including the takeaway, which Manolis had hoped would be serving big country breakfasts. Ordinary business hours, it appeared, meant nothing in Cobb. That certainly wasn't how Manolis remembered it; he remembered decorated shopfronts, crowded pavements and his diligent father opening the milk bar at seven o'clock every morning without fail. Customers would arrive five minutes later.

Manolis pulled up at the station with dirt in his eyes and flies in his nostrils. Sparrow heard the loud backfiring outside, emerged. He flashed a pearly smile.

'Wow,' he said. 'Now *that* car is a great cover.'

Manolis slammed the door hard. It rattled on its hinges before coming loose and sagging at a crooked angle. Rex had told him it needed fixing, the hinge pins and bushings were due for replacing. It was on the repair list alongside the car's engine, body, interior and electricals.

'Where'd you park the Val?' Sparrow asked. 'Hide it under a pile of old rags in Rexy's shed?'

Manolis didn't respond, his irritation growing by the minute. Instead, he called for Fyfe as he walked through the station, trying to summon him from the oceanic depths of whatever bottle he'd crawled into.

Sparrow followed him. 'He's not here,' he said.

Manolis stopped and turned. 'Where is he?' He pronounced each syllable very precisely.

'He's not far. Sit. Coffee?'

'No,' he replied firmly. 'Evidence locker. *Now.*'

Sparrow eyed his senior officer, whose gaze was unflinching. 'OK, mate. Right this way.'

Christ, thought Manolis. Was he the only cop in this wretched town who realised this was a murder investigation? Did no-one in Cobb respect the badge, the thin blue line, not even the police themselves? Everything in town moved at half-pace, including human evolution. He wondered whether they actually taught the topic in the local schools.

'And what about a search of Molly's house?' Manolis said. 'Organise one ASAP, please.'

70

'Righto.'

'I also want to see the autopsy report.'

'Doc hasn't finished it yet.'

Another bullshit excuse, thought Manolis.

Sparrow led the way down a long corridor that seemed to narrow the further they walked. The linoleum floor was covered in all manner of stubborn stains that someone had unsuccessfully tried to remove. Manolis picked up a scrap of paper from the floor and recognised it as being from his notepad. It was the names of the boys who had vandalised his car, given to Sparrow the previous day.

The drunk tank was again empty, its door wide open. So was the door to the room where the evidence was kept. Manolis was shocked.

'Lock's stuffed,' Sparrow said flippantly.

'I see that. No-one's ever come to fix it?'

Sparrow scoffed. 'You think the government gives two shits about us out here in Woop Woop? Nope. Outta sight, outta mind.'

'But aren't you worried about people tampering with evidence?'

'Not really, nah. And besides, there's locks on the front door.'

The evidence room had a large metal shelving unit against one wall. The shelves were bowed beneath the weight of overloaded milk crates containing an assortment of spanners, knives and misshapen wooden implements. A rack of shotguns sat against the opposite wall, with handguns tossed into a distinctive red milk crate. None of the items were tagged in any way or enclosed in sealable containers or bags. A filing cabinet stood against the far wall, its drawers half-open, papers arranged haphazardly.

Sparrow stepped through the room with purpose and dragged back a shopping trolley parked in the far corner. It had a wonky wheel.

'Here,' he said. 'Good to go.'

Manolis scratched the prickly new growth on his chin as he examined the trolley's contents. There were two black garbage bags, one bulging more than the other.

'Rocks in that one, tape in this,' Sparrow said, pointing.

'Tape?' Manolis said.

'Yair, we found a twisted roll at the scene. Oh, and this.' Sparrow held out a Bowie knife that was so long it was nearly a sword.

'Jesus. Where was this?'

'Sticking out of the tree she was taped to. Wait, the file . . .'

Sparrow rooted around in the filing cabinet's middle drawer and retrieved a recycled manila folder, covered in biro and scribble. 'Notes and photos,' he said.

'Thank you,' Manolis said, flipping through the file. It felt incredibly light. He tapped the trolley with his other hand. 'You run out of milk crates or something?'

Sparrow chuckled. 'Actually, mate, that's evidence too. Be hard-pressed dragging someone to an oval in a milk crate.'

Manolis instinctively snatched his hand from the trolley handle. He glared at the constable with large, incredulous eyes.

'Relax, I already dusted for prints,' Sparrow said quickly. 'Not a single one, not even on the rocks or tape or knife. Killer must've worn gloves.'

'So, she was pushed to the sportsground in the

72

trolley?'

'Reckon so. There was a trench in the grass leading to the oval.'

How ingenious, thought Manolis. A trolley was the easiest, least suspicious transport available. A car meant the potential for hair, spit, blood, DNA, which could all be traced. A shopping trolley belonged to no-one. And if anyone had come across the murderer and victim, well, it was probably just some drunk being wheeled home by a considerate mate.

Sparrow showed Manolis to the spare office at the back of the station. It had a small desk but no computer. There was a landline telephone with the number seven missing and a dead line. Sparrow flicked on the light switch. A fluorescent tube buzzed to life after a delay of several seconds, then flickered like a strobe. Sparrow struggled to lift the first garbage bag onto the desk, bringing it down with a loud thud. A succession of softer thuds followed as he emptied the contents. Manolis turned off the fluorescent tube and opened the window's venetian blinds. Shafts of light fell across the desk, illuminating the rough, bloodstained rocks.

'Her blood,' Sparrow said. 'And bits of her insides. Christ, talk about being stoned until you're dead.'

Manolis took his first proper look at the murder weapon. He'd been hoping for something more distinctive, a unique colour or shape or texture. But as he examined the rocks one by one it dawned on him that they could not have been a more ordinary collection of grey and white angular stones. The land was littered with a billion of the nondescript bastards. It was the most uninspiring weapon, and Manolis had known of people killed with teaspoons and ballpoint pens. The only thing that made the rocks in any way distinctive was the gruesome ritual they'd been used for.

Sparrow held up the gaffer tape. It was black, two inches wide, and still thick with supply. 'You can buy these at the supermarket, this exact kind. They'll be all over town. I got a few rolls at home myself. Hell, we even got some here at the station.'

'So, you think the killer was a local? Or what are the chances of someone passing through town who bought tape from the shop?'

Sparrow leaned against the doorframe, thought a moment. 'Unlikely.'

'Oh?'

'The only things people stop for in Cobb are petrol and directions out of Cobb.'

Manolis picked up the rock nearest to his favoured right hand, held it in his coarse palm, felt its weight. It was the size of a cricket ball but twice as heavy. He folded his fingers over the projectile and felt little stabs of electricity shoot up his forearm. He imagined throwing it with all his might at someone's head from a short distance. Closing his eyes, he held the rock up to his face, pressing it hard into his cheek until his mouth contorted. Sparrow's whole face did the same thing in horror at the detective's unorthodox methods.

Jesus, thought Manolis. This was Old Testament shit. Not what he usually handled. Not what anyone usually handled.

He continued to feel the rock's unforgiving weight. The clank of metal on wood broke his reverie. He opened his eyes to see the silver blade of the Bowie gleaming in the sunlight.

'This here's a bit more interesting,' Sparrow said.

Manolis picked up the knife, blade in one hand, handle in the other. It was impressively heavy, particularly the handle. He held it at eye level, rotated it. It had a cross-guard to protect the user's hands. The blade was as wide as the gaffer tape and as long as a wooden ruler. It was spotless, looked brand new. The beauty of it steadied him, grounded him.

'Unfortunately, I reckon there's at least one of these per house in Cobb, probably more,' said Sparrow. 'Blokes carry 'em round town all the time. They make no effort to hide 'em.'

Manolis sat back in his chair, the well-worn spring squeaking beneath his weight. He rotated the knife in his hand. 'How do you conceal something so huge?'

'The blokes at the abattoir compete for who has the biggest blade, but they're harmless. It's the jobless pricks on ice you gotta worry about. Angry, paranoid lunatics slash anything that moves.'

Manolis paused to think. 'And where was this found again?'

'Stickin' out of a tree.'

'She wasn't cut?'

Sparrow shook his head. 'Not from what I saw.'

Manolis made one final examination of the knife before placing it back on the desk. He wondered why it had been left at the scene.

Sparrow wheeled in the shopping trolley. 'From the supermarket. Same place what sells the tape.' Like the rocks, the trolley bore no distinguishing features. It was metal, slightly rusted, with swivel wheels. 'They even left their dollar coin in the lock.'

Manolis bent down, leaned in, squinted. 'So they have.' He tried to pull it out but couldn't.

'Jammed tighter than a nun's nasty,' said Sparrow.

'Did you fingerprint the trolley?'

Sparrow shook his head. 'No point. It'd be covered. We found some long strands of hair twisted around the bottom, probably hers. But that's it.'

'Was she carrying anything, any personal belongings? Purse or wallet or keys or phone?'

'Nope.'

Manolis stopped. 'Doesn't it seem strange she'd go out without at least one of those items?'

Sparrow thought a moment. 'Not really, I wander round town all the time without any of those things. Maybe it's only strange in the city.'

'And you say someone pushed her to the oval in the trolley? She was probably drugged, unconscious or semiconscious.'

Sparrow nodded. 'There was a trail of flattened grass from her body to the trolley, which was tipped on its side.'

Manolis paused. He knew the answer but still asked the question. 'What about DNA samples, can we collect those?'

Sparrow gave a small sarcastic laugh. 'Sure, mate. Absolutely we can. I'll send them down to the boys in our forensic lab, chop-chop. They'll work around the clock to get us an answer.'

Manolis considered the resources at his disposal in the city: controlled laboratory conditions, microscopes, sequencers, all state-of-the-art machines, cutting edge. He was certain that evidence from regional homicides was usually sent to the city for DNA testing. But it was likely a lengthy process, and Sparrow, in a roundabout way, was right: the trolley could have been contaminated with half the town's prints and DNA.

'So, that's it?' Manolis said. 'That's all there was?'

'The rest was as nature intended,' Sparrow replied.

Manolis picked up the thin manila folder that was carefully balanced on one corner of the desk. He opened it and saw a collection of square photos of poor quality, randomly arranged in different orientations, some on their side or upside-down, others backwards.

'What's this?' He squinted. 'Are these . . . are these Polaroids?'

He took a second to arrange the photos in order, like unshuffling a deck of cards. Before his eyes flashed his first sighting of the bloodied and broken head of Molly Abbott. The photos were spattered red and black. Manolis's fingers felt grubby. He wanted to wipe them.

'Yair, Polaroids,' said Sparrow. 'It's the easiest way.'

'Jesus. I haven't seen Polaroid photos in twenty years. Didn't realise they still made the film.'

'Can't develop photos in town no more since the pharmacy closed,' Sparrow said matter-of-factly.

'And the station doesn't have a digital camera?'

Sparrow let out a wry laugh. 'We had one years ago, but it broke and was never fixed or replaced. The Polaroid's more reliable.'

Manolis scanned the images. They were gruesome, even for an experienced homicide detective. And he had seen bodies that were decapitated and dismembered. Part of his reaction came from knowing the brutal way she had died. The rest came from the eerie style of photography that made the images look like a faded memory.

Next, Manolis consulted the sketches of the crime scene, as there was only so much he could glean from photographs. The drawings had been done on scraps

77

of paper. An elevation view was drawn on the back of an old mechanic's receipt blackened with grease stains; someone had bought spark plugs. The field sketches were bereft of measurements and looked as though they'd been done by a five-year-old. Manolis analysed the pencil-drawn diagrams, rotating them in his hands. The papers were much-handled, grimy and creased. The field notes, written on the back of a serviette, were just as illegible, as if the author had had a seizure.

'Are these your notes?' Manolis said.

Sparrow swished his hair. 'Sarge's.'

'Can you read this chicken scratch?'

Another swish.

Manolis re-examined the sketches and notes, then closed the folder with a snap. The rocks remained on the desk. He considered the room for a moment and tapped two fingers to his lips, searching his rabbit thoughts, while Sparrow searched his holey pockets. After finding a cigarette and lighter, he was about to bring the two into contact when Manolis said:

'Right. Take me to the scene.'

10

They went in Sparrow's car after Manolis explained what had happened to his. Sparrow was unperturbed, claiming that vehicles used for kindling were not uncommon in Cobb.

His own car exploded to life at the third attempt. Manolis reached over his shoulder for a seatbelt that wasn't there. Even with worn brake pads and no discernible suspension, Manolis still thought it was a smoother ride than Rex's jalopy.

As they drove, the young constable fiddled nervously with the smoke tucked behind his ear.

'So how much looks familiar to you?' he said, making conversation.

He was referring to the town, but Manolis wasn't focusing on the passing scenery, or even listening closely. He was still picturing the bloody stones strewn across the desk, even though Sparrow had safely returned them to the unsecure evidence room. Manolis thought about his cremated Valiant and why he'd really been housed in the sheriff's office. There was still no sign of Fyfe. A cloudless day meant another scorcher, the air dry and dusty, the asphalt road turning tacky.

'Detective . . . ?'

'Sorry, what?' Manolis said.

'The town. How old were you when you left?'

Manolis stared out of the passenger window, saw the boarded-up shops and derelict facades. These were the wrecks of long-closed businesses that had once flourished. His shoulders slumped in a kind of sigh and he half-closed his eyelids.

'Town looks the same,' he lied.

'What about the brown house?' Sparrow said.

'What about it?'

'That wasn't there. At least, not like it is now.'

'No. What did it use to be?'

Sparrow took a moment to respond. 'You don't remember?' he asked suspiciously.

'I think I do,' Manolis said, playing dumb. 'But it was such a long time ago. Freshen my memory?'

Sparrow's lip curled. 'Before the nice white men in nice grey suits came making promises about nice new jobs and money and bullshit, it was a technical college. You know, welders, plumbers, sparkies, chippies — that kinda actually useful stuff.'

Manolis smiled knowingly, thinking about his son's new father figure. 'Yeah,' he breathed. 'Trades. Not suits. Real jobs.'

'Yair.' Sparrow swerved to avoid a pothole large enough to swallow a truck. 'To think, though, the brown house almost didn't happen.'

'Oh?'

'It was the deciding issue at the last council election. People wanted to believe the lie, that it would do the town good. So they voted yes.'

'How'd you vote?'

'Didn't,' Sparrow said, almost proudly.

Manolis shifted in his seat. 'I remember when the detention centre was a migrant camp. It's where they put all the Europeans after the war.'

'Must've been before they made it a tech college. Well before my time.'

'My dad apparently stayed there when he first

80

arrived in Australia.'

'No shit, eh. Your dad?'

'Apparently. So what it's being used for now is nothing new. It's just the next wave of immigration, the second one, after the Europeans.'

Sparrow let Manolis's remark settle a moment before he said, 'You mean the third wave.'

'Huh?'

Sparrow counted with his fingers, grinning as he extended each long digit. 'Third wave, towelheads. Second wave, wogs. First wave, *whitefellas*.'

A knowing smile appeared on Manolis's face. 'Actually, I forgot the Asians. They came after the Vietnam War, during the '70s and '80s, from what they called Indochina.'

'No gooks ended up in Cobb.'

'Most migrant camps had closed by then. Like today's asylum seekers, they also came in fishing boats and against great opposition.'

'It doesn't matter where you came from,' breathed Sparrow. 'You're all bloody invaders. Nobody asked us what we blackfellas thought when you all started turnin' up.'

'Why, what would you have said?'

Sparrow smiled broadly. 'Fuck off, we're full.'

A man appeared on the road ahead, limping, crossing the burning asphalt in bare feet. Recognising the approaching car, he lingered in the middle of the street and Sparrow slowed down. The man had a broad nose and a goatee and was wearing a fraying T-shirt, drainpipe jeans and a black baseball cap turned backwards. He leaned down to Sparrow's open window and bumped fists. A short volley of mumbled exchanges followed in a language Manolis didn't understand.

81

He traded glances with the man, who appeared to be in his late teens or early twenties. They laughed. Manolis knew he was the topic of conversation. A second fist bump ended the discussion.

'Who was that?' asked Manolis.

'No-one. Just a mate.'

'Just a mate saying hi, eh?'

'Yair.'

'What's his name?'

'Eddie.'

'Eddie who?'

'Eddie Rogers.'

'Thought you said all your people considered you a sell-out?'

'Guess I lied. Some don't.'

'And what's that you were speaking?'

'What, the language?'

'Yes.'

'Australian. I'm like you, mate, English is my second language.'

The sedan took the corner at speed. The black outline of a roo skipping along the hot asphalt appeared in the middle of the windscreen. The Ford accelerated. Manolis assumed Sparrow was trying to shoo the animal away, or backed the kangaroo to be agile enough to escape. But he wasn't, and nor was the roo. It zigzagged down the centre of the road but lost ground with every desperate stride. Sparrow had the roo in his crosshairs and a grin on his face. It grew ever larger in the windscreen and was just about to disappear beneath the bonnet when Manolis cried, 'Hey!' and reefed on the steering wheel. The car veered left, the roo shot right. Sparrow planted his foot, smashed the brakes, slamming sideways into the gutter. It was a few seconds before the car came to a skidding stop beneath the shade of a drooping birch.

'What the hell?' Sparrow shouted. 'What was that for?'

With the sting of burning rubber in his nostrils, Manolis looked up. In the near distance, the roo was frantically skipping away.

'You wanna kill us or something?' Sparrow went on. In the background, the engine idled with a harsh vibration.

'No,' Manolis said at last. 'But running down helpless animals is *not* OK.'

Sparrow's breathing was stolid. 'Helpless my arse. They're pests. They rip up crops, tear down fences, attack locals and spread disease.'

Manolis paused. 'I don't remember them being so bad.'

'Not when you lived here. Plague proportions now, mate.'

Manolis considered the empty road ahead, remembered the journey to town that morning. 'I doubt that,' he lied.

'My oath, they are. Look, just be glad my weapon of choice is a car. Some bastards lay poison — slow and painful death.'

'I thought your people had a deep spiritual connection to all wildlife, including kangaroos.'

'We do. But we still bloody hunt. And anyway, tell that to me cousin.'

'Your cousin? What happened?'

'Last year, this big red boomer bastard tore his whatchamacallit . . . oesophagus. Flyin' doctor came, took him straight to the city. He spent eight days in hospital, first two in intensive care. Still can't talk right.'

Manolis went quiet, picturing the injuries. He'd never heard of such aggression in normally docile animals.

'And this year Kate's fiancé died when he swerved to avoid a roo and hit a tree.'

Manolis raised his eyebrows, looked at Sparrow in disbelief. 'Jesus. Really?'

So Kerr was grieving too. Manolis would need to tread gently, be mindful of her loss. So many lives touched by death. In Cobb, a long life appeared to be the exception, not the rule.

'Yair,' Sparrow said. 'You've seen the roads out 'ere. Once you're off the bitumen and onto the shoulder, you're stuffed. It's actually safer *not* to swerve for roos. You're better off to just keep ploughin' right through 'em, drivin' straight.'

Manolis did not respond. He was thinking.

'We're supposed to serve the community, right?' Sparrow said. 'Well I consider the eradication of pests, of traffic hazards, a community service. I'm savin' lives.'

Manolis moistened his lips. Finally he said, 'That's awful news about Kerr.'

'Yair. Kate's gotten the rough end of the pineapple.'

They kept driving, past the war memorial and cenotaph. Manolis recognised them both, although the soldier's rifle had been snapped off at the end, a prized trophy for vandals. By contrast, the empty smoke packet and long neck of beer cradled in the digger's forearm were gestures to recognise service.

The road opened up ahead, downhill to the Alfred Crapp Reserve, named after another local war hero recognised for travelling to a foreign land and killing many foreign troops. Manolis used to run on the oval in school sporting carnivals, surrounded by crêpe-paper streamers and coloured balloons, sprinting until he couldn't breathe. His dad had even taken him there to kick the football. His memories were beginning to stir.

Sparrow parked at a right angle to the street and led Manolis onto the oval. The detective turned, examined the road with narrow eyes. He tried to imagine the route the trolley would've taken, likely to have been deliberately mapped to avoid detection. He wondered if the trolley's hard plastic wheels had somehow marked its course — probably not.

Sparrow walked him through where they'd found the trolley, the narrow strip of flattened grass and an area of widely spaced trees behind the scoreboard. A pair of rabbits, their eyes swollen with myxomatosis, scurried off. The eucalypts took Manolis by surprise: their trunks were bleeding, covered in thick rivulets of deep-crimson sap.

'Christ,' he said. 'You sure there was just one person killed here? Looks like mass murder.'

'It is,' said Sparrow. 'Of trees.'

Run down with drought, the eucalypts had been attacked by boring insects who were eating them alive from the inside out. The trees fought back as best they could, seeping their defence, trying to stay alive, to no avail. They were dying a slow death.

In front of the thickest eucalypt was a patch of darkened dirt. The tree was also stained with what appeared to be spray marks. Manolis was careful to step around a bull-ant nest that was shaded by the broad-trunked tree. He examined the crime scene from multiple angles, high, low, and listened to the young constable's descriptions, looking everywhere he pointed. All the while, Manolis tried to mesh the indecipherable diagrams in his hand and reconstruct the events in his mind. But something was niggling at him.

'Why isn't the area taped off?' he asked eventually.

Sparrow's shoulders rose up and down in time with his breathing. He looked at Manolis as if he were mad. 'You being serious?'

'Deadly. The area should always be taped off to preserve the crime scene. That's basic police work.'

Sparrow chuckled. 'Mate, that was the last thing on our minds. We needed to clean up this crap before the mob arrived. And I don't mean 'my mob' — I mean 'the mob'. They didn't need any extra incentive.'

'Not sure I know what you mean.'

'I mean rocks. I mean a knife. I mean a white woman's body lyin' in a pool of white woman's blood.'

'But taping off the area preserves the evidence. What if the offender had dropped something, a clue?'

Sparrow shook his head. 'We already got the clues. You saw 'em. That's it.'

Manolis pictured the stones on the desk and again consulted his sketches.

'Besides, it's not like we got anyone who could've stayed and secured the scene,' Sparrow continued. 'They'd only have gotten lynched themselves.'

'For what? For doing their job?'

'For being seen as hiding something, or even as a sympathiser. Strung up yellow tape only attracts trouble round here, mate. Best way to secure a scene like this is to not make it a scene. This ain't the city, our streets aren't swarming with people. The chances of someone stumbling across it randomly and giving a toss are pretty low. So, for all intents and purposes, you can consider this scene before you as 'secure'.'

Manolis considered the small-town logic. 'Shame that won't stand up in a court of law.'

'Kangaroo court here, mate.'

Manolis wiped his oily forehead with the back of a sweaty hand. He needed to get the case under control, and fast, or Detective Inspector Paul Bloody Porter would have his guts for garters.

'Constable,' Manolis said calmly, 'I've had cases that I worked on for years thrown out of court for not following the book. I've seen rapists and murderers walk. I've learned lessons the hard way.'

Sparrow ignored all the warnings of extreme fire danger and lit the cigarette he'd been denied earlier.

'Mate,' he said, inhaling a lungful, 'if we went by the book here, we wouldn't make half the arrests that we do.'

'Perhaps,' Manolis said. 'The only problem is that half of zero is zero.'

Sparrow smirked. 'I like yer big city mathematics, professor. Look at it this way. The brown house was singed the night after Molly's death. But it would've been razed to the fucken ground if we hadn't done our bit to clean up this 'ere mess on Saturday morning.'

Manolis considered the crime scene: the oval leading up to the scoreboard, the area beneath the trees, the dry creek next to the oval. He saw small scraps of rubbish that were easily recoverable, cigarette butts and food wrappers, perhaps even a footprint or two with a little work. All of it was evidence. Or none of it was. It was now all the same. He imagined what might happen if he dared call in the forensics boys. He pictured them laughing their heads off — at the situation, at him — then returning to their real coffee and real police work in the city. He was operating inside a parenthesis where nothing seemed rational: a strange, logic-free zone. A trickle of sweat ran down his hairy neck.

A gust of hot wind scattered the dry leaves around his feet and nearly blew the worthless notes from his hand. Sparrow sucked hard on his smoke to keep it alight, making the end glow a violent orange. The ash vanished into thin air.

Manolis consulted the Polaroids, saw the bloodied remains of the schoolteacher's head. 'You know,' he said, pointing at the ground, 'I actually expected more of a bloodstain.'

Sparrow screwed up his features. 'Huh?'

'From a stoning. A human head holds many litres.'

The young constable shrugged. 'Must've dried,' he said, cigarette in mouth.

'Sure, but there'd be a stain.'

Sparrow gave him a long look. 'There is a stain,' he said flatly. 'Right there.'

Manolis wasn't convinced. Something didn't add up. 'And who found the body again?'

Sparrow stamped out his smoke. 'Ida Jones. Local busybody.'

'Take me to her.'

'Sure.' Sparrow paused. 'Only thing is, Ida's old and tends to treat us darkies with contempt.'

'Oh?'

'Greets us with a fully loaded shottie if ever we come within sight of her place.'

'Really . . . ?'

Sparrow snorted. 'Ha. Well maybe not every time, but she's definitely done it a few times. So, we'd sooner

88

not risk it. Plus it's now after twelve, which means Ida will already be drunk. She's up with the sparrows and into the gin by morning tea. Best time to get to her is before noon. In fact, that's the only time to get to Ida.'

'Tomorrow, then.'

'Sure. Kate can take you. She likes Kate. Won't shoot Kate.'

11

'Let's go to the pub. My shout.'

Sparrow had started walking to his car before he'd even finished his sentence. Creature of habit, thought Manolis. Or a fully committed drunk. Either way, not much of a working day for a full-time police officer, though Manolis knew cops in the city who did less and drank even more.

He was a step behind Sparrow as they crossed the oval. The constable was walking with determination and faster than he had all morning, as if he planned to start the car and drive away with or without his superior officer. Not that rank appeared to concern him.

'I'll give it a miss,' Manolis said.

Sparrow stopped in his tracks, then turned and glared at Manolis as if mortally wounded. For a second, Manolis prepared to defend against a flying fist. To refuse someone's shout in Cobb was downright criminal. But then Sparrow's eyes softened and he turned away.

'Suit yerself,' he said simply, and continued to his car.

Manolis looked to the sky, felt the sun scalding his exposed body. Endowed with Mediterranean genes, his skin was inherently olive in colour and had only ripened over time, becoming darker and more etched with wrinkles. His swarthy appearance meant he was often mistaken for Middle Eastern, which elicited all manner of insults. But he still burned, and it didn't take long beneath the harsh antipodean sun.

He caught up with Sparrow as he engaged gear and began reversing. 'Can you at least give me a lift back to the station?'

Sparrow glanced past Manolis's shoulder. 'You don't wanna hang round here no more? You know, scope the scene?'

'Think I got all I need.'

A pause. 'Take you as far as the pub. Hop in.'

The town was reluctantly coming to life, and Manolis reasoned it was probably due to liquor licensing hours. Groups of men wandered around, led by their livers. Eyeing Sparrow crookedly, Manolis hoped that any road-bound wildlife had already sought shade from the noonday heat.

'I met Constable Kerr last night,' Manolis said. 'At the barbecue.'

'What'd she say?'

'Not much. She reckons the killer's an outsider, not a local. Or maybe someone passing through town, which means they'll be long gone.'

'Prob'ly, dunno.'

'Any idea who that might be?'

Sparrow kept dodging potholes. 'The roads have always been bad, but they've gotten worse with the extra traffic since the brown house opened up.'

Manolis repeated his question.

Sparrow crunched the gears. 'Passers-by, eh? Well, lemme see. There's no fruit pickers cos there's no fucken fruit to pick. And I think all the slaughter-house workers live here now. We had some issues with truckies recently, hmm . . . '

'Truck drivers? Like what, when?'

Sparrow drummed the steering wheel nervously. Manolis got the impression the constable had said too much. He pressed him for more information.

'Aw, you know,' Sparrow said finally. 'A few dumb truckers thought it was a good idea to offer our local girls drugs, food, money for sex. They used to do it in their trucks.'

'Illegal prostitution. That's nothing major.'

The car slowed noticeably. Sparrow glared at him with bulletproof eyes. 'Some of the girls were eight years old. Hadn't even bled yet. Me sister was one.'

Manolis arched his bushy eyebrows in shock, before lowering them in dismay. 'I'm sorry, I had no idea.'

Sparrow eyed the road. 'Worthless white scum. Preyin' like that.' His tone had changed into a cold, hard bark.

'That's terrible. Did you at least catch the guys who were doing it?'

A satisfied smile settled around Sparrow's eyes. 'My oath we did. The cousins brought justice with baseball bats and star pickets. Bastards won't be back anytime soon.'

That wasn't quite what Manolis had asked. But point made.

They drove on. Manolis found himself recognising more of the town. A group of trees he used to climb when he had supple knees. An old house, now barely standing, that all the kids once avoided. Blinking hard, he pushed away the memories.

'You think Molly might've been involved in something like that?' he said. 'The sex game, I mean.'

Sparrow shook his head. 'Doubt it. What's in it for her?'

Manolis moistened his lips. He was pensive. 'Maybe she was turning tricks as well. Nice little earner, till she ticked off a client?'

'Like I said, doubt it. Big difference between wanting a middle-aged schoolteacher and one of her students.'

'Each to their own. Not everyone's a paedo.'

'Bullshit. Everyone's a paedo.'

The car ploughed towards an angry murder of crows, feasting on the remains of something dead stuck to the road. They scattered at the last second. Sparrow scowled.

'Look at the way Molly was killed,' Manolis said. He was speaking with his hands now, gesturing his thinking. 'Aren't women normally stoned to death for adultery? Maybe one of her clients was infatuated, thought they owned her or something. You even mentioned that one bloke who carried a torch for her?'

Sparrow stayed quiet, thinking.

'I'm just talking off the top of my head here,' Manolis said.

'Maybe,' Sparrow said. 'But to stone her to death? Who even does that? Doesn't that say something to you?'

'It does.'

'Yair, so?'

'I just didn't think it could possibly be that cut and dried.'

'Mate, I hate to admit it, but those religious nutters at the tourist park have a point here. They're only sayin' what most of the town is thinkin' — even us blackfellas, and we don't wanna agree with anything the whitefella says, ever. Kate's wrong if she calls this an outside job. But I don't reckon it's an inside one either. It's a bit o' both, if you get me.'

The line for the drive-thru bottle shop came into view, twice as long as the day before. Trev would be raking it in. Sparrow waved at him as he puttered past with thumb extended, teeth exposed.

'I'll say one thing,' Sparrow said. 'People round here are always lookin' for ways to make an extra buck. Look at Trev and his little operation. They know it's the only sure-fire way outta this craphole. So it wouldn't surprise me if Molly was chargin'. Blokes round 'ere would pay top dollar for a nice, clean white woman.'

Manolis considered this information as they arrived at the top pub. Sparrow had to use both hands to wrench on the handbrake. Reaching for the doorhandle, Manolis asked, 'And you'd say, in your opinion, that Molly was attractive?'

Sparrow stopped. 'As in, good-looking?'

'Yes.'

He laughed. 'Well, I wouldn't go there. But that's only cos I'm not into that sort of thing.'

His words hung in the air. Manolis couldn't read the young man's flawless, emotionless face. His eyes looked sheepish, appearing larger than usual, or perhaps that was just a trick of the light. Sparrow's cheeks burned; he sighed and turned his gaze down to his hands.

The realisation dawned on Manolis. 'Oh,' he said. 'Well, good. Good for you, mate.'

Sparrow studied Manolis's face warily, searching for a hint of expression. When finally he spoke it was barely a mumble.

'Best that come from me. I'm used to it. It's another reason most people in town give me a wide berth.' He paused, then narrowed his eyes. 'But fuck them. And fuck you.'

And with that Sparrow slid off the seat, took a giant

step and slammed the car door. Manolis's ears rang for several seconds and he was again made to chase his host, this time grabbing his arm as it grasped the pub door and spinning him around. Sparrow brushed Manolis's hand away with a swipe.

'Hey.' Manolis met his gaze. 'Look, I'm not sure what you expect me to say here. I don't know what you've been through but I reckon, at a guess, I'm not like the people here in town. In the city, we don't give two shits what you do outside work. We don't care if you like men or women or both or neither. All we care about is that you're a good cop and do your job.'

Sparrow's pupils flicked from side to side, his breath heavy, his chest heaving.

'Is that clear?' Manolis asked, his tone calm.

The young man didn't move. Then, after a few seconds, his breathing steadied and his eyelids half-closed.

'I asked you, Constable, is that clear?'

Sparrow looked away. He swallowed hard and exhaled lightly. 'Yair.'

'Good. Now, a few questions so I can make the most of my afternoon . . .'

'Shoot.'

Manolis leaned against a weathered old post holding up an asbestos verandah. Sparrow slumped on a park bench, the wooden slats either coming loose or missing altogether. He lit a smoke to calm himself, his nerves surely razor-wired. Manolis wanted to do the same but fought the urge.

'OK. Who are the persons of interest, the main suspects? Who was close to Molly? Come on, you know this town.'

Sparrow's eyes remained fixed on a small patch of

dirt behind Manolis. His limp cigarette turned to ash in his lips. 'Er,' he mumbled. 'I'll have to get back to you on that one.'

'Do you know of anyone behaving differently recently, either just before Molly's death or since?'

'Nope.'

'Is there any CCTV footage anywhere in town?'

Sparrow chuckled at the mere suggestion.

'Where's this bloke she slapped in the pub?'

'Joe? Again, get back to you.'

Manolis exhaled his frustration. 'How was the detention centre last night, any trouble?'

'Dunno.'

'I thought you said you were going there last night?'

'Yair. Didn't.'

'Where's Fyfe?'

'No idea.'

There was a long pause as Manolis gathered his thoughts and Sparrow inhaled his tar. Then Manolis said, 'OK, this conversation is over. But tomorrow morning, nine o'clock, I want to see you, Kerr and effing Fyfe at the station for a briefing. You tell them. Enjoy your drink.'

Sparrow stood abruptly. 'Thank God. Dyin' of thirst . . .'

He flicked his butt at Manolis's feet, narrowly missing his leather shoes, and disappeared inside the top pub. Manolis felt a cold blast of air conditioning as the door slammed in his face.

12

Manolis's walk back to the station took much longer than he'd imagined. Not because he got lost — there were only so many streets, and only one memorial hall and post office that he remembered as landmarks. It was more the heat that slowed his progress, combined with an unexpected feeling of nostalgia. He couldn't quite put a finger on it but he suddenly felt much younger, which created the illusion of having all the time in the world. He lingered on street corners, kicked a crushed beer can as if it were a football. He came across the local school, his old school, everything smaller than he remembered, play equipment, water bubblers. Stopping to smell the leaves on a heavy old ghost gum that reached across the road, he felt transported. The crisp, sweet smell of eucalyptus grounded him, helped release his tension. It all looked entirely unfamiliar yet felt so recognisable.

Stumbling across a cemetery, Manolis pondered life and death, age and youth. He thought of his own son, and then considered young Sparrow. The kid projected as relaxed and carefree, but in reality was all kinds of messed up. And no wonder — he'd been shoved into a sack and beaten with a small-town stick. His reaction to Manolis was itself a reaction to the prejudice he'd faced his whole adult life. It was automatic, learned behaviour. The kid had some fight in him, and in spades, that was clear. He refused to live a lie, and was every day simply trying to play the cards he'd been dealt. In a town like Cobb, Manolis deemed this to be worthy of the utmost respect.

Manolis spent almost an hour in the graveyard, walking casually through the rows. He always found cemeteries curiously calming, something about all those departed souls resting in peace, even though he imagined that some had died violently. He read the inscriptions on the headstones — those he could make out — and recognised more family names than he would ever have been able to remember.

'The last shirt has no pockets,' he told himself.

In the city, Con's grave still required work. Maria, who kept a weekly vigil to light a remembrance candle, was already bothering Manolis about it. The grave had collapsed on the day of the funeral due to heavy overnight rain and needed to be dug out again. It was now 'naked', as Maria called it, just the hard Australian soil that her husband had been buried under. It needed some cover, some protection from the elements. Manolis pictured himself filling up a car boot with white stones from a landscape supply shop and taking to the task with one of Con's old shovels. It was an interim measure before the erection of a pair of matching his-and-hers marble monuments. Con had already paid for them, more than ten thousand dollars.

By the time Manolis reached the station he felt dehydrated, and quenched his thirst from an outdoor tap. The water tasted hard and metallic and probably wasn't fit for human consumption, but he drank until his stomach groaned. His sweaty shirt clung to his chest and back, transparent, revealing thick ringlets of black hair.

The station was secured with its trio of heavy locks. No sign of life. Manolis sat to rest on the step, began talking to himself in Greek, thinking out loud, processing. He stopped when two young Aboriginal men walked past, staring at him as if he was mad. Maybe he was.

Needing to move on, he decided to take his chances back aboard the rolling deathtrap. A drive would clear his head and help him properly scout the scene.

Driving along the main drag he was overtaken by speeding utes flying Australian flags and bearded bikies on rumbling choppers. Groups of shirtless men — all black or all white — roamed the filthy streets. Some loitered in pockets of shade, while others appeared to be walking with a clear direction and intent. The end of sobriety was nigh. Did I really come from this place? Manolis asked himself. And yet, the air in his lungs tasted sweet and felt right.

He was back at the abandoned takeaway shop, once his father's bustling milk bar. Pulling over, he went and pressed his face against the grubby glass. Even with bright sunlight the shop's interior was dark, but Manolis could make out the long counter running almost the entire length. This was where customers had paid their bill, often to Manolis's mother who had stood in a starched white uniform and hat behind a shiny cash register. It was where they sat on chrome swivel stools slurping his father's vanilla milkshakes and eating his home cooking. Manolis's aunt had been there too, in matching white uniform. She was Con's unmarried younger sister who had come out from Greece, supposedly to find a husband and have a family, but hastily returned after only a short while. Manolis's memories of Theia Penelope were hazy but he did remember she loved children and would pinch his plump youthful cheeks to bursting.

With the younger generation craving American food, Greek cafés were a Trojan horse for the Americanisation of Australia. Con dished up hamburgers, hot dogs, fries, spiders, malts, sundaes, banana splits and cordials. The older generation, on the other hand, was still comforted by Mother England and wanted traditional British fare: steak and eggs, chops and eggs, fish and chips, meat pies and boiled sweets. Con cooked it all, this 'food for white Australia'. He even had a jukebox in the furthest corner from the door. The milk bar was where most people first heard rock 'n' roll, well before it was on the radio. Closing his eyes, Manolis pictured a room full of people, all eating his father's cooking, a few dancing the twist, while his mother collected notes and coins, and he collected plates and glasses. Manolis remembered so much, but for the life of him couldn't remember what the café had been called. He would ask Rex when he next saw him.

The other memory Manolis struggled to recall was the day his family had left town. He remembered being in his room one evening, lying on his bed, hearing his father return home, slamming the back door. His mother was soon arguing with him, yelling, frantic. Their suitcases were packed in haste, their departure under cover of darkness and at high speed. They just locked up the café and left, only stopping once on the southern outskirts of town for his father to have a pee in the scrub by the roadside. Too tired to keep his eyelids open, the young Georgios Manolis fell asleep in the back of the station wagon, listening to his parents quarrel. When he woke the next morning, he was surrounded by pillars of concrete and glass.

The whole episode had left him bewildered. He'd

never told anyone about how he came to move to the city, and never found out why his parents left country Australia. His father's only explanation, over many years, was: 'Life is better in the city.'

Ever since that day, Manolis had never felt quite as stable. The earth always seemed to be shifting beneath his feet, his connections with the world fleeting, his trust wafer-thin. Or was that just the reality of being an adult? Nothing was secure, friendships and relationships only ever superficial, and no-one could be counted on. Geography had nothing to do with it. Returning to Cobb, seeing how things had worked out for Molly and for the town in general, had left the grown-up Manolis torn. He wondered whether he should have been grateful that his parents left when they did.

Driving north, Manolis saw the Cobb Friendly Grocer with its collection of murderous shopping trolleys. Young men were milling in the car park, smoking, drinking, swearing, spitting and staring at Manolis sideways as he idled past with the window down. He had only to follow his nose to find the abattoir further up the road. The stench was rank and meaty, at its worst in the height of summer. The stockyards contained a handful of cattle, all looking malnourished, the outline of their spines and hipbones prominent, some with ribs showing through their hide.

Then, on the horizon, the immigration detention centre loomed. It appeared unfocused, hazy. A pole flew an Australian flag the size of a swimming pool. Beyond the fences, prefabricated Nissen huts were distinctive with their half-cylindrical snakeskin of corrugated steel. It was cheap, ready-made housing for post-war migrants, and now even cheaper shelter for desperate asylum seekers.

Manolis approached with trepidation, driving guardedly, unsure of what to expect. He'd never been called out to an immigration facility before. Other cops had gone to centres in the city to deal with reports of civil unrest and assault, but there'd never been anything with the gravity of a homicide, let alone a stoning. As he got closer, Manolis pictured his young father emerging from the gates with a single suitcase in his hand, and an earnest hope in his heart for his new country and its people.

Manolis parked near the entrance, not far from the charred remains of two vehicles and a dumpster. He winced at the sight, remembering his own burnt wreck. He sat a while listening to the mufflers tick as they cooled, considering his next move. Finally, and with some unease, he approached the small demountable office building.

It was locked, empty. Coffee mugs, newspapers and cigarette packets were strewn across the front counter. There was no intercom and no number to ring. Manolis wasn't sure if this was normal for a Monday afternoon; it could very well have been.

The chain-link perimeter fence was about three metres high. Manolis examined it, noticed there was no razor wire on top, which reflected the centre's low security and the fact that some detainees were children. Being so new, the fence was sturdy but appeared easily scalable, either through climbing or with a boost from below. Around the perimeter, an arrangement of spectral trees showed their crooked limbs against the clear-blue sky.

Manolis followed the fence east. For the purposes of reconnaissance he planned to complete a full circuit of the rectangular centre. He walked casually, but with an alertness in his eyes. The accommodation blocks lay silent, which again may have been normal, perhaps a daily siesta. But it felt altogether too quiet as the dry earth crunched like cornflakes beneath his soles.

Suddenly, a spate of raised voices rent the air. They were coming from the direction in which Manolis was walking, although he couldn't tell from which side of the fence. Whatever they were saying was incomprehensible. He moved faster, breaking into a half-jog, stumbling, nearly twisting his ankle on the uneven ground.

Crouching and peering through some needle-sharp spinifex, Manolis now saw the source of the voices. It was a group of men, white, on his side of the fence. They were arching their backs, hurling stones and torrents of abuse at the detention centre. The rocks were landing on a vast expanse of dead lawn and falling a long way short of their intended target. Behind the men lay cases of grog, one per drunk, ripped open hurriedly, with discarded empties encircling them in a delicate ring of shiny aluminium. The men were making an afternoon of it, settling in, enjoying their sport. Empty cans didn't fly as far as empty glass bottles. But rocks did.

'Stone us? Fucken stone them!'

Manolis turned to the detention centre and squinted into the near distance. On an outdoor basketball court, enclosed with its own separate fence, he saw a small crowd of detainees, around twenty or thirty. But there was no basketball being played and no shade from the sweltering sun. Most of the detainees were trying to stand upright but losing the battle. They clutched at the chain-link fencing with outstretched arms to avoid the searing-hot asphalt surface, and silently watched the drunken spectacle unfold before them. Manolis kept looking at the detainees, wondering why they weren't inside during the hottest part of the day. A few slumped against the wire with obvious exhaustion. There were no guards or other officials in sight.

Manolis stared intently. The longer he watched the basketball court, the more it dawned on him that its occupants weren't there voluntarily. It was as if they'd been herded up, and he bet his life that there was a thick steel padlock on the gate. Such sweltering heat, he thought, would surely boil the brain.

'Cop that, ya terrorist scum.'

It was a surreal sight. From what Manolis could discern, there wasn't a great sense of community in Cobb other than for retaliation. Only when there was a common enemy did people unite.

Manolis considered booking the men with trespassing, vandalism, criminal damage. But no-one was where they weren't supposed to be, and only sobriety was being damaged. It was merely the displacement of organic matter, which had no owner, from one place to another. A nuisance charge, maybe. But not worth the paperwork. Careful not to be seen, Manolis crept away.

Walking towards the car park, the detective saw a figure crossing the asphalt and heading to a parked four-wheel drive. The man looked familiar. It took a moment for Manolis to recognise him. And then, skipping over the spiky grass tussocks, Manolis could not move fast enough.

'Hey. Hey, Sergeant . . . ? Oi, Fyfe. Wait, stop!'

Manolis was almost sprinting by the time he reached

the hot asphalt, his breath ragged. But the car door slammed, the engine fired, the tyres spun, and Manolis was left choking in a dirty cloud of diesel exhaust.

13

Manolis couldn't keep up with the four-wheel drive in Rex's pickup, which took multiple attempts to get going. He watched until Fyfe disappeared into the distance and then slowly began the long drive back to Olde Cobbe Towne, to rest and gather his thoughts. His mind was humming, connections being made, possible lines of enquiry opening up.

As he drove through the heat and flies, he considered all he'd seen, and all he'd not seen. The physical evidence was completely underwhelming. There was no murder weapon to trace, nothing the killer had left behind, and a grossly contaminated crime scene. But Manolis thought it strange that there was only a relatively small bloodstain to be found there, and that Molly would have left home without personal items, her wallet and phone and keys.

'That can't be right,' he told himself. 'No matter what anyone from around here says.'

There was always a chance the items had been retained by the killer as some sort of sick souvenir, which Manolis knew was common. In fact, this was an outcome he preferred — it meant the items were out there, somewhere, linking an individual to the murder. A search of Molly's house would confirm if they were missing. It was downright negligent that one hadn't already been conducted, but it wasn't altogether surprising for Cobb. The unorthodox was customary, the book barely followed. And that was a whole separate issue that niggled Manolis like a rock in his shoe. Securing a conviction based on evidence alone would be nearly impossible. Hardly a procedure had been adhered to. Defence barristers would queue up to take the case, the media would have a field day, headline after headline. Cobb would be the great detention experiment gone wrong. And Manolis would be forever linked. His career would dive-bomb faster than his marriage.

There were even more roos at dusk. Manolis saw several pairs of boomers boxing by the roadside as he drove back to the tourist park. He found Rex asleep in a camping chair outside the office building. Beside him, a hammer and a box of nails. Above him, a gulp of scraggly hot magpies on dead branches aired their rumpled wings, their mouths half-open as if panting. Manolis closed the car door lightly but it still rattled on its loose hinges and woke the proprietor, his ear attuned to a sound so familiar.

'Sorry,' Manolis said. 'Just returning your car.'

'It's your car now, Kojak,' Rex said, rubbing his eyes. 'For as long as you need it.'

'Thanks. Better to park it here, though. Cars spontaneously combust near me.'

Rex chuckled. 'I was just getting some kip after trying to fix a fence. Bloody thing's rotted, about to fall over. How'd you go today?'

Manolis sighed heavily and leaned against the rusted fender. 'First impressions. Every time you come into a case cold, there's a lot to get your head around.'

'I can imagine. Make it up to the brown house today?'

Manolis paused, considering his answer. 'I did, actually.'

'How was it?'

He was careful with his words. Rex had an obvious interest in the case, but the investigation needed to proceed without any further intervention.

'Quiet,' Manolis said.

Rex cleaned his ear with a black-rimmed fingernail. 'Ma can go on. Sorry about that. She doesn't want to admit it, but she loved Molly, she really did. Personally, I think she was heartbroken.'

'Heartbroken?'

'Because we'd drifted apart since Patrick's death. But it was always on the cards. After all, there was no blood between us.'

Manolis nodded. 'Can you think of anyone who'd want to hurt Molly?'

Rex shook his head. 'Not a soul. The entire town was at Patrick's funeral. Everyone knew that Molly had suffered enough, having already lost her husband.'

Manolis momentarily thought of Kerr. A town of widows, like in war.

'What about this Joe bloke, do you know him?'

Rex snorted. 'You mean Joe Shrewsbury? He's harmless. He and Patrick were mates. Molly saw him as a friend, but that was all.'

Manolis rubbed his coarse chin. 'Hmm. OK. And was Molly's recent behaviour different in any way?'

Rex exhaled. 'Couldn't tell you. Honestly, we hadn't seen her round here for a while. We've been flat out dealing with the new arrivals, no pun intended. Ma can go on about that too. But the truth is that without all this extra business, we'd have closed the park yonks ago.'

Looking around at the scene of dilapidation and disrepair, Manolis wanted to say perhaps that wasn't such a bad idea.

'Be a shame to lose all this local history,' he said instead.

Rex pointed towards the caravan section. 'See all those people over there? They'd be homeless. They're all pensioners, and I don't charge the oldies any rent.'

Manolis acknowledged the proprietor's generosity. There were certainly a large number of discoloured caravans baking in the sun, the vast majority with long grasses and weeds encircling their jaundiced sides like funeral wreaths.

'Your dad did the same, you know,' Rex added.

Manolis looked puzzled. 'The same what?'

'Like I said yesterday, when someone couldn't afford to pay their bill at the milk bar, Con let them eat for free.'

A memory cut across Manolis's mind. Hushed conversations by the cash register, embarrassment, then understanding and kindness. He smiled.

'That reminds me,' he said. 'I ended up going past Dad's old shop today. You wouldn't happen to remember its name?'

Rex's knees made a cracking sound as he stood. He stretched and scratched.

'I'm pretty sure it was the Manhattan Café,' he said. 'No wait, the Niagara Café. Something American, anyway.'

'Really, an American name . . . ?'

'Apparently your aunt's idea.'

'I remember Dad cooking American food, British food, Australian. Didn't realise he went the whole hog and called the café something American too. You sure it wasn't something Greek, like the Parthenon or Olympia?'

A gear clicked in Manolis's brain. Niagara did sound familiar.

'The name reflected most of the food,' Rex said. 'I remember your dad tried adding traditional Greek food to the menu a few times, things like stuffed peppers, moussaka, even souvlaki. But people didn't like it, they complained, said it was too oily and too rich. So he stopped.'

Manolis didn't recall that. He certainly remembered his father's vegetable garden, which produced tomatoes that tasted like real tomato, and eating Greek food with his parents. Roasted gemista vegetables, tomatoes and peppers filled with mincemeat and rice and mint. Spanakopita, spinach pie. Dolmades, which Manolis even helped make, collecting vine leaves bigger than his hands from around town with his mum and Theia Penelope. But it was all prepared and eaten behind closed doors, away from prying, judging eyes.

'Greek food was considered peasant food,' Rex said. 'No-one wanted it.'

That all changed in the city. Building on his experiences at the Niagara Café, Con ran a successful Greek restaurant serving authentic Greek fare for which people paid top dollar. His son waited tables there too, the handsome gadabout in a crisp white shirt and tireless charmer of flirtatious female diners. Con would've preferred his son take over the business, but the police academy — the chance to protect and serve the public — proved too strong a draw. The café was never meant to be inherited and was purely to lay a foundation in the new country. But the restaurant was different; it was something more legitimate and long term. Con was understandably disappointed with his son's career choice but supported him nonetheless, as

110

any loving parent would.

Manolis stared at Rex blankly. 'I better go,' he said.

'Go? But Ma's cooking her famous lamb curry tonight. It melts in your mouth.'

'Thank you, but no. I need rest.'

Rex held Manolis's gaze a moment before half-closing his eyes. 'I understand.' He sounded disappointed and resumed his seat. 'We'll see you later then, Kojak.'

'See you.'

The blackened shell of the Val remained beside the sheriff's office, the wreck still releasing toxic vapours. Manolis sat on the verandah and rolled his nightly smoke. Expelling his own noxious air, he pictured his father doing the same, hunched over a horseracing form guide, studying it fastidiously, making his selections with the precision of a surgeon.

'*Signomi, Baba*. And sorry about the car, too.'

Manolis had usually visited Con in hospital in the early evening. He often found him sitting up in bed, staring into space, or sleeping. Maria sat there for hours waiting for him to wake up. She was then barked at for doing something incorrectly or not to his liking, and limped home in disgust and disappointment. Manolis knew that much of his father's anger was frustration at himself, at his ageing body failing him. As hard as it was to witness, Manolis knew it was healthy. It was a spark. It was life.

But it was also wrong. Having given up her entire day, Maria often shambled home in the winter chill wondering why she'd bothered. And yet, she stayed devoted to the very end. Although Maria often drove her son crazy with her old-fashioned ways, Manolis remained firmly of the view that Greek women were the strongest on the planet because they'd endured a lifetime of Greek men.

With a light sigh of contentment and a pang of guilt, Manolis extinguished his cigarette butt. He took out his notepad and wrote down his thoughts in preparation for the next day, then went inside and showered with his eyes closed, imagining the streams of water as pummelling rocks. For a brief moment, just before he fell asleep, Manolis thought he smelled the moisturiser his wife normally applied before bed each night.

His furry possum friend did not visit that night, no doubt still scared by the fumes and the fear of fire. But the sound of explosions came again, in the near distance, somewhere in town. Manolis stepped outside for a better listen and look, but by then the world had gone quiet. The quick series of bangs, two nights in a row, left him pondering their significance.

14

In the morning, the sky was so blue that it overloaded Manolis's brain. A cloud of grasshoppers swarmed across the verandah, leaping like sprung mousetraps as he walked to the pickup. On the drive to town, he saw something wholly unexpected. Overnight, bright-yellow ribbons had appeared on trees, tied around trunks or dangling from branches. It made for a slightly less depressing journey but only raised more questions in his mind.

He arrived at five to nine expecting to find the station locked, empty. But it was open, manned. Stunned, he went into the tearoom with a look of both determination and surprise. Sparrow had his feet up on a plastic chair and was gingerly sipping water from a stained mug. He reeked of alcohol, his hangover plainly visible. His eyes were red-rimmed, squinting against the sunlight streaming in through crooked venetian blinds. Kerr looked much the same, minus the smell. Her ponytail was decidedly askew, as if tied in haste. Her eyes were the deep cornflower blue of a vein, her skin biscuit brown.

Manolis stood before them with several pages of handwritten notes. He quietly bemoaned the lack of a whiteboard.

'Where's Fyfe? Where's your mythical sergeant?'

His question was met with stony silence. Sparrow refused to look him in the eye.

'Well, whatever,' Manolis said. 'I've tried. From now on, you take orders from me. That's official.' He tapped the invisible chevrons on his shoulder. 'No-one here is as qualified as me. You want to stop me, you're welcome to step up and try.'

Sparrow and Kerr looked at Manolis mutinously, and then exchanged uncertain sideways glances. Neither constable had the desire or energy to debate with their senior officer.

'Excellent,' Manolis said. 'We have unity, we're a team. Now, before we begin, I need to ask whether anyone else has heard any late-night explosions.'

He waited for a response. Blank faces blinked at him.

'Quick-fire bangs, like a bunch of firecrackers or a car backfiring? Any reports of a disturbance, or is it just some kids practising to be arsonists and starting a bushfire?'

The constables finally cracked, snickering like children. Manolis knew it wasn't because they thought he was funny.

'That's the sign,' Sparrow moaned.

Manolis waited. 'Don't make me ask,' he said firmly. 'Speak.'

Kerr sat forward. 'Whenever a local drug dealer takes delivery of a fresh supply, they let off a burst of firecrackers late at night. It's their way of delivering the news to their clients that they're open for business.'

'Word spreads like a cancer, yair,' Sparrow said. 'Meth heads come runnin'.'

Manolis folded his arms across his chest. 'Clever. But it doesn't surprise me.' Methamphetamine was running rampant across the city as well, taking over from heroin as the cold, malevolent new scourge.

'There's so much ice in town these days that the

locals have started calling us 'Little Antarctica',' Sparrow said. 'Twenty bucks a hit. Cheaper than a slab of piss, and no risk of a hangover.'

'And what about crime?' Manolis asked, half-expecting the answer.

'Up,' Kerr said. 'Way up. Burglaries, robberies, assaults, all off the charts. Junkies desperately trying to feed their habit.'

Manolis bit his lip. There were a lot of drug-filled dead bodies in his rear-view mirror. To be told his home town was being cannibalised was something he took surprisingly personally. Having not given Cobb a second thought in years, he'd reconnected with the place, with his parents, and his childhood. It was an outcome he almost feared.

'And what have you been doing about it?' he said. 'Any major seizures or arrests?'

There was a moment of heavy silence. Sparrow sipped his water. Kerr adjusted her hair tie. Finally, she said, 'We asked residents for tip-offs, said they could respond anonymously. We got nothin'.'

'Crackers used to go off two, three times a week,' Sparrow said. 'Now, it's almost every night.'

Manolis shuffled across the grimy lino, stood before the window. He stuck two fingers through the dusty slats, peered in both directions. The street was strewn with garbage but otherwise empty. He wanted to go outside with a dustpan and broom.

Returning to his original position, he sighed. There wasn't even a corkboard.

'OK, I may as well use this to segue into why I'm . . . we're here. Local schoolteacher Molly Abbott. I understand you each have your own theories. Here's one that just occurred to me — an unpaid drug debt.'

115

There was laughter.

'For a primary school teacher?' Sparrow said. 'Doubt it.'

'Don't be so presumptuous,' said Manolis. 'I've seen fully functioning addicts who worked in child-care centres with babies.'

Kerr turned to Sparrow. 'Did you check her arms for acne or scratch marks?'

'Bugs crawling under the skin,' Manolis said. 'A common hallucination.'

'We saw her arms,' Sparrow said. 'She was clean.'

'Did she have any tattoos?' Manolis asked. 'That's a tactic they sometimes use for hiding bad scratch marks.'

'She had a couple, but not on her arms.'

Manolis recalled the oral and dental decay that came with long-term meth use. 'What about her mouth, her teeth?'

'Broken,' Sparrow said. 'But not otherwise abnormal.'

'And when can I see her body, where is it now?'

'Hospital morgue,' Sparrow said. 'In fact, there were a few people at the pub yesterday askin' about a funeral.'

Manolis shook his head lightly. 'No. Sorry, but the funeral has to wait until we've found everything we can, and preferably when there's someone in custody. Her body's probably the most valuable piece of evidence we have, and I haven't even seen a bloody report yet. We just can't have her in the ground.'

Sparrow leaned over to Kerr. 'See the yellow ribbons this morning?'

'Yellow balloons, too,' she replied. 'Her favourite colour.'

116

Manolis was quietly pleased to see the locals finally expressing their grief more appropriately than with rocks and roaming gangs and wooden bats.

'There's been tributes posted online, too,' Sparrow said.

'I saw,' Kerr said.

'Can you show me?' Manolis asked.

Kerr retrieved her phone and began scrolling through images of Molly that had been lovingly posted by the local community. 'Molly didn't have any social media accounts herself. She was very private, especially after poor Patrick died, and didn't buy into the need to post about what she ate for breakfast.'

It was Manolis's first chance to see the schoolteacher as she had been in life, instead of clobbered by death. With sandy-blonde hair and ocean-blue eyes, Molly was a quintessential Australian beauty, the kind who belonged on a postcard of an endless beach with an idyllic sunset backdrop. Instead, she was a bloodless corpse strung up against a gum tree.

'All this'll send a message to the brown house,' Sparrow said. 'Loud and bloody clear.'

'OK, enough,' Manolis snapped. 'I know people think they've got it all worked out, but our investigation starts right here, right now, with basic, honest police work. Who was the last person to see Molly alive? That's an obvious question. We need to retrace her steps. The people closest to a murder victim are often the killers, so we need to seek them out and ask for an alibi.'

The constables looked at each other, then the floor.

Sparrow finally said, 'Yair, but we know the town. I woulda thought that'd be worth somethin' to ya.'

Manolis took a step towards Sparrow, who seemed

117

to shrink an inch in his chair.

'It is,' the detective said calmly. 'But I need definite lines of enquiry, specific persons of interest, not broad speculation. Still, I hear you. On the one hand we have the theory she was killed as punishment for infidelity. I believe that's traditionally why married women are stoned under Islamic law.'

'Men too,' Kerr said swiftly.

'Yes, men as well,' Manolis said. 'So with that in mind, persons of interest would be lovers and jilted lovers. And yes, given the way she was killed, it's clear why the brown ... the *immigration detention centre* would be of interest. So we'll check that out too.'

Sparrow's lips formed a satisfied smile.

'But then there's the theory of something random. Wrong place, wrong time. Drunks, drugs, et cetera. Being stoned is an especially violent and brutal way to die, and I've seen people high on meth who would stone you for a laugh.'

Manolis let his reasoning sink into the room. Sparrow drained his water mug, wiped his wet mouth with a hairy forearm.

Kerr looked up from her hands. 'Have you ever worked a homicide where someone was stoned to death?'

'Mercifully, no,' Manolis said. 'Have you?'

Kerr shook her head solemnly.

'Look, the way Molly died is absolutely important, I'll give you that,' Manolis continued. 'Clearly stonings are a form of punishment in some cultures. But I can hardly go up to the detention centre and arrest everybody based on that reasoning. And as I said, given the number of addicts in town, it could just as easily have been some random, drug-fuelled attack.

118

Meth gives its users insane strength and hyper-aggression, a wicked combination. So I want to make that clear, and I want you to make that clear to everyone you speak with if it helps keep the peace. This is not a witch hunt. Is that understood?'

The constables nodded slowly.

Sparrow exhaled and scratched the back of his head. 'I still reckon we're wasting our time. She wasn't beaten or stabbed. She was *fucken stoned to death*. Am I the only one who thinks that's a big deal . . . ?'

'It is significant, I acknowledged that,' Manolis said. 'But experience has taught me to not jump to conclusions. Now, I'm led to believe that Molly may've been involved with a number of men. More suspects make our job more difficult. And adding to that, we can't enter the detention centre easily.'

Kerr thought a moment. 'We can request entry if we're investigating a crime. But we can't just go up there making wild accusations.'

'That wasn't my intention,' Manolis said, proffering his notes. 'We need something firm, a lead. So, with all that in mind, here's my plan . . . '

15

Manolis charged a disgruntled Sparrow with the task of chasing down Molly's phone records and supposed suitor, Joe Shrewsbury. Her workplace, home, computer and the morgue would all come later. The school was closed for a second day anyway, the children having been offered counselling for the loss of their teacher. In the meantime, Manolis would accompany Kerr to meet with seventy-six-year-old Ida Jones before her gin took effect.

Before Manolis left, he offered Sparrow an olive branch in the form of a cigarette. It was freshly rolled, thick and straight, one of his finest. He was genuinely disappointed to give it away but wanted the young constable to have it. Sparrow stared at it for a long time before snatching his cap and trudging off. Manolis watched Sparrow walk away, the unwanted gift still hanging from his fingers.

'Ida's actually a friend of my mum,' Kerr told Manolis as they prepared to leave.

'They're of the same vintage?'

'Roughly. Same level of intolerance.'

'Were you looking after her yesterday?'

She exhaled, exposing her heavy heart. 'It's not easy.'

'You live with her?' Manolis was careful not to mention Kerr's fiancé.

'She lives with me.'

As they locked the doors, a four-wheel drive skidded into position outside the station, engulfing Manolis and Kerr in a thick cloud of dry dust. Hacking away the outback spores, Manolis saw the car door fling open and the elusive Sergeant Bill Fyfe fall to the earth with a cold thud. Manolis and Kerr ran over and helped the senior policeman to his feet before walking him inside, arm in arm. They laid him on the tearoom sofa, which shunted on impact then bowed in the middle.

'City mouse!' Fyfe sputtered. 'Good to see ya.'

'He's been on a bender since Saturday,' Kerr said. 'Stupidly driving around town half-cut. Haven't ya, ya dumb bastard?'

'Shaddup,' Fyfe spat. 'Bring us some water, would ya, sweetheart?'

The lines on Kerr's face appeared darkly. She went to fetch a clean mug while Manolis stood over Fyfe, watching him groan and struggle to breathe. A small bird whacked into the cop-station window, making the glass rattle and shake. Fyfe didn't budge.

Manolis was unsure where to begin, or if this was even the right moment to ask. But there never seemed to be a good time and there was still a killer at large, something only he seemed to acknowledge.

'So . . . how goes it?' Fyfe spoke with his eyes closed.

Manolis looked at him guardedly. 'Um, good. We're just off to interview Ida now.'

Fyfe chortled. 'Ida, eh. Well good luck with that.'

'She found the body, right?'

'She poured the petrol on the fucken fire, yeah.'

Kerr returned with a full mug and thrust it into Fyfe's waiting hand. She told Manolis she'd wait in the car, stomping away in a grim huff. Still horizontal, Fyfe downed the water in two gulps without spilling a drop.

'You settlin' in alright? Like your quarters?'

Manolis placed his hands on his hips. 'Yes, thank you. Constable Smith . . . Sparrow, said it was your idea.'

'Vera and Rexy will look after you. They're good people.'

'Hmm.'

'My heart goes out to 'em. Two kids, and now a kid-in-law, dead. Can you imagine?'

'Tragic. Rex said he remembers my father.'

'Is that right?'

'Dad owned a milk bar in town. We lived out the back.'

Fyfe's head rocked from side to side. He appeared to be concentrating hard on keeping the water down, the sudden lack of alcohol proving a shock to the system.

'I saw the evidence you collected from the crime scene,' Manolis said. 'And then the scene itself.'

Fyfe snapped his eyes open. 'You did?'

'Sparrow showed me.'

'What'd ya reckon? Any ideas?'

'I reckon you should've locked the evidence and secured the scene.'

Fyfe chuckled. His languid gaze dropped to the floor.

'Protocol, eh,' he slurred. 'Good one, city mouse. Look, son, no-one gives a toss about protocol in a one-horse town.'

'Well, you should. We've now got Buckley's, no chance, if this ever goes before a judge or jury.'

'Thass not gonna happen.'

No-one said anything for a while. Manolis watched Fyfe, all gentle-eyed and useless. Having caught his breath, the local sergeant looked down at his hands, inspecting them as if surprised to find them there. Finally, Manolis extended his arm, offering a refill.

'Ta,' said Fyfe, passing the empty mug. Manolis topped it up from the dripping tap and handed it back. One gulp this time.

'Cruel way to die,' Fyfe breathed. 'Being stoned. Imagine it.'

'I tried. I can't.'

'Ever seen anything like this before?'

'A stoning? No.'

'Might be a first then, eh? For Australia, I mean.'

Manolis folded his arms. 'I don't think that's anything to be proud of.'

'Really?' Fyfe said. 'I do.'

Outside, an outlaw bikie gang thundered past, all exhaust pipes and attitude. The window shuddered in its wooden frame. Manolis momentarily lost his train of thought.

'I thought there'd be more of a bloodstain,' he said.

'Huh?'

'At the crime scene. More blood.'

Fyfe's forehead creased in confusion. 'You said this was your first stoning. How would you know otherwise?'

Manolis was about to reply when Fyfe held up a hand to stop him. He then cocked an elbow and extended his arm as if throwing a dart. 'I hear the Aboriginal fellas spear each other in the leg for payback. Like this. It's usually done in the thigh, sometimes calf.'

Manolis paused, thinking. 'But isn't spearing in that part of the body really dangerous?'

'Hell yes it's dangerous. Spear goes in wrong and you cut the main artery, the femoral one, and bleed to death.'

Manolis thought he'd test the water. 'Ever heard of a bloke named Jimmy Dingo?'

Fyfe smiled hyena teeth. 'Course I have. Everyone has. And I know why you're askin'. Don't even bother. That story's bullshit, a myth, it all happened years ago. It's got nuthin' to do with Molly Abbott.'

His words were firm. Manolis expected it, and eased off.

'Anyway, thass what the Aboriginals do, they chuck spears,' Fyfe said. 'I don't think they chuck rocks. I'm pretty sure thass just the carpet kissers.'

'Up at the detention centre?'

'Thass right.'

'Is that why you were there yesterday?'

Swinging his legs onto the floor, Fyfe sat up steadily. 'Yesterday?' he asked quizzically. 'Dunno what you're talkin' about.'

'You weren't at the detention centre yesterday afternoon?'

Fyfe looked at him for a long while. 'I was home all day yesterday,' he said finally. 'In bed, sick, hungover. A hangover a hundred times worse than any stoning.'

Manolis wondered why Fyfe would lie. Probably the same reason he hadn't stopped the previous day — he was hiding something. Or was Manolis mistaken? He was almost certain he wasn't. Almost.

'Oh,' Manolis said, 'I thought I saw you.'

'Not me, mate. So you went up there?'

'I went to check it out, yes.'

'You catch the murderer?'

Manolis looked away. 'Did Molly have anything to do with the detainees?'

'Dunno.'

'I thought you said you were close.'

'More with her dad. Graham was an alderman, a war hero and mate. I promised him I'd take care of his little girl. Now the bastard's gonna bloody kill me when he sees her up in heaven before me.'

Manolis found a chair. 'I hear there's a drug problem in town. Methamphetamines.'

Fyfe raised a caterpillar eyebrow. 'No way,' he said, fake smile. 'We're a good little community.'

Manolis looked at the ceiling, frustration curling his top lip into a sneer. 'What about the theory that Molly might've been killed by a raging meth head?'

'Thass a theory, sure,' Fyfe said. 'But it'd be wrong.'

'Oh?'

He bared his yellow incisors a second time. 'We're a good little community.'

'Who's in charge at the detention centre?'

'The devil incarnate.'

'He got a name?'

Fyfe produced a tobacco tin, shoved a brown blob in between his lower lip and gum. Manolis watched with some disgust.

'Yeah,' Fyfe said. 'Onions is his name. Francis Onions. Frankie Fucken Onions. Prick from the city. Like you.'

A sudden clamour of voices sounded on the street, wolf-whistles, swearing, anger, an argument. Before Manolis could investigate, the ruckus died down, a horn blaring and a car revving into the distance.

'Best you don't keep the little lady waitin'.' Fyfe smiled. 'She tends to get stroppy, especially at this time o' the month. We'll talk again.'

Manolis stood to go, then turned back. 'One last thing, have you spoken to the media yet?'

Fyfe folded fat fingers into each other. 'Media? What, you mean, like newspaper reporters?'

'Yes.'

'You assumin' they made contact?'

'A beautiful blonde woman stoned to death in an outback town . . . ? I imagine they would.'

'Well, now you mention it, there's been a coupla calls from nosey city journos sniffin' about. But we've dodged 'em so far.'

'Doesn't the whole town know?'

'Prob'ly. But that means shit, son. We don't give a toss about the city or anyone from it in the same way they don't give a rat's arse about us. No-one really knows we exist outside the detention centre. We're like a pimple on an ugly arse.'

This unexpectedly good news made Manolis feel lighter. Immigration detention was often in the headlines, a political hot potato. Perhaps people high up in government had threatened lawsuits if the media printed anything substantial on the case so early on. Still, it was only a matter of time before the truth came out. And Manolis loathed reporters. He often saw city journalists loitering around the station, notepads and recorders at the ready, or after something off the record. They were getting younger and pushier by the day.

'Anyway, good luck, city mouse. Let me know how you get on. I'll start making a few enquiries of my own.'

'Who'll you be speaking to?'

Fyfe smiled. 'I got some folks in mind. Tell you more later.'

* * *

Manolis found Kerr leaning against the bonnet of an old Holden ute. Its doors and windows were open to allow for airflow. She was biting her nails and wore a scowl.

'Get in,' she said gruffly. 'Ain't got all day.'

She proceeded to execute a befuddling combination of pedal pumps and choke pulls until the engine whirred to life. She reversed without looking in her rear-view mirror, then floored it. They drove in silence for a while, heading east, past entire streets of houses with windows made of bricks. The ute's tray rattled with its collection of unsecured items. Kerr drove as recklessly as Sparrow had; getting to Ida in time was a desperate race against inebriation.

In the brilliant midmorning light, Manolis stole glances at Kerr from the corner of his eye.

'You OK?' he said.

'Never better,' she replied.

'Is it far to go?'

'No. Ida's house is one of the oldest in town, handed down through the generations. Shame it'll end with her.'

'No kids, then.'

'You don't remember her?'

'No.'

'She never married either.'

'Ah,' he said. 'An old maid.'

Kerr thrust her chin at him. 'What's that supposed to mean? Fuck you.'

Manolis snapped his neck right. 'Steady on, Constable. What was that for?'

'What do you reckon it was for?' Kerr blinked slowly and deliberately. 'When you see the animals in this town, is it any wonder she never married?'

Manolis looked out the window, thought a moment, then gently but directly asked what had happened before they left the station. At first Kerr denied it was anything, before finally loosening her tongue. Manolis was an outsider and this was her confessional.

'I'm sick of it,' she said. 'Just bloody sick of it.'

16

A group of men had pulled up in a car with no licence plates and about half a brain between them. They were young, their bodies hastily assembled and alive with budding testosterone. They let fly in Kerr's direction, a combination of catcalls and gestures which abruptly became sexual insults, all in squeaky singsong voices.

'They're getting younger all the time,' she said. 'It's a rite of passage.'

She had returned fire but that only seemed to work them up even more. Taking crap from a woman was a sign of weakness, a cardinal blokey sin.

'I'm sick of it,' Kerr said. 'Sick of the ugly, disgusting words. Sick of their sense of sexual entitlement. They invade my space and violate my privacy. I can't walk down the street anymore, it's like I'm trespassing, like I'm their prey. They used to do it behind my back — now it's to my face. The uniform means nothing, only eggs them on.' Anger dripped from her every word.

Manolis wrinkled his face in sympathy. 'That's harassment. Lock the little pricks up for a night. Teach them a lesson about respect.'

'Waste of time and energy,' she said, scoffing. 'If anything, they'd just go harder next time.'

'Then lock them up again.'

'Ha. Of course.'

'Ignoring them might work. But you shouldn't have to.'

'I tried that. I can't do it, it's not in my DNA. I bite

129

back. I get too upset.'

Manolis narrowed his eyes. Young, bored men were the bane of his existence. In the country, they appeared younger and more bored than anywhere else. Other men were bodies to destroy, while women were bodies to conquer and then destroy.

'Disrespectful little bastards,' he said. 'You know someone vandalised my car the day I got here?'

'You got off lightly,' Kerr replied.

'I did, till they came back to cremate the bastard. I'm still furious.'

'That makes two of us. As my dad would say, we've got a lot of shit on our livers.'

'Greeks would say that we're ready to drink blood.'

Kerr sighed. 'Really, given what happened to Molly, I guess I should be grateful they're only throwing insults, not rocks.'

'No,' said Manolis. 'No, you shouldn't.'

He reflected a moment. Could a common, basic hatred of women have been a motive for Molly's stoning? It was certainly possible. He'd seen it too many times before.

The car decelerated as they turned into Crawford Street.

'This wasn't just a murder, Detective,' Kerr said. 'This was violence against women. And if it was done by a detainee as some kind of sick punishment, it's culture and religion being used to excuse violence.'

Manolis nodded. The crime was a homicide, first and foremost, but it wasn't lost on him that the victim was female.

'This is why I take a hard line on the issue,' he said. 'It's comments and insults today, domestic violence and rapes and murders tomorrow. And I'm sorry for

130

the old maid remark.'

Kerr smiled gently, acknowledging his apology. 'These little snots identify in opposition, no matter who the opponent is. They relish it, then go express themselves with anger and violence. The parents do bugger all. Boys'll be boys.'

Manolis felt an ache of guilt as his thoughts drifted to his young son. He'd heard that children always noticed a parent's absence more than any presence. At that tender age, absences were not readily forgotten.

Kerr pulled into a gravel driveway and applied the brakes with a loud squeal.

'Look, I know I'm police, and we're fair fucking game in this town — you should hear what poor Sparrow cops. We're targets for other reasons, of course. We try to stick together, look out for each other, be mates and watch each other's back. But the thing is, as much as I try not to be a woman, I'm still just a bloody worthless woman. And you see what happens to women in Cobb.' She slammed the door with enough force to shake the vehicle and end the conversation.

They found Ida on the front porch with a tall glass in her hand and a sharpened cricket stump by her side. A large wooden crucifix was on the wall behind her, weeping Jesus in agony. Her gaze was distant, staring up at the sky.

Kerr said a polite hello and introduced Manolis, who asked what Ida was looking at. She told him she was 'trying to work out a way to get up there'. She wanted a loophole, a painless way out that didn't come with the price of eternal damnation. It appeared gallons of gin may have been the answer. She offered

131

the officers a drink but both declined. Casting her eyes over Manolis, she referred to him as 'Inspector Poirot' with a lopsided grin. Ida's voice was gravelly, her nails chipped. She smelled of aniseed. An enormous goitre rested on her right collar.

A mangy cat, whiskers criss-crossing, ears torn off, fresh from rolling in the dirt, appeared at Manolis's feet. It snaked between his legs, rubbing furiously. He leaned down and patted it, liberating a cloud of dust from its matted coat. It purred and flopped onto the dead brown grass, exposing its belly and writhing for more attention. Ida stared at the feline with a look of disdain.

'You're a slut,' she rasped. 'Ya slut cat.'

Manolis heard the clack of her tongue in her dry mouth. He stood with notepad in hand and asked about the events of Saturday morning.

'I went and stole my morning paper, then came home.' She uttered her words flippantly, like it was any other day, and returned to methodically slurping her gin. Eventually, Kerr had to prompt her.

'Godless whore,' Ida spat. 'Got what she deserved.'

'Did you see anyone in the area when you found the body?' Manolis said clearly.

'Not a soul,' Ida said.

'What time was that?'

She stared at the grass. The cat was still rolling around, playing cute. 'Quarter past six,' Ida finally said.

'You know that for sure?' Manolis asked. 'You checked your watch?'

She looked at him as if he were slow. 'No, Inspector. But trust me. Every morning, God willing, I wake up at exactly five-thirty, and leave to get my paper at six.'

'And you're certain she was dead when you found her?'

Ida laughed into her drink. Her false teeth slipped in her mouth as she swallowed. 'She was a doornail.'

'Was the victim known to you before the morning in question?' Manolis asked.

'To the extent she was the local floozy, yes.'

'And what made her a floozy? Do you have the names of any of the men she'd been seeing?'

Ida's thin lips formed a tight smile. 'Why yes, Inspector. I've got them all written down in my little black book. Their phone numbers and measurements too.'

Manolis scratched behind his ear in frustration. 'So, other than that, you knew nothing more about her?'

'No. I knew her parents more. Wonderful people. Respectable. Served both town and country. God-fearing.'

'Did you touch the body?'

'Yes.'

'With what?'

'My stump.'

'Why?' Manolis's questions were clipped.

Ida tightened her eyebrows, thin black millipedes. 'To make sure my cataracts weren't deceiving me. I see many things at my age, including dead bodies and ghosts.'

Manolis asked Ida where she was the night Molly died.

She cackled like a witch. 'You have got to be joking.' She turned to Kerr. 'Kate, dear, how's Mum?'

Kerr hoicked up her belt and positioned her hands on her hips. 'Not good,' she exhaled. 'I can bring her by sometime if you want to say hello.'

'Don't bother. I don't want to see what that poor woman has become.' Ida turned back to Manolis. 'You know, Inspector, your skin's rather dark. You're not related to anyone at the brown house, are you?'

Her mouth creased into a sour smile. Manolis clicked his pen closed and narrowed his eyes. He saw the bones in her fingers, the skin over them as thin as crêpe paper. Activated by gin, ropes of saliva hung in her mouth like rigging on a sailboat.

After pocketing his notepad, he offered his card. 'Thank you for your valuable time, Mrs Jones. Please call me if anything else occurs to you.'

Ida slipped the card into her breast pocket without looking at it. She massaged her goitre and kept sipping at her drink, which by now was running dangerously low.

'Waste of time,' Kerr whispered as they walked to the car.

'It's never a waste,' Manolis said. 'People are sometimes scared to talk, or things only occur to them later. Meeting them face to face makes all the difference.'

★ ★ ★

Driving back to the station, they encountered Sparrow coming in the opposite direction along Broad Street. He flashed his only working headlight and flagged them down outside Saint Christopher's. The two cars sat idling in the middle of the road beneath the shade of a drooping coolibah tree, each driver with an elbow out the window. There was no risk of them blocking traffic; there was no traffic.

In order to be heard over the rattling engines, Manolis leaned across Kerr. She pinned her shoulders to

134

the seat.

'How'd you go?' Manolis said.

Sparrow spoke with a half-burnt smoke stuck between his lips, ash evaporating in the breeze. 'So I drove out to Joe's place — he's got a farm just north o' town. Breeds greyhounds.'

'What did he say?'

'Bashed on the door for ages. No answer. In the end I found him snoring out back in a hammock. I woke him up. He was pretty dusty . . .'

'Dusty?'

'Well, no. More like drunk. Had to squint to focus on me, as blind as a welder's dog. Couldn't tell if he was in mourning or if it was just another Tuesday. Prob'ly the latter. Anyway, didn't get much out of him, although he said he hadn't seen Molly in months.'

'Did he say where he was the night she died?'

'Said he was at the pub all night. Left at first light, drove straight home.'

For as long as anyone could remember, Joe Shrewsbury's life was a murky lament of beer, wine and country music. Sparrow said the whole town could hear Joe's bin being emptied on recycling day from the echo of shattering glass. It was like a thunderclap.

'Anyway, Joe's lying,' Sparrow said. 'I checked with Turps, and he said he'd barred him from the pub. Hasn't seen him in yonks, let alone last Friday.'

Manolis smiled faintly. 'Does he have a record?'

'Public drunkenness,' Sparrow said. 'But that's pretty much standard issue for Cobb.'

'Why was he barred from the pub, what did he do?'

Sparrow flicked his cigarette butt into the hot day and said, 'Punched a woman who spilled his pint.'

Kerr sucked at her teeth. Manolis quickly asked

whether Joe had ever hit Molly.

Sparrow shook his head. 'Nuthin' I know of. All I know about is the time she slapped him in the pub. It's not like he pressed charges.'

Manolis nodded gently, digesting the information.

'So anyway, I went and rang the phone company,' Sparrow said. 'Turns out they've no record of any number owned by a Molly Abbott with an address in this state.'

Manolis cursed to himself in Greek. 'She had no social media but she owned a bloody phone, right?'

'Prob'ly. But the phone could've been under another name. No Molly Abbott.'

Kerr piped up. 'Is Molly her real name? Isn't it usually a nickname for Mary or Margaret? I once had an Aunt Margaret who we always called Molly.'

Sparrow stared blankly from under his sweat-stained hat. 'Didn't check those.'

'Check,' Manolis said.

'Check her married name too — Boyd — in case she might've been using that,' said Kerr.

'She changed her name back?' Manolis asked.

'After she was widowed, yes,' Kerr said.

Manolis shot her a look of approval. 'We'll search her place. There's bound to be a phone somewhere. In the meantime, get this Joe fella down to the station for interview.'

'Not today,' Sparrow said. 'Let him sleep it off. He's bloody useless today.'

The detective tapped his chin in thought. 'Breeds greyhounds, eh?'

'Yair, sells 'em for racin'.'

Manolis's father had spent hours at the betting shop every weekend. Manolis never understood the allure of animal racing, let alone of emaciated canines. Poor men bet their hard-earned on races about which they knew little, briefly cheering on a mutt with an unlikely name as it ran after a non-existent rabbit. It seemed as cruel on the punters as it was on the dogs.

'At least he's no longer live-baitin' the hounds,' Sparrow said. 'It was whatever he could get his hands on for a while there — possums, piglets, lambs, bunnies. All tender juicy meat.'

Manolis shuddered, a sharp pain stabbing into his thoughts. Joe sounded like a real piece of work. No wonder Molly hadn't returned his advances.

'Intoxication, assault, harassment, animal cruelty,' Manolis said. 'Right, got it, thanks. Good work.'

Sparrow paused, surprised by the compliment. Eventually, his ferrety face relaxed.

'No worries,' he said nonchalantly. 'So anyway, when I was at the pub, two other things tickled my ear. First, more talk of reprisal attacks against the brown house, only worse. A few blokes were sayin' that they'd give anyone they found roaming the streets 'the punishment they deserve'. And by anyone, they meant kids.'

Manolis closed his eyes and shook his head as the image crystallised. The stakes had just gone up a notch. All he could utter was: 'No.'

'And second,' Sparrow said, 'I bumped into ol' Ian Searle.'

Manolis blinked hard, returning to his body. 'Who's he?'

'The headmaster,' Kerr said.

'Yair, Molly's boss,' Sparrow said. 'He was busy drownin' his sorrows. Ian was my teacher when I was at school. He's got a soft spot for me, feels for the fate of the little black poof destined to die in Cobb. Ha, he's probably a closet bender himself, all teachers are, benders or paedos. Anyway, I buy the soppy ol' bastard a beer, and he gets to talkin'. Turns out Molly had a second job. She worked at the brown house in the evenings teachin' English to the reffos.'

'What?' Manolis said. 'She worked at the detention centre?'

'But wait, it gets better . . .'

17

Manolis told Sparrow to return to the top pub and promptly escort the headmaster to the station. This time there'd be no booze present during questioning.

'I dunno,' Sparrow said. 'The old bloke had had a few by the time I reached him.'

Manolis saw a theme in Cobb. Grog was king. It anaesthetised the residents into a constant state of inebriation and denial about their collective plight that ultimately became destructive to themselves or others. They wanted death. They wanted oblivion.

'As a little tacker, I remember watching planes struggling to land on the airstrip cos they were so heavy with beer,' Sparrow said. 'When they finally made it down, we helped unload them, ten flights a week. I carried a slab of beer on my shoulder before I even carried a schoolbag.'

During the 1950s, local Aboriginal communities had been taken from their ancestral lands, loaded onto tractors and left to rot on the outskirts of Cobb.

'Most of me mob died during the move,' Sparrow said. 'We're refugees in our own land, mate. Like them blackfellas in America who fled from the south to avoid gettin' hung.'

Manolis nodded, then said, 'We'll give Searle the breathalyser.'

Sparrow turned in his features, confused. 'What? We have a breathalyser?'

★ ★ ★

At the station, Kerr showed Manolis to a back room where a broken breath tester was buried under a pile of junk.

'Can't remember the last time we used it,' she said, whacking it with an open hand. 'But it's not like we've needed it. If you've been drinking in Cobb, you're over the limit.'

Ian Searle was a big, bluff man with deep, soulful eyes and sheepily thick sideburns. His manner belied his appearance — he spoke in a soft tone and admitted to feeling anxious about making a formal statement. He'd never spoken to the police about anything, not even a neighbourhood noise complaint. Manolis felt slightly nervous too; something about speaking with the headmaster in his home town. He remembered once being summoned to the principal's office for hitting a classmate who had called him 'a greasy wog'. He remembered the principal being ancient then, and likely dead now. The kid probably was too.

Sitting on the plastic garden furniture in the station tearoom, Manolis reassured the current principal that there was nothing to fear and kept feeding him mugs of strong, sobering black coffee. To calm his nerves, Manolis offered him a pre-rolled smoke, which he declined. Kerr took notes. Fyfe retired to his office to make some calls. Sparrow went outside and chain-smoked on the verandah.

To gain his trust, Manolis let Searle have the air. The headmaster spoke in short spurts, all the while playing with his fingers, intertwining them anxiously.

'Um, well she liked singing and dancing, which she did a lot with the kids. I still don't know how we'll replace her. She loved life, loved people, and was very approachable. The kids adored her, and the parents

140

did too. Everyone did. She had a bubbly personality and a wicked sense of humour. I still don't know how I'm going to explain to the children what happened to their lovely teacher. Why do the good always die young . . . ?'

It was the first description of Molly which made her sound like an ordinary, likeable person. Manolis hated this moment of an investigation, properly meeting the victim for the first time and seeing their personality, when he couldn't help but become momentarily human. It made his job immeasurably harder.

Manolis closed his eyes. He needed something to come to him that would make this bloody investigation easier.

'She was a green thumb but claimed she hated roses,' Searle was saying. 'I thought that was both unique and funny. Who hates roses? No-one hates roses, everyone loves roses. She once looked after my garden when I visited my brother and threatened that I'd come home to find my roses with their heads cut off. She didn't, of course, and I returned to find a lush, green garden, better than ever.'

Manolis snapped open his eyes, refocused on the principal. 'Did you live far from Molly?'

'Two streets over. I'm on Wellington Road, she's Henry.' He sipped the hell-dark brew, wincing at the taste. 'Molly had a warmth and generosity that drew people near. She wanted to know who you were. But that came at a price. She had an unwary trust in others.' His voice cracked with the weight of those words, at the thought that a local might have killed her, or someone as good as local.

'Tell me about her other job,' Manolis said.

Searle told him that Molly had walked into his office

one morning and asked for a raise. 'I told her that if I had my way, I'd double her salary, triple it. She was worth every penny. But as it stood, the school didn't have enough money to whack two blackboard dusters together. A week later, she came back and said she'd gotten a job teaching English at the immigration detention centre. Because it didn't impact school hours, I gave my blessing.'

The tourist park had increased bookings. Local teachers got second gigs. The centre was exactly as it had been sold to the town — jobs, the local economy, improvements to infrastructure, lucrative contracts. Manolis thought that was clear. But as Rex and Vera had told him, the dark side was harder to see.

'Not long after Molly started her second job, new faces started appearing at the school,' Searle said. 'I had to tell a few to leave because they were loitering during afternoon pick-up time and the parents complained. Well, they did more than just complain.'

'What did they do?' Manolis asked.

'They started arguments, picked fights.'

'With you?'

'With the detainees. Not the first time, mind you. These were the same people who snatched their kids away when they saw them playing with the detainees' kids.'

'So the detainees' kids attend the local school?' Manolis said.

Searle said there was an agreement with the government for detention centre kids to attend state schools. It was cheaper than sending teachers up to the centre. Teaching English to adults, on the other hand, was different.

'That's actually how Molly heard about the job,

through one of the parents,' the headmaster said. 'I know all the parents who come to collect their kids, and those new faces who'd started turning up weren't there as parents. They were there for Molly. So I told her to tell them to stop coming, they were becoming a nuisance. She said she tried but they wouldn't listen. And they were overwhelmingly male.'

Searle turned his head in the direction of the school, as if picturing what he'd just described.

'Do you know what the new faces wanted?' Manolis asked.

Searle shook his head. 'Molly never told me. Course, it wasn't the first time local men came looking for her. But I figured this mob might've had questions about homework or something. She taught there twice a week, on Mondays and Thursdays.'

'And you say she took the job just for the extra money?'

Searle paused, breathed heavily. 'Molly, well, she didn't show her pain to most. But I saw it. Losing a husband, losing her parents. It changes a person. She needed to get away from those memories, needed a fresh start. And to do that, she needed money.'

Manolis sat back in his garden chair, folded his hands behind his head, considered the ceiling. It was stained black in places, had panels missing and wires dangling. Kerr's pupils darted between interviewer and interviewee. Searle anxiously pulled at his thick sideburns.

The headmaster certainly painted a grim picture of what seemed an otherwise cheerful individual. But Manolis was aware that Molly's cheer may have been no more than a mask. She'd certainly had her share of tragedy. And if she was truly promiscuous, that suggested she either loved sex or was, more likely, trying to fill an emotional hole in her life.

Manolis returned his attention to the room. 'How did she like working at the detention centre? Did she ever talk about it?'

Searle emptied his lungs. 'She said she enjoyed the teaching — after all, she is . . . she was a teacher. But she thought the conditions were poor. The education area was cramped, non-exclusive. She was trying to teach while other detainees were busy having conversations and arguments.'

'Which probably caused more arguments,' Manolis said.

'Exactly. Some detainees saw learning English as pointless — they imagined never being allowed into Australia, not even after their detention.'

Manolis coughed into his hand before nodding in agreement.

'Molly thought the detainees were getting a bum deal,' Searle went on. 'At least, that's what she decided after working there a while. At first it was just about the money. But she told me she'd gotten to know the people and quite liked them.'

'So maybe it wasn't just homework questions they were coming to ask her about?'

'No. I mean yes, agreed. Sadly, that outlook made her more of a target in town.'

'A target?'

Searle fired a look at Kerr, then back to Manolis. 'There are many people who want to see the detention centre closed down,' he said. 'If you're on the side of the detainees, you're on the outer.'

Manolis nodded again.

'I especially remember what Molly said about the

children she taught,' Searle said. 'How she saw them progressively deteriorating, as if a light was going out behind their eyes. They were changing with prolonged detention, but so was she, as it turns out.'

'How so?'

'She was more upset than I'd ever seen, like she herself was traumatised. And this was a woman who was already grieving.'

Manolis leaned forward, placing his elbows on his knees and his thumbs under his chin. He was trying to retrace Molly's final steps and work out who was the last person to see her alive. For the time being, that man was sitting in front of him, polishing his bifocals with the frayed ends of a shirtsleeve.

'Let me ask you specifically about last week . . .' Manolis said.

Searle swallowed hard, his palms leaving damp marks on the table. He was brought another mug of strained mud, which he sipped pensively.

'How was Molly over the past few days?' Manolis said. 'Did she seem to have anything on her mind?'

'She was fine. And not really, no.'

'Can you think of any reason why she might've been out at that hour of night?'

'No. But why is anyone out at that hour? Nothing good ever happens after midnight.'

'Did she have a phone?'

'Yes. Actually, now you mention it, I remember her getting some nuisance calls.'

Manolis's eyes lit up. 'Nuisance calls . . . ? She told you?'

'No, but she sometimes looked at her phone when it rang, recognised the number and didn't answer. That's usually someone you don't want to hear from, right?'

'Usually,' Manolis said. 'But nuisance calls are something else. These could've been from a friend or relative she was avoiding.'

'That's still a nuisance.'

'Did she ever tell you who was calling?'

Searle shook his head. 'Molly seemed fairly unflustered by them, whoever they were from. She just looked down at her phone, saw the number and got on with her day.'

Manolis sifted through his thoughts. 'Did she ever mention a man named Joe Shrewsbury?'

'Shrewsbury? No. I know who he is, of course, but she never mentioned his name.'

'What about Molly's friends?' Manolis said. 'Did she have any confidants, maybe a close girlfriend or two?' Someone like that would most likely have known who Molly was sleeping with or dating, or if any men were bothering her.

Searle pinched his strawberry-red nose. 'She did have one good female friend I remember, Amy Wilkins. She was a mum of one of the schoolkids, a single mum. They used to walk home together after school.'

'Can I speak with her?' Manolis said, sensing an untapped resource.

'That, uh, may be difficult,' Kerr broke in.

'Oh?' Manolis turned to her.

'I knew Amy too, she's no longer in Cobb,' Kerr said. 'She and her daughter left town a year ago.'

Searle shrugged. 'We don't actually know where they ended up.'

'I see,' Manolis said slowly. He needed to find Molly's phone, it might at least contain Amy's number.

146

'And when was it that you last saw Molly?'

'Friday afternoon, as she was leaving work. She was by the front gate, talking to two men. I was in one of the classrooms.'

'Two men?'

Searle described a middle-aged man with sharp blue eyes and a shock of thick blond hair. He wore a white shirt and tan trousers and had a muscular chest and arms. His face was clean-shaven, his jaw chiselled and square. Kerr scribbled furiously.

'I didn't recognise him,' Searle said. 'I suspected he was a local based on appearance, only I'd never seen him before.'

The second man was younger than the first — Searle estimated twenties — and much taller and thinner. He also had a full head of hair, though black, combined with a hairy sheepdog moustache and five o'clock shadow that the headmaster thought made him look quite menacing. He wore jeans and a check shirt, half-unbuttoned, that revealed a dark-brown chest bristling with even more hair.

'I'd never seen him before either, but he resembled a lot of the men I'd told to go away.'

Manolis fixed his eyes on the headmaster before asking the question to which he already knew the answer. 'How so?'

Searle's tone was measured. 'They stick out like dogs' balls.'

'Who do?'

'They do. *Them.*'

Scratching the back of his scalp, Manolis exhaled a long, tight stream of air. 'I see.'

'Detective, I'm a Catholic with very strong beliefs,' Searle said. 'I don't know who Allah is and why they pray to him. I know we pray to Almighty God and Jesus and Mary.' His words sounded heavy, a deadening force.

'And did you approach these men, find out what they wanted?' Manolis asked.

'No,' Searle said. 'I just stood at the window and watched the three-way conversation unfold. These two men were a very different pair, but they had one thing in common — it looked like they were both arguing with Molly.'

'Arguing? What were they saying?'

'I couldn't hear the words, but the body language was clear. The taller man was gesturing passionately about something and appeared almost angry. He had a sinister face, shifty. The other man tried to talk to Molly, but she wasn't interested in whatever he was saying and kept trying to walk away. I nearly banged on the glass to shoo them like a pair of stray dogs. After a few minutes, Molly stormed off, walking south towards Henry Street, likely heading home. I was going to give chase and see if she was alright but I couldn't keep up. Fortunately, the men ended up leaving in the other direction, heading north. Had they followed Molly, I would've definitely gone after them, slow as I am. I watched until they disappeared. I don't think they saw me.'

Searle paused. Manolis waited. Kerr stopped writing.

'I was just glad the children had gone home for the day,' the headmaster added. 'They didn't need to see their teacher upset like that.'

Manolis looked at Kerr. She glanced up from her notepad and nodded gently. It was another lead. Who were these two men? One of them sounded like he would be easy to locate, but the other? And what about the nuisance calls? Manolis needed to find Molly's phone more than ever. He turned back to Searle, who was again mumbling to his criss-crossed digits, eyes half-closed.

'That poor, poor woman,' he said glumly. 'Broken by tragedy, our beloved Molly was drifting. The detention centre only opened up after the last town election. And Molly's job there was an attempt to save her life. Little did we realise it would only cause her death.'

18

Dusk was approaching by the time Searle left the station and returned directly to the top pub. Sparrow escorted him back, insisting on ensuring the headmaster's safe passage and complaining of dehydration.

Searle had replied he was 'in bed sleeping' when Manolis asked his whereabouts the night Molly died. His wife could verify.

'Happily married for as long as I can remember,' Kerr later said. 'No kids. Maybe that's why.'

The headmaster had looked aghast when Manolis queried him, offended even. It was a concern that seemed to grow when Manolis added that he would confirm his alibi with Mrs Searle.

'You don't suppose I had anything to do with it?' Searle stammered.

'We just need to rule people out,' Kerr said quickly.

Manolis stared at Kerr coldly, reprimanding her only after the headmaster had left. 'You can't say that. You've got to be objective. Look at your community as an outsider.'

From the vacant look in her eyes, Manolis wondered if he was asking the impossible.

'And what do you think, is he telling the truth?' he said.

'Can't see why he wouldn't.' Kerr tightened her hair tie, fixed her ponytail. 'What about you?'

Manolis rubbed his sandpaper chin. 'Not sure yet. It's all very neat. Very neat and tidy. That usually sets off an alarm in my head.'

Kerr huffed. 'Christ, not everyone's a suspect.'

'Everyone's a suspect . . . '

Manolis grabbed his car keys with one location in mind. Kerr said not to bother, that everyone would've already gone home for the day, except for the two bored security guards on the front gate who monitored curfew and read pornography.

'Tomorrow, then,' Manolis said. 'Right after we interview a sober Shrewsbury.'

A thorough search of Molly's house was absolutely essential. But experience told Manolis that searches were best conducted in daylight; fumbling about at night risked missing clues or contaminating evidence.

Kerr wanted to call it a day. Her frail mum was waiting, and the witching hour was approaching. The old woman often went wandering at dusk, looking for her childhood home or dead relatives, and Kerr sometimes encountered her en route, inching forward in her lavender nightgown and house slippers. On other occasions, finding her mum missing when she got home, Kerr had spent hours traversing the town in darkness before discovering the old woman sitting patiently on a park bench, waiting for a bus that never came.

'I understand,' Manolis said. 'You can go. But before you do . . . '

* * *

Manolis was familiar with the notoriety of Cobb's murderous base hospital: a string of recent fatalities, doctors and nurses suspended, the coroner permanently investigating. The community's trust was gone; they would sooner drive hundreds of kilometres to the

151

nearest neighbouring hospital than visit their own. At least there they stood a chance.

Adding further strain to the hospital's stretched resources was the detention centre. The detainees were rumoured to receive better medical care than the locals — comprehensive health checks, specialist doctors, access to prescription medicines, sterile bandages, clean needles. Not to mention all the paramedic call-outs to the centre when a detainee was found hanging from plaited rope or bedsheets. It all came from the duty-of-care arrangement, which meant the government could be sued if they failed to discharge their duty. This was why an adult detainee with a cut finger got priority over a local newborn baby struggling to breathe.

Kerr led Manolis through the hospital's emergency department, which better resembled a shantytown. The waiting room smelled of urine and carbolic, and held a deepening chill. Families camped out on long gang chairs, huddled in each other's arms, subsisting on a near-empty vending machine in the corner of the room. At the triage counter, a woman — dragging a child behind her and carrying twins within her — argued with an overtired, disinterested nurse.

Manolis recalled the one time he'd been brought to this hospital as a child. It had been late at night with a raging fever, his body limp and carried by his father while his distressed mother spoke hurriedly to doctors. He remembered seeing, through half-closed eyes, the emergency room as uncrowded, clean and calming. He was seen to promptly, given medication and rest, and he went home the next morning with his colour restored.

Kerr led him down darkened corridors where

barefoot in-patients trailed intravenous drips. Bypassing a lift stuck between floors, they took the stairs to the basement that was reserved as a morgue. There Kerr stopped at the heavy double doors, refusing to go further. She spoke hurriedly and splashed back through water puddles along the corridor, picking up speed as she walked. It was clear that she felt uncomfortable. Manolis reasoned that she'd probably identified the body of her fiancé beyond those double doors.

An Aboriginal man with coarse hair and an iron-grey beard appeared from the gloom. Manolis instantly recognised him as an elder. He wore a patriotic T-shirt in the national colours of red, black and yellow. Manolis introduced himself and shook the man's hand firmly. The man carried with him an air of indifference as he handed Manolis a clipboard, pointed to a wall freezer and trudged away. Manolis tried to talk to him but his queries went unanswered.

The detective looked about him. A corroded mortuary slab dominated the middle of the room. The furthest wall housed a collection of rusted bone saws and bottles of embalming chemicals. It was immediately clear to him that the room was not washed frequently — if ever — and had poor ventilation. The odour was overwhelming: dense, wet, vile and almost shockingly sweet. Manolis felt it coat his skin in a thin film. Feeling nauseous, he considered leaving the room, but instead he just retched.

'Be strong,' he told himself in Greek. '*Thynami.*'

Composing himself and breathing into a cupped hand, he consulted the clipboard under a fizzing fluorescent light. It contained a number of reports, most notably Molly's medical records and the autopsy report. Her medical history was uninspiring: no mention

153

of antidepressants or abuse of prescription or illicit medications, no history of major illness. The external examination revealed a pair of tattoos on her calf and upper back. Compression marks around her wrists and ankles indicated that she'd been bound when she died. Manolis wanted to see toxicology results but there were none; it was still too soon. He was, however, concerned that there was no record of specimens being collected and sent for analysis — this was standard for any suspicious death.

The internal examination was the briefest autopsy report he had ever seen. The body cavity and internal organs remained untouched. He imagined that broken bones were likely, a clavicle or ribs. Not all the rocks would have hit their desired target, even at close range. He often missed the bin at work with his banana peel from half a metre; stones were much heavier, and if flung with enough force introduced a greater margin of error. It was simple physics.

He was most interested to see if the injuries suggested blows from two or more sources, as was the case with 'traditional' stonings. This approach sought to diffuse responsibility; to prevent an individual in the group from being identified as the one who had dealt the death blow. It was the same in a firing squad where one or more guns were loaded with a blank. Or an electric chair with two activation levers, so neither guard knew if they were flipping the actual switch.

Unsurprisingly, the autopsy report contained no mention of blows from multiple sources. It listed the time of death as 'between midnight and dawn', the cause of death as 'homicide', and the mechanism as 'blunt trauma, head injury, stoning'. Death came from a range of medical issues including 'intracranial

154

haemorrhage, swelling to the brain, exsanguination'. Mercifully, there were no signs of sexual assault.

And that was it. Manolis leafed through the pages a second time but found no more to the report. He was annoyed that it had taken so long for such a short report to be finalised. It was signed with an indecipherable scribble, but at least it was signed. To his knowledge there was no electronic copy.

Breathing deeply, he took a moment to find his centre, to compose himself. Over his career, he'd seen more dead bodies than he cared to count, examined victims killed in the most gruesome and cruel of ways, even small children. But he'd never seen the outcome of a stoning before, and suddenly felt inadequately prepared. For individuals who dispensed stoning punishments, this wasn't murder — it was an act of moral self-righteousness. It was also a twisted mode of entertainment that came with a party-like atmosphere. Like picnics at Wild West hangings or packed Roman coliseums for the throwing of Christians to lions.

Manolis shook his head, as if to erase the thoughts in his weary brain. He badly needed a smoke.

The fluorescent light continued to flicker with maddening irregularity. Deep in the bowels of the hospital, the morgue's eerie silence now hurt Manolis's ears. He held his breath, clasped the freezer handle and twisted.

The metal tray slid out in one swift motion, making a cold, hollow clank. He exhaled and let his tired eyes fall upon the dead body of much-loved local schoolteacher, Molly Abbott.

His breath escaped as if he'd been king-hit in the guts. '*Theos kai Panagia . . .*'

It wasn't often that Manolis invoked God and the Holy Virgin. But he did then.

The woman's head and chest were gravely bloodied and bruised, her forehead split open. Her lips were swollen, she had lost teeth, and her head drooped at a grotesque angle. A purple halo ringed her neck, the dead blood trapped, unable to seep down into her back with gravity.

And yet, Manolis could not help but feel surprised. He'd expected the victim to be more disfigured. Perhaps he'd built stonings up in his mind. Were they, by their nature as a punishment, somehow less injurious than an aggravated assault? More controlled, with a purpose, and thereby less violent?

Manolis stopped. He reminded himself that this was no retribution or entertainment. This was murder. An appallingly vile and savage homicide perpetrated by a sick, sadistic individual. It could be nothing else. At that moment, in that silence, Manolis vowed to Molly, to her body and memory, that he would catch the party responsible and bring them to swift and severe justice.

'Let he who is without sin cast the first stone,' he whispered to himself.

Casting his eyes down, he examined the torso and limbs: covered in dried blood, but largely untouched, incredibly. He scrutinised every inch of her lifeless body, the yellow-white skin, looking for something, anything — a cigarette butt, a fingernail, toenail, piece of skin, eyelash, stray hair. Whatever shred of foreign matter might provide another lead. But she was, regrettably, incredibly, clean.

Something doesn't add up here, Manolis thought. What was he missing?

Fast running out of ideas, he worked his way back up the body. Delicately, he lifted the fragile head and inspected the underside.

And then he found his first real clue.

19

When he returned to the tourist park, Manolis heard Rex and Vera arguing inside their cabin. He couldn't make out what they were saying but their tone was unquestionable. She seemed to be contributing most to the discussion, her voice shrill and hectoring, like fingernails on a blackboard. It bounced off the walls of their cabin, which had its doors and windows closed tight. Manolis considered knocking on the sliding door and asking if everything was OK, but in the end decided that a mental note would suffice. They were private citizens on their own property, and no-one had complained about the noise. And besides, he was too dog-tired to deal with a bloody domestic.

He made a toasted cheese sandwich, ripped through it, ravenous. As the stale bread dissolved in his stomach, he savoured his nightly smoke on the verandah and regarded the night sky. Constellations emerged like a photograph sinking into a bath of developer, gradually becoming known to the eye. Every drooping gumleaf, every dry blade of grass, every rooftop was soon etched in radiant silver starlight. It was almost as if the moon was out.

Hearing Rex and Vera quarrel made Manolis's mind wander, and he was grateful to put Molly out of his thoughts for a while. He considered the institution of marriage, of a life shared with one other, as his parents had shared theirs for some fifty years. In that time he'd seen peaks and troughs, happiness and sadness, joy and frustration. He pondered his own marriage — or, at least, the union that had once been. No doubt his neighbours had heard them arguing too, often late at night.

Emily was a quiet, introspective solicitor whom Manolis had met working on a case. Her forebears hailed from the British Isles as so-called Ten Pound Poms. The cracks of their relationship, their marriage, which they'd once successfully plastered over with work and ignorance, had become gaping chasms with the arrival of children. It was the sleepless nights, the perpetual lack of time, and the extra duties and responsibilities. Manolis had expected it all but was never fully prepared. Having been one herself, Maria had warned her son to marry 'a good Greek girl' and have 'good Greek babies'. He had ignored her. Now, for the rest of their lives, she would always be right.

Manolis stubbed out his cigarette with minor disgust and went inside. He showered, flopped onto his mattress and was asleep in seconds.

* * *

His possum returned later that night, rousing him from a deep sleep with a clatter of cutlery. He was pleased to see that it had escaped the wrath of the car fire and returned with the same curiosity and hunger. Its damp eyes were clear and trusting.

'Hey there, buddy. Good to see you're OK. Want a snack? I've got a real treat for you tonight.'

He again fed it saltines, this time smeared with crunchy peanut butter, which it approached cautiously at first, then ate with gusto, licking its sticky lips.

Manolis heard the fireworks again and fell back into

159

bed with a long sigh, extending a bare arm across the scratchy sheets. He missed Emily. He missed her in bed, her deep breathing, her steadying presence and warmth.

Closing his eyes, he waited for his nightmare to restart: a bloodied, disfigured Molly Abbott being pelted with stones and screaming for her life. At times, he clutched his own head and face, or ground his back teeth into pulp. The image would not dislodge; it interrupted his sleep. He feared it would be with him for some time. He wanted to forget it.

★ ★ ★

In the morning, the sky was yellow and rotting. Manolis could feel the heat coming out of the ground as he walked to his car. The sun hung in the sky like a red-hot stone, dust in the air as hot as metal filings. Vera was in her front yard, trying to tame some weeds. Her plastic goggles, vinyl gloves, rubber pants and gumboots made Manolis wonder if she was using Agent Orange. She waved when she saw him and went to remove her respirator mask. He waved back but kept walking.

She stood, goggles on forehead, mask hanging loose around her neck. A dark mark of sweat trailed between her breasts.

'Lamb curry tonight, love?' she asked. Her Jekyll voice was light, airy, and in stark contrast to the harsh screeching of the night before. 'Or I can grill some lamb chops or a juicy T-bone? The steaks from our abattoir are thicker than your arm.'

Manolis wrestled with the starter motor, swore at it in Greek. Bloody car wouldn't kick over on purpose,

160

he thought. God was punishing him for being such a heathen. Vera was waiting, face bright, hopeful. He'd better answer.

'That's a very generous offer, Mrs Boyd, but unfortunately I suspect I may be working late tonight.'

'Sounds like you've got some leads then, eh? We sincerely appreciate it, Detective, thank you.'

'No thanks necessary. I'm just doing my job.'

'Are they Muslims?'

Manolis did not respond.

'I knew it . . . ' She spoke with a sudden hateful smile, turning her head west, to the direction of the devil.

Manolis looked at her blankly. Vera was short and dumpy, the size of a garden gnome. Her cheeks were ruby red, glowing like hot coals in the roasting sun.

'I can't talk about the case,' he said simply.

Her smile evaporated, her face turning down. Twice in two minutes he'd disappointed her. He continued to grind the key into the ignition, cursing both Jesus and God in the process. Vera looked at him with wrathful eyes. She wanted to scold him for his rampant blasphemy but held her tongue. In the end she turned the other way, facing east, to confirm her faith.

'Tell you what, whatever I cook, I'll leave a plate in your fridge, yep,' she said. 'You can enjoy it whenever you get home.'

The car started. Hallelujah, praise the Lord.

'That's very considerate, but no thank you,' Manolis said. The gear engaged with a crunch. 'Sorry, but I have to go.'

He floored the accelerator with determination, hands clenching the wheel as the cold engine roared in agony, and he sighed with relief.

The flyblown cop shop finally resembled a working police station for Wednesday morning's nine o'clock briefing. Manolis was momentarily stunned. He stood before the constables and spoke briefly but assuredly. He told them what he'd seen on Molly's body during the morgue examination. He said the pattern of trauma suggested injury to the back of her head as well as the front.

Sparrow and Kerr looked at each other blankly, then at Manolis with the same expression.

'So?' Sparrow finally said. 'She was stoned to death. With rocks. What a newsflash. I reckon that'd involve a fair amount of head trauma, don't you?'

'Well, yes, obviously,' Manolis said. 'But she was tied to a tree. Don't you find injuries to the *back* of her head surprising given she was tied to a tree?'

Sparrow let out a laugh. 'Did you see the final position of her head? All drooped. Her bloody neck was broken.'

'I guess it's not that hard to imagine her head slumped forward after she died,' Kerr added, 'and then copped a few more rocks to the back, is it?'

Manolis agreed that was plausible. 'I just didn't expect it. I didn't imagine someone would keep raining blows after she died.'

'They would if they got pleasure out of it,' Sparrow said.

'She might've also turned her head away,' Kerr said. 'I know I would.'

Manolis looked at his feet, was reflective. 'Yes, also possible. But just hear me out when I say I found it odd — my sixth sense was tingling. I've seen more

162

brutal assaults in my time in the city. There might be something in it, there might not. But keep an open mind to all possibilities. I will too.'

Sparrow was soon hunched over his desk, simultaneously working a handset and filling an ashtray, searching for the phone records of a Mary Abbott or Margaret Abbott, or Molly or Mary or Margaret Boyd, her married name. Kerr went out doorknocking and chasing up alibis; Principal Searle was her first stop. Manolis expressed some concern over her house-to-house enquiries, which she was going to do solo — this wouldn't have been allowed in the city. She told him in a fierce tone, 'Piss off, I'll be fine.' He backed down.

Old Geoff the chicken farmer made an appearance — apparently a frequent occurrence — to report more missing poultry from his coop. He was ancient, bent, dressed in soiled overalls, no shirt, trucker's hat to protect him from the cancer-causing sun. Manolis took down his details and said that an officer would visit soon. Geoff stood silently a moment, then trudged away grumbling.

Fyfe soon arrived, escorting a reluctant Joe Shrewsbury into the tearoom for questioning. Sparrow had described Joe as 'always kinda drunk' and with a liver the size of a small car. He never went to sleep, 'he always just passed out'. Joe arrived shirtless, in shorts and thongs, sporting a proud beer gut and complaining about the early hour. It was ten-thirty.

Manolis was wary. This interrogation would need to be textbook in order to avoid a false confession. The local cops had breached multiple codes of practice; there was no way any defendant could possibly have a fair trial. So a confession was crucial, but it

163

needed to be watertight.

Fyfe stopped Manolis at the entrance to the tea-room.

'The prick's guilty,' he muttered, rubbing palms together. 'His alibi's bullshit. He's got a history of pestering the victim. Let's lay a murder charge and go to the pub to fucken celebrate.'

Manolis quickly discerned that Fyfe and Joe had bad blood between them. He thought a moment, but in the end decided to retain the local sergeant in the interview.

'We're gathering information, not eliciting a confession,' Manolis reminded him firmly. 'If we happen to get one, that's different.'

'We're wasting our bloody time, city mouse. The bastard lied. Only a guilty prick with something to hide would lie.'

'Even innocent people lie when they're scared.'

'Scared? Joe? Ha. Scared of sobriety, maybe.'

It was as if Fyfe had done an about-turn and completely exonerated the detention centre. Perhaps all he wanted to do was drink, so he was happy to clear his schedule. Manolis repeated that he planned to visit the detention centre in the afternoon, to investigate Searle's report of a man resembling an asylum seeker in heated discussion with Molly the day before she died.

Manolis and Fyfe entered the tearoom and took their seats with Joe around the rickety table. Joe's first utterances were more grunts than words, there was a looseness to his body. He wolfed down the last of the supermarket doughnuts that Fyfe had brought in, ceremoniously licking the remains of sticky pink icing from his stubby fingers. He took one gulp of sour coffee, swore and hurled the polystyrene cup towards the bin, missing it by a long way. Dark-brown liquid sprayed across the lino.

Joe was in his forties but didn't look it. He was like many men who grow up in small communities: looking forever like boys, then suddenly old. There is never the gradual corrosion of features as they age. He scratched his smooth chin and ran his blue eyes, still lustrous, over Manolis.

'Hi, Joe,' Manolis said kindly. 'I'm Detective Sergeant George Manolis. You already know Sergeant Fyfe. Thanks for coming down. First of all, sorry about the seating arrangements.'

Having removed the excess garden furniture from the tearoom, Manolis had offered Joe a plastic milk crate as a seat. It was a tactic sought to heighten the suspect's discomfort and set up a feeling of dependence.

'Don't mind,' Joe said casually. 'The base of me bed is crates.'

Fyfe let out a derisive laugh.

Joe ignored him. 'Look, this gonna be quick? I gotta get back to me dogs, they're hungry.'

After assuring him it would not take long, Manolis opened with a series of non-threatening questions. Joe looked at him from a long way away, pausing before he spoke but ultimately answering all that was asked. Fyfe shoved a blob of tobacco under his upper lip and sat quietly chewing, brooding, sneering.

Eventually, Joe interrupted Manolis's questioning. 'Look, Dick Tracy, save it. I know why I'm here. I didn't kill her, orright?'

Manolis held up his left hand in a stopping gesture. 'No-one's saying that, Joe. One thing at a time.'

Joe scratched at his flabby pectoral. 'Honestly, ever since she slapped me in the pub that night, my dick went limp,' he said bluntly. 'I lost interest, never called her again. Frigid bitch. Check my phone records if ya want.'

Manolis remembered the supposed nuisance calls Molly had been getting and decided to call his bluff.

'Go right ahead,' Joe reiterated. 'I got nothin' to hide.'

There was a long pause as the three men looked at each other. Manolis consulted his notepad, flipping through the spiral pages. 'Joe, do you have any idea who might've wished Molly harm? Even if it's just a feeling. A sense of unease about someone, something you heard her say, something that didn't quite sit right?'

Every single question was met with a headshake. 'Like I said, ain't seen her in ages. I haven't a clue about any of that stuff. What she did, who she saw.'

Manolis sketched in his pad, pretending to write notes. He was drawing lines, connecting them, doodling. Fyfe cracked his knuckles so loud that it sounded like he'd snapped a finger. A pentagram soon materialised on Manolis's page. He stared at it a moment, becoming aware of what he'd accidentally drawn. Looking up, he asked Joe about his whereabouts the night Molly died.

Joe folded his freckled arms across a hairless chest. 'I already told that young copper you sent over. I was at the pub.'

Manolis tore out the pentagram page, screwed it up into a tight ball. 'What time? How long were you there?'

'Got in about eight, stayed all night. They turfed us

'No,' Manolis said coolly, flicking back through his notepad. 'We've been told you weren't at the pub on Friday.'

Fyfe gave a deep grunt, cold and loathsome. 'Only a guilty prick would lie,' he growled.

The lines on Joe's face darkened. 'Get your hand off it, Bill. Half the town's on the run for somethin' or other.'

Manolis again checked his notepad, as if to jog his memory. But he already knew what he was going to say.

'You told Constable Sparrow you were at the pub last Friday, but the publican says he hasn't seen you in a long time, let alone on Friday. In fact, he said you're barred from the pub for hitting another woman who spilled your beer. So, care to try again . . . ? Where were you on Friday night?'

Joe's eyes darted. He arched his back and slapped his chest like an ape, letting out a long exhalation of hot, tight air. 'So, what, now I'm a suspect?'

Manolis clicked his biro. 'Everyone's a suspect unless they can provide an alibi. You tell me where you were on Friday and who you were with. Once I confirm, I rule you out as a person of interest. I'm sure this is all very straightforward.'

His calm words were a soothing balm. Joe's breath steadied, his eyes stared dead ahead. Fyfe continued to glare at the topless man with a combination of hostility and disgust. In the harsh morning light, Joe's fleshy love handles appeared sickening.

Eventually, his face cracked. The expression was accompanied by an incredulous laugh that escaped tight, blistered lips.

167

'Look, I dunno what to tell ya. I was at the pub. Ya sure *the publican*'s not lying? You sure *he*'s not the killer? Bloody useless blackfella . . .'

Manolis recalled the publican at the top pub. Turps was his name. Hair was albino white, skin the colour of ice. Didn't look like no Aboriginal fella to him.

'Hang on a minute,' Manolis said. 'At which pub were you drinking?'

Joe looked insulted. 'What, can't a whitefella drink at the bottom pub? There a law against that now as well?'

Fyfe whacked the plastic table with an open hand, making it shudder. 'Smart arse,' he spat.

Joe turned his head coolly in the local sergeant's direction. 'Hey, Bill,' he said calmly, 'screw you too.'

Manolis leaned forward, placed his palms on his knees and cocked his head. 'So you're telling me that you were actually at the bottom pub last Friday night?'

Joe eased back onto his crate. 'Exactly like I said.'

'And the publican there can attest to this?'

'Reckon so. Aboriginal fella with a shaggy beard served me all night. I paid off the mortgage on his mud hut.' Joe scratched his scabby scalp.

Manolis glanced over at Fyfe. 'Blokes have been known to move between pubs,' the sergeant conceded. 'Depending on which one they're banned from at the time. There's no law against it.'

A pause. 'Right,' Manolis said. 'I'm off.'

Time was running out.

Manolis looked at Fyfe, motioned to Joe. 'But he stays here. You boys play nice.'

The two men eyed each other with distrust and suspicion, and with pure, burning hatred.

As Manolis walked away he swung back to Joe,

addressing him with a pointed index finger. 'And if I find out you're lying, I'm arresting you for obstructing a murder enquiry.'

Manolis turned and walked on.

Joe raised his voice to ensure he was heard. 'This is exactly what they want, Detective. Those camel jockeys who stoned Molly to death, those sand niggers. It's their plan. Isn't it a sad bloody day when Australians are fighting among Australians to save Australia . . . ?'

20

Fyfe tried to talk Manolis out of going. 'Don't be pig-ignorant and stupid,' the sergeant said. 'And take Sparrow. *It's what he's for.* Use him.'

Manolis disregarded the advice and drove straight to the bottom pub. Sparrow was busy working the phones, and Manolis wanted to see things with his own eyes.

As he drove, he kept a close watch for any unaccompanied children wandering the streets. But he hadn't seen anyone who looked like an immigration detainee since arriving. The streets were empty anyway — no people, only rumours and accusations.

An accumulation of outstretched comatose bodies ushered his arrival to the bottom pub. The majority were still clutching grog containers, bottles and cans and cardboard boxes of goon, silver bags of happiness.

By the time Manolis reached the epicentre, his whitefella car had been identified as foreign. It was pelted with a barrage of racial epithets and drink receptacles, bottles and cans clattering into the already heavily dented bodywork. Manolis dodged and weaved, accelerated and decelerated. With no windscreen, his main concern was a bottle smashing through a side window.

The bottom pub did not look at all familiar to Manolis. It resembled a toilet block. All concrete and windowless, the flat-roofed pub was on what felt like the hottest edge of town, as if somehow nearer the sun. The smell inside was similarly latrine-like, tangy and acrid, a thick brown stench of ammonia that made Manolis want to tear the nose from his face.

There was a hush as he entered the room, quiet whispers of discontent. All sets of eyes instantly locked on to him; bleached white against dark skin, they appeared to hover in the gloom. Manolis met their gaze and shunted with clear purpose past the mismatched chairs and tables. He pushed the over-flowing ashtrays away and leaned against the bar to take in the scene. The killer, he told himself, could very well be inside this godforsaken shithole.

Manolis counted about a dozen souls of differing size, shape, age and level of animosity. Voices were soon heard, swearing and threatening the stranger with eviction — even violence. Others murmured to their drinking partners, a few muttered to themselves under their breath, and the rest just cocked their elbows, swallowed and stared. Most were seasoned drinkers, nursing new beers and old grievances. But there were also some minors, and a few junkies rattling with nervous energy. Two of the patrons were white, huddled together in a corner. Manolis drank it all in, straightened his spine and waited for an approach with his piece at the ready.

But none came. The bar was not the hell on earth Fyfe had claimed. Instead, it was an abyss of desperation and despair, the end result of a community ruined by grog and overrun with hopelessness. Quietly, Manolis's heart broke.

Eventually, someone walked over: a bearded man from behind the bar. He was wearing the unmistakable look of someone who had drunk to excess. His eyes were deep and wounded, dolorous and heavy. Manolis watched his tobacco breath emerge from

171

somewhere within his wild beard and form a distinct cloud before the detective's eyes.

He inhaled deeply, letting his brain swim. 'You the owner?' he asked, coughing.

The man's dark eyes took the measure of Manolis. Without warning, he hoicked up a great gob of spit and deposited it noisily into an ashtray.

'Could be,' he said. 'Who's askin'?'

Manolis reached into his shirt pocket and casually retrieved his wallet, flashed his badge.

The man squinted his red-rimmed eyes and scoffed. 'How'd I know that's real?'

'Relax, mate.' Manolis's face softened. 'I'm not here for you or your business. I need to ask about a man. Do you know a bloke named Joe Shrewsbury?'

The man's eyes smiled knowingly. 'Shrewsbury,' he sneered. 'That white cunt.' He spat each syllable with precision and disgust.

Manolis cleared his throat. 'So you obviously know Joe. Good. Was he here last Friday night?'

Lighting a cigarette, the man let it dangle from the corner of his mouth as he spoke. 'This about that white bitch got stoned to death?'

'Maybe,' Manolis said. 'First, answer me. Was Joe here on Friday?'

'Maybe,' the man breathed. 'Or maybe not. What's it worth to ya?'

Manolis wanted to tell the drunk it was actually worth more to him. That if he didn't answer Manolis's questions, there was a jail cell with his name on it. Manolis was a senior detective investigating a homicide, not some private dick hired by a suspicious lover to source some dirt — he was above needing to bribe people for information. Still, he did not relish the

172

thought of slapping a pair of cuffs on the burly elder's wrists and trying to haul him outside. The locals were quiet now but the air was simmering, and he didn't want to start a full-scale race riot. The sight of a white cop in a black bar dragging away a black man was not a good look.

Manolis opened his wallet, slid a pineapple across the bar. The man's dark eyes sparkled and grew large. A wrinkle of ash teetered at the base of his smoke. He went to snatch the fifty-dollar bill with a grubby paw before Manolis slapped down the money.

'First, tell me.'

The publican's bright eyes remained firmly on the money. He spoke to it, addressing the currency, not the detective. 'Shrewsbury wasn't here on Friday night.'

'Not at all?'

'Nope.'

Manolis's hand remained on the fifty. He suddenly felt like he'd been ripped off, that he should've offered less, a lobster, a twenty. He wanted more bang for his buck.

'So where was he on Friday night?'

The man's pupils flicked up to meet Manolis's. 'That's not what ya asked,' he said firmly. 'Ya asked if he was here. And he wasn't. Ya got what ya came for. Now, if ya don't bloody mind . . . '

Manolis assessed him, in case he too was hiding the truth. After a few seconds of intense glaring, he relaxed his eyes, then fingers. The money had vanished by the time he looked down.

The publican showed his teeth, a set of crooked but dazzlingly white choppers. 'Drink?' he offered. 'On the house.'

173

Manolis's nostrils flared. At least he had an answer: Joe was lying, and without a verifiable alibi would remain a person of interest.

Checking his watch, the detective saw it wasn't yet noon, but it had been a long morning. 'Got any whisky?'

The publican's face stretched in astonishment, confusion. He extinguished his butt in the nearest ashtray.

'Might have an old bottle out back,' he grumbled. 'Wait here.'

Shambling away in bare feet, he disappeared behind a concrete wall and into a darkened room. Just as Manolis leaned across the bar to get a better view, he felt a hard tap on his shoulder.

'You ask about Shrewsbury?'

Manolis swung around. The voice was deep, so he expected to be greeted by a big man. The bloke turned out to have the dimensions of a fridge and appeared just as solid, perhaps even as smart. His bald skull was the size of a beer keg and had a violent architecture of indentations and scarring.

'I did,' Manolis said. 'You know something?'

The man looked uncertain, his coffee-stain eyes growing wider. He paused, scratched the back of his non-neck, then asked quickly, 'You a cop?'

His words were slippery and small. Manolis again showed his badge. The man's face lit up, his eyes widening even further and now burning with a maniacal light. Manolis recognised that look and took an instinctive backward step, as if to prepare for an oncoming fist or knife or broken bottle or blood-filled syringe. All had been thrust upon him at one time or another during his career in circumstances not dissimilar to these.

'Good,' the man-fridge said. 'Cos I wanna report the bastard.'

'Report him?' Manolis said, unable to hide his interest. 'Report him for what?'

The words fell out, heavy and solemn. 'For what he did last Friday night.'

Manolis swallowed hard.

He bought the man a beer, and together with his soft, flavourless whisky they sat on a misshapen table in the least depressing corner of the pub and talked. The man identified himself as Joe's neighbour. He owned a farm on the western side of a small, dry creek that acted as the boundary line between the two properties. He explained that he and Joe had bonded over alcohol for years. They were mates and looked after each other.

'But not anymore,' he said. 'Not after Friday.'

Manolis made notes and listened attentively. The neighbour's slurring made his words increasingly incomprehensible. He talked in circles, repeated himself, got distracted, spilt beer, cursed, spat. He described the evening that unfolded, a night spent drinking with his long-time friend, and how he left the room to get more drinks and came back to a scene that stopped him dead. His eyes welled up as he spoke.

'I swear, I nearly killed the bastard there and then . . .'

Every few minutes, some or other drunk staggered up to the table to hurl an insult at Manolis's white face or accuse the neighbour of being a lying prick or plead to be bought a beer or bum a smoke. Others offered car stereos for sale, or counterfeit watches or drugs.

Manolis sipped his whisky thoughtfully, listening to his informant. When it was all over, the detective sat back in his chair, digesting all that he'd been forced to hear.

He was boiling with rage, his hand close to snapping his pen in two. But then he remembered he had a job to do, a crime to solve. Two deep breaths quelled his emotions. A good cop remained cool, calm, he told himself. So did a good husband.

Manolis reflected on what had been laid out before him: a clear impression of what Molly's former suitor had been doing the night she was stoned to death.

'Did Shrewsbury mention a woman named Molly Abbott on Friday?'

'The dead woman? Nah, mate. Not once.'

'And he was with you all night?'

'Unfortunately, yes.'

Thanking Joe's neighbour for his time, Manolis bought him a final beer. He finished his whisky, his tongue feeling deadened, and returned to his car. With the echo of abuse in his ears, he left the bottom pub in his dust, navigating through another hailstorm of beer cans and speeding back to the station.

As he walked in the door, he heard raised voices — Fyfe and Shrewsbury, arguing like unruly siblings over something only they could understand. Manolis hushed them like an irate father and recommenced his line of questioning.

'Since we talked earlier, I checked on a few things,' Manolis told Joe.

Joe didn't move; his mouth gaped open, inviting the circling blowflies.

'Your alibi is bullshit. The publican said you weren't there on Friday.'

'I knew it,' Fyfe said instantly, viciously. 'You lying piece of shit. Why'd you kill her?'

Joe laughed. He pressed his palms into his eyes. 'I didn't kill anyone,' he said in exasperation.

'Not kill,' Manolis said. 'But you did do something.'

Lowering his hands, Joe blinked. His face lightened in colour.

'Ha,' he said. 'Find my neighbour, did ya? Yeah OK, I admit it. I was with him at his house. But she led me on, orright? His daughter, wearing clothes like that.'

Manolis felt his fingers tightening, his fist clenching. But then he let out a long, stinging sigh of despair. He stood up and turned to Fyfe. 'Sergeant, please lock this *diavolos* up.'

Fyfe looked at him with wild eyes. 'What charge?'

Manolis turned to leave. 'Sexual assault,' he said, 'of a sixteen-year-old girl.'

21

It had been a trying, confronting morning, and Manolis's lungs were itching for the calming embrace of sweet tobacco. He sat on the steps of the police station, his jittery fingers rolling a long, thick cigarette. When it was ready, he admired it for a moment before igniting and smoking with the nonchalance of a silent film star. The nicotine balm soothed his nerves, cleared his mind and settled his soul. He'd never encountered such an investigation before. It would be too soon if he ever had to deal with one again.

Like his dad, Manolis's wife hated that he smoked, a hatred that strengthened when young Christos arrived. But he was such a poor sleeper that Manolis found himself leaning hard on the crutch of tobacco, which only furthered Emily's distance. Sooner or later, something had to give.

On Manolis's instructions, Fyfe had driven to the bottom pub to arrest Joe's neighbour for irresponsible supply of alcohol to a minor. Joe had said everyone at the neighbour's house was drunk last Friday, and the man had allowed his underage daughter an unlimited quantity of vodka. Joe had pleaded his innocence, claiming he'd done nothing wrong, that she'd led him on and he'd just fondled and kissed her. Either way, Fyfe took Sparrow to the bottom pub as insurance policy.

The detective recounted the details to Kerr as they drove to Molly's house.

'This is the outback,' the constable said curtly,

sounding unsurprised and unperturbed. 'This is how we treat our women. Like animals.'

Searle's alibi that he was home had been confirmed by his wife. 'Only problem is that she was sleeping,' Kerr said.

Manolis scratched his rugged chin with a leathery hand, feeling the sharp bristles emerging.

'So we've got no-one who can verify his whereabouts the night Molly died. Is his wife a heavy sleeper?'

'Straight through,' Kerr said. 'Dusk to dawn.'

'Hardly a confirmed alibi, then.'

Sparrow's morning had been equally fruitless — he was unable to locate any phone records for Molly's other names. Finding the dead woman's phone was now crucial.

★ ★ ★

Situated halfway along the street, Molly's house was a weatherboard with an iron roof and small chimney. It was a crude, cold construction, a rundown cottage, all asbestos and peeling paint, close to collapsing. It didn't appear at all familiar to Manolis, who thought it looked just like any other decrepit dwelling in Cobb. Approaching the building, he couldn't help but notice ghostly wind chimes dangling from the eaves, being blown about by a gentle breath of wind. He had to hack his way through the thick, high grass that overran the front yard. He recalled Searle's testimony that Molly had a green thumb and was left somewhat bemused. Had that story been fabricated too?

'Have you been here before?' Manolis found himself whispering to Kerr as their heavy-soled workboots crunched up the dirt driveway.

179

'Never had reason to,' she said at normal volume.

'And she and Patrick lived here?'

'Yes, this was the marital home.'

Snapping on rubber gloves, they first circled the cottage, checking for signs of forced entry or disturbance or physical altercation. But everything appeared normal — the house was in order, the doors locked, the windows intact, the blinds and curtains drawn. No bloodstains. Manolis briefly considered whether anyone had spare keys. It was as if Molly had simply left of her own volition, with every intention of returning.

'Shouldn't we take fingerprints?' Kerr asked.

'If we find something of significance. We can't take prints of the whole house.'

Kerr prised the back door open with a gentle twist of her crowbar. It splintered ajar with minimal effort. Again, there was no indication of any conflict or unlawful entry. The furniture was in place, no broken chairs or upturned tables; the beds were made, and the cutlery was neatly balanced in the drying rack. There was even a carton of soon-to-be expired milk and a plate of leftover casserole in the fridge.

'Check drawers and cupboards,' Manolis said. 'Keep an eye out for anything unusual.'

They worked methodically, moving from room to room, searching through cupboards and drawers, under mattresses, behind curtains. For such a crumbling house, Manolis thought it had been kept meticulously clean and retained a certain warmth.

He scanned the photos on the walls and bookshelves and TV unit. He could see why Molly's students had adored her — she appeared easy to love, a natural beauty, her face striking yet warm. She would have been the subject of many innocent schoolyard crushes. He lingered on one framed photo in particular. She was much younger, perhaps early twenties, her face and eyes bursting with youth and joy. She was wearing a white bikini and doing a star jump on a lush green lawn under a summer sprinkler.

'Should I check this room?' Kerr asked tentatively. 'I don't really want to. It feels wrong.'

Manolis poked his head around the corner. She was referring to one of the bedrooms. There were posters of Hollywood blockbusters, a stereo and TV, bass guitar in a stand, bar fridge, and a collection of merchandise from a favourite football team. It was Patrick's room, his man cave, presumably just as he'd left it, regularly dusted and maintained in pristine condition.

'Absolutely check it,' Manolis said.

The room had clearly not been altered in years, save for regular dusting and the addition of a small shrine in the furthest corner. A collage of photos was pinned on a corkboard, and there was a collection of personal items on a table in front: wallet and keys, necklace and rings, toothbrush and comb. Manolis noticed the room was a degree or two warmer than the rest of the house, likely due to its northerly orientation.

While Kerr reluctantly searched the room, he returned to examining the photos on the walls. There were a number of framed pictures with Patrick, including of their wedding day. He was certainly handsome, thought Manolis, square-jawed and clear-eyed. Molly may never have looked happier, embracing and kissing him in all white. A group shot revealed her parents, the war hero and housewife, and parents-in-law, the tourist-park operators. Rex and Vera appeared so much younger and genuinely joyous at their son's marriage to a much-loved local girl. In many respects, he and Molly appeared the perfect couple.

Returning to the kitchen, Manolis examined the photos stuck to the fridge door. By virtue of their high-traffic location, fridge photos were seen more often; it was why he had put pictures of his son on his own fridge. These were the newest ones, those yet to be framed, if they ever would be. Manolis was hoping to find photos of recent boyfriends or lovers on Molly's fridge. The two male suspects Searle had earmarked were at the forefront of his mind. In the past year alone he'd seen the faces of two murderers for the first time under fridge magnets.

Instead, he saw a sad-eyed cocker spaniel, a beloved, recently departed pet. Smiling kids in school uniforms. Proud girlfriends and their young babies. Manolis wondered why Molly and Patrick never became parents. Maybe they didn't want to. Maybe they couldn't.

There was also refugee activism paraphernalia, stickers and pamphlets, slogans and catchcries. *Let Them Stay. No Human Is Illegal. Stop War Not People.* For a brief moment Manolis felt like he'd found an oasis in the desert. There were also mementos from the detention centre, colourful thank-you cards with childlike lettering. But no photos.

'Interesting,' he told himself. 'So it's true, she was very much — '

Kerr appeared, her expression confused. 'Who are you talking to?'

'No-one,' Manolis said. 'What have you got there?'

In one hand she was holding a bundle of material. 'I found these.'

She held it out to Manolis, who eyed it suspiciously.

He gripped an inch of cloth between his fingers and let it unfurl with gravity.

'Y-fronts,' she said.

But he could already see what they were. More importantly, he could see what they meant. There was a man out there to whom these belonged, a lover, who had recently been in Molly's house and left them in haste, or out of routine.

'Could they be Patrick's?' Manolis asked. 'Are they from his room?'

'Could be,' Kerr said. 'And no, I found them folded up in the cupboard in her room. See, thing is, this is a specific brand they buy in bulk.'

Manolis examined the underpants, rotating them before his nose. They certainly had the hallmarks of an ordinary pair: white, cotton, with an elastic waistband and supportive pouch. They would need to be sent off for DNA testing. But he was confused. 'Buy in bulk? Who buys in bulk?'

Kerr's face tensed as she realised the magnitude of what she was about to say. The words dropped from her mouth like lead weights.

'The immigration detention centre, for all their detainees.'

22

Manolis had to use all his powers of persuasion to get past the front gate of the detention centre. The security guards stared at him with pothole eyes. As employees of a private company, they did not take kindly to having their authority usurped and their kingdom invaded. Manolis was searched for contraband, a process that took an inordinately long time. He was given a laminated pass and signed in. As he was led through the checkpoint, he heard one of the guards joke about Molly's stoning while the other laughed and mentioned 'solitary'. From above, CCTV cameras captured every move.

The administration building had a newness about it, but also a sterility and a sense of misery. There was a lack of natural light, and it was near silent. What little noise there was echoed through the bare corridors — footsteps on concrete, a slamming door, a ringing phone. It felt eerie.

Manolis was handed on to a second pair of bulky security guards and escorted to the facility manager's office. Their tall frames cast long shadows across a dirt quadrangle in the late afternoon sun.

'No photos,' one of the guards told Manolis. 'Photos inside the centre are prohibited.'

Manolis eyed his ID badge. It bore a single name: Deacon.

'I'm a police officer,' Manolis said.

'Your badge means nothing here,' Deacon barked. 'You can still be prosecuted.'

184

Manolis again saw the outdoor basketball court, now empty. Beyond the court, makeshift washing lines sagged, heavy with cheap polyester and rayon. There was also row upon row of the same white underpants that had brought him there that day. The huts had been painted in parts, the detainees having tried valiantly to make their incarceration more tolerable. Their sketches included murals and foreign flags of origin. Gardens had been planted, airless rooms decorated. The detainees' lives were monitored closely, their transitions between sections controlled by a phalanx of private security.

The guards themselves spoke in hushed undertones. They eyed their visitor with suspicion as his pupils darted to every corner of the common areas, examining holes in walls and broken windows and charred remains. Walking further, he overheard Deacon mention a 'blindfold' to his colleague. It was an offhand statement with an ounce of truth, and certainly would've kept Manolis from noticing what was in the next building: canisters of tear gas and boxes of rubber bullets and stun grenades and rows of batons and shields, all locked up securely in wire-mesh cages. Manolis kept looking for a children's playground that wasn't there.

In the mess area, the kitchen appeared derelict. There were signs of numerous maintenance jobs, including extensive patchwork. The floor was uneven and precarious in places, with insufficient storage space and old equipment piling up on benches.

They were now towards the very back of the detention centre, at its northern-most point. An aerial drone hummed ominously overhead. As Manolis and the guards crossed a final patch of grass, a little girl ran across their path. Her mouth was sealed tight with sticky tape, an older woman in a black hijab in tow. Manolis instinctively went to the girl's aid before her hand was snatched by the woman, who swiftly bundled up the girl and carried her away.

'Her mum,' said the second guard.

'Keep walking,' Deacon said. 'Eyes front.'

The manager's office was in a new building, up one flight of stairs. It was sparsely decorated, bland and functional, with two rubber plants contributing the only splash of green. Their glossy leaves shimmied in the gentle air conditioning. A poster-sized image of the Queen hung watchfully on the wall. Next to it, a suffering Christ melted from his cross. Manolis was offered a seat in a hard plastic visitor's chair. He was not offered tea or coffee or water. The cool, crisp air stroked his hot sticky face.

The facility manager, Frank Onions, kept his visitor waiting. When the man finally appeared, his first words to Manolis were a query tinged with irritation.

'What took you so long?'

He eased into the cushioned seat of his ergonomic office chair, seemingly forgetting to shake Manolis's outstretched hand. Onions was unsmiling and wore an expression that said: 'My time is worth more than this.'

Behind the large mahogany desk, Manolis saw a prepossessing figure with strong cheekbones. Onions had broad shoulders but was thin, the sinews of his neck stretched to their very limits. His close-cropped hair was turning silver at the temples, and his long, crooked nose looked like it had been broken a few times in the past.

'Thank you for meeting with me,' Manolis said politely. 'You probably know why I'm here.'

186

'I probably do,' Onions said, showing teeth. 'So why aren't you out there doing your job?' He had a steady gaze and spoke with a soft but self-assured delivery.

Manolis proceeded to detail the crime, the victim and the investigation so far, all in broad strokes. The more he spoke, the more the manager's expression changed from uninterested to confused, and finally incredulous. His fingers, which had thrummed the desk with a military beat, stopped dead still.

At first Onions spoke in great bureaucratic detail, words designed to bewilder and bore. He spoke about visa systems and processing times and advisory bodies and independent agencies and global population movements and budgets. He outlined infrastructure and resources and duty of care and bipartisan political support and nation-building. His speech sounded pre-written and well-rehearsed. When he finally took a breath, he fixed Manolis with striking blue eyes and a sharkish smile.

'Of course, you do realise you're only wasting your time here,' he said. 'Whoever you're looking for isn't here. Here in the facility, I mean. The culprit is beyond these walls, out there.' He pointed over Manolis's shoulder, back towards the town.

The detective cleared his throat. 'Thank you for that, Mr Onions. I need you to realise I'm just doing my job.'

'Your job is to restore law and order in this town. That's why you were called in, to tame the wild animals that run rampant through Cobb and sort out the cowboy lawmen who are supposed to protect us.'

Manolis sat forward and stuck out his chin. 'Mr Onions, I was sent here to solve a murder. I'm a homicide detective. That's what I do — I solve murders,

I catch murderers, I bring them to justice. I'm not a circus trainer of animals, and I've no time or patience for incompetent police.'

Onions paused, smiled. 'I knew you'd be good.'

Manolis sat back, studied the manager. 'Just doing my job,' he repeated.

The smile disappeared. Onions narrowed his eyes. 'But Fyfe put you up to this. You're on a witch hunt, like all the others.'

Manolis's glare was steely. 'I'm a police officer,' he said firmly. 'I'm following leads.'

'And what lead is this, what scenario are you proposing? That my English teacher was involved in a relationship with one of her students and that he stoned her to death when it went sour?'

Manolis took a moment to answer. 'I was never told she'd been teaching English here.'

'Figured you were a good detective. Well done on working that out.'

'And yes, that is certainly one possibility, that she was involved with a student. There are many lines of enquiry that we, the police, are following. It would be remiss of us not to ask what happened here. She was, after all, a person in your employ.'

Onions considered the detective's face, clearly searching for any sign of doubt, a hint of uncertainty, a chink in his armour. Something that told the manager that this was just some bureaucratic hoop that needed to be jumped through, a box on a form that needed ticking. This man from the city had been summoned to restore order to a lawless town ravaged by alcohol and racial tension, not to falsely accuse already distressed and persecuted people of crimes they couldn't possibly commit.

The manager stood to his full height of nearly two metres, neatly buttoned his suit jacket and strode to his big office window. His step was heavy on the boards. The window was south-facing and overlooked the rest of the detention centre. He placed his hands on his slender hips and spoke to the view.

'Do you know about the people who live here, Detective?' His voice was resonant and rich with authority.

An espresso machine gurgled in the corner.

'Let me tell you about the people here. These people are *asylum seekers*. They have fled persecution in their home countries and come here for a better, safer life. For *asylum*. Now, the practice of granting asylum to people fleeing persecution is thousands of years old. It was first implemented during the rise of empires in the Middle East, the Egyptians and Babylonians.'

'No need for a history lesson, Mr Onions.'

Onions looked at him with minor irritation. 'Very well,' he said, smile tight. 'Today, Australia is obliged to protect the human rights of all asylum seekers and refugees who arrive in our country, regardless of how or where they arrive, and whether they arrive with or without a visa. Our obligations to vulnerable people fleeing persecution arise from our commitment to international treaties and a shared sense of justice and fairness as a safe, prosperous and humanitarian nation.'

Manolis nodded his understanding.

Onions continued. 'My job and the job of everyone here — the guards and cooks and doctors and psychologists and teachers — is to ensure the physical and mental needs of these current-day asylum seekers are met while their claims are being processed. We

189

conduct full background medical checks for parasites, bacterial infections, typhoid, malaria, measles and hepatitis. We X-ray for tuberculosis, do blood tests for HIV/ AIDS, check dental hygiene. Those asylum seekers who are approved become refugees and are offered protection under international law. So we're a halfway house — nothing more, nothing less. And yet, I see myself as following in a noble tradition and continuing an ancient practice.'

Onions swung his head around, his neck joints creaking like weathered floorboards. Manolis's eyes were down as he wrote his spidery notes, but he looked up briefly.

Staring him dead in the eye, Onions urged him to reveal his thinking, his agenda.

'The accusation that we're harbouring a murderer is utterly preposterous,' the manager went on. 'It's the detainees who are the vulnerable ones — I'm genuinely more worried about them. They're abused and attacked when they walk through town, and even in here, where they're meant to feel safe, they're fire-bombed from the outside. They're the ones who need protection from the townsfolk, not the other way around.'

Manolis stopped chewing his pen. 'But you do have riots here in the centre. People are angry, they're violent, they're protesting their incarceration. How do you explain that?'

Onions ran a finger across his forehead, collecting a thin veneer of sweat.

'Well, in this heat, people tend to go a little troppo. Look at the town itself if you want proof. Though I admit that a lot of it in the centre is behavioural. If the detainees don't get their way, they act up. I'll concede

190

that. And between you and me, I don't blame them. The legal system and courts and bureaucracy in this country are all obscenely slow.'

The detective nodded sagely. Onions was humming a familiar tune. Manolis had seen criminal lawyers add additional storeys to their palatial homes with every extra year that a murder case was dragged through the court system. Defendants died before they saw their trials completed. Their defence teams blamed the prosecution, the prosecution blamed the judges, the judges blamed the politicians, and everyone upgraded their postcodes.

Manolis leaned forward in his chair, cupped his hands. 'Now, I understand that most of these boat people — '

'They're not 'boat people',' Onions interrupted. 'They're not people 'made of boats'. They're people who come to Australia in boats. Officially, they're referred to as 'irregular maritime arrivals'.' His voice was full of menace, of annoyance, of a history of correcting people.

Manolis held up a palm in apology. 'I'm sorry,' he said. 'I was merely being brief.'

'If you must do that, be brief, please call them 'IMAs'.'

'These IMAs,' Manolis said, starting again, 'I understand they haven't arrived by proper means.'

Angry red smudges appeared on Onions's cheeks. He tightened his eyes into thin slits.

'But that, Detective, is not breaking the law. As an enforcer of the law, you should know that. IMAs simply haven't arrived with the right paperwork. If you ask me, when you're fleeing a war zone that's not really the number one thing on your mind, now is it?

191

It's an administrative issue. Arriving without a visa is not a criminal offence, and these people are not criminals.'

'That's not what I was insinuating. I meant to say — '

Onions interrupted again; he wasn't having a bar of it.

'I can tell you there are over two hundred people in this detention centre, which includes nearly a hundred children. I've met each one of them individually, I've heard their stories and I can assure you, they're absolutely harrowing. I don't for one second believe that a single person in this facility could possibly be responsible for what you're investigating. It's ludicrous.'

Manolis paused, waited. He wanted to make sure Onions had finished speaking before risking being cut off again.

'With no disrespect,' Manolis finally said, 'people like the ones you describe sound like they've got nothing to lose.'

Onions turned back to the window, to the slowly fading light of the day. He chuckled to himself.

'You're wrong, Detective. Dead, dead wrong. These people have risked everything. They've survived torture and trauma. They've come here for help, which is why they're so relieved to arrive, even if it's aboard a rickety fishing boat. They made it, they survived.' His voice was close to cracking. 'They're not the terrorists, Detective. They're *running from* the terrorists. So we make a big mistake to fear them. If we fear them, we cast them out, and that's precisely the moment they could be preyed upon by the people who we *should* truly fear. If we send them away, they're more likely to be the victims of terrorism. Or, in worst-case scenarios, we gift criminals and terrorists a limitless supply of desperate people whose exploitation then funds attacks on us all. Put emotion to one side, Detective. This isn't about emotion. This is about crime. As a man of law, I thought you might appreciate that.'

Manolis tapped his notepad thoughtfully with his pen. He did not like being dictated to.

'Mr Onions, I do appreciate that. But a woman has been murdered in cold blood. I would say that a murderer among us is someone to fear, wouldn't you?'

Onions's face relaxed. 'Of course they are.'

'Then that's all this is about. Gathering evidence for a prosecution, bringing a criminal to justice and ensuring the community is safe. No politics or agenda. As I said, this is one line of police enquiry, one of many, so I'd appreciate your assistance. Without it, I can't close the book on all the people here.'

The colour in Onions's face lightened a fraction, red to pink. He returned to his chair, posture ferociously erect, and invited Manolis to continue.

'Can you think of anyone who'd want to hurt Mrs Abbott?' the detective asked.

Onions did not hesitate in replying. 'No. I can't remember hearing a single bad word said about her. She was a well-respected teacher, she did an excellent job, and will be sorely missed.'

'Did she have a boyfriend or lover?'

'I don't know. I understand she was widowed, but I made no enquiries about her private life. That was none of my business.'

Manolis nodded. 'Was her behaviour any different recently?'

'No.' Onions scratched his chin. 'I can't say that it

was.'

'What about the detainees?'

'Nothing I've heard. I get daily updates from the guards if there's any trouble, and weekly updates from our psychologist. Of course, their behaviour has changed since Saturday night's fire, they're all frightened, but that was to be expected.'

'Hmm,' Manolis said.

'Problem?' Onions asked.

The detective paused, considering how to reply. In the end he decided to try to make an ally of the manager, who was clearly his only way in.

'No killer behaves normally over time. If you look for what's strange, uncommon, unusual, they'll usually reveal themselves.'

'I see . . . .' Onions said warily. Sweat beaded on his upper lip.

Manolis consulted his notebook. 'Out of interest, what interactions do your staff have with the townspeople?'

Onions pressed his hands together, forming a steeple with his long fingers.

'Well, I encourage my employees to mix with local residents as much as they can. I think it engenders a sense of community, connection and belonging. But it's always been difficult because of the irregular hours they work, shifts and the like. And given recent events, I know that many of my staff now feel very uncomfortable socialising with the locals. They're blamed for some of the events here.'

'Events?' Manolis asked.

Onions shifted in his seat, the chair squeaking beneath his weight. 'Riots, protests,' he said plainly.

'And I understand the detainees are allowed to

194

move around town.'

'Only at certain times of day. It's a way of gradually integrating them into the community, and the country. The children attend the local school, the parents shop at local businesses. Normal life, in other words.'

'When is the curfew?'

'Ten o'clock each night.'

'Is there a record of exits and entries?'

'Yes, a logbook, and CCTV footage. We've got fixed cameras at the front. And in emergency situations, our guards wear portable cameras to cover all bases.'

Manolis sat forward, straightening his back. He had the manager on side now.

'I'd like to see the logbook and security footage. I want to see if anyone was absent last Friday night.'

'Of course, I'll make sure they're available ASAP. We do the daily muster and head count at seven o'clock, right before breakfast.'

'Thank you. Are people often out all night?'

'Not usually, but it happens. It's a condition of their detention that they don't break curfew.'

'And what happens if they do?'

Onions paused, his mouth as tight as wire. 'Suffice to say, we restrict their freedom of movement. They also jeopardise their application for a protection visa to stay in Australia, which is, I imagine, a much worse consequence.' His voice had zero emotion.

The manager's words settled in the room a moment, dropping the temperature a degree. Manolis wanted to ask about the level of restrictiveness of movement, and what happened if detainees were caught rioting. He also wanted to ask if Onions or any of his staff ever borrowed or stole underwear from the laundry.

In the end, Manolis decided to curtail his curiosity

195

and stick to the case.

'Where were you the night Molly died?'

The manager looked at him with shock and disbelief.

'This is a standard question I ask of everyone,' Manolis added calmly.

Onions wiped a broad hand across his mouth before replying. Manolis was surprised to hear that he admitted to being at the detention centre all night.

'Last Friday was the end of a fortnightly roster, so the staff changes over,' Onions said. 'We usually have a few drinks here to celebrate — a happy hour, if you will. Last Friday ended up being a lock-in. It's safer than letting people drive back to town drunk.'

Manolis scribbled. 'I see. So, you were all here last Friday night?'

'Yes.'

'And you had been drinking?'

'Yes, I had a few drinks with my staff to unwind. But I can vouch for them and they can vouch for me. We were all here.'

Manolis thought that was rather a convenient outcome. He finished drawing the last two lines on the stick body of a hangman swinging from gallows.

'I need to ask one more thing. I know this is somewhat of an issue in the town, but do you at all have a problem with drugs here in the centre?'

Onions's reply was unequivocal. 'No. Searches are conducted daily, and whenever people return to the facility. Contraband is confiscated on the spot, while drugs are illegal and would jeopardise visa applications. Even the children are searched when they return from school. That may sound harsh, but we are thorough and run a tight ship.'

The facility manager stood and showed Manolis out, walking swiftly and via the shortest, most direct route. At the gate, he shook the detective's hand firmly and said he looked forward to his next visit. Manolis did not tell him that would be the very next morning.

23

The cop station was locked, in darkness. His face slicked with sweat, Manolis peered in through the windows but heard no sound and saw no movement. A single crow harked mournfully in a nearby tree. Another day was done. Manolis drove home.

Against his better judgement, he parked outside the front office. Inside, there were raised voices again. Manolis walked on. He soon heard a screen door slam, and Rex muttering prayers and curses to himself.

In the sheriff's office, there was a plate of rubbery chops waiting in the fridge. They were stacked high to the point of toppling over, swimming in a pool of their own blood. Manolis decided to leave the meat on the verandah and let nature do its work. The carbonised wreck of his Val lay silent. He made another cheese toastie, left a black thumbprint on the butter. He rolled and smoked a slow cigarette, watching a flock of spinifex pigeons forage for vegetable matter and insects in the disappearing light. The stars soon came out. He stared longingly at them, in awe of the whitish smear, the mighty Milky Way.

Was his father up there, looking down on him? No, probably not. Manolis had been raised in the Orthodox Church and dragged to Sunday services by his pious mother. He understood little of the ceremony but always stood and sat and crossed himself a few seconds after his mum. He now saw the Church in his life as more custom and tradition than anything religious. Maria was the opposite; she continued to light candles and recite ancient incantations and fast on holy days. But she knew no other way.

Con's final phase began on a Wednesday. Manolis and Maria were summoned to the hospital, which hadn't happened before. A stony-faced senior doctor updated them on Con's condition, frankly and without self-censorship. The old man's heart was failing and he was unlikely to go home. Maria cried. She knew she was losing her life partner.

Gathering around the bed, the family watched its patriarch refuse all food and water. Con was soon seeing visions, including of the dearly departed: his parents, sister Penelope, aunts, uncles, friends. He kept repeating the name 'Dimitrios', which confused mother and son alike; there was no such name in the family. And then, the dreaded death rattle emerged from Con's throat. By that stage he was too weak to cough up the fluid filling his lungs. Manolis remembered it as perhaps the saddest moment: watching his father trying to make his body respond to the simplest request, and seeing it fail. Con now had no more anger at the world. Manolis was absolutely heartbroken to see it gone.

'Ah, Baba,' he said. 'If only you were in Cobb with me now. I'd like that, even if you might not.'

Feeling tired, insignificant beneath the heavens, Manolis extinguished his cigarette and retreated inside the cabin. He showered and fell asleep to the sound of exploding firecrackers punching holes in the night. He dreamed of thirst, of bashing on a vending machine somewhere in the town, trying to buy a cold drink to wet his whistle but unable to because something was stuck in the slot. He woke dehydrated, his sheets sweated through.

Returning to the station in the morning, Manolis saw a thin figure waiting on the steps. It was Sparrow, solemn like an undertaker. His left eye was darker than usual and horrendously swollen, a knot the size of a hen's egg, to the point of being closed over. He flicked his smoke and anxiously lit another.

'Jesus,' Manolis said, 'what happened?'

Sparrow considered him with a reptilian gaze. He spat congealed blood onto the dry ground and dabbed at his split lip. 'Nuthin',' he said flatly.

Manolis waved a clutch of flies from his face. 'Oh, right. You just woke up like that, did you?'

The young constable appeared stricken, far beyond the obvious bodily pain. He looked tired, his soul weary. He ran a sandpaper tongue across his chipped incisor and said, 'Let's just say that a little poof like me gets regular reminders of what this town really thinks of him.'

His voice was thin and reedy; he had a hunted look. Manolis considered his words of support delicately. The kid was clearly hurting, physically and emotionally. But every beating was a measure of his loyalty to himself.

Without warning, a grin appeared on Sparrow's face. Manolis watched it grow into a smile and then a laugh. 'But you should see the other guy.' Sparrow chuckled. 'My eye may be purple, but it'll heal. His broken teeth won't.'

Manolis's forehead uncreased. He was pleased to see the kid showing his fight, his spunk, a backbone. 'Nice one.'

Sparrow arched an eyebrow in surprise. He extinguished his smoke. 'And here I was thinking you might try to spin me some hippy-dippy city bullshit about political correctness.'

'I don't always live by the book.'

They went inside. The station was empty. Joe was gone and there was no sign of his neighbour either. Manolis was stunned. He enquired as to their whereabouts.

'We let 'em go,' Sparrow said.

'You . . . what?'

'About an hour ago. There was too much bad blood, they were gonna kill each other in the same cell and Sarge didn't want another death in custody, no matter how it came about.'

Manolis stopped in his tracks. The hull of his ribs ached as if he'd been kicked. There was still work to do to restore law and order.

Sparrow took a plastic seat in the tearoom and helped himself to a crooked strip of jerky from an old jam jar. He laid it precisely into his swollen mouth, tore it with back teeth, chewed methodically. Manolis checked the holding cell, saw the open door, the fresh bloodstains on the floor. Mumbling Greek curses under his breath, he reluctantly joined Sparrow.

A hot silence thickened in the room, a warm slice of light falling across the plastic table. Sparrow said not to expect Fyfe anytime soon — he'd called in sick. Kerr would be in later after taking her mother grocery shopping. It was what they did on Thursday paydays, assuming her wages came through.

'Kate told me what you found at Molly's. Still no sign of her phone though, eh? How'd you go yesterday up at the brown house? You meet with Onions?'

'I did,' Manolis said.

'He's ex-military. Could you tell? Was once stationed somewhere remote. It's why he got the gig here as facility manager, along with being a former army sergeant and complete bastard.'

'The job needs a firm hand.'

'My oath it does. Think about it, all those desperados crammed in together. Liars, thieves, rapists, and who knows what else before they got here. Just like all the whitefellas who first came from England — convicts, murderers, rapists.'

Manolis pulled at his earlobe. 'Of course, you know that my family once came here from another country too. Are you calling my grandfather a murderer and rapist?'

The young constable laughed, which made him wince in pain and clutch his ribs. 'Prob'ly. But don't worry. I bet you mine was too.'

'They all were back then. Life was cruel.'

'But your family didn't come to Australia as reffos, did they?'

'No. But my grandfather was once a refugee.' Manolis talked about his father's father, his *papou* Georgios, after whom he was named. 'He was living in Turkey in 1923. There'd been a war; Greece lost, so the Turks kicked them out. He had to walk to the coast before boarding a tiny boat across the Aegean.'

'How far did he walk?' Sparrow asked, mouth full.

'Hundreds of miles, through heat and rain and snow. One out of four refugees died. And then, when he arrived in Greece, my *papou* discovered the Greeks didn't want him either.'

Sparrow swallowed the black ball of jerky in his mouth. It visibly avalanched down his drainpipe throat. 'Who told you all this?'

'My dad. I never got to meet my *papou*, he died before I was born. Dad said the Greeks coming home

202

were all dirty and diseased. They received no medical attention. So at least we give that to new arrivals here.'

'Yair, sure.' Sparrow scoffed. 'Even when they swallow razor blades or nails or screws. Or eat washing powder or drink bleach or snort insect repellent.'

Manolis said his *papou* escaped just in time. 'He had forged papers that said his family had already left.'

Sparrow licked his bloody lip. 'Most reffos today get forged passports too. And pay bribes.'

'My *papou* bribed the Turkish guards as well,' he said. 'Part of the game.'

Sparrow laughed again, winced.

'The native Greeks spat on him, beat him up,' Manolis said. 'They didn't trust his odd dialect. '*Tourkosporoi!*' they yelled at him: 'Seed of Turk!' The fact he'd lived in a Muslim country made his adherence to Christianity suspicious.'

Sparrow smiled to himself. 'Boy, treated like crap in your own country. I can't imagine how that must feel.'

Manolis stood, preparing to return to the detention centre.

'Dad eventually came here as a migrant to a new land, not a refugee returning to an old one like Papou. Both were fleeing war or the effects of war, like asylum seekers are today. But there's a difference. Unlike migrants, refugees have no choice. And yet, the treatment my dad received was exactly the same as was given to my grandfather — distrust, fear, 'go back to your own country'. You've got invasion and genocide coursing through your veins, young Sparrow, and rightly so. But these are the experiences, the history, which I have in mine.'

24

This time, Onions met Manolis at the front gate. Sparrow remained at the station, his swollen face pressed to a packet of frozen peas, which was rapidly thawing and dripping.

'Good morning, Detective,' Onions chirped. 'I trust you slept well.'

Manolis grunted. 'When you wake up, it's a good sleep.'

Onions smiled salesman teeth, unnaturally white. 'I agree. I wake up every day and thank the Lord for the gift of life and this wonderful, safe country. I'm sorry I kept you waiting, I was receiving my daily sitrep.'

Manolis closed an eye in thought. It sounded like an exercise routine.

'Situation report,' Onions explained. 'It's an executive summary of all major incidents in the preceding twenty-four hours — adverse events, missed meals, behavioural management, that kind of thing. Fortunately, today is a good day.' Again he bared his teeth.

The logbook and CCTV footage from the night Molly died had been retrieved.

'As it turns out, we had two people break curfew on Friday,' Onions said, offering the thick, ink-stained notebook.

'Sorry, two people?'

Manolis remembered the individuals Searle claimed had been with Molly on the Friday afternoon, and consulted his notes to recall their physical appearance.

'It's more common on weekends,' Onions said.

From what Manolis had seen, there was very little distinction between weekdays and weekends in Cobb.

'And you say you had a staff party on Friday night?'

'Yes, due to changeover. But the gate was manned, always with two security guards.'

Manolis examined the logbook and was then shown the CCTV footage in a darkened back room. Due to the camera quality, the images were of limited use. Faces were in poor resolution and variable light. He questioned the cauliflower-eared guard on duty at the time; he confirmed the entries in the book, then corroborated the grainy footage. It was only when he paid more careful attention to the names of the two detainees who had broken curfew that his eyes grew large. The names were both male, and distinctive alongside one another. His pulse sped up in the hollow of his throat.

'I'd like to ask these two individuals to come down to the station for official questioning,' he said to Onions.

The manager shook his head gently. 'Afraid I can't allow that. It's not in our protocols.'

Manolis considered the manager, his starched white shirt and perfectly straight-hanging tie. 'Here then,' he said. 'But I need somewhere secure, ideally a private room.'

Onions turned away, eyed the corridor guardedly. A few seconds passed. Finally, he snapped his needle-like fingers. 'Actually, on second thoughts . . . yes, I can approve an official escort to the station.'

Manolis was surprised. 'Here's perfectly fine, really. I'm flexible.'

'No,' Onions said firmly. 'Your request can be arranged. I'll organise the two men to be at the station within the hour. You can head back there now.

Thank you and good day.'

He barked an order straight from the parade ground, and the bull-necked guard hurried away. Onions followed. Manolis watched them leave with a questioning, unsettled gaze.

* * *

On his return to the station, Manolis found the bag of peas sitting on the collapsible tearoom table, now watery and malodorous in the heat. Sparrow had gone. Manolis guessed he might have left to fetch another variety of frozen vegetable or meat, but more than likely he'd gone home.

The detective cleaned up and prepared the tearoom for interview. He soon heard a large vehicle pull up outside. Doors slammed, voices were raised, argumentative and full of protest. The station door was flung open and a uniformed, sunglassed Deacon bundled a limp body inside, presenting it to Manolis like a beaten old tyre.

The man stopped arguing with Deacon the moment he saw Manolis. He was tall, slender, dark-skinned, with unkempt shaggy hair and a thick moustache that concealed much of his mouth. The canyon of an old scar shone in the sunlight. He was just as Searle had described. The look on the man's face was one of sheer terror, his eyes wide, body not moving a muscle.

Manolis walked over to the window, peered through the open blinds. The outlines of two individuals remained seated in a four-wheel drive, unmoving.

He looked back to the moustachioed man and his square-shouldered escort. 'Right this way,' he said, showing them the tearoom.

Manolis sat, offered the man a flimsy plastic chair. He remained standing, frozen. But Deacon sat down, pushed sunglasses onto his head, exhaled. He crossed a leg and made himself comfortable. Manolis fired him a cold stare.

'I'd prefer to conduct the interview alone,' he said.

Deacon smiled canine teeth. 'Consider me his lawyer.'

Manolis considered him. 'Well, because you're very clearly not his lawyer, I'd appreciate if you sat over there,' he said, indicating the furthest wall. 'I'd like some privacy during questioning. This is a police station, not the detention centre, and this is now official police business.' His voice was strong, categorical.

Deacon mumbled something under his breath and reluctantly dragged his garden furniture away. He lit a cigarette, repositioned the sunglasses on his pushed-in face, and turned to the window.

Still standing, the detainee watched his private security escort closely. He peered out of the window as if checking that the street was empty, that he would not be seen by passers-by. Eventually his gaze returned to Manolis, who gestured again to the chair.

The man did not move. His trust was not going to be won easily. Manolis reasoned that he had likely come from war, seen many dead. This was a streetwise tomcat he was trying to coax into being petted. Haunted eyes stared at Manolis from a face lined beyond its years, gaunt, the body beneath it incredibly thin.

The detective fetched two mugs sitting upturned in the nearby sink. He rinsed them, filled them from the tap, offered one. The man stared, a statue.

'Hello, Ahmed,' Manolis said. 'Would you like to sit

down?'

The sound of his name elicited a sharp blink. Ahmed Omari took the mug cautiously and began to speak. The words tumbled out in imperfect English, broken and anaemic. The first thing he said was:

'You will help me?'

He pulled out a battered wallet and showed faded photos of the wife and young daughter he'd left behind in Iraq.

Manolis briefly forgot the investigation and went along with him, asking the relevant questions at the appropriate moments like a new acquaintance.

'I was home eating dinner and then start to hear grenades. They come and beat my father and brother. They rape my wife and sisters, threaten to kill my daughter. So I go north to Turkey to find us new life. I am three years in refugee camp. They give me food, but local people come at night with guns, take the food. I am in prison for six months, tortured everywhere, my body. They pull out my two front teeth with pliers.'

He opened his mouth wide to reveal an empty black gap, the rugged pink endings of exposed gum. Manolis could not help but recoil. The surrounding teeth were dull and brown like old ivory; the overgrown moustache was strategic.

'From Turkey, I pay money to go to Greece. Then plane to Malaysia and boat here.'

'Why didn't you stay in Malaysia?' Manolis asked.

Ahmed shook his head wildly, his hair swishing from side to side.

'Turkey is for escape. But Greece is for Europe, how to get to Germany and Denmark and Sweden. But is now very hard, it all changes. In Malaysia, we live in commune in Kuala Lumpur, all refugees put there. Very tough life, fifty people use one toilet. Very dirty. We dig all day the fields for little money, then sleep on floor at night.'

'Why did you come to Australia without documents?' Manolis asked.

Ahmed shot out a long arm, pointing in a random direction, at an unseen force.

'They take it. The smugglers when you get on boat. Many problems on boat, gangs take our bags and people who pretend they police. But they all liars and take our money, it was big plot between smugglers and gang.'

'And what would've happened if you didn't hand over your passport?'

Ahmed paused, exhaled, and said, 'They kill me.'

His shoulders slumped like those of a man at the gallows. Dragging his feet across the floor, he finally sat down. Bending forward, he held his face in his hands as the dark memories came to him. Deacon, unmoved, smoked on.

Ahmed proceeded to detail a harrowing sea journey to Australia, in an old fishing boat overcrowded with Arabs, Kurds, Syrians, Afghans, Sudanese. Adrift for days, vomiting, sunburn, fever, drownings. Indonesian pirates boarded their boat, smashed their engine and left them to die, until they were rescued by the Australian navy.

'You will help me?' Ahmed said again.

Manolis paused, wanting to choose his words carefully. Eventually, he asked Ahmed what would happen if he returned to his homeland.

Ahmed's face froze with horror. 'I can't go home. They will shoot me dead in a day. We think Australia is the place of freedom. But what freedom? There are people in centre on their third and final asylum, like me. If that fails, then, we have no choice . . . '

'No choice in what sense?' Manolis asked.

Ahmed looked down at his hands, like claws. He spoke to them almost reluctantly. '*Aintihar*.'

Manolis shook his head. 'I'm sorry, I don't understand Arabic.'

Ahmed spoke again. 'Suicide,' he said gravely. 'We not go home to die.'

His words settled in the room. They seemed almost to echo, resonating for longer than anything said before.

Manolis leaned forward and placed his hands together in a contemplative pose.

'You don't want to do that. Think of your daughter.'

Ahmed met Manolis's gaze, his eyes suddenly alive.

'I do,' he snapped. 'Every day, I do, all the time. But we have no future here. Here is nothing, it is not even death.'

Ahmed stared at the floor. Manolis sat upright, digesting what the detainee had said. Was this man a killer? Could he kill? What life had he led before arriving illegally? How much was truth and how much lies?

'I feel I go crazy,' Ahmed said softly. 'I don't want to go back to Iraq as crazy man. Dying is better.'

Ahmed's eyes were soon closed, his voice mumbling. Deacon turned, fired a glance, then returned to staring at the vacant street. It took a moment before Manolis realised what the young asylum seeker was doing.

Ahmed was praying.

25

'Molly Abbott,' Manolis said.

Ahmed snapped his eyes open. 'A tragedy. We all very sad. Mrs Abbott taught me, she taught us all. Our visa applications need good English. Mrs Abbott helped.'

'So you were in her class?'

'Yes. She care for us, for our English. And we knew people would come for us after she died.'

'What people?'

He pointed out the window. 'Out there in the town. They blame us for what happened to Mrs Abbott. They say we done it.'

Manolis nodded knowingly. 'And that's all Mrs Abbott was to you, your teacher?'

Ahmed's face went blank. 'Yes,' he said hesitantly. 'What else?'

'Not a lover, a girlfriend?'

Ahmed stiffened, a look of acute irritation crossing his face, eyebrows turning in. 'I am married,' he said firmly, 'I have wife.'

'To some people that means nothing,' Manolis said. 'I need to know if you were at all romantically involved with her.'

The detainee fixed the detective with a long, steady gaze. 'No,' he finally said. 'A hundred times no. I not romantic with her. I am married. I have wife. We have child.'

Deep inside his chest Manolis felt a nasty beat to his heart. He sat forward and said, 'Ahmed, now listen.

211

I need to ask where you were last Friday night.'

The detainee's face darkened. Manolis could see his pupils dance, his brain working. Ahmed's eyes narrowed, the muscles in his jaw twitching beneath the skin.

'First you ask if I love her, now you think I kill her? Because I am Muslim and because we stone people?' His voice had raised an octave.

'Please, Ahmed. Yes, I'm here to help. But I can't help you if you don't help me. So please, just tell me where you were last Friday.'

Ahmed stood, his broad sandalled feet spaced the width of his shoulders.

'Who is saying this?' he demanded. 'Are you asking others? Many Muslims are in facility. Why me?'

Deacon stood, reached for his holster. Manolis gestured that he should sit down, that everything was under control. The detective held up his hands to Ahmed, his open palms requesting calm.

'It's not just you,' he reassured him. 'We are asking others.'

Ahmed took two steps towards the door, as if preparing to run. His face was blotchy, red and white at the same time.

'If I kill someone, they send me home. If I kill, I die.'

His voice broke on the final words, and he appeared to visibly calm down. The guard sat.

Manolis thought a moment before speaking again. He'd wanted to tell Ahmed that he was being questioned because he broke curfew. Instead, he approached from a different angle.

'Maybe if you kill someone, you stay here. If you go home, you may not serve jail time. So you stay here and go to jail, swap a death sentence for a life sentence. Sounds smart to me. When you're released, you go home. The war will probably be over.'

The detective's logic settled in the room. The two men watched each other for some time, their breathing deep and steady. After a while, Ahmed smiled. It was a smile that cut his face into segments; Manolis quite liked it.

'I never think like that. But jail is no change from here. This already jail. In fact, jail maybe better. At least jail is jail. Here is nothing.' His tone was resigned, his arms hanging by his sides like those of a puppet with cut strings.

Manolis's eyes settled on a spiny black insect inching its way across the floor; it did not look friendly. He scratched the back of his neck. He was struggling to find an angle. This suspect was like no other. If anything, murder made the most sense — it guaranteed him life in a law-abiding land.

'Do you know about stonings?'

Ahmed's question struck Manolis like a blow. It was wholly unexpected. He looked up to see a face that was calm, but held intense sorrow.

'I do,' Ahmed said. 'I see them, many times, in the hills near my village.' The detainee sat down and began. Stonings, he said, never took place in cities where victims were usually publicly hanged. They were more common in the countryside and mountains, away from prying eyes.

'Revenge by blood, is what people say.'

Pits are dug using shovels and pickaxes. Ahmed made digging motions with his big brown hands. The condemned individual is lowered in, their arms tied with rope, their body wrapped in three pieces of white

213

shroud in accordance with Muslim burial practices. The head is sometimes concealed. A mullah oversees the ritual. A crowd gathers, fists clenched, implements ready. Stones have to be the right size.

'Too big and they kill too fast,' Ahmed said. 'But too small, like pebble, and they do nothing.'

Manolis pictured the desk down the hall, the murder weapon strewn across it. In terms of size, its many separate pieces sounded comparable, if not optimal.

'They don't have to be stones,' Ahmed said. 'People throw bricks, tiles, broken concrete. All things heavy, Allah does not care.'

Crowds whistle as items hit their mark. Shouts of joy ring out with every strike, every spray of blood. Dogs bark, hungry for flesh. A medical doctor periodically stops proceedings to check if the victim is dead. Most stonings take place at dawn.

'How long do they last?' Manolis's voice was weak.

Ahmed shrugged. 'Depends. Sometimes five minutes, sometimes two hours. And you can tell the people who are guilty.'

'How?'

Ahmed said the innocent look straight ahead, lift their heads, hold them high. 'Only the guilty look away.'

Manolis thought that sounded like superstition and inwardly shook his head. But he then recalled the strange location of the wounds on the back of Molly's head, and the surprising lack on her face. Kerr had explained them by saying she would have turned her own head in that situation. Did that make sense? Was Molly guilty of something? Guilty of what? Or simply terrified?

'One time I see, the pit is too shallow. The woman

214

has to wait for death, listening to the sound of shovels digging a deeper pit.'

When the ritual is over, fists shoot into the air in triumph and celebration. Villagers boast of what they've done and receive blessings for their magnificent act.

'People say they do their duty in the name of Allah,' Ahmed said. 'They are not the ones throwing the stones. Allah throws them. He guides their arms.'

Afterwards, the body is disinterred and taken away. The hole is filled in, the area flattened and raked clean to remove any trace of blood. Fresh soil is scattered.

Raked clean to remove any trace of blood . . . ? Manolis wondered whether that might explain the noticeably small bloodstain at the scene.

Ahmed said that adulterers who confess are allowed to go free if they can escape the pit during their execution, and Manolis realised this was a quirk of the ritual that put women at a distinct disadvantage. Pits were dug deeper for women than men, up to their chest, not waist. The death game was loaded.

Manolis again considered the evidence. Molly was tied to a tree, not buried in a pit. She had not been wrapped in cloth, and her head was left exposed. He imagined the horror of seeing stones approaching, even in dim light. The uncertainty, their indistinct outlines no doubt making it worse. This could indeed explain the trauma to the back of her head if she'd been trying to dodge their trajectory. But there were similarities in ritual, too. It had taken place in the countryside, and it could very well have been at dawn.

He recalled a distinctive feature about a stoning: that it was perhaps the only form of execution in which no single person delivered a fatal blow, but where a community became de facto executioner. Had he been wrong to suspect a killer operating in isolation? Was Cobb itself the culprit?

'You certainly know a lot about stonings,' Manolis said.

Ahmed smiled gently, almost modestly. 'Most of us from these countries do,' he said. 'Stonings, whippings, burnings, beheadings, all happen, all the time. We grow up with them all around us, even as children — it is part of everyday life. We fear them so we know right from wrong. But this is my yesterday. And today, I have nothing to hide.'

'So, tell me, where were you last Friday night,' Manolis said.

There was a long pause before Ahmed replied. A deep sigh preceded his answer. 'I was in jail, of course.' He drank his words down thirstily, draining the mug in a single motion.

Manolis sipped at his own mug pensively, considering the young man's emotionless face. His reply was equally protracted. 'So you were there, in the detention centre?'

'Yes.'

'What were you doing?'

'The same as any other night . . .'

He wasn't sleeping. He explained that most detainees rested during the day because it was too dangerous to sleep at night.

Glancing over his shoulder, Ahmed checked whether Deacon was listening. Behind his dark sunglasses he appeared to have fallen asleep, his breathing steady, slow. Ahmed turned back, watched the floor with intense concentration. Careful with his words, he began.

'In the dead of night, blood pours from the bodies

216

of young men, as it did on the Friday she was killed.'

Arterial gushings — in their trembling brown hands were orange razors, disposable, single blade.

'This is the men,' Ahmed said. 'For women, is even worse.'

He said the female detainees avoided the toilet block after dusk for fear of being raped. They would sooner wet their beds than go to the toilets, which were some distance from the accommodation dongas and didn't have locks.

'This is what goes on, what happens,' he said.

Manolis cringed. He was beginning to form a picture.

'I very happy my family not here,' Ahmed went on. 'I did not promise them this, to come to be raped. You can stay in Iraq for that.'

Manolis stroked his chin, heard a scratching sound. 'How old is your daughter?'

'Four when I leave, now ten.'

Manolis looked at Ahmed's arms, tried to see if there were slash marks, but his sleeves were too long. Instead, the detective wrote in his notepad. He was deeply concerned about the reference to sexual assaults.

'Did this happen on Friday?' Manolis said.

'Yes.'

'And you were there all night?'

'Yes.'

'You were asleep or awake?'

'Both.'

Ahmed checked over his shoulder again; Deacon remained still. The detainee turned back and said the facility staff regularly cut off their electricity and water when detainees self-harmed, as punishment to others.

'I sleep two hours, maybe three. The rest is night-mare.'

'And when did you last see Mrs Abbott?'

Manolis expected Ahmed to say Thursday, which was Molly's last scheduled English class. But he didn't. Instead, he told the truth.

'Friday afternoon. I go to her school, we talk about my visa.'

'Your visa?'

'Yes. She is helping.'

'What happened?'

'We talk, me and Mrs Abbott, and with another man. After we talk, I go home.'

'And all you did was talk?'

'Yes.'

'What time was this?'

Ahmed scanned the cracked ceiling. 'Three o'clock, maybe four.'

'And you didn't leave the detention centre again that night?'

'No. I mean, yes, I not leave. I still not leave, only to come here today. No-one leaves anymore. We too scared.'

Manolis consulted his notepad. 'And this other man you were with, he's also at the centre?'

'Yes. He is not like us. He is white.'

His mouth dry, Manolis took a slug of his drink. The water was tepid, tasted faintly of rust. He let the liquid coat his insides, burning like mild acid and tried to swallow the tense lump crowding his throat. Dragging a forearm across his lips, he prepared his words deliberately and delivered them slowly.

'Ahmed, please listen. The security records show

that you did not return to the detention centre on Friday. That you left and broke curfew and were out all night.'

A weighty silence filled the room. Ahmed's limbs perhaps felt heavy, as he did not move. He stared at the floor, processing the information. Manolis watched him, waited.

After some time Ahmed looked up at Manolis. 'So, I am liar?'

Manolis paused. 'This is the evidence I have before me. You need to prove to me otherwise. Show me proof that I am wrong.'

A quizzical look swept across Ahmed's brown face. He opened and closed his mouth, then stared at the floor. When finally he opened it again, a solitary word fell out.

'How?'

Manolis felt a profound sadness wash over him. The whole time he'd been speaking with Ahmed, he had pictured his own refugee grandfather and migrant father sitting beside him. They were judging his interrogation, grave looks of disappointment across their weathered faces. They too had once been strangers in a foreign land and had likely been accused of something or other. Manolis felt enormous guilt and shame but remained professional. He shook off the vision and returned to task.

'You need to show me something that says you were at the detention centre on Friday night. Something that shows you weren't at the crime scene. Something that shows you were somewhere else. Only then can I consider ruling you out as a suspect.'

A soft frown appeared on Ahmed's face. He blinked, and the light of an idea seemed to ignite behind his eyes. He leaned in close to Manolis and spoke in a barely audible whisper.

'It is guards. They must be. They have party Friday, everyone drinking, drunk. You see what they do in toilets.'

Manolis looked at him soberly and with clear eyes. 'If that's true, I need proof,' he whispered back. 'Words are not enough. I'll do my best to find out more about the other things you said, but those are some very serious accusations.'

Ahmed stood, shunting his chair back across the floor. It startled Deacon and perhaps even woke him. He was abruptly by Ahmed's side, restraining the detainee's arm and preparing to march him out the door.

Ahmed eyed Manolis directly. 'I bring proof,' he said bluntly. 'Praise to Allah, *inshallah*, and thank you to you.'

Manolis nodded his gratitude. The Iraqi was shoved forward, told to 'move it'. After a few metres, he turned back, a half-turn.

'What about other man, the white man in truck with me?'

Manolis clicked his biro. 'I'm about to speak with him.'

Ahmed smiled dark teeth, exposing jagged gums, and extended his free arm. Manolis stepped forward and shook his hand, matched his pressure. It was hefty and strong with a firm grip. The detective could not help but imagine how a rock might sit in that strong and hefty hand.

26

'Drive him straight back to the centre right now. We can't leave him sitting in the car in broad daylight — people might see him.'

Deacon was growling at his colleague in the station doorway, giving him clear, unequivocal instructions. They each held a detainee before them, two arms pinned behind two backs.

'You hear me? No more cock-ups here, Baz. This is now very bloody serious. Drive him straight back, drop him off, and then get back here to wait for me to finish up.'

Ahmed was loaded into the four-wheel drive like cargo and told to lay low. It sped away, tyres squealing. The second pairing of guard and detainee came down the hall and took up position in the station's tearoom. Again Manolis had to explain his desire for privacy. Deacon was again reluctant to grant it, and in the end sat by the window to grudgingly stare outside.

'Mr Lee Francis Cook?'

The detainee's sun-crinkled features tightened. He glared at Manolis with intensity.

'Yes, sir. And you are?'

His voice was deep and husky, like that of an old crooner. It was a patently Australian accent, and yet his words were clear and precise with a certain refinement that hinted at pedigree and schooling.

As with the young Muslim, the middle-aged Caucasian suspect was almost exactly as the observant headmaster had described. Manolis watched him run his hands through his scarecrow hair, tensing a pair of thick biceps in the process. His blue shearer's singlet exposed fine hair on his forearms, shoulders and chest. Cook retained a healthy pink vigour that was in stark contrast to the washed-out Iraqi.

Manolis stood, offered water. 'Hello, Mr Cook. My name's Detective Sergeant George Manolis.'

Cook took the mug and they shook hands. Manolis noticed he had hands like laundry buckets. The grip was solid, meaningful.

'Detective, you say? Then I must be here for one reason.' Cook sniffed the contents of the mug, and only then took a swig.

Manolis reached for his notepad, his questions. Cook spoke freely and without prompting. He took uncertain sips from his mug as if expecting the worst.

'We were lovers,' he said. 'Once. Until she ended it a few months ago. She said she did so reluctantly, and I believed her. She loved me and I loved her. Still, I can't blame her for ending things — it's not like our relationship could go anywhere.'

Cook explained that it was his incarceration that came between them. With such an uncertain future, he could offer her nothing.

'Given my circumstances, I found that I was invariably at Molly's beck and call. We always went to her house. Never up there in that godforsaken hellhole.'

In Manolis's experience, such a direct, candid disclosure of information was either a sign of innocence or a finely rehearsed charade orchestrated to the nth degree. It was the same for Ahmed's recollection of stonings he had witnessed. Cook's admission was welcome, but did it identify the owner of the Y-fronts found in Molly's cupboard? They *may* have been his . . . once. Or someone else's, an as-yet-unidentified lover.

'And where did you meet Molly?' Manolis asked.

Cook ran a rough tongue across his dry lips. 'At the detention centre, of course.'

'Not in town?'

'No.'

'Were you in her class? Your English sounds perfect.'

'No, I wasn't. We met after one of her classes, in the northern courtyard. She approached me and we just started talking.'

'When was that?'

A long pause and a light sigh preceded his response. 'Nearly a year ago, not long after I arrived. I stood out like a sore thumb. I still do.' His eyes jittered, an unnerving tic.

Manolis struggled to keep up, his hand sore from writing. But he was intrigued. He sat forward. 'Where exactly are you from?'

'Originally? North London. A place called West Hampstead, to be more precise.'

Manolis felt bewildered, his face creasing. With a heavy exhalation, Cook rolled his neck until there was a satisfying crack.

The youngest of four sons born at the Royal Free Hospital, Cook spent his toddler years chasing his older brothers across the lush green expanses of Hampstead Heath. Then, on his third birthday, the family immigrated to Australia as Ten Pound Poms.

'My parents had hoped the drier, warmer climes would help cure my brother's bronchial pneumonia,' Cook said. He added, with a wry grin, 'All that wonderfully clean London air. Particles inhaled and exhaled a billion times over.'

Ever since, for fifty-five of his fifty-eight years, Cook had lived and worked in Australia. He'd never once returned to the British Isles, not even to visit.

'I served as a volunteer in the Australian army reserve,' he said, with a faux salute. 'Can you believe that? I pledged my undying allegiance to this damned country . . .'

His entire family still lived in Australia. The eldest brother looked after their now elderly parents.

Having listened intently, Manolis extracted the moist biro from his lips. 'So, you're an Australian citizen?'

Cook's face grew heavy with disappointment. 'No. I had a child visa through my parents. And after being here so long I can't see myself as anything other than Australian. My whole life has been here, family and friends, work and memories. But officially no, I'm not Australian. On paper I'm British. And that's the problem.'

It had all started two years earlier. Cook admitted he'd had some 'previous driving convictions, minor drug and alcohol offences, but nothing that attracted more than a fine'. Then he lit a fire. It was in bushland near his property, ostensibly to clear some old growth that itself was a fire hazard. The blaze was promptly extinguished by the Rural Fire Service, burning less than an acre of scrubland. It did not destroy any property or threaten life. It wasn't even during summer. It was late April, autumn.

'I was convicted of arson,' Cook said. His words were muted, had an airless quality.

Manolis listened, wrote notes, but there was something in Cook's voice that made him question his

224

conviction. The detective nodded, but didn't feel certain. He remembered the fire at the detention centre and his burnt car.

'Did you have a permit?' he asked.

'No.'

'Then fair enough,' said the pragmatic lawman. 'You do the crime, you do the time.'

'Oh, I agree. No complaints there. I deserved to go to the nick. But it's what came after . . .'

Cook claimed he'd been a model inmate, completing all the necessary rehabilitation programs and counselling. The prisoners' review board noted that he'd demonstrated 'a strong motivation to change his offending behaviour', while a limited criminal history indicated 'an ability to lead a pro-social life when returned to society'. After fifteen months, he was free.

'Yes, I was free,' Cook said. 'Free as a bird.' Then his face shadowed, his eyes sharpened. 'I was free as a bird *for all of two minutes.*'

As his lungs inhaled the air of freedom, Cook was apprehended at the prison gates. Only this time it wasn't by police officers — it was by government immigration officials. He pointed out his visa but to no avail. He was immediately trucked to Cobb and handed over to the guards at the detention centre.

'As it turns out, the immigration minister can now cancel the visas of people who've been convicted of a crime and sentenced to at least a year in prison,' Cook said. 'This is on the grounds of the so-called 'national interest'. Apparently, I fail the character test. The man who sits before you is a person of poor character.'

Manolis had heard stories of people being refused visas for not passing the character test. American rappers wanting to tour often made the news. Their

225

colourful pasts inspired their lyrics, earned them street cred and sold millions of albums, but they also jeopardised visa claims. Being a member of a motorcycle club was similarly frowned upon. Cook's circumstances were unusual and somewhat astonishing to Manolis. He wrestled with the idea that permanent residents were suddenly being removed for being of questionable character, even after they'd served a prison sentence.

'It's a new power,' Cook grumbled. 'They amended an act of parliament. Never mind all the earlier acts that let me stay.' A smile trembled at the side of his mouth. 'Do you know, I've even heard about people who avoided prison time altogether after being deemed by a judge to have 'good character' only to have a bureaucrat later *disagree* and have them locked up?'

Manolis raised an eyebrow. 'Who told you that?'

Cook gestured over his shoulder at a dull-eyed Deacon.

'One of those knuckle-dragging gorillas,' he said, voice low. His smile broadened and he chuckled to himself. 'The locals round here think I'm a complete joke. Here, Britain, have your convicts back! It's so funny that they buy me beers at the pub as thanks for the laugh. I can't blame them. If this situation wasn't so real, and if this wasn't me, it would be highly amusing.'

No-one said anything for some time. Looking at Cook, Manolis thought his appeal to a girl from outback Australia was obvious. He was handsome and refined, and the antithesis of ordinary, familiar Joe Shrewsbury. Cook had an air of 'other' about him due to his British heritage. He was exotic. But then again,

226

so was Omari.

Eventually, Manolis wiped the perspiration from his brow and said, 'Did Molly ever think you were a joke?'

Cook's hard blue eyes softened. 'No,' he said fondly. 'She didn't. Not once. She sympathised.'

'I heard she was a kind woman,' Manolis said.

'She was. Even after she broke up with me, I can say that. She was genuinely concerned for me, how I would survive the centre; she knew I wasn't a rotten apple. There's no-one in there for being a career criminal or murderer. Instead, you've got people with traffic offences or who had run-ins with the law a decade ago.'

Cook said he was trying to keep his head down, even more than he had in prison. He did not participate in strikes or riots and altogether steered clear of the gangs who ran the place.

'The gangs are ten times worse than in prison,' he said.

'What kind of gangs?' Manolis asked.

'Just like prison, drawn along racial lines. But there's religious lines in there too. People go slightly crazy when you throw different gods into the mix.'

Manolis pretended to cross himself. 'My god is better than your god.'

Cook snorted. 'Don't believe a word they say. They're all no-good cheats and liars.'

'You're not religious?'

'My religion is no religion. I'm an atheist.'

Manolis thought a moment. 'So how do you know all this if you keep your head down?'

Cook scratched his nose. 'Molly would tell me. She came to me on my second day. She saw a clueless white man and knew I'd get eaten alive. Do you know what the local residents call that place?'

Coughing dryly, Manolis cleared his throat. 'The brown house,' he said reluctantly.

'It's humiliating,' said Cook with a knowing smile. 'I feel like I'm being made to do two sentences for the one crime, except the second one's much worse.'

Manolis tensed his bushy eyebrows. 'Really? Immigration detention is worse than prison? With detention you get to go out into the community every day. You were having a romantic relationship with a woman. It can't possibly be worse than prison.'

Cook fixed him with a soulful gaze. 'Spoken like a man who's never been in prison,' he said, voice muted.

Looking away, Manolis studied the floor.

'They're called immigration detention centres, but they're basically prisons for immigrants and asylum seekers,' Cook said.

Manolis let his tired eyes drift back to the detainee.

'In prison you've got a start date and an end date, you know how much time you have to serve,' Cook said. 'Mentally, that's huge. But with detention, the sentence is open-ended. Being a model detainee means nothing, there's no incentive. And there's never any information about appeals.'

'I find that surprising,' Manolis said. 'Even prisoners in supermax get news about appeals.'

Cook nodded. 'Exactly.' He proceeded to compare his incarceration to a natural disaster or terrorist attack. 'Not that I've been in one, but at least there, you hear positive stories about survival and bravery and rebuilding. There's optimism. But there's none of that in detention, no sense of 'moving on'.'

They stared at each other for some time, sticky heat

licking at their faces. Manolis dragged a finger across his forehead, wiped away another oily film of sweat.

'And then, when it's all over — whenever that is — I may end up being sent to England,' Cook added. 'I'd have to leave my job, my friends, my family and the life I have here to go to a country I don't know. I'd have no family, no support, no accommodation and no employment.'

A hot flush of panic pooled in Manolis's stomach, and tension spidered through his veins. He looked at the striking Englishman who now sat motionless, watching the tearoom floor. There seemed no reason to doubt his story, impossible as it sounded. Regardless, Manolis made a note to check Cook's background, place of birth and full criminal history. Did it start with driving, drug and alcohol offences and end with arson, or were those just the beginning? Was there assault, grievous bodily harm, violence against women? Was there more behind Molly's reason to end their relationship? Or was there something political, against the state?

Cook's punishment was another matter. He was a product of Australian society, yet the solution was to ship him abroad . . .

'At least you'd be going to Britain,' Manolis said. 'There are detainees who dodged bombs and pirates and nearly drowned to get here. Every day they fear being returned to war zones in Iraq and Syria and Afghanistan.'

Cook looked up, his eyes shining. 'But they're not Australian,' he said firmly. 'I am.'

27

'Just a moment . . . your surname — Manolis, was it? What country is that from?'

Manolis cocked his head. The direct and personal nature of Cook's question had caught him off guard. The suspect answered questions — they didn't bloody ask them.

'It's Greek. My father came to Australia after the war.'

'Ah, the war,' Cook said. 'A topic close to every Brit's heart. They fairly romanticise it nowadays. But it was a massive humanitarian disaster, tens of millions displaced in Europe alone.'

'Dad wasn't so much displaced,' Manolis said. 'He just saw a tired old country and compared it to a new country far away from invasion and conflict.'

'My family did too. So you and I are more alike than we realise.'

Manolis sucked on his teeth. 'Except that I was born here. I'm an Australian citizen, not a Greek one.'

'That's just luck. Do you speak Greek?'

'I do.'

'And you can get a Greek passport? Through your dad?'

Manolis paused. 'Yes,' he said warily.

'You just never have. It's an oversight.'

In mild frustration, Manolis leafed through his notepad. 'It's not a requirement, no. It's optional. However, I suspect that if I went to live permanently in Greece, I probably would have. It only makes sense.'

Cook inspected the back of his hand, thick with blue veins. 'I must say, though, it's incredible to see how the Greeks are dealing with this latest refugee crisis, with all the boats arriving across the Mediterranean. For such a poor country to show such compassion and understanding, it's astonishing. How is it that a country with so little to give can show such humanity?'

Manolis looked at Cook directly. Why would he know or care about such details with all his own problems?

'When you find yourself stuck in an immigration detention centre,' he said, 'you take an interest in how other countries handle things.'

Manolis shrugged. 'I suspect the Greek people's generosity has got a lot to do with memory. They remember what happened a hundred years ago when Greece was flooded with refugees from Turkey. There are many people today with a refugee parent or grandparent. They want to honour them.'

Craning his neck to check on Deacon, Cook saw the guard now playing with an enormous key ring heavy with metal. On his other hip swung a hook-nosed rescue tool, a Hoffman knife.

'See that?' Cook said, voice lowered. 'They call it a 'cut-down knife'. They use it on inmates found hanging from nooses.'

Manolis swallowed. Cook gestured in the direction of the detention centre.

'There's a bloke up there who's dug himself a six-foot grave behind Lilac Compound. He lies in it all day and all night.'

Cook said the various detention centre compounds had been given anodyne titles like Lilac, White and

Gold. Primary colours were apparently too provocative.

'And you should see the children,' Cook said. 'Can you imagine, being a young kid in that place?'

'I can't.'

Manolis mentioned the little girl he'd seen at the centre with sticky tape over her mouth.

'Her mother put it there,' Cook said. 'It was after the other detainees in her donga had complained about the girl's constant crying. The mum didn't want further conflict.'

Manolis was appalled.

His horror turned to dismay when Cook said, 'The children don't know how to play anymore. I watch them, they don't know what to do with puzzles and picture books. They don't explore, don't even talk. They just sit there numbly eating bits of foam rubber and paper. It breaks my heart.'

Manolis let the image settle in his mind. To make it go away, he pictured his son playing with the wooden train set he'd bought last Christmas.

'Molly was especially troubled by the kids,' Cook went on. 'As a teacher, she was kept away from the worst conditions. But she saw them at the school where she taught and asked me about them all the time. I was candid with her, and because she cared about me, this had an impact.'

His sentiments echoed what the principal had told Manolis during interview.

'Molly was a woman with a conscience,' Cook said.

Manolis nodded.

'Are you a parent?' Cook asked.

Another personal question. Manolis paused. This time, when it came to his own child, he didn't want a part of the conversation. 'No,' he lied.

'Just as well. This isn't a country to bring new life into, let alone a world.'

Manolis refocused. 'Where were you Friday night?' he asked directly.

Cook lifted his mug, drank deeply. Manolis watched his throat bob as he swallowed. 'You know I broke curfew,' he said openly. 'That's why I'm here. You know I didn't get back until the morning.'

Manolis half-closed his eyes and nodded.

'It was the end of the working week, time to unwind,' Cook said. 'There was a staff changeover, which means absolute chaos. On those nights especially I want to be a million miles away from that place. They're the worst. Like a college party. Unfortunately, after our conversation that afternoon, I knew that spending the night with Molly was not an option.'

'Your conversation?' Manolis was brief, careful not to get in the way of key facts as they revealed themselves.

Cook's eyes clouded. He was fighting to compose himself.

'Well, it was more of a disagreement, really. I went round to ask if she was free on Friday night. I didn't expect it would be the last time we'd speak. Have you ever had that, Detective? Regrets over the last things you said to a person?'

Manolis nodded and sighed. 'Many times.'

'It's new to me. Molly was a ray of sunshine in my otherwise dark existence. She made me feel human again. It's a constant struggle to keep your sanity in detention. To maintain who you are without falling into the depths of despair.'

'What did you disagree about?'

233

'Sex,' Cook said frankly. 'I wanted to spend the night with her. I missed her. Is that wrong? But she said no, she'd moved on.'

'To?'

'You mean ... ?'

'To another person?'

Cook scratched his neck, rich with freckles. 'I'm not sure, she never said. Probably didn't want to hurt my feelings if she had. She was like that. All I know was that she said no to me, so I backed down. She saw no future with me in indefinite detention, and potentially with deportation.'

'So you were harassing her for sex?' Manolis said, remembering the nuisance calls Molly had been receiving.

Cook shook his head lightly. 'That makes it sound so sordid, so sleazy. I was merely enquiring as to whether she was free to spend a lovely evening together.'

'She had something else on?'

'Again, I don't know, she didn't say.'

'So what did you do next?'

'The same thing I've always done since arriving in Cobb. I dove to the bottom of a bottle.'

'You went to the pub? The top pub?'

Giving him a quizzical look, Cook said, 'If you mean the pub at the northern end of town, then yes.'

'Can anyone confirm your presence there?'

Cook thought a moment. 'I'd say there were probably about fifty people who could confirm my presence there. But I couldn't name a single one. They were just faces that blurred as the night went on.'

'Did you drink with anyone in particular?'

'I drank alone. Since being condemned to life in Cobb, I've gotten quite used to my own thoughts and company. At the pub, people irregularly staggered up to me, breathed on me, fell on me, laughed at me, bought me another, staggered away. There was nothing major or especially memorable about the evening. It was just another night trying to outrun the thought of detention.'

'What about the publican?'

'He may remember me, I don't know for certain. I don't remember him. My mind's shot since I came to Cobb.'

Cook lamented a worsening memory and concentration, a mounting fatigue and loss of vitality, and a reduced ability to act purposefully, all of which he blamed on his indefinite detention.

Manolis considered his suspect, who appeared collected, unflustered, with nothing to hide. Or was that because he didn't remember what he'd done on the night in question? People high on meth often didn't remember their actions. At times, Manolis had been forced to sit with horrified addicts and watch their faces turn white as he imparted details of a brutal homicide or rape committed during their high. Ice zombies, they called them: aggressive, violent and unfeeling. Those who killed were ultimately convicted of manslaughter instead of murder, but the prison sentences were just as lengthy.

The tearoom felt suddenly narrow and airless. An urgency swelled inside Manolis, left him dizzy.

'What time did you leave the pub?'

Resting his chin on his palm, Cook exhaled. 'It's hard to say. Whatever time they kicked us out. One o'clock, two o'clock, maybe later, I don't know. I remember it was still dark, so it wasn't yet morning, but that's about all.'

'And where did you go after you left the pub?' Manolis asked.

Cook coughed into a tight fist and smiled. 'I know this sounds somewhat bohemian, but I slept under a tree. There's no way I could've walked home in that state. I was tired and drunk.'

'Did anyone see you?'

'Again, I don't exactly know.' Cook scratched his ear. 'It was one of the many trees between the pub and detention centre. If it helps, I think it was a gum tree. Whichever tree it was, it was mercilessly uncomfortable for my aching neck and back. I'm terribly sorry I can't be of more assistance, Detective. It was dark, there was no moon. And I was very, very drunk.'

They stared at each other intently. Finally, Manolis blinked and summarised the situation for Cook: his alibi was weak, he was once in an intimate relationship with the deceased, and he'd been seen harassing her the day before she died. Quite deliberately, Cook said he understood why Manolis would be making further enquiries, and welcomed them. He had nothing to hide. What Manolis did not vocalise were the detention centre jocks they'd found in Molly's bedroom — he would carry around that little nugget in his head a while longer.

But he did ask one more thing. 'Who do *you* think killed her?'

Cook looked instantly downhearted, his features slumping. With a quick glance over his shoulder, he checked the coast was clear.

'One of them,' he whispered, before adding, 'One or more.'

Manolis eyed Deacon, now absently playing with his cut-down knife. 'Any idea which one?'

'No. They all look alike to me.'

'And why, for what reason? Was Molly in a relationship with a guard?'

'Beats me.' Cook shrugged. 'Why does anyone kill anyone else?

Rage, jealousy, money, revenge . . . religion.' He said the guards were the worst of all. 'All blundering idiots, fresh out of high school, backpackers, overseas students, you name it. Hiring is rushed, job ads on websites and social media, no training or preparation. One minute they're driving a forklift in a warehouse or flipping burgers, and the next they're in charge of a compound with a hundred angry men.'

Manolis glanced at Deacon again, the back of his bald head bandaged, his neck thick with fat.

'Wouldn't you want more social workers at the detention centre, people who understand human behaviour?' Cook said. 'The privatising of all this immigration detention is simply the government distancing itself from the practices that go on. Day-to-day, there's either nothing to do or a major incident. Calm or chaos. The guards are a mix of people who either can't handle the monotony or can't handle the incidents. Those who are compassionate burn out quickly. If you want to last in that job, you disconnect.'

It was the same with police, thought Manolis, and particularly those who worked homicide.

'Anyway, let's see how I now fare when I get back,' Cook said. 'They talk, you know. The guards, the detainees. I bet you they're talking about me right this minute — it's enough they know you dragged me here for questioning. The guards shoot first and ask questions later, while the detainees have their own tribal law. But I pity more the other man you spoke with. He'll be judged more harshly than me, even by his own people, because his skin's the wrong colour.'

Manolis stood, shook Cook's hand firmly and with genuine understanding.

Cook looked him in the eye. 'Stiff upper lip, eh, old chap?' he said in a very British way. 'Cheerio then, mate.'

Deacon took a calculated step forward, grabbed him by the arm. The guard eyed Manolis sternly through narrow, letterbox eyes the colour of slate. He appeared to be barely in his twenties but had the weathered face of an old man.

With head tilted slightly, Manolis watched as Deacon manhandled Cook along the corridor. The guard prodded him in the back whenever he dragged his feet and surreptitiously jabbed him in the kidneys. They fell out the station door and into the waiting four-wheel drive, which drove away at top speed.

The street was empty, quiet. Manolis stood in the doorway. A hot, scouring breeze whipped up, unfurling a discarded tabloid and scattering the sheets like paper tumbleweeds. Galahs flung themselves into the air from tall eucalypts, shrieking like banshees. Crows dive-bombed something unseen and likely dead.

Clutching at his neck, Manolis exhaled away his tension. He'd seen enough, time to go home. And yet, the distant, impenetrable detention centre drew him. He'd been denied proper access and desperately wanted a good look inside.

'You've got to get in there,' he told himself. '*Ta matia sou dekatessera.*' It was an old Greek phrase his mother used to say, meaning to pay close attention with fourteen eyes. It made no sense, but Manolis still liked it.

He locked the station, fought his way into his vehicle through the jammed door and wrenched the key clockwise in the ignition. Angling the steering wheel in the direction of the road heading north, he pushed his foot down and accelerated away. The town disappeared behind him, the asphalt unfolded before him, dotted here and there with potholes and clumps of rubbish. Manolis rubbed at his midriff, a low, grieving pain having taken up residence in his abdomen. He needed to rest. But he also needed answers.

He thought with distaste of the new fragments he'd seen of the world. One suspect had a strong reason to stay in Australia and intimate knowledge of stonings, while the other was a jilted ex-lover with no alibi. Manolis needed to reflect on all this new information. He felt drunk and sober at the same time, and painfully human. He wondered how Sparrow's bruised face was feeling. No sign of Kerr or Fyfe. No surprises there.

'Something's not quite right here,' Manolis said to the empty cabin.

He pushed his foot harder. It was an automatic action, done without thought, to hasten his journey to the detention centre. The speedometer stayed flat; the needle was broken, but he knew he was smashing speed limits. The engine groaned. The car shook. Better back off, he told himself. He was being unnecessarily reckless, and a dip and bend in the road was approaching.

He went to tap the brake.

And felt no resistance.

He pressed harder, felt the impotent gulp of the pedal, then his foot collapse to the floor.

Before he could react, the bend was upon him, the

wheels shuddering across the uneven ground, and the windscreen was filled with bushland and the thick white trunk of a fast-approaching gum tree.

28

This was not the first occasion time had stood still for Detective Sergeant George Manolis. Death had come for him in the line of duty before. He'd been shot at twice, had a druggie lunge at his jugular vein with a butcher's knife, and narrowly missed colliding with a crowded inner-city bus during a peak-hour pursuit. To Manolis, these were occupational hazards, and inseparable from the notion of a long and decorated police career. Compared to death's previous incarnations, the twisted trunk of a stoic old gum seemed like an anticlimax.

Incredibly, driver training at the academy had prepared him for this very situation. The gears could be used to slow down, or the handbrake, or guardrails by the roadside, even steering gently from side to side. A more impressive manoeuvre was to drive into the back of another car. On a country road, running through a series of wire farm fences would also provide ample resistance to reduce a car's speed. And finally, simply turning off the engine and letting the car come to a natural halt. Of course, all these solutions anticipated a driver's brain having time to choose the right course of action. But where a car had run off the road and was hurtling towards the unflinching trunk of a tree, the instruction manual was useless.

The dry dirt and long grass through which the car ploughed did little to shave any speed off the dial. The earth was still dropping away, almost launching the car towards a headfirst collision with the sturdy gum.

The car's safety features were minimal, if not non-existent. No modern airbags or crumple zones. This was no car — this was a coffin on wheels.

Manolis's survival instinct took over. He clenched the steering wheel with white knuckles, trying to regain control. He wanted to curse but there was barely enough air to speak. With the trunk drawing closer, larger, he sucked in a final breath. His chest burned and his throat tightened like a garrotte.

He braced for impact.

With what little strength remained in his forearms, he gave the steering wheel one last desperate heave.

The crash was swift, sharp and surprisingly ineffectual. The right-side mirror was ripped from its bracket and sent flying through the air like a cannon shot. The gum tore past, dry branches scraping the car's body, bark peeling like old wallpaper. The margin was so close that Manolis felt the shockwave ripple his hair. His windpipe relaxed; he grunted and swallowed, his Adam's apple lurching down his throat. The car was still careering down the grassy slope.

Camouflaged against the dry backdrop, a second hazard loomed in the scrub. It was a pod of smoke-grey roos, boomers and joeys, foraging for food on an otherwise uneventful afternoon. Sensing the speeding vehicle, they scattered in all directions, darting and hopping like furry maniacs. Manolis dodged left and right, turning the wheel frantically. Only by some miracle did he manage to avoid the mob; it would've been easier if they'd just stood still.

In the end he turned the wheel hard left, sending the car fishtailing to the right. Up on two wheels, it came close to tipping and running aground in the serrated tussock weeds that strangled the barren land.

Perhaps a preferable outcome over the car spiralling onwards and only coming to rest when it concertinaed against the trunk of another gum tree.

The earth shook. A scatter of white cockatoos spread themselves across the sky like a throw of salt crystals. Dead branches fell, small logs teased free, smacking against the metal roof and echoing around Manolis's ears. Flung hard against the steering wheel, the detective heard a dull crack implode in his chest. His kneecaps instantly burned, lacerated by the underside of the dashboard.

Had he blacked out, even for a second or two? Manolis could not be sure but he didn't think so. He credited the missing windscreen for sparing his head. Looking over to the passenger side, he saw it folded back onto itself like a crushed paper cup. He expressed silent gratitude to whatever unseen force of physics had caused the car to drift a few merciful metres and spare his life.

Slumping back into his seat, he felt his body pounding. Unspent adrenaline pulsed through his head and limbs. The bonnet and engine were smashed beyond repair. This was a problem, he reasoned, not from the perspective of how to get home, but because of possible evidence. As he shook his head from side to side, hearing his neck vertebrae click and clack, the question gradually crystallised in his mind: was the truck's sudden lack of braking power a random accident or something more deliberate? The vehicle was old, practically falling apart, held together with chewing gum and electrical tape. And the brakes had always felt spongy. But for them to fail altogether over the course of half a day was worthy of suspicion.

Forcing the stubborn door open with two kicks,

Manolis got out. But then the planet spun; he lost his balance and toppled to the ground with a thud. He tried to stand again, but this was suddenly an unexpected challenge. He rubbed his head, checking for signs of swelling or blood. But he was smooth and clean.

'You're fine,' he whispered to himself. '*Ola kala.* Keep going.'

Clutching the truck's cargo tray, he dragged himself to the rear of the vehicle, its uncrumpled end, and slumped to the ground. He calmed his breathing and heart, felt his pulse — it was low. His blood pressure was probably the same, which likely explained the issues with balance. His hands and feet felt cold, slightly numb. The early stages of shock, he reasoned. Unwanted, but nothing to fear.

The sound of a low-rumbling, fast-revving engine punctured the outback silence. Manolis fixed his eyes on the western horizon, squinting into the drooping orange sun, and saw a vehicle approaching at a dangerously rapid pace. It was driving erratically, following in his chaotically laid tyre tracks, and itself coming close to losing control in a skidding, sideswiping heap.

The vehicle continued to accelerate. For a panicked moment Manolis wondered if its driver planned to stop at all. He briefly considered his options, which included crawling back to the truck and sheltering in the driver's seat or climbing up the same tree that had been his own undoing.

But the car did ultimately stop, braking at the last second only metres from where Manolis sat. The fallout enshrouded him in a thick cloud of bulldust and made him cough through several seconds of suffocating air. When the haze finally cleared, he wiped his eyes and peered into the fierce light.

29

Kerr sprang from the Holden ute and ran to his aid. Her face was ghost white.

'Jesus,' she stammered. 'Are you OK?'

She crouched, gripping Manolis's shoulders warmly, running her panicked eyes all over him. He took some time to reply, her words settling into his adrenaline-soaked brain. When he answered, it was as if his utterances had been dredged from some muddy depth.

'I'll . . . be fine. It's just shock, minor shock.' He spoke in a small voice. Wincing at a pain in his side, he added, in an even smaller voice, 'Maybe a rib or two.'

'Shit. Your knees.'

Looking down at his legs, he saw rivulets of deep red streaming the length of his shins. He looked up again, finding relief in Kerr's sea-green eyes.

'They're just cuts, no damage,' he said.

She leaned in, tore his already ripped shirtsleeve and wiped his outstretched legs clean. 'What happened? Was it roos?'

'Yes and no. What are you doing here?'

'I ran into Sparrow — he said you went to the detention centre this morning for questioning, so I came to check on you.'

'Oh. Right. Thank you.'

'Did a roo jump in the way of your car? I saw a mob in the grass back there. I swear, those animals are the devil.' She went on to describe a bloke she once found dead after rolling his vehicle. 'A roo had smashed through the windscreen before panicking in the confined space and kicking him to death.'

Manolis waited until she finished fussing and met her gaze.

'Did you manage to buy groceries for your mum?' he asked.

Kerr knitted her eyebrows together, a perplexed look dawning across her honest country face. 'Come on, let's get you to a doctor. Can you walk?'

She helped him up, draped his arm across her bare shoulders for support.

'I'm fine,' he said, steadying his feet one after the other.

'You may be concussed or have internal bleeding. You wouldn't realise either. Let a professional decide.'

He clutched at his side, grimaced in pain. 'I said I'm fine,' he snapped. His tone was sullen, irritated by his new discomfort and status as an invalid.

Kerr eased him into her passenger seat. Her face was mask tight with concern.

'I wasn't asking you,' she said testily. 'I was telling you. Now shut up, you bravely stupid man, and let the bloody stubborn woman take charge.'

And with that, she slammed the door, started the engine and spun the wheels in the direction of Cobb's infamous base hospital. Resigned to his fate, Manolis ceased his protests, held his tongue and tried to ignore the sharpened dagger twisting into his ribcage.

They drove in an uncomfortable silence: the reluctant patient and his well-intentioned nurse. Kerr was careful to avoid potholes, of which there were many of considerable size. After some time, Manolis got to talking. He described the detention centre — what little he could — the suspects' interviews at the station, the guards, the accident, and finally the brakes, or lack thereof. In contrast to Manolis, Kerr seemed only vaguely interested in the likelihood of sabotage, and even less so in the murder investigation; she was solely focused on Manolis's health and wellbeing. He found it touching and frustrating at the same time. Again he reassured her that his injuries weren't serious, but he could tell her mind was elsewhere.

At the hospital, they had to talk their way past an imposing triage nurse fighting off an angry crowd tired of waiting hours in emergency. Their police badges meant nothing alongside claims of a child who had drunk paint and a bloodied woman punched in the face by her partner. The officers were pelted with profanities as they pushed in the queue. Manolis apologised, insisting to Kerr that this was all unnecessary, overkill, he really was fine, but she was single-minded.

It was at that moment that Manolis felt decidedly uneasy. He couldn't fully explain it but knew it was more an emotional reaction than anything physical, and all to do with his father. Even though he'd been back to several hospitals since Con's death, he was now, for the first time, just like Con — a helpless, vulnerable patient. The association momentarily terrified him.

Eventually, behind a thin paper curtain, Manolis was given a cursory examination by a kid doctor in a vaguely medical uniform. He had the bedside manner of a drill sergeant. Manolis was discharged with an opened box of non-prescription painkillers — four pills were missing — and a hastily packaged roll of loose bandages.

Kerr was furious, energised. Manolis was measured,

spent. Ultimately, he was just glad to be leaving hospital. It had been a formidable day and he needed to rest.

'You'll stay at mine,' Kerr said.

'But what about your mother?'

She jangled her car keys. 'Mum's fine. I lock her room overnight so she doesn't go wandering. You may have delayed concussion, so you're not staying on your own tonight. And besides, we should probably start to entertain the notion that you have a target on your back. What if someone *did* cut your brakes? What if someone *did* torch your car? Accidents happen. Or, they don't.'

Her focus had returned, broadened. Manolis wanted to reassure her, tell her he'd been hunted before. But he hadn't. He'd been threatened, of course, by junkies, wife beaters, rapists, paedophiles and murderers, though they never had the balls to follow through. The only truly unnerving incident involved an underworld figure Manolis had locked away: a hit man. From the dock he had promised to make Manolis his first assignment on release. He was still behind bars; Manolis was sure of it.

And yet, a strange restlessness and anxiety had taken up residence in his marrow. He didn't want to admit that this tiny mote of a town, his first ever home, had utterly shocked him. It had appalled and dismayed him. Did he really sprout from this rotten soil? Was this the 'true Australia' that so many proudly put forth as the nation's indomitable identity, the iconic outback plastered across tourist posters to entice overseas visitors? Were the resourceful small business owner, the wise Aboriginal elder and the resilient outback farmer no more than bigots, drunks and sexual predators? No wonder his father had left for the city; he'd seen the writing on the wall as a new migrant and decided to spare his young son the same ordeal. It was time for Manolis to leave too, steal a car and drive until he ran out of road.

But then he reminded himself to not be so impulsive, or act so surprised. After all, the reason he was on assignment in Cobb was because a woman hadn't simply been killed — she had been brutally stoned to death.

At least Kerr seemed normal. Manolis empathised with her silent but obvious mourning.

'It was arson yesterday, cut brakes today,' she said. 'What will tomorrow bring?'

Her blunt assessment of the situation rattled around inside Manolis's head as she drove. He decided not to mention the box of firelighters found near his torched Valiant. Had it really been cut brakes? Either way, with the pain in his ribs intensifying, he suddenly felt acutely mortal.

★ ★ ★

Kerr's house was a rabbity bungalow with a bay window, small porch and sun-faded picket fence. Despite Manolis's objections, she showed him to her bedroom, declared she would sleep in the spare, and went to check on her mother.

'Sorry the house is so stinking hot,' Kerr said. 'Our air con's broken. We used to be able to get it fixed fairly fast, but the detention centre ended that. The tradies all go there now as first priority.'

Manolis kicked off his shoes, made fists with his toes and tried to quieten his mind. He wanted to inspect the pickup, take a look under the chassis, see what remained of its brake cables. He also wanted to examine the parking space outside the station for leaked brake fluid. Next, he had a number of pointed questions to ask Facility Manager Onions. And lastly, he had to deliver an apology to Rex; old and useless as it was, the smashed-up vehicle was still his property.

Manolis wondered how bruised young Sparrow was feeling.

As he showered, his grazed kneecaps burned under the acid sensation of hot water. He changed into the men's T-shirt and shorts that Kerr had laid out for him with no further explanation. Examining his face and head in a large wall mirror, he checked for obvious signs of trauma, then lay on the bed. The light in the day was all but gone and his eyelids were heavy. Hearing a noise nearby, he snapped them open again. A big glass of water and hearty bowl of vegetable soup appeared under his nose, a saintly Kerr hovering behind.

'Made this earlier today,' she said. 'Two big pots. It's Mum's family recipe.'

With every generous spoonful, a soothing current of warmth gradually flowed through Manolis's veins. He slurped hungrily under the watchful eye of his benevolent host. He couldn't quite place his finger on it but there was something deliciously different about this simple bowl over all other meals in his recent memory. It smelled and tasted like earth.

'Mum and I have a small garden out back.' Kerr smiled proudly. 'All the veggies came from there. Fresh fruit and vegetables cost a bomb since the detention centre opened, and so does eating out. The garden is about the only thing Mum seems to genuinely

250

recognise and take joy from these days.'

Manolis looked down at the empty, soup-stained bowl.

'It was delicious,' he said. 'I'm vegetarian.' His tone was sheepish.

Smiling, she took the bowl with one hand and held out two painkillers with the other. 'Rest. Take a night off. The case will still be there tomorrow.'

Manolis gulped down the small white pills, then half a glass of water. They exchanged smiles. He thought about his wife, and about Kerr's former fiancé. He felt decidedly awkward lying in the bed where the man would once have laid, wearing what he assumed were his old clothes. The room was sparsely decorated, with not a single photo of cherished loved ones. Manolis initially found this strange but on reflection understood why a person might have chosen not to be reminded of their past, particularly if it was racked with heartache and pain.

'OK,' he said reluctantly.

Kerr held a finger to her lips to silence him. She smiled her snaggletooth smile and softly closed the door behind her. The rushing of the shower was soon heard across the hall. Kerr came across as an old soul; Manolis liked that.

30

Manolis promptly fell asleep in Kerr's achingly comfortable bed. But his slumber was brief, his sore ribs donkey-kicking him awake every time he rolled over. He heard the midnight fireworks again, closer now, only several streets away. Another shipment had arrived.

In the morning, the light through the curtains was thin, aquatic, the house several degrees cooler. Sitting up in bed, Manolis felt a dark and medieval pain muscle through his body. He rubbed his eyes, waited a beat, then gingerly got up, stretching every angry sinew.

After changing back into his own clothes, which had been magically washed and dried overnight, he went searching for his colleague and host. He overheard her on the other side of a bedroom door, speaking gently. Manolis didn't want to intrude; he only wanted to thank her and bid her adieu until the station. In the end he nudged the door open. Through the crack, he saw Kerr with an arm around her shrunken, blanketed mother, stroking her grey hair and gently asking, 'Do you remember?' over and over. Her mother's eyes were closed and she was breathing deeply. Kerr looked over, acknowledged Manolis through the gap. The detective nodded and quietly let himself out.

He walked to the station, the movement in his arms and legs making him feel instantly better. Breathing deeply, he filled his lungs with fresh country air. As usual, the day was inexorable, cloudless, the mercury cocked and ready to soar. The streets were empty, a great hush having fallen over the town. Manolis pictured Ida Jones with her cricket stump on her way to steal her morning paper. He thought about Rex and needing to explain why he was now walking and not driving.

As he rounded the corner into Endeavour Street, his vision became reality: Ida, splintered stump in one hand, newspaper in the other, head down, goitre out, plodding. Manolis thought the end of her stump looked decidedly sharpened, as if she'd whittled it to a deadly sabre point. When she raised her head and stump to face the oncoming threat, she recognised Poirot instantly and referred to him as 'the Arab'.

'You know, Inspector, something occurred to me after you left,' she said. 'There's been a stoning in Cobb before.'

Manolis froze.

'It was a long time ago,' Ida said, her turkey throat gobbling.

He pressed her for details: year, location, victim, perpetrator. There was every chance the old lush was imagining her today as yesterday, and simply remembering the case of Molly Abbott. Or it might just have been the gin talking.

'Long time ago,' Ida said. 'Happened outside town late one night.' She sounded utterly convinced by what she remembered, even though it was little.

'Another stoning . . . ? Are you sure, Mrs Jones?'

She didn't reply, walked on, stump by her side. Her civic duty completed, she now had drinking to do.

★ ★ ★

253

Manolis's route proved to be surprisingly direct thanks to some navigational tool long dormant in his subconscious. Unsurprisingly, the station was locked, empty. He sat on the steps and rolled the meditative cigarette he'd forgone the night before. He savoured the taste as if it was his last. You never know, he reminded himself.

Briefly, he mused on Ida's extraordinary claim of a previous stoning, before the two key suspects in the Molly Abbott case re-entered his mind. As far as he knew, Ahmed and Cook were the last two people to see the schoolteacher alive. One was a desperate individual who came from a country where such executions were known to take place. The other occupied the conspicuous position of ex-lover and almost boastfully had no alibi.

Ahmed's story and plight tore at Manolis most of all. To have endured all that he had and survived, only to find himself where he was. Maybe Ahmed should have stayed in Greece, thought Manolis. Maybe Con should have too. Quietly, Manolis was immensely proud of the response by his grandfather's country to the refugee crisis, his chest swelling with robust Greek blood. But, deep down, somewhere near his bile duct, dwelled the shame that he carried at his own country's reaction.

Ida's recollection continued to niggle at him like a horsefly bite. 'An earlier stoning,' he repeated to himself. Was that possible? He forced himself to think, swore that something didn't add up. He made a mental note to look into police records in the city.

Sparrow arrived in his jalopy, eased up outside the station with a mechanical shuffle. His face was even more swollen, an extra day's coagulation of blood.

Purple golf balls now clung to his eye and cheek.

'Look away. I'm hideous.'

'Horrific,' Manolis said.

'It was always gonna get worse before it got better,' Sparrow said heavily. 'How'd you go yesterday? And hey, where's your car?'

Taking up position in the tearoom, Manolis briefed him on the interviews.

Sparrow squared his jaw and helped himself to jerky. He chewed thoughtfully and deliberately through the inflammation.

'I've heard of that Pommy bloke,' he said. 'I'm not so sure about him.'

'How'd you mean?'

A blank expression washed over Sparrow's face as he scanned for facts to back his swift character assessment. Then he shook his swollen head.

'Dunno. Can't place him. Maybe that's the problem, yair. He's neither here nor there. Plus he's a whitefella. And not just any whitefella, he's the very first whitefella who invaded my people's country, an Englishman. I mean, c'mon, even his name is Cook.'

Manolis chuckled. 'That never occurred to me. Related to Captain James, you reckon?'

Sparrow went quiet a moment. 'Gotta be, direct line. Did he tell you what he was in for?'

The detective looked at him with alarm. 'Arson?'

'Really?' Sparrow snorted a laugh. 'Arson, eh . . . '

'No?'

'I heard aggravated assault. Bit different to arson.'

Manolis stared into space, worry etched on his brow. Had it all been a lie, a precisely honed charade? He could normally tell fact from fiction, but ever since arriving in Cobb he felt out of his depth.

'There's all sorts of hardcore felons and thugs at the brown house,' Sparrow said. 'I'm talkin' killers, rapists, paedos, kidnappers, dealers. All mixin' with the nice brown folk.'

'What, they're all in there together?'

'They used to be in protective custody in prison, then in a segregated unit at the brown house. But not anymore. Some are still awaiting their trials.'

'And they let these people roam free through the town?'

Sparrow paused. 'No-one knows that about 'em,' he said quietly. 'Outta sight, outta mind. The paedos are the worst. The reffos who have kids 'specially don't appreciate bein' housed with 'em. Can you imagine that, havin' kids and a paedo sleepin' a few metres away? You'd never rest.'

Strange, Manolis thought. That wasn't how Cook had described the felons at the detention centre; he'd said they were summary offenders, up for traffic violations and vandalism.

Manolis hitched up his trouser legs, showed his torn knees. Sparrow regarded them through pained, puffy eyes before looking away with disdain.

'You'll survive,' he exhaled.

As Manolis remembered the damaged vehicle, a vague panic buzzed inside his chest. He stood with purpose and gave his bony knuckles a brisk crack.

'Come on,' he said. 'I need a lift.'

★ ★ ★

Sparrow chewed as he drove, one lazy finger nudging the wheel. Manolis scratched at his dark dusting of new beard and eyed the road with an intense focus.

The roos were retreating with the rising sun, looking for anything that cast a shadow. Manolis asked where the other cops were. Sparrow said Kerr had the day off and that Fyfe would be in later. The detective wanted to ask Fyfe how his investigation was progressing and what he'd learned.

Manolis brought up Ida's vague recollection of a stoning from yesteryear.

'The old bat's brain has rotted,' Sparrow said. 'Or finally been pickled in all that gin.'

'So you don't remember one, or hearing about one?'

Sparrow shook his head. 'Another stoning? Are you serious? I'd bloody remember something like that.'

As they approached a sharp bend in the road, Manolis felt a clot of heat form at the back of his head. Pinpricks of sweat erupted on his forehead and the nape of his neck. It was an emotional reaction, a fresh memory of trauma. Having scanned the scrub by the roadside, his eyes following the wayward tyre tracks, he seemed to lose his bearings the further his gaze wandered from the road.

'Here,' he said uneasily. 'Stop here.'

Sparrow pulled over. Manolis got out and started walking, then stopped. He eyed the land, suddenly unfamiliar.

'You OK, boss?' Sparrow said.

Manolis touched his throbbing temple as if calling up a memory. What else was he forgetting?

'I'm fine,' he said. 'Just stood up too quickly.'

He walked on, muttering to himself in Greek and English, retracing the path of what might have been his last ride. He was shocked to see how far he'd travelled, the land had blurred past in mere seconds. He had to stop on several occasions, turn and look over his shoulder, then forward again to be sure he was on the right path. For a moment he thought his concussion was more serious, more delayed than he could possibly have suspected. He cursed his addled brain and walked on, soon jogging past tyre marks and scattered car parts. Finally, on seeing the executioner tree, he ran with relief.

The wreck was where he'd left it, now part of the landscape itself. Bending down, Manolis examined the wheels first, looking for weeping brake fluid and stripped chassis paint. But there was no fluid and no marks in the paintwork. It could be that the brakes had just worn away. It did happen. There was only one way to find out.

Easing himself down, mindful of his tender ribs and stinging knees, Manolis squeezed his cumbersome frame beneath the crumpled chassis. The brake cables were hidden at first, the pickup's underbody had been contorted by the impact, but when he found them their condition was unequivocal.

They had been severed, their hollow black ends appearing like sinkholes to hell. But had they been cut with a blade or snapped by the force of the accident? The latter was certainly a possibility.

'Only one way to find out,' Manolis told himself.

He had to stretch his arm further and run a callused fingertip across the cable's exposed nerve endings to diagnose. Feeling the smooth end, he smiled grimly.

31

Manolis stood, grimacing at the pain in his legs, his slowly scabbing knees. As he walked back to the road, his circulation returned, his muscles loosened. By the time he reached the car he had a target on his back but a distinct spring in his step. He was clearly making progress, and someone was scared.

Sitting on the bonnet, Sparrow acknowledged his superior's purposeful stride and promptly extinguished his half-smoked cigarette. They got back into the car and continued driving north.

They were escorted into the facility by a pair of guards, Deacon and a colleague. They heard men yelling, women wailing and children crying. Sparrow kept glancing over his shoulder and being reminded by Deacon to 'look straight'. Manolis asked if everything was OK and was told, 'Everything's fine.'

The cops were soon parked in the manager's office. Sparrow quietly mentioned that Onions had started working at the detention centre having been unable to handle life 'on the outside', and Manolis felt unnerved by the prospect of a personality who needed to return to a militarised zone for normality. Sparrow flipped Queenie the middle finger, which he hurriedly turned down as the door swung open.

Onions entered swiftly, glowering at them from his height.

'Detective, good morning,' he said, sitting. 'So, how did you go yesterday? I trust the detainees were escorted to your station in a professional manner, and that your interviews were worthwhile?'

'Yes, thank you.'

Onions refused to make eye contact with Sparrow or acknowledge him in any way. Manolis had to formally introduce his colleague and Onions fired a dismissive glance at Sparrow's purple eye.

Manolis flipped hastily through his pad. 'Before I begin, I wanted to ask about a few serious issues raised during interview. The first of these concerns allegations of sexual assault in the facility.'

Onions pressed his palms together, as if preparing for prayer.

'Go on,' he said uneasily.

Manolis recounted the details in a measured, dispassionate tone. It took a certain degree of concentration and self-restraint given his feelings on the subject. He was careful to pause to scan Onions' face for any reaction, whether appropriate or inappropriate. But he managed to remain stony-faced throughout the description and blinked only twice, lowering and raising his eyelids unhurriedly like a calm predator.

'Detective, has anyone actually visited the police station and officially filed a report of sexual assault?' he said.

Manolis looked at Sparrow, who was shaking his head.

'Well then, until there is such a report, I will take your concerns on advisement and have a precautionary word with my staff.'

Turning his head, Manolis pinched his earlobe in mild annoyance at the platitudes he was hearing.

Sparrow found his voice. 'I heard rumours of a gay asylum seeker being raped by two other detainees,' he said, before adding, 'But nuthin' official.'

260

The director fired a combative look at Sparrow, the lines on his face dark and menacing. 'I don't operate on rumours.'

'Perfectly understandable,' Manolis said. 'But it's also my understanding that these cases are rarely reported for fear of consequences. That's something that I, personally, believe to be true because I've seen it in broader society. Underreporting happens a lot in small ethnic communities where a social stigma is cast on the victims.'

'Same with gay men labelled a disgrace by their families,' Sparrow said.

'Women can be disowned by their families, or subjected to further violence,' Manolis added. 'In the most extreme cases, this has resulted in honour killings.'

Onions stared at Manolis for some time, his eyes fixed like lasers. 'Honour killings?' he said eventually. 'You mean, like being stoned to death?'

His words hung in the air. Manolis's brow creased. Sparrow's mouth fell open.

'I'm sorry,' Onions said. 'That was highly inappropriate.'

'Actually, no,' Manolis said, forehead softening. 'In fact, it was quite accurate. That's precisely what happens.'

'But inappropriate, given recent events,' Onions said. 'And far be it for me to speculate on a motive for Mrs Abbott's unfortunate death. But you'll have to excuse my cynicism, Detective. We hear lots of personal stories inside these walls, many of them contradictory and confusing. I am, of course, well aware that we have homosexual detainees and that they engage in activities beyond our control. Sometimes that turns ugly. Homosexuality is illegal in many detainees' homelands, with people imprisoned, tortured or even executed for homosexual acts.'

Sparrow snorted his contempt.

Onions ignored him. 'Other stories are complete fabrications, designed to enhance an individual's application for refugee status and asylum. I hope you can see why some people are motivated to make false complaints.'

Onions went on to detail some examples. Detainees who lied about their country of origin, their circumstances, even their names. Detainees with forged paperwork.

'My colleague here has mentioned fake passports,' Manolis said.

The director looked at Sparrow, now with a combination of surprise and admiration.

'In . . . deed,' Onions said with some hesitation. 'I once had a whole drawer full of them. Some were remarkably good copies, worth a lot of money on the black market.'

Manolis thought laterally a moment. 'Didn't you say the guards here wear portable cameras? Can I view some footage?'

'They do, but only in emergency situations, during riots and the like,' Onions said. 'The footage is routinely deleted if nothing significant is noted.'

Sitting forward, Manolis ran a hand down the front of his shirt, as if ironing it flat. 'Would you mind if I interviewed a few of your female detainees?' he said tentatively.

Onions' face pinched tight. 'As it happens, I would. It's a duty-of-care matter. Without an official report of an alleged assault, sexual or otherwise, I'm afraid

I can't allow it. I would risk breaching my government-appointed duty.'

Manolis felt decidedly powerless. Kerr had warned him though, told him that incidents were handled in-house. The centre was its own little country, and Manolis was a foreigner, an interloper, invading their territory, asking questions, sniffing about, causing trouble. His presence was tolerated at best. A murder enquiry under sufferance, as if he was being told: 'Consider yourself lucky we've let you see this much.'

He raised the assertion that utilities were cut off in the centre when detainees self-harmed.

'Again, those are standard operational procedures implemented by the Federal Government for the safety of those vulnerable persons in our care,' Onions said. He looked down, admired his blood-red tie, pulled it straight. 'Would you prefer we turned a firehose on our detainees instead? I'm afraid this isn't 1960s America.'

'Yes, but isn't it a punishment to the others, too?' Manolis said.

Onions moistened his lips. He stood, walked over to his rubber plants and squirted one of them with a light shower from a spray bottle.

'Self-harm is a weapon,' he said nonchalantly. 'Cutting arms, hunger strikes, drinking shampoo — they're all attempts to get out of immigration detention and into an Australian hospital. It's a bargaining tool, a form of currency.'

'It's a protest,' Sparrow interjected.

'Something I'm sure that you, as an Aboriginal person, would know a lot about,' Onions muttered.

'What?' Sparrow said. '*What did you just say?*'

Manolis held up a big hand to calm his colleague,

263

whose own hands were now balled tight.

'My colleague's right,' Manolis said. 'People are so desperate, they have only their bodies to protest with.'

'Or *negotiate* with,' Onions said. Gently, he wiped excess water from the plant's leaves with a soft tissue. 'It's attention seeking, all intended to expedite their release or otherwise work the system.'

'So what you're saying is that these people aren't actually suffering from mental illnesses?' Manolis said. 'No anxiety, no depression, no PTSD?'

'Put it this way,' Onions said. 'There's a reason they cut *across* their wrists and not lengthways.'

Sparrow leaned forward in his chair, spoke with controlled venom. 'So I guess sewing their lips together is a new fad diet, yair?'

Onions' own lips formed a half-smile. 'Look, son, I see what you're saying. And I do have a heart. I know Aboriginal people have been treated poorly over many generations, so you've every right to protest. But this place changes people over time, I see that too. Once-healthy relationships start to sour. People bounce from one detention centre to another; they get caught in an endless system, become more irritable and impatient. They withdraw socially, start to distrust others, doubt themselves. That then manifests in a number of ways. I've seen a grown adult man in my care stick paperclips in his eyes. I've seen others try to suffocate themselves with plastic bags and douse their bodies with boiling water. I've seen them slice their chests open, beat their heads on concrete, set themselves on fire and scream for their mothers. You don't see those things, but I have. And here's one more thing you haven't seen: me, spending long periods of time with all these people, sitting and talking and trying to convince them their lives are still worth living.'

He sat down. Sparrow relaxed his hands, let the blood return to his fingers.

'But there are good days as well,' Onions said. 'Recently, we've had some of our detainees start helping out at the abattoir. A job's a good thing, isn't it?' He smiled, baring wolfish teeth. 'Gives a man a sense of worth.'

Manolis agreed with the broad sentiment regarding employment, although he imagined the detainees' mental state was not helped by the fact they were in the business of death.

'And speaking of jobs,' Onions continued, 'here's something I think may be of interest for yours . . .'

He leaned to his right, disappeared for a moment behind his vast mahogany desk. Manolis heard him opening the bottom drawer and fossicking about inside.

The detective and constable glanced at each other.

When Onions reappeared, he held two sealed plastic bags that he plonked on his desk blotter. 'I pre-empted you wanting to search the two suspects' lockers. Naturally I can't allow that, although we do conduct regular locker inspections ourselves. Yesterday, to be thorough, we searched under their mattresses too. This is what the guards found.'

Manolis lifted an unruly eyebrow, immediately suspicious. He always preferred to source his own evidence, particularly in an environment where so much was controlled. Still, he realised he was limited in what he could do.

Onions disappeared a second time, now to his left, rummaging about in another drawer before returning with a box of prophylactic gloves that he held under Manolis's nose.

'The guards did the same when they conducted the searches. So you know.'

Manolis prised four mismatched gloves from the sticky, tangled agglomeration of rubber and latex. He handed two to Sparrow. They snapped them on, then each selected an evidence bag and began extracting items, laying them out one by one on Onions' impressively large desk, careful not to mix them. The bags were unmarked, though it was assumed Onions knew the owner of each.

Examining the first bag, Sparrow found clothes, stationery, three dog-eared paperbacks, a chrome wristwatch, a stainless-steel thumb ring, an overcrowded key ring, sunglasses, headphones, a pocket torch, a toiletry bag, batteries and guitar picks. Manolis's bag contained a bar of soap, bandages, painkillers, sunscreen, sunburn ointment, ginseng, a hat, a T-shirt, a pair of trousers, shoes, socks, nail clippers, a comb, hair gel and a jar of face-whitening cream.

'Some people, after they lose everything, try desperately to get it all back,' Onions said. 'Others realise they can never replace what's gone and learn to live with what's important.' He sat back in his chair and rotated his signet ring, set with a black bevelled onyx.

The officers had barely got through half the contents of their respective bags before the owner of each became clear. But it was the final three items, buried in the depths of one, that proved the most unexpected — and valued.

A full roll of black gaffer tape, a purse and a mobile phone.

Onions pointed a slender finger at the phone. 'Phones, cameras and assorted electronica aren't allowed in the facility, so that's contraband. We sourced the number, then asked the phone company the name of the owner to which it was registered.'

This was, again, police work by proxy. Manolis would have done precisely the same. He was surprised at the investigative power the detention centre wielded. But he reminded himself it was simply another institution of government, albeit at the forefront of the supposed war against foreign invaders. At least now he could independently verify the phone owner's information and confirm with the company.

'It turns out this phone is registered to one Margaret Abbott,' Onions said. 'Also known as Molly.'

Air forced its way from Manolis's lungs. 'And I take it that's her purse?'

'Correct,' Onions said.

Manolis opened the purse, checked inside. It was devoid of cash but still held identification, business cards, bank cards. The plastic sleeve was empty, without even a photo of a loved one.

'But wait,' Onions said. 'There's more.'

He reached into his jacket pocket and produced a single piece of A4 paper with official government letterhead.

'It turns out the owner of this bag had his third and final visa application rejected last Friday morning. That was his last chance to stay in Australia. He's due to be deported within thirty days. Molly had been helping him with his application. And can you guess why it was rejected?'

The officers shook their heads in near unison. Manolis took the paper, read.

'Our department did some searching,' Onions said. 'As part of our background checks, we needed a penal clearance from overseas — from Greece, actually. It took some time for it to come through. Greek bureaucracy is, shall we say, slightly less efficient than Australia's.'

'Noted,' said Manolis, looking up. 'What's the bottom line?'

'We found no evidence of an immediate family,' Onions said. 'So it turns out he doesn't have a wife and young daughter after all. He's lying. Ahmed Omari made up a family to improve his chances of a protection visa.'

32

Manolis requested a second interview. Onions acquiesced, though this time it would not be at the police station.

'What's your personal opinion of Omari?' Manolis asked. 'You said you've met each detainee individually.'

The manager thought a moment before replying. 'In my experience, detention brings about two kinds of personalities. The first become more reclusive, they stop talking, go into their shells. The second are the opposite, they're vocal and loud and boisterous. They're natural-born leaders who can bring together a group to support their cause, which is when you end up with twenty shirtless men on a rooftop refusing to come down.'

'And in which category is Omari?'

This time, Onions did not hesitate. 'The second.'

* * *

Deacon was soon leading Manolis to a part of the detention centre he had not seen before. Sparrow followed, evidence bag in one hand, second hulking security guard on his other side. Their destination was some distance away from the main centre, through long, untamed grass, towards the western perimeter fence. Their primary suspect was already waiting, and had been told he would not be returning to the main donga area anytime soon. Manolis had expressed

269

some concern at the prospect of a forced confession, but Onions had reminded him that the punishment was appropriate for breaching detention centre rules.

They walked about a hundred metres. Heat pulsed from the ground beneath Manolis's feet. They passed a small building, which Deacon explained was 'an ammunition hut, heritage listed'. When Manolis asked where they were being taken, the guard replied, 'The managed accommodation area.' It was not on any of the centre's official infrastructure maps. The four main compounds were clearly marked. But not this one.

The managed accommodation area was three blue shipping containers arranged in a triangle formation. Each container was secured with a series of thick steel chains and padlocks the size of fists. The containers were windowless and appeared to have no openings for daylight. They had structural damage and a collection of minor dents. Manolis wondered why there was a need for shipping containers when millions had been spent to upgrade the detention centre, and there was no shortage of space. Perhaps the very idea of baking in a dark box was in itself a deterrent.

The locks were unfastened, the chains rattling free like headless snakes, and the police were shown inside. Manolis stepped into the gloom with trepidation, his nostrils flaring at the smell of stale sweat that clung in the thick container air. A cluster of blowflies, fat and moist, rushed to feast around his mouth and nose. As he waited for his eyes to adjust to the darkness, a raspy cough resonated from a distant corner, echoing off the bare-metal walls before fading into insignificance.

'Crap,' Deacon said. 'Wrong box.'

'Jesus,' the other guard said.

Deacon pulled hard on Manolis's arm, yanking him back into the daylight. The other guard reapplied the chains and locks to the sound of continued coughing, then the guards led the police to the next shipping container.

'What was that?' Manolis asked.

'Nuthin',' Deacon said bluntly.

'Who is that person? Are they OK? Was that Omari? What's going on here?'

'Look, mate . . . ' Deacon frowned. 'You're here to investigate a murder. So just do that, orright? Anything else has got nuthin' to do with you.'

Manolis approached Deacon, stood in his personal space and smelled alcohol on the man's heavy breath, the remnants of a night of binge-drinking, of stress management.

'Bullshit,' Manolis said. 'Answer me.'

Deacon stared him down with small, crooked eyes. 'In accordance with operational policy within the centre, detainees who become abusive, aggressive, antisocial, noncompliant, who incite mass unrest, or who have undertaken real or threatened acts of self-harm are monitored in the managed accommodation area.' He spoke lethargically, as if reading from a work manual. 'Reasonable force can and will be used to ensure the safety of all persons in immigration detention, staff and property. The use of force is considered to be reasonable if proportionate to the risk faced. This includes use of the enhanced escort position.'

Manolis looked at Sparrow. His expression was blank; this place was new to him too. But the detective was incredulous at what he was hearing and asked Deacon about screening for mental illness, fearing the damage that such conditions could do.

'Standard operational policy, sir,' the other guard said in a reassuring, peacekeeping tone. 'It's for their safety and the safety of others.'

The second container door was opened. Manolis and Sparrow were shown inside.

The metal door slammed, plunging Manolis into a darkness blacker than any he'd ever experienced. It was immediately disorientating, his hands invisible before his face, even when he held them right before his eyes. The door's echo made his ears ring. And then, when the ringing had faded, there was not a scintilla of sound. Not a voice outside or the wind whistling or a bird flying overhead. The blackness was suffocating and seemed only to intensify the heat of the weathering steel. Manolis felt light-headed and detached from his limbs.

'Boss?' Sparrow said, voice faltering.

'Wait,' Manolis said. 'Just wait.'

Then, a voice, muffled. 'Hello? Is someone there?'

Before Manolis could react, the door reopened. Fierce sunlight spewed in. Struggling to focus, he held up a hand before his eyes. Blinking away the glare, he turned back and now saw the inside of the shipping container. There was a single bed in one corner: metal frame, foam mattress, military blanket, no sheet. The plywood floor was heavily stained. The walls were marked in certain places, deeply scratched, as if bodies had been purposely flung against them with force. The ceiling was painfully low.

And then, in the furthest corner, restrained in a chair with small rear wheels, was a man. He was facing the corner, his back to the door.

Ahmed's face was obscured, his entire head wrapped

in a white cloth. It was what Deacon called a 'spit hood'.

'He's taken to spitting,' Deacon said. 'Became agitated and hostile.'

Deacon untied the hood, removed it, wheeled Ahmed around. The detainee blinked wildly, his face brightening as Manolis came into sharp focus.

The second guard leaned into the container, his silhouette placing a portable floodlight and small battery-operated fan on the floor. He switched them on, and Manolis felt the thick air move, the cool relief, and began a gradual return to his body. Three plastic bottles of tepid water followed, rolling across the plywood. Sparrow picked up a bottle and offered it to Ahmed with a courteous smile. He gulped thirstily and clumsily, water dribbling down his chin and chest.

Deacon freed Ahmed's restraints. The detainee immediately stood and stretched his back.

'If you need anything, we'll be outside,' Deacon said. 'Give us a yell if there's any trouble.'

The door slammed again.

Manolis went and sat at the head of the bed. The mattress felt hot, almost damp with humidity. Around his shoes, big black cockroaches scuttled for cover.

Laying out the clear plastic bag on the bed, Manolis asked the asylum seeker if he recognised the items inside.

Massaging blood into his serrated wrists, Ahmed studied the items a moment, wide-eyed, then said, 'No.'

His one-word response resounded through the bare shipping container, as if to underscore his proclamation of innocence.

'Ahmed, these were found in your possession,' Manolis said. 'It is very serious.'

The detainee carefully re-examined the bag, clutching each item inside the protective plastic with analytic fingers. Manolis watched Ahmed's eyes closely to determine if his mouth would soon be speaking untruths.

Again he responded, 'No.'

The security guards outside — if they were still outside — made no sound. In the corner of the container, the fan whirred away, shunting around the lethargic hot air molecules.

Manolis went on the offensive. The detainee's monosyllabic answers had roused his ire. Energy leached from his body.

'No? What does 'no' mean?'

Ahmed looked at Sparrow, who now stood metallically, his warmth having faded to a leaden-grey glare.

'It means no, these not mine,' Ahmed said. 'Did guards find them?'

'They did,' Manolis said.

Ahmed rubbed his jaw, sat gingerly on the bed. 'I don't use phone. Not allowed. Is this why I am here, because of phone?'

Manolis straightened his back. 'You don't know why?'

'No. Guards come in middle of night, wake me with sharp stick in ribs, bring me here.'

In sympathy, Manolis felt his own ribcage, still tender to touch.

Suddenly, Ahmed grabbed at his back, rotated his trunk. His spine crunched and he let out a satisfied sigh. 'Better,' he said.

Manolis looked down at the wheelchair. 'That looks

painful.'

'Is not because of chair . . .'

Ahmed spoke dispassionately, factually. After the guards had woken him, they'd taken him to a darkened storage room. Using cable ties, they secured him to a bed frame with metal bars at the base. They then threw the bed up in the air, let it fall. It struck the cement floor with a crack. They called the game a strange word, something like 'zipping'. That was when he spat at them.

Sparrow smiled knowingly, nodded. His people had faced similar treatment. Manolis felt a sudden pain in his gut.

He shook it off and held the evidence bag before Ahmed's eyes. Clinically, he explained the gravity of the situation. It was the claim of a false family that incensed Ahmed the most, the personal affront. A thick vein seemed to grow in the centre of his forehead. Manolis thought to add that it was this revelation that made Ahmed's other claims harder to believe.

The detainee looked away, avoided eye contact, then hung his head low and began to mutter under his breath.

'In the name of Allah, I pray.'

Slumping forward, Manolis gave a long, tremulous sigh. Sparrow stepped from foot to foot, seemingly unsure of his place. The container boiled. Manolis fanned his face with his notepad and explained to Sparrow how the detention centre staff refused to tolerate religious practices. There were seventeen nationalities living together, and they were all made to feel like one generic unit.

'Let him finish,' Manolis whispered.

It was another minute before Ahmed looked up.

His eyes were clear, free of rage. He spoke calmly, his words measured and even.

'If items are mine, they must have my fingerprints.'

Manolis had asked Onions about that. 'We found no prints.'

'So they cannot be mine,' Ahmed said.

'Unless you cleaned them or wore gloves,' Sparrow interrupted. 'I found the same at the crime scene, not a single print.'

The detective shot the constable a stony look. Too much information, young Sparrow.

Setting the plastic bag to one side, Manolis moved a few inches closer to the detainee. 'Ahmed, you said you would bring me proof that you were here at the centre on Friday night. Do you have any?'

The young man looked down solemnly at his hands, before shaking his head.

'Then I'm afraid I can only go on the evidence before me.'

Manolis didn't want to say what was really on his mind, the credibility of the evidence found in Ahmed's possession. Could a guard have planted it, or was there a conspiracy that went all the way to the top . . . ? Manolis couldn't prove anything as yet, and he feared that if he tried to question Onions, he would be kicked out of town and off the case.

'I scared,' Ahmed said. 'I cannot tell between a nightmare, dream and awake. I have difficulty talking about yesterday, today and tomorrow. From when I arrive till now feels like one day.'

Sparrow scoffed. Manolis felt torn. The electric fan droned on.

'Ahmed, I know this isn't easy, but you can help us by telling us *truthfully* what you know,' Manolis said.

'Where were you the night your teacher died? Do you have a family?'

An uneasy silence filled the tightly packed container. The only sound was insects colliding with the flood-light, making noises like tiny circular saws. Ahmed's pupils jittered with shock, panic, fear. His hands were clasped together like he was holding a gun, his lips pressed tight in a hard, straight line. When he finally spoke, it was to his hands.

'When a Muslim makes pilgrimage to Mecca to ask Allah for forgiveness, they pass Mount Arafat. On top is small cement pillar. The bottom is dark from human touch, handprints. Muslims see pillar as Satan. Between sunrise and sunset on last day of pilgrimage, under the hot burning sun, we throw stones at pillar to banish Satan. It brings us closer to God and virtue.'

As if feeling that desert sun's very rays, Ahmed wiped the slick from his brow. Manolis saw a tear running down his cheek.

'One day, in future, mountains will be flattened. There will be no shade, and people will walk through heat to present their deeds before Allah. Everyone will be equal and same, no kings or presidents or businessmen. We can make amends now, when we pass Arafat, but not later.'

With tired eyes, he looked up at the officers one by one and added:

'This is what I know, and my soul is at peace.'

He stood, walked to the door with a slow, assured gait, and bashed on the wall three times. His powerful fist produced a clamour that reverberated off the metallic interior.

The guards appeared promptly with attitude and

277

impatience, faces like granite. Ahmed bowed lightly and gestured to Manolis and Sparrow, who were hastily accompanied from the grounds; short of making an arrest, they were powerless inside the facility. As Manolis was led away, he saw Ahmed being returned to his chair, his restraints and hood swiftly reapplied.

★ ★ ★

At the front gate, Manolis asked Deacon about the sickly sounding occupant in the first shipping container. His concerns were dismissed with the curt response:

'He'll be fine.'

Manolis folded his arms. 'Will he? Why don't I believe you?'

Deacon placed his hands on his hips, leaned forward, cocked his head. 'We get bugger-all help from you cops when we got trouble here,' he spat. 'Gimme one good reason why we should now give a toss what you bastards think?' He didn't wait for an answer, turned his broad back and retreated into the centre.

There were a handful of vehicles in the car park, all left at haphazard angles. Sparrow fumbled for his keys.

'Christ,' he said. 'Omari, eh? What a headcase.'

'Steady on,' Manolis said. 'The bloke's traumatised, scared to death. I would be too.'

'So you believe him?'

Manolis thought for a moment. 'I prefer to believe in evidence. That's where I'm stuck. What do you think?'

Sparrow shrugged. 'Headcase ... '

They got into the car, rolled down the windows, let

it breathe.

'What about the other fella, the Pommy crim, you gonna interview him again?'

'No.' Manolis pocketed his notepad. 'No point. I'm in no way convinced by this evidence, but right now it's all we've got to go on. And anyway, the Iraqi's done nothing to help his cause.'

'I've been on that side of the fence, yair. The last thing you wanna do, even if you're innocent, is help the bloody pigs do their job.'

Manolis was 'allowed' — as Onions had reminded him — to take the bag of evidence items. He wanted to compare the roll of gaffer tape with the one stored at the station, but he could already tell they would match. The purse might have provided some new information. But the key piece of evidence was the mobile phone.

These three items sat uncomfortably with Manolis. It wasn't unexpected for a killer to keep a souvenir or trophy of their victim, but these were unusual circumstances under which such a morbid memento couldn't be kept. Only a fool would try.

After a reminder to first check his brakes, Sparrow eased the car into gear and drove south. The ramshackle ugliness of Cobb appeared, expanding into the surrounding bushland like a malignant disease. My glorious home town, thought Manolis.

He still hadn't seen a detainee outside the centre. It felt like the mother of all ironies — the hostile local environment meant the detainees now retreated to the centre 'for asylum'. The townspeople had calmed too, perhaps sated by the progress of the investigation, or tranquillised by the continual intake of grog and relentless heat. Manolis was relieved. He'd grown tired of the fear-stoking, race-baiting, red-meat brain-washing that had been carefully calculated to appeal to residents' basest instincts. It had been annoying at first, but now it was just plain exhausting.

The station was locked; someone had already come and gone, their identity unknown. Sparrow said it was likely Kerr and not Fyfe because 'it looks like some work's been done'.

'Honestly, how do you put up with him as your boss?' Manolis asked.

Sparrow shrugged. 'Yair, we know the bastard checked out a while ago. Can't blame him, really — I mean, look at this town, only gotten worse since the brown house opened. Don't be so hard on him, he was once a great cop, feared by crims and respected by the community. He's just got one eye on the finish line now. And he'll be right, he's on a cop pension. Me and Kate are just waitin' for his liver to pack it in.'

'So who takes over?' Manolis said.

Another shrug. 'Dunno. Might have to flip a coin. Loser becomes sergeant.'

33

They stored the items in the evidence locker. As Manolis had anticipated, the seized gaffer tape was identical to the roll found at the scene. But as Sparrow had pointed out, the same brand of tape was available at the local supermarket, and otherwise 'all over town'.

Manolis decided against leaving the phone in an evidence room of questionable security — the device's contents were far too valuable. He kept it, along with Molly's identification, safely inside his shirt pocket. He had already placed a call to the phone company to chase up its records.

While Sparrow sat outside and smoked, Manolis made the most of the opportunity to pore over the evidence with fresh eyes. He scrutinised the items under the annoying flicker of the fluorescent tube. The tape, the Bowie knife, the rocks, the shopping trolley with its jammed coin all still appeared as generic as they had the first time. Inroads had been made with evidence found at the victim's home and in a suspect's possession, but Manolis ideally wanted something at the crime scene to better link the investigation directly with the murderer. Because the scene had not been secured, the items recovered from the area behind the oval were his best bet. And it was the rocks that intrigued him most of all.

He acknowledged that they were a random selection, literally the garden variety. But he doubted the ability of any killer to have simply collected them at the scene without some prior scavenging and storage. He wondered whether a witness might step forward who had seen someone gathering rocks. At the time, such behaviour would not have aroused suspicion, but it would be of great relevance now. Surely there had been some preparation involved. Or had there? Manolis doubted himself. How hard would it be to gather rocks?

Sparrow appeared, leaned against the doorframe, watched. Manolis's other thought was of a landscape supply centre or nursery in town, if they had any record of sales or perhaps even stolen supplies. Sparrow laughed at the mere suggestion of such legitimate, worthwhile businesses in Cobb. According to the young constable, the only plants that thrived in town were 'weeds and pot'.

'C'mon,' he said. 'I'm hungry. Let's get some tucker.'

Manolis exhaled, stood from the old banker's chair. 'Good idea. But first ...'

* * *

Rex and Vera were sitting down for supper when Manolis arrived to apologise for the loss of their pickup truck. This time, there was no turning down their welcome and hospitality, particularly when a casserole dish overflowing with Ma's famous lamb curry was presented as the centrepiece. Manolis thought the meal was a rather unnatural shade of orange. Adding to the sickening aspect was the wooden picnic table, which appeared a watery shade of green beneath the corrugated plastic pergola. Rex completed the dining setting with his home-brewed long-necks, to which Sparrow helped himself without invitation.

282

Rex took the news of his truck with indifference. 'It was a bomb,' he said. 'Just glad you're not hurt, Kojak, especially after what happened to your car. I'll go collect the wreck sometime, maybe get some scrap money for it.' He smiled.

Manolis was curious about this reaction, but at the same time unsurprised. The truck had been a heap.

After saying grace, Vera pushed hefty spoonfuls of goopy curry into Manolis's bowl. He resisted and stocked up on fluffy white rice and emerald-green peas. 'Mm,' he hummed, 'delicious, Mrs Boyd.'

She smiled, pleased to have again won him over with her honest country cooking. 'It's my own recipe, yep. The lamb's from the abattoir, with my own secret blend of herbs and spices. One hundred per cent local, all natural tucker.'

Rex spoke with his mouth full. 'I reckon that's why your dad's food at the café was so tasty,' he told Manolis. 'Back then, he would've sourced only local ingredients.'

Manolis recalled his father's cooking. Looking out across the barren land, he tried to picture a thriving vegetable garden. For a brief moment he could taste the richness of a slow-cooked moussaka on his lips, only to be left with an aftertaste of nostalgia, sadness.

'It's been good to come back to Cobb, to see the place where I've so many memories,' he said. 'I can still remember kicking a football with Dad on the oval.'

Sparrow laughed sarcastically and wiped the corners of his mouth. He chugged his ale and, suitably refreshed, loosened his tongue.

'Look, sorry. That just reminds me why I became a copper. Ya see, I never got to kick a footy with me old man, cos me old man was dead. Most of me family died young. And they didn't just die — they were killed by whitefellas. Whitefellas who then got off scot-free. Like the bloke who stabbed Jimmy Dingo.'

Mention of the name seemed to suck the air from the party.

Refilling his stein, Sparrow detailed the ritualistic, cold-blooded killing of his kin in retribution for such transgressions as 'bashing a whitefella' or 'sleeping with a white woman' or 'spearing a milking cow' or simply 'being Aboriginal'.

'Coppers didn't treat the deaths seriously,' he said. 'Bastards turned a blind eye. Dingo was the worst, though, cos the cops bloody blamed us. They wouldn't listen when we said it wasn't our tribal punishment.'

Rex scoffed. 'What crap. I know the events you're talking about, and they were a hundred and fifty years ago.'

'No,' said Sparrow firmly, angrily. 'This was less than fifty years ago, one generation, especially Dingo.'

'No it bloody wasn't — '

'So, Detective,' Vera said, 'There's good news, I hear.'

Manolis sat forward with interest. 'What's that?'

Her lips formed a tight smile. 'A likely arrest. One of those reffos up at the brown house. We're so very, very relieved. Patrick would be too.'

The detective stiffened, feeling wary. 'An arrest? Who told you that?'

There was a nervy pause as glances volleyed around the table. Manolis had reminded his deputies on several occasions that their work was confidential, that there was to be no gossip.

284

It was Rex's soothing voice that restored calm. 'Everyone in town knows,' he said coolly. 'It's all anyone's talking about. I just hope the bloke's in a secure part of the complex in case a lynch mob turns up.'

'Boat people who arrive without paperwork should be sent home without hesitation, end of story,' Vera spat. 'And particularly if they're caught destroying documents. It looks as if they've got something to hide.'

Manolis coughed, cleared his throat. 'I actually think you'll find that many 'irregular maritime arrivals' are threatened with death if they don't hand their passports over.'

Rex extended an index finger. 'Don't tell me about the hard time you've had, sonny boy,' he said to an invisible new arrival. 'The first thing you've shown me is that you have no respect for the laws of this great land. Why should we let you in? End of story.'

Manolis said that people who had fled their countries in a hurry were likely unable to gather the means to establish their identities.

Holding up his wallet, Rex said, 'What, they can't pick up one of these before they leave the house?'

Sparrow moaned and drank more beer.

Vera gesticulated wildly, almost theatrically. 'This country's had droughts, fires, floods and cyclones, our kids are self-harming and suiciding, and where's all our money going?' she asked, before answering her own question. 'To countries who wish to cause us harm, and to housing queue-jumping criminals.'

Clearing his throat again, Manolis said, 'A lot of these asylum seekers are stateless.'

Rex shook his head. 'I'm sorry, but that's crap too. No-one's stateless, everybody comes from somewhere.

Asylum seeking is organised crime. It's a racket, worth hundreds of millions.'

'A Royal Commission into Islam,' Vera proclaimed. 'That's what we need, a bloody Royal Commission. Molly's death can be the reason. Can you order that, Detective?'

Manolis gave her a long, ponderous stare. 'Leave it with me.' A blowfly circled his head sluggishly, like a floating balloon. He batted it away.

'Don't get me wrong, Detective, I'm a strong believer in being compassionate, yep,' Vera said. 'But our compassion should end at our borders.'

He wanted to ask when compassion had become a geographical concept, and what was its precise latitude and longitude. Instead, he ate some peas.

'If we take in these people, we encourage more to come,' Rex said. 'Cut off one head, another grows in its place.'

Manolis was loath to admit it, but the old man made practical sense. The global flow of human traffic was enormous, and criminals were exploiting and profiting with every rickety boatload.

'But have you actually seen the detainees' conditions?' Manolis said. 'I'm not sure where you heard they have air conditioning and flat-screen TVs. I've just seen the exact opposite. In some respects, it's more depressing than prison.'

Rex swallowed another mouthful of syrupy lamb. 'I don't believe anyone who says detention centres are harmful to a person's mental state. What mental conditions did they have before they came here?'

The detective found himself nodding. For all Rex's intolerance, at times he came across as rather informed.

'In that respect, you're right,' Manolis said. 'It's likely that most experienced significant trauma before their flight — torture, imprisonment, separation, rape, kidnap, murder. And probably deprivation of food and water, as well as homelessness. But to make it worse by housing them in cruel, inhumane conditions . . .'

Rex listened with reluctance, his brow tense. 'Sorry, but I still think a lot of it is behavioural. They don't get their own way so they act up. It's the same with children.'

'Hmm,' said Manolis, remembering Onions' insider assessment.

'Pa's right,' Vera said. 'When you stop the boats, you stop the deaths, yep.' The words sounded like poison on her lips.

Sparrow sucked his teeth. 'Dunno about that, Mrs Boyd. They still die. You just stop them dying at *sea*.'

She looked flustered, her face pink with defiance and anger.

'Well, a woman is dead,' she said flatly, her voice controlled. 'And not just any woman — she was our lovely schoolteacher and daughter-in-law. Here, in our little town, stoned to her brutal death. And more will die. We've got a human bomb on our soil with this whatchamacallit, Sharia law. There's absolutely nuthin' moderate about Islam; somebody needs to rewrite the Koran, write somethin' more peaceful. Like the Bible.'

Sparrow laughed. 'The Bible,' he said, wiping his eyes, 'as if. Fucking racists . . .'

The words had clearly been brewing in the young Aboriginal man's throat for some time.

Rex turned, eyed him coldly. 'Andrew,' he said calmly, 'criticism is not racism.'

The old man pushed away his empty plate and stood, turning his back on the dinner party and retreating into the confines of the office demountable, mumbling under his breath.

'Pa's right, yep,' Vera said solemnly. 'The word 'racist' has lost its meaning nowadays. It's just used to shut down free speech, you can't say anything anymore without offending people.'

The table fell silent. Sparrow turned sideways to stubbornly sip away at his beer and contemplate the vast nothingness of outback Australia. Vera watched him, unblinking, hateful. Manolis didn't know where to look. On the one hand, his hosts had been hospitable and were entitled to their opinions, which at times made sense.

And on the other, young Sparrow had read his mind.

* * *

The three of them sat there for some time, listening to the sounds of early evening. In the near distance, a trash of currawongs cawed happily from the branches of a swaying gum. They fell comically from branch to branch, appearing inept, clumsy, even drunk, before something startled them and they shot into the air like tracer fire. Vera began clearing the table. Overhead, the bug zapper fizzed, claiming another victim in its deathly blue bulb.

Manolis prepared to excuse himself, the evening over, until Rex surprised him by reappearing in the doorway of the demountable. Sparrow, now smoking a slow cigarette, looked up languidly, then away. Disregarding him, Rex approached the table and thrust

288

an old photo into Manolis's hand. 'Your dad and me,' he said. 'At the migrant camp.'

Manolis raised his brows. 'What migrant camp? You were with Dad at the camp here in Cobb?'

Rex looked surprised. 'Thought you knew. I first met him there. We were all single men at the time, so the camp was it. Once you got married, you could leave. So when your mum arrived from Greece, your dad moved out, and they started the milk bar. The rest is history.'

Manolis looked at the photo. The black-and-white image was grainy and torn at one corner. It was actually of four men in shorts and sandals — three of them shirtless, one with a towel slung across his shoulders, one holding a broom — standing in front of what appeared to be an army barracks. Their faces were indistinct, in shadow on a sunny day, but their wide smiles were obvious, proud and puckish. Rex pointed himself out — broad chest, hairy arms — and the man he identified as Manolis's father. Manolis, who had seen photos of Con in younger days, instantly recognised him from his hawk nose and cleft chin.

'Who are the other blokes?' Manolis asked.

Rex re-examined the photo. 'Can't remember. Poles, Maltese, Slavs, could be anything. Everyone was from somewhere.'

Manolis paused to consider his immediate thought. 'I didn't realise you were from somewhere,' he said.

Rex leaned in close. 'I'm Dutch,' he said under his breath.

Sparrow's cigarette glowed.

'The camp was actually a pretty grim place,' Rex said. 'It was horrible to live in and with mostly bad people. Getting married was your ticket out.'

Vera, collecting the last of the beer-stained glasses, smiled broadly, her grin both exuberant and terrifying.

'Too bloody right I was, yep,' she said proudly. 'Pa would be dead without me.' They'd met at a bush dance one warm summer evening. 'He was an excellent dancer,' Vera added, gently pecking her husband on his sweaty bald head.

Sparrow groaned, clearly tired, bored, sickened. With one final cock of his elbow, he drained the dregs of his beer. He looked around to see if any more bottles were forthcoming. When they weren't, he seemed to decide he was weary of the conversation, and the evening.

'I'll come by in the mornin',' he told Manolis as he got up, before turning to Rex and adding, 'Thanks for the grub and grog.'

At this opportunity Manolis also took his leave, asking if he could make a copy of the camp photo. Rex said he could have the original, that it was a time in his life he actually preferred to forget.

'Ma's right,' he said. 'She saved my life. And I am a bloody excellent dancer.'

Manolis thanked Rex for the photo, Vera for the meal, and Sparrow for the hard work and company. He took a few steps up the road before doubling back. Something had occurred to him.

'I know there's a Chinese laundry right next to my cabin, but I'd prefer to not have to mangle my clothes to get them clean. You wouldn't happen to have a washing machine I could use?'

Rex chuckled, wiped a fat finger across his top lip. He explained there was a small laundry room not far from the office, then showed Manolis the way. The

290

room was locked overnight but would be open at first light. Clotheslines were out the back, pegs provided. Manolis thanked him. He said he had a week's worth of sweaty shirts and was down to his last pair of clean jocks.

'In this bloody heat, the first shirt you hang on the line will be dry by the time you hang the last,' Rex said.

The brushtail possum was waiting for Manolis on his verandah, practically tapping its paw with impatience and hunger. Pleased to see his companion, he prepared another delicacy of stale crackers with peanut butter. Now familiar with the sweet and salty taste, the possum ate them heartily, even the tiny crumbs that fell around its paws. Manolis rolled his evening cigarette, smoked it as he watched. Above, the nighttime country sky began to appear, the stars and planets and moons.

'You know, mate,' Manolis said, 'it's actually not so bad out here, is it?'

The possum kept chewing.

Manolis looked again at the photo. How young his dad appeared, his brown face, bronzed torso, his whole body full of life and hope and vigour. How it would all fade to nothing.

Flicking his butt into the charred remains of his former car, Manolis sighed and went inside. He stripped, showered and was in bed before he heard the first explosions announce the nightly narcotic shipment.

Closing his eyes, he let his mind wander, replaying the day's events, the evidence, the conversations, things said, things left unsaid. He felt awful — a man he believed was innocent was being locked up and tortured by uniformed thugs, while the guilty party

was free. Could it be Cook? A guard? Onions himself . . . ? Manolis swore he was missing something,
something significant; something didn't fit. In the
brief moments before he lost consciousness, as the
darkness and silence closed in, he imagined his small
sheriff's office was the inside of a shipping container,
and that his head was wrapped in a tight, suffocating
hood.

34

Saturday morning came too soon. Manolis slept as if clobbered over the head. He heard the kookaburras first, laughing like madmen. He opened his eyes slowly, reluctantly, eyelids sticky with sleep, the morning heat suffocating. It was enough to sap his energy before he was even vertical.

Every morning since returning to Cobb, for a moment or two Manolis could not help but be reminded of Greece. With each sunrise, more boatloads of refugees arrived on its shores. The Greeks welcomed them, gave them shelter in disused hotels, fed them nourishing soups and stews, provided clothing and blankets, all without any government support. But how was this possible? As a country, Greece was bankrupt. The thought invigorated Manolis, gave him strength.

His mind switched swiftly to the case. He rose unsteadily, dizzy for a moment. The beginnings of a headache were kicking against his forehead. His neck was unexpectedly sore. Delayed whiplash, perhaps? He dressed and rolled his morning smoke. Leaning against the doorframe, staring out into the new day, he thought the decaying tourist park appeared rather serene, exquisitely dilapidated, a tableau of former glories and faded dreams. He had no idea how Rex kept the park running; it came across as a money pit.

Unsure of when Sparrow was arriving, Manolis decided to gather his dirty clothes from the cabin's various corners. Bundling the garments into a garbage

293

bag, he slung them over his shoulder like a swaggie with a bindle and set off for the laundry. The door was open a crack, a choice of four top-loading machines on offer, all with various dents and smelling of stagnant water. Manolis sighed. No chance of his clothes smelling any different, but at least they'd be clean.

There was no sign of any detergent. He scratched the back of his head and dumped his bag on the floor with a whump. Would he need to scrape together the leftover sludge in the four machines? He began searching the room for washing powder. The single shelf above the machines housed nothing more than a collection of faded women's magazines turning to pulp. Behind the machines, some old sheets of cardboard were stacked upright against the wall. Intrigued, Manolis pulled them out, held them up. They were posters, placards, slightly water-damaged from a leaking pipe. But the image was unequivocal: Rex's beaming moonface, airbrushed to make him look several years younger.

Manolis was now even more interested. A slogan at the bottom of the poster revealed its purpose — it was from an election. *Vote One, Rex Boyd*, in bold, dynamic lettering.

The man himself arrived carrying a washing basket overloaded with guests' sheets and stained towels. He saw Manolis examining his enlarged face and laughed.

'Like 'em? Bit embarrassing, really. They came from the city. Mate o' mine runs a printing company.'

The detective kept studying. 'Oh, that's right. From when you served on the council alongside Molly's dad.'

Smiling wistfully, Rex said, 'My platform as mayor was the local economy, and especially improving tourism, of course.'

Manolis stopped. 'What's that . . . ? You were mayor?'

'Bet you didn't know that, eh? But it's hardly an achievement in a one-horse town. I only narrowly lost the election, though.'

Manolis was momentarily transfixed by Rex's computer-enhanced eyes. 'Narrowly lost,' he repeated, mind working.

'Yep. But that's politics. Mug's game.'

Now slightly embarrassed, Rex grabbed the posters, put them to one side. He shot a foot out, kicked Manolis's makeshift laundry bag.

'Washin' ya garbage, are ya?'

Manolis explained what had led him to discovering the posters in the first place.

'Sorry about that, Kojak,' Rex said. 'Forgot to tell ya, we keep the detergent in the office these days. People nick it otherwise, snort the stuff, get high — I dunno, kids these days.'

He reached into his basket, poured a sprinkling of snowy-white powder into Manolis's machine like it was fairy dust.

'On the house,' he said.

Manolis smiled in gratitude before encountering a second challenge: loose change for the coin-operated machines. All he had were notes and small silvery shrapnel, five and ten cent pieces.

'Actually, these machines are old school, they take special tokens,' Rex said, reaching into his back pocket. 'We also sell 'em at the office, a dollar a pop. My shout again.'

Rex's wallet was leather, thick, much-loved, bursting with business cards and shop receipts. With a light metallic crash, he emptied the contents of the coin pouch into a heavily creased palm. Finding a token, he held it up between a stubby index finger and thumb.

'Cheers,' Manolis said, letting it drop into his soapy, slippery hand.

The token was a shiny copper colour, much like a dollar coin and about the same size and weight. But the edge was smooth, unlike a ridged dollar. Manolis found himself studying it for some time. It looked somehow familiar.

'Sorry about last night,' Rex said. 'Ma can go on.'

Manolis gave a noncommittal grunt, distracted.

'But I'm glad I found that camp photo for you,' Rex said. 'Hopefully it's a nice new memory of your dad. I know I really appreciate it when people show me photos of my kids I've never seen before. It takes me back.'

'I love it, thank you.'

Rex turned, began loading his linen into the nearest machine with some endeavour, the sheets tangled into unwieldy balls.

Manolis looked again at the contents of his palm, absorbed by the gleam of the token.

'Do any other machines in town use these tokens?'

It was a question that seemed to come from nowhere; Manolis hadn't seen a local laundromat.

Rex appeared to find the query strange but remained preoccupied, still fumbling to load his laundry.

'Other what, other machines? No. No other machines.'

There was a long pause.

'Oh,' Manolis said. 'Right.'

After Rex finished emptying his basket, he searched his wallet for another token. Manolis stood motionless a moment, garbage bag at his feet, eyes on the old proprietor.

'What's up, mate?' Rex said. 'Forget something?'

Manolis gave him a long stare, then blinked hard.

'Actually, I think I have,' he said, peering into his bag. 'I can't see my fitted white shirt here. It's brand new, Italian. You know us wogs, our fashion. I think I know where I left it, in my cabin behind the bathroom door. Back in a minute.'

He turned and left the laundry, footfalls crunching along the dirt path.

At that moment Sparrow's white sedan with blood-red bonnet pulled up. No windscreen. Manolis waved him down, threw himself into the passenger seat, garbage bag on his lap.

'You takin' out the trash, eh, boss?'

'What happened to your windscreen?'

'Incredible stroke of luck,' Sparrow said with a shrug. 'Some thoughtful bastard left the gift of a house brick on my passenger seat. It was just what I needed to smash against my head.'

Manolis fished some glass fragments out from under him, tossed them onto the bonnet like he was scattering seeds.

'Drive,' he said, his tone anxious.

'Drive? Drive where?' Sparrow said, cigarette in mouth.

'Actually . . . wait a sec . . . '

Manolis got out of the car, came around to the driver's side.

'I'll drive. You stay here. Keep him company.'

35

The voice of reason told Manolis to ease off. He was pushing Sparrow's engine too hard, the car's side panels shuddering, threatening to break apart like a spacecraft on re-entry. White cockatoos scavenging by the roadside flapped and squawked in alarm as he shot past. Roos scattered, for a change, as if sensing his urgency and recklessness.

'Slow down,' he told himself. 'Better late than not at all.'

He'd taken Sparrow's keys in case the station was locked, unmanned. For the first time ever, he prayed it was. But he needed to get back to the laundry room before suspicions were raised. How long did it take to find a shirt?

'Step on it.'

He saw it from a distance as he turned the corner on two wheels. Outside the station, a white truck, door open. Now easing off on the pedal and pulling up alongside, he saw fresh skid marks, could almost smell diesel exhaust.

Diffusing the engine gently, he eased from the vehicle with no sound, left his own door unclosed. He took three swift steps to the station doors. Locked, as expected. Fortunately, he had keys.

The racket could be heard from the entrance — swearing, clanking, complaining, banging. The single voice sounded on edge, panicked, distracted, the words emerging half-formed, simian. Manolis saw no-one, heard only echoes bouncing down the corridor in the sour morning light. Moving catlike along the hallway, he drew his weapon, kept it down by his side.

'Fucking hell,' said the voice with an air of resignation.

It was coming from the evidence locker. Manolis turned the corner, stood in the doorframe.

'What the hell are you doing?'

The man spun around. He held a screwdriver in one hand, mobile phone in the other. Seconds earlier, the screwdriver had been wedged into the shopping trolley — Molly's trolley — in a desperate effort to remove the washing-machine token stuck inside the lock.

'Are you tampering with evidence?' Manolis asked.

Sergeant Fyfe did not respond. Dressed in jocks and singlet, obviously roused from a drunken slumber, he appeared grim and pale-faced. It was patently clear he wasn't armed. The tendons in his neck stood prominent, knotted. His twitching pupils hinted at a racing mind, struggling to register what had just happened, and what should happen next. Manolis kept his arms by his sides, tensed, ready. Neither spoke for a few seconds, the conversation played out through silent but deafening stares.

Fyfe made the first move, dropping his phone, letting it shatter. He swung back to the trolley and continued to grind away at the coin slot with his screwdriver, as if Manolis was somehow invisible. The detective watched him for a moment, astonished by Fyfe's complete disregard. In the end, he extended his arm, flicked his wrist and whistled. With the light catching the gun's silver barrel, Manolis now had Fyfe's undivided attention.

The sergeant stopped straining, relaxed his arms

and held up his palms in mock surrender. 'What, you gonna shoot me?'

'Rather not,' Manolis said. 'Make a mess. But you can stop that now. I already know what's jammed in the trolley.'

'Yeah, but you need proof,' Fyfe said.

Manolis fished around in his pants pocket, extracted the laundry token. 'This is all I need.'

Fyfe focused on the metal disc gleaming between Manolis's fingers like a ninja star. 'Planting evidence, hey. Thass low.'

'Well, it was good enough for you at the detention centre,' Manolis said.

Lowering his hands, Fyfe looked at the cold concrete floor, tarnished with years of scratches and scuffmarks. He stared at it for some time, steadying his breathing, slowing his mind. Eventually, he started mumbling, cursing, blaspheming, a hateful mantra growing ever louder as his thoughts bubbled to the surface, spilled over.

'I told 'em they shouldn't have done it . . . Bloody told 'em, said to let it go . . .'

Manolis regarded him anew. 'Who? Told who?'

He already knew the answer. He just wanted it confirmed.

Fyfe tossed the screwdriver against the dented filing cabinet, let it rattle and roll to a halt. The trolley with its wonky wheel did the same, coming to rest at an angle in the middle of the room. Fyfe looked around, wanting somewhere to sit.

'Christ,' he grumbled. 'Need a drink. Too old for this shit.'

He found the least-full milk crate, emptied it of its contents — tools, knives, implements — and sat with a long, drawn-out exhalation that seemed to empty his whole body. His frame sank with gravity, then expanded, like a blob of jelly released from its mould.

With a casual flick of the wrist, and a firm 'ahem', Manolis reminded him of the cold metal object that was facilitating their conversation.

Fyfe waved his hand in dismissal. 'Put that bloody thing away, city mouse. You'll hurt someone. We're just talkin' here.'

'So talk,' Manolis said. 'Who was on the phone?'

The sergeant wiped his dry mouth with a big country hand. 'You know who.'

Retrieving Molly's driver's licence from his pocket, Manolis held it up. 'So why her, why their own daughter-in-law?'

Fyfe swallowed hard, summoning the saliva to speak. 'Politics,' he said softly, no tone. 'Bloody power and politics.'

The sergeant looked at Manolis with red-ringed eyes and spoke with the relief of someone in a confessional.

'Poor ol' Rexy. He ran his little tourist park for years. Good little business it was, honest and true, but it was dyin' a slow and painful death. So was the whole town, really. So he did what any loyal citizen would do — he ran for local council. He won, became mayor. Happy days. But then, the brown house loomed. Some people wanted it, some didn't. Rex didn't, but his opponent did. In the end it decided the election. People thought it would turn our busted-arse town around.'

Manolis nodded. 'Let me guess. They were wrong.'

'Been payin' attention.' Fyfe showed yellow teeth. 'Good.'

He explained that Rex returned to the tourist park,

but the issue burned inside him.

'As time went on, he saw he was right. That bloody place was eatin' our town alive. Shops were goin' broke, the extra traffic was ruinin' the roads, services and medicines and fresh food were in short supply. And crime was risin'.'

'Wait,' Manolis said, cocking his head to one side, 'when's the next election?'

Fyfe rubbed his eyes, screwed up his nose.'Later this year. Rexy plans to run, of course.'

Manolis blinked hard. 'Well, given what's happened to Cobb, he'd be a shoo-in. So why stone a poor woman to death? And why single out Ahmed Omari?'

A grin crawled across Fyfe's blotchy face.'As guarantee. Couldn't risk it bein' close. As for Omari, this is where it got messy . . .'

Fyfe looked away, tugging a thickened, gnarled earlobe. He explained that the idea came to Rex following an argument with Molly, after he'd discovered she was helping Ahmed with his visa negotiations.

'Poor Rexy felt betrayed, ashamed. Vera did too. Their kids were dead, their business was buggered, they had only Molly left. So they invited her round for tea last Friday night and confronted her for helping the reffos. But she didn't want a bar of it.'

'So he stoned her to death in retribution?' Manolis was stunned. It seemed like an extremely disproportionate and violent response, no matter the provocation.

'Nah,' Fyfe said. 'Not even Rexy's that bad.'

'Then what, how did she die?'

Fyfe smiled lightly. 'Well, you're half-right . . .'

He explained that Molly had begun to leave.

'She was really upset and wasn't payin' attention.

302

As she was backin' away, she tripped and fell on a step, hit the back of her head on some concrete.'

Manolis stared into space a moment, then blinked hard. It seemed to trigger his brain into action, his thoughts swiftly filling in the blanks. He was familiar with new 'one-punch' alcohol laws, which had come about from drink- or drug-fuelled assaults ending in death, often from a person's head hitting the pavement. The punch would concuss the victim, but it was the impact against the concrete that killed them, often from extensive bleeding on the brain.

'Molly fractured her skull and died instantly,' Fyfe said solemnly.

Manolis found himself subconsciously lowering his weapon, as if removing his hat out of respect for the dead. One by one, the pieces fell into place. The scenario Fyfe was describing explained both the trauma to the back of Molly's head and the lack of blood at the crime scene. She hadn't died there, beside the oval; she had died much earlier and elsewhere.

'Rexy said that he and Vera tried to help the poor girl, but there was nuthin' they could do. Nuthin' anyone could've done. That's when Rex got the idea for the stonin'.'

'So,' Manolis said tentatively, 'Rex stoned a dead woman to death?'

Patting his distended gut, Fyfe said, 'Thass what he told me. Made the best of a bad situation. Ultimately, Rexy only has the town's interests at heart.'

Manolis let the reasoning settle in his brain. Finally, he asked, 'So why'd you get involved, why help? Why not leave Rex to swing in the wind?'

Fyfe looked at him sternly, bullet-hole eyes. 'Why? Cos I hate the bloody brown house too. They're the real criminals here, not poor Rexy. Town's gone to shit ever since that place opened. Nuthin' but trouble — we police are run off our feet. I thought this might end things once and for all, close up shop. But all we've been doing ever since the bloody stonin' is puttin' out spot fires.'

Fyfe's description made Manolis realise he'd been away from the tourist park too long. He needed to get back, to make the arrest. He was confident that Sparrow could handle himself; he was bold and pugnacious. But Rex had proven to be more than capable too. Manolis had to go, and he'd take Fyfe with him if necessary.

The station's front doorhandle rattled. Light poured in as the solid wooden door creaked open. Manolis listened, unsure of who to expect. The rasping voice he heard was familiar, guttural and ragged. 'Bill? Bill, mate, you here?'

Fyfe called back. 'Geoff? Zat you, mate?'

The man's features upturned slightly. 'Yeah. Wanna make another report. Two more of me chickens, last night. Thievin' cunts.'

Turning towards the door, Manolis was about to approach the farmer, tell him to come back later to make his report, when he felt a sharp whack against his wrist and arm. It had been preceded by a near-instantaneous rumble, too quick to register. The impact of the hurtling shopping trolley made Manolis drop his weapon. It was seized upon by Fyfe, who now stood, barrel pointed squarely at Manolis's broad target of a chest.

'Yeah no worries, Geoff, mate,' Fyfe called out. 'Er, just a bit busy right now. I'll come by later on, see for myself.' He sneered at his new bunny with undisguised satisfaction.

Old Geoff the chicken farmer stood silently a moment, grey cogs creaking inside his brain, before ultimately shifting his weight and shuffling outside.

36

The station door clicked closed, a sombre, desolate sound. Fyfe motioned with the gun barrel, directing his new prisoner to the tearoom. On their way, he turned the knob, locking the station entrance.

The back of Manolis's neck began to sweat. His stomach felt greasy.

He fell voluntarily into a garden chair.

'So,' he said. 'Now what?'

Fyfe took up position a metre away, handgun still drawn. He stared blankly into the space behind Manolis's head.

'To be honest with you, city mouse, haven't given it much thought. I never pictured us here. You were s'posed to be Rexy's assignment.'

Manolis couldn't help but smile painfully.

'He burned your car, cut your brakes,' Fyfe said. 'But Rexy was only tryin' to scare ya off. Not kill ya. He's no killer.'

Pressing his hands together, Manolis interlocked his fingers, breathed. 'Either way, this has gone far enough, don't you think? Don't make it worse by acting irrationally against an officer of the law.'

Fyfe looked down at his steeled hand, hefted it, admired it. 'Mate. I don't think you're currently in any position to tell me what to do.'

He added a light whistle of approval.

'Nice. Solid, cold. So this what they give you in the city, eh? Bugger me. Stop a bull with this. Stop a truck. Out here, we're still usin' muskets.'

He aimed it above Manolis's head and pretended to pull the trigger.

'Bang!'

He laughed, a demented kookaburra, the pink fat under his chin wobbling uncontrollably.

They sat for a moment, tense silence, listening to each other breathe. Manolis couldn't tell whose respirations were shallower.

He thought again about the tourist park, about young Sparrow. His arse was on the line too, a situation of Manolis's engineering. It would be the wrong way to die, so impotent, so inconsequential. Being beaten to death was more worthy — abiding by his true self. Christ, the kid's bruises hadn't even healed yet.

'So how'd you get the detention centre to go along with it?' Manolis asked.

Fyfe grabbed his own piece of outdoor furniture, plopped himself down. Resting the piece comfortably on his hip, he pointed it squarely at Manolis's heart.

'Now the reffo, Omari, well, he was startin' to be a problem. Onions said he was becomin' a troublesome and dangerous figure among the other reffos.'

Manolis struggled to comprehend. This description of Ahmed didn't at all sound like the self-effacing young man he'd interviewed twice.

'How exactly?' Manolis said. 'Was he threatening them?'

'The opposite.' Fyfe snorted a laugh. 'Omari was becomin' vocal, political, argumentative, which began to fire up the other detainees. Onions was worried about his authority bein' undermined, about the peasants stormin' the gates, about a mutiny, bad press, and his arse bein' fried.'

The sergeant explained that Ahmed had been stirring the pot, talking to his colleagues, plotting, protesting, rioting.

'And for that, Onions blamed our darling school-teacher cos she was actually encouragin' Omari to speak up.'

Manolis nodded subconsciously. He'd have been speaking up too. And loudly.

'On top of that, I gave that prick Onions no choice,' Fyfe said proudly. 'I threatened to blow the lid off his little operation.'

Manolis looked at Fyfe blankly.

'What, you think I don't know what's been goin' on up at the brown house all this time?' Fyfe added.

Without warning he slumped forward. He pinched the bridge of his light-bulb nose and squeezed his temples, deep like irrigation ditches. Exhaling, he began to mutter. He spoke of a young girl, unkempt, bare feet, big black eyes. She'd one day run into the station and into his very arms, her slick, teary face leaving a wet imprint on his work shirt. This hadn't been long after the detention centre opened. He gave her food, water, wiped her snotty nose and moist cheeks. She stayed silent for a long time, unwilling to speak, not even to share her address.

'But she didn't have to tell me where she lived,' Fyfe said. 'I could tell.'

He returned the girl to the centre, met with her mother, asked her what had happened. Her daughter had needed to use the toilet, but the woman feared to take her there after dark. So she'd taken her outside and pulled down her pants, holding her in a squatting position near the ground. A security guard on routine patrol shone a torch at the young girl's vagina.

Embarrassed, she was unable to finish. The guard then refused entry to the staff toilets. The girl later wet herself.

'Pretty traumatic for a little kid,' Fyfe said.

Manolis nodded solemnly. He eyed the gun barrel, still aimed at his vital organs.

'The woman told me another guard asked to see her daughter havin' a shower,' Fyfe continued.

The guards had offered the woman dope in exchange for sex. When she said no, they offered her extra shower time. When she said no again, there was nothing more they could offer, so they raped her. They then told her that rape was very common in Australia and that perpetrators didn't get punished, so there was no point reporting it.

'The same thing happened in the town a while ago,' Fyfe said. 'With some truckies flyin' through.'

'Sparrow mentioned that. His sister,' Manolis said.

Fyfe coughed hard, avoiding his hand. He said 'that military fuckwit Onions' had given him seemingly sincere assurances that 'all complaints would be thoroughly investigated in a timely and sensitive manner'. In every instance, the end result was assured: 'Insufficient evidence to warrant further investigation.'

'Onions reckons the incidents are cooked up,' Fyfe said. 'That they're all just hype.'

'And what do you think?'

Fyfe waved a dismissive hand. 'Mate, I gave up listenin' yonks ago, gave up carin'.' He breathed, heavy. 'Grew immune to the horror, like in war.'

Manolis considered his colleague. And Fyfe was still his colleague, even with a gun between them. They were all one force, fighting the good fight. But this was an unfair fight, rigged from the outset.

'What about the Bowie knife?' Manolis said.

'My little touch. Wasn't sure the plan would work, so it was insurance. If it all went to shit, we could just pin it on that lowlife scumbag Joe.'

'Did Onions know who killed Molly when I was summoned to Cobb?'

'Nah. He genuinely wanted some outside help after the arson attack.'

Manolis rubbed the bristles on his chin. 'Omari. They stuck him in solitary.'

'Fuck Omari.' Fyfe's eyes grew wild. 'Fuck all reffos. They're no angels either. They lie, steal, riot — we're called to clean up fifty shades of shit. Guards do bugger-all, only fan the flames.'

He described detention centre workers who'd been caught robbing local shops, starting pub fights, crashing cars, all with impunity.

'Ya can't touch 'em, can't do nuthin',' Fyfe spat. 'They get sent home on medical advice or compassionate grounds or stress leave or some bullshit before we can get to 'em.'

He leaned forward menacingly.

'Can't blame the reffos. They're desperate, only fightin' back. Can't blame the guards, they're idiots, boys pretendin' to be men. So what was I s'posed to do? This is where Rex's stupid idiotic plan actually started to make sense.'

Manolis furrowed his brow. 'Made sense . . . ?'

Fyfe was tugging an ear, a dried apricot. 'I tried to do things by the book. Fuck the book. It all adds up to a pint of warm piss. Better to take care of business yourself.'

His gunmetal eyes smiled. Manipulating his fat clumsy fingers, he cocked the weapon.

'I'm really sorry, city mouse,' he said, shaking his head lightly. 'I can't. I just can't let this shit get out.'

Manolis swallowed hard, his throat dry, working noisily. His breath quickened, pulse surged, heat radiated from his cheeks. Should he rush at Fyfe? His muscles twitched at the thought, began to prime themselves. He would likely overpower him, push him backwards, crash to the floor. But the gun would flash, fire, the chamber would empty, smoke, hot lead. Was he prepared for a bullet tearing his skin, burrowing through arteries and veins and embedding itself deep in his internal organs? Or it might sever his spine, exit his back, drag viscera in its wake and leave him paralysed. That was, of course, if he didn't haemorrhage to death first.

Manolis hadn't been shot before. Cops who had said the pain was unimaginable.

'Can't,' Fyfe repeated. 'Just can't . . .'

The hollow in his voice, the repetition, were unconvincing. Manolis sensed he was trying to persuade himself.

'Then don't,' Manolis said calmly. 'Don't. Don't make this any worse.'

Their eyes locked, debated, wrestled. This was how animals solved conflicts, through imperceptible adjustments and complex micro-movements. Psychological warfare, more with self than with other, the physical act secondary, less important.

Fyfe's eyes were full of blood, his stare weak. He looked weary, as if he wanted no further part in this, but also unhinged. The gun trembled in his hand.

'Don't,' Manolis repeated. 'Give it to me. We'll go arrest Rex.'

Fyfe blinked. 'And then what? He goes down, I follow. This isn't some pissy traffic offence.'

He was right, of course. But Manolis couldn't admit that. He sat up, leaned forward, prepared to deliver his sales pitch.

Fyfe thrust the gun, met his advance. 'Back. Get back.'

Manolis got back. The gun seemed to hover between them, growing in size. He felt himself falling, losing what may have been simply the illusion of control.

'OK,' he murmured. 'Relax. We're just talking here.'

Standing up, Fyfe shunted his chair back. It tipped onto its cheap plastic side. 'Enough talk. You're fucking with me.'

'No, I'm not. I'm trying to find a solution, a way —'

'There *is* no solution, and only one way out. You die, I disappear, this all gets forgotten.' He extended his arm a final time.

Manolis tightened his hamstrings, tensed his calves and prepared to charge headlong into certain death. The air in the room was as tight as a held breath.

And then, from the near distance, past Fyfe's shoulder, came a sound. Barely audible at first, it grew ever louder, tapping, moving swiftly across the linoleum floor. Distracted, Manolis glanced. Not wanting to fall for that old trick, Fyfe didn't, until it was too late.

A swift swing and a firm blow were delivered with the fattest part of a baseball bat. It clipped the lowest point of the chin, sought to maximise the shaking of the brain in the skull. Separated from his senses, Fyfe's eyes rolled back into his head and he crashed to the floor, losing consciousness. The liberated gun landed easily at the feet of its owner.

Kerr was suddenly hyperventilating. The surging

adrenaline had caused her body to visibly pulse. Her words came out staccato, in broken pieces.

'Two cars ... out front ... doors open ... knew there was trouble. I keep a bat in my boot for emergencies, and sometimes for everyday errands, when the men of Cobb try to express their undying love for me.'

Manolis struggled to find his own air to breathe. 'Jesus. Sweet Jesus Christ. How much of that did you catch?'

She fell onto the sofa, clutching her chest. 'Enough.' She had station keys, of course, one of only two other people.

They went quiet a while, watching Fyfe's unmoving body, collapsed onto itself in an awkward origami.

'Dear God,' Manolis said. 'Thank you.'

She looked at him. 'No rest for the wicked. Next stop, the detention centre.'

He met her gaze. 'Indeed. Omari's still in solitary. But it's not just him who needs us now.'

37

They dragged the senior sergeant's comatose body to the drunk tank, each pulling on a flabby arm until his underpants crept down. Manolis tugged them back up again, stretched him out flat across the floor. Ducking into the equipment room, Manolis helped himself to two pairs of handcuffs. Kerr locked the door with an old iron key, added a bicycle U-lock around the metal bars.

'He'll rejoin the land of the living soon,' Manolis said. 'I'll pick him up some aspirin.'

Kerr secured the station. She was to drive north to the detention centre while Manolis went west. The detective felt torn. But he needed to get back to the tourist park and prayed he would find it just as he'd left it.

'You don't need me to come as backup?' Kerr asked.

He considered a moment, his eyebrows forming a tight chevron. 'Best you get to the centre. We need someone reliable there, trustworthy, to release Omari. I'll be fine.' He turned to leave. 'Just one more thing — and this may sound crazy — but has there ever been any report of a stoning in Cobb before Molly Abbott?'

Kerr looked at him blankly, her head tilted to one side.

'No,' she said at length. 'Not to my knowledge, neither as a cop nor as a lifelong resident. What makes you ask?'

He swallowed hard. 'Nothing. Just a theory.'

They drove in opposite directions, peeling away at dangerous speeds, skidding and fishtailing, competing engines revving into the distance.

* * *

Olde Cobbe Towne's rickety wooden archway threatened to topple over with the velocity at which Manolis drove beneath it. Slowing his final approach, idling to a stop, he surreptitiously parked behind a thick gum tree not visible from the office, then advanced on foot.

The tourist park was deserted. Not a soul amid the rack and ruin. A stray newspaper blew about in the hot wind, scattering sheets like flyaway dandelion seeds. No sign of Sparrow.

His gun poised by his thigh, Manolis first checked the laundry. It was empty. Rex's load was still spinning, humming like a centrifuge. Good, thought Manolis. As he came back out he heard a noise and drew his gun before being greeted by a stray dog, a blue heeler, all yaps and yips. It jumped up, paws prodding his knees, dry nose sniffing his crotch. Startled, he nearly unloaded his weapon into the innocent beast, which scurried away whimpering, tail turned inwards.

'Shit,' he breathed. 'Sorry, boy.'

The canine's enthusiastic bark alerted Manolis to the likelihood that his cover was now blown. He needed to move decisively, and fast. He felt his ribs, still a dull ache.

This was the first time he'd seen the office building with door closed, curtains drawn. Knees cracking, he crouch-ran to the demountable, circumnavigated it once. Peering into tiny windows, past sheer curtains and multiple Australian flags, he saw only slivers of ordinary domesticity: floral-patterned furniture, used newspapers, uncapped sauce bottles. No sign of movement or life. The boxy white station wagon normally parked under the carport awning was absent, deep tyre tracks in the dry dirt.

Returning to the sliding door, Manolis steadied his breathing, raised his gun to his ear and with his other hand knocked firmly, twice.

'Police,' he said. 'Rex, Vera, c'mon now, open up.'

No response.

He tried again, firmer, a steeled knuckle.

'Open up. Police.'

The sound of wind in the surrounding bushes and trees, a magpie warbling.

'Sparrow . . . ? Andrew, you there?'

The carport flapped.

Manolis briefly considered the time it would take to execute a search warrant, before drawing back his hand and shattering the glass door with the butt of his revolver. Careful to avoid the angular glass shards, he reached inside, flicked the lock, flung the door open and entered through the multicoloured plastic strip curtains.

Gun first, finger poised, twitchy, he searched the rooms one by one, moving swiftly, precisely. The outdated front office, the messy back room and overcrowded storage room. Then the cabin with its poky kitchenette, airless bedrooms and musty bathroom. The whole space had an interrupted feel, with opened clothes drawers and half-drunk coffee cups and uncooked slices of white bread still resting in the toaster.

Stopping at the fridge, Manolis lowered his gun. He rubbed his eyes, pinched the bridge of his nose

316

and felt the weight of the new world absorb into his bones.

'*Gamoto*,' he grumbled. Then, after a beat, 'Right.'

They couldn't have gotten far. He pictured a dour-faced Sparrow, palms raised in surrender, at the end of a muzzle or blade.

Not far, but where? Manolis ran outside, jogged down the centre of the tourist park's main street, now more than ever a ghost town. Surely there was a resident who had seen or heard something — a confrontation, an argument — or knew where they'd gone? The cattle dog reappeared, snapped playfully at his heels.

He passed half a dozen cabins, the general store, pub, barbershop, chemist, calling out whenever he caught his breath. He soon doubled back, returning to the first cabin, rapping on the sliding door. No answer. He tried the second, the pub, with more determined knocking, bashing, announcing himself as police. It was a risky move. In Manolis's experience, revealing his identity when knocking on doors kept hidden those with something to hide, or they were shortly thereafter seen leaping a back fence. In rare circumstances, cops were welcomed with flying bullets.

A half-face finally appeared from behind a curtain, its single eye big and bloodshot. Brilliant, thought Manolis, a junkie; probably high on meth, up all night, ready to fly through the door with a meat cleaver or disease-laden syringe.

'Yeah?' the eye asked.

Manolis pointed back towards the office demountable. 'See anyone leave recently? A car drove away, you see where they went?'

The eye jagged sharply sideways, revealing a splatter of swollen vessels, then back to centre. The words came slow, laboured.

'Yeah . . . three of 'em . . . two whiteys, one black . . . drove off real fast — '

'Any idea which way they went?'

The eye blinked once, twice.

'Umm . . . nup. They just left.'

Manolis checked his watch, precious minutes slipping by. Sensing his informant had run out of information, and potentially vocabulary, he bolted for Sparrow's car.

Manipulating keys, ignition, gears, steering wheel, accelerator, Manolis drove, the wind blasting his eyes and face. Fumbling for his phone, he dialled Kerr's number. She answered on the first ring.

'They've gone,' he said. 'Took Sparrow with 'em.'

'They took Sparrow . . . ? What, you mean they kidnapped him?'

'Seems that way. Big, stupid risk. I'm driving. But where do I go? Which way, what's to the north, what's south?'

Kerr sucked her teeth, scanning her local knowledge.

'Not much, really,' she said. 'You've pretty much seen it all. Detention centre in the north, then nothing. Aboriginal community south, then more nothing.'

The car dodged a pothole, clumps of rubbish, roadkill. The rotting carrion was covered in scavenger birds now trying to avoid becoming roadkill themselves. Manolis coughed exhaust fumes, spat flying insects and bugs. The town was fast approaching, growing ever larger in the car's non-windscreen. He would need to decide which way to spin the wheel:

318

left to go north, right for south.

'Can you get here?' he asked, his mind on a solution.

A pause. 'Not really. Got my hands full.'

'What's the problem?'

A longer pause. 'It's Onions. He won't release Omari.'

Manolis's forehead clenched. 'Jesus. Why not?'

'He said Omari was in the managed accommodation area for being abusive and aggressive to his staff.'

'Did you explain that he was innocent?'

'I did, but he doesn't believe me, doesn't trust me, I'm too junior.'

Manolis heard his breath, heavy, ragged.

'I told you,' she said. 'They do what they want here.' Her voice had taken on a sudden tightness.

Manolis breathed thickly, anxiously down the phone line. 'Just stay where you are. I'll be there as soon as I can.' He was about to hang up.

'Wait . . . George?'

'Yes?'

'There is some good news.'

'Oh?'

'Omari's wife and daughter just arrived.'

Manolis nearly ran his car off the road. 'What? You saw them?'

'It was fortuitous timing — one of the guards let slip.' She explained that Ahmed's wife and daughter had been intercepted aboard a fishing boat two nights before and brought to shore on a navy warship. 'It's a bit hectic here now, everyone's distracted, trying to work out what to do.'

'So Ahmed wasn't lying about his family,' Manolis said.

'No.'

He smiled, instantly lighter and energised. 'Be there soon as I can.'

Arriving at the T-junction, the town's major artery of Queen Street, Manolis sat, engine idling. Hands clasped in his lap, he closed his eyes and centred his breathing. He consulted his sixth sense. If he was on the run, which way would he go?

'*Ela*,' he told himself. 'Slow down. Think.'

Ten seconds passed. Twenty, thirty, sixty, scanning his mind, replaying recent events, even dredging his childhood, all in the hope that an arm muscle would involuntarily twitch and decide for him.

Eventually an arm shot out, grabbed the wheel. He turned it left, to the north.

The outskirts of town, the yellow remembrance ribbons still tied around trees and the turn-off to the detention centre were soon all in Manolis's wake. An increasing number of roos littered the roadside, starving, looking for scarce nutrients, or deceased, their carcasses splayed flat. Manolis drove recklessly, regularly crossing into the oncoming lane, eyes far into the distance, scanning the horizon for the rear of a speeding station wagon. The noonday heat blasted into the cabin like a hellfire furnace. His skin seemed to blister, his eyes burned. There was barely any traffic on the road, only the occasional chicken truck spewing feathers or rusted horse float that he overtook with ease.

What began as an indistinct dot on the horizon turned out to be a roadhouse, a last bastion for fuel and supplies. A hand-drawn chalkboard sign out front declared: *Last fuel, five hundred Ks*. There were two cobwebbed petrol bowsers beneath a metal roof that extended from a large tin shed. The signage was from yesteryear — extinct brands, promises of 'full driveway service', 'friendly, courteous staff' and 'home-style cooked meals' in florid cursive lettering. In its heyday this would have been more than just a place to refuel; with so many services on offer, it was a destination in itself. The proliferation of multinational burger chains had put paid to that, just as they had to quaint little Greek cafés in outback country towns.

Manolis parked, entered through a door with a large jangly bell. It roused a snowy-haired proprietor from his morning nap with a start, hand clutched to his chest, mouth gasping. When his breathing had calmed, he focused his rheumy cataract eyes on his customer, blinking through the milky-white. 'Help ya, son?'

Manolis asked the man if he'd had any other customers that morning, or seen a dirty white station wagon drive past with three occupants. The man looked out the window, then at the space above Manolis's head. He mumbled that he had, although admitted he wasn't entirely sure it hadn't been a dream.

'Are you real,' he droned, 'or is this a dream as well?'

Manolis gauged the proprietor was likely under the influence of some substance, illicit or otherwise. He didn't have time to find out. He thanked the old man for his time, bought bottled water and continued up the road.

He drove on, further into the great unknown, the badlands. The earth grew hotter and drier as if he were approaching its very core. The land was coarser now, the conditions harsher, the grasses shorter, tougher, trees stunted, clinging to life. Animals appeared more

321

primal and desperate: larger, more muscular roos, broad-shouldered, barrel-chested wombats like land-mines, hardened by the conditions, emboldened to take on anything.

It took some fifteen empty minutes before Manolis began to question his instincts, along with the dependability of the heavily medicated old man. He hadn't seen a single vehicle since leaving the roadhouse and had been flooring the sedan to its limit. He imagined he would have caught up with anything short of rocket-powered by now. Would he have to drive for hours, days? He might need to call for reinforcements here. Perhaps he should have already — not that his phone had any reception.

Another dead animal loomed ahead, this one stretched precariously across the centre of the road. Manolis narrowed his eyes, assessed the oncoming hazard and subconsciously eased his foot off the pedal. Normally he would have swerved past the beast and continued on, but there was something about this carcass, its orientation, its shape. As he came closer, he realised what it was.

He applied the brakes late, the car screeching and sliding to a halt, rubber burning off bald tyres. He sat a moment, inhaling the cloud of toxic gas, eyeing the mass with trepidation and panic, coming to terms with what lay before him. On the road, a trail of deep crimson snaked from a pool that haloed the body's head.

The arms and legs were flared in unnatural positions, the face down, eyes closed.

But above all, it was the clothes. Powder-blue shirt, navy shorts, white socks and sensible black shoes.

38

Manolis scrambled from his car, rolled the body over, face up. He cradled the man's limp frame in his arms, felt the head go slack.

'Hey,' he said. 'Hey!'

Constable Andrew Smith was unconscious. He was breathing — barely — in occasional agonal gurgles and gasps. His face was blackened, bruised, bloody, bones broken, clothes torn, grazes on his elbows, arms and knees. It was clear he had fallen from a car travelling at high speed. Whether it had been a voluntary or forced exit was harder to discern.

But it didn't matter how he'd fallen, all that mattered were his injuries. The weak pulse in his throat, the chill in his skin, even against the blistering hot asphalt. Sparrow was dying. This ghastly realisation dawned on Manolis in the same instant he ascertained that he was, indeed, on the right track. He eyed the road ahead: empty, but he swore he could smell petrol fumes on the wind. They weren't far.

He turned back to Sparrow, his handsome, damaged face, his twisted arms, bent at hard-to-view angles. The detective shouted the young cop's name, slapped his sunken cheeks, tipped water into his mouth. But his voice only echoed, the cheeks turned red and water dribbled out. Sparrow remained unresponsive. Time ticked.

Easing him flat, Manolis tilted his forehead and lifted his chin to open the airway. Blowing a large rescue breath down Sparrow's throat, he began CPR.

Waited, gave a second breath, watched for the chest to rise. No response. Manolis tried again, waited, same outcome. He slid his fingers into the opening of Sparrow's shirt; with one swift rip, the buttons leapt like hot popcorn, scattering across the warm tarmac. Locating the position of Sparrow's heart, Manolis began chest compressions. He counted thirty, gave two more breaths, repeated, waited.

No response.

Time ticked on. The fugitives got further away. And Sparrow drifted further from life and closer to death.

Manolis considered his options. All of them were bad. The hospital was miles away. There was no guarantee he would make it in time, he might already be too late. Perhaps it was better to drive on, to cut his losses and ensure that Sparrow's demise was not completely in vain.

Manolis stared at the road, at Sparrow, the road, Sparrow. He saw his father dying, blocked it out. He looked to the sky, to the boundless burning blue.

'*Gamoto*, fuck!' he cried in exasperation.

He needed to decide. He sucked in air, tried to clear the obstruction in his throat, coughed, spat, coughed again. He considered the expanse, the likelihood of the outlaws disappearing into the outback's vast nothingness. He'd heard accounts of criminals found hiding in the bush after many years, even decades, having assumed new identities or with no identities at all. Of others who had never been found. It was the rich convict beauty of the southern continent, the welcoming embrace of space in which to run and hide and disappear.

Sparrow's head grew more leaden in Manolis's palms.

'Fuck!'

The adrenaline hammered through his veins, his fight response in overdrive. How could he put the value of a good man's life beneath the pursuit of two worthless criminals?

The senior detective knew he would likely live to regret what he was about to do. But he had to try, even if ultimately it proved pointless.

Dashing for his car, he flung the rear door open. Returning to Sparrow's body, he manipulated it into position, took the weight and carefully lifted the young constable in a textbook fireman's carry. Ensuring even distribution across both shoulders, Manolis commenced a slow walk to his car, puffing like a powerlifter awaiting three white lights. He nearly collapsed for the pain in his ribs. Squatting, knees popping, he bent forward and eased Sparrow into the back seat. Only then did he hear the low rumble in the distance.

It was an engine, another car, driving at speed. They were coming back. They wanted to finish off poor Sparrow. And any witnesses.

Manolis hurried to buckle Sparrow in, lie him flat, make him safe. Then, removing his revolver, cocking the hammer, he crouched behind his vehicle, ready to spring an ambush.

The wind picked up, a hair dryer out of the west. Hot and harsh and unnatural, it blew coarse outback dust into Manolis's face, stinging his already-burning eyes. He closed them, which also helped to sharpen his hearing, allowing him to better discern the vehicle's final approach.

The sound of the car's fast-revving engine, unwavering, suggested it was not going to stop. Manolis's ears pricked, his muscles tensed. He was about to step out when he heard the brakes squeal, the tyres skid. He waited for the sound of opening doors, voices, footsteps, more voices, questions, doubts, 'What the fuck's going on here?', 'Where the fuck is he?'

Instead, he heard nothing. He stayed patient. He didn't want to face a pair of fugitives tucked away behind a steering wheel and a layer of protective glass; that would be complicated. He wanted this to be clean, calm and ordered. Hands in the air, give yourselves up, it's over.

But still, he heard nothing. Just the engine idling. Had they seen him? Were they preparing their own surprise attack? Manolis listened, tense, a current of sweat snaking its way down the canyon of his spine.

When he heard the engine pick up, he finally made the decision to stand, gun drawn. It wasn't what he wanted. He'd only fired his gun twice in twenty years, both times in response to being fired upon.

'Joe . . . ?'

It was Shrewsbury. The man killed the ignition, raised both hands in surrender. He was guilty-faced, as if he'd been caught doing something unlawful.

'Well, bugger me,' Joe grumbled. 'If it isn't Dick bloody Tracy.'

'Jesus,' Manolis said. 'I nearly blew your head off. Here, help me, quick.'

They carefully transferred the constable to the back seat of Joe's vehicle. Shirtless Joe shook his head and grumbled.

'He's not gonna make it,' he said flatly. He turned the key, made the cylinders hum. 'He's a goner.'

Manolis wasn't having a bar. 'Drive,' he said. 'Straight to hospital, fast as you can. Don't stop for anything, man or beast.'

Joe eyed the road ahead, shimmering with heat. 'Dunno, mate. Fucken roos on the road, fucken everywhere. You shoulda seen the mobs back there earlier. I had to slow, beep, swerve, beep again, stop. Dumb bastards pay no mind, they do what they want.'

Manolis looked back in the direction of Cobb. 'Just drive.'

'Yeah righto, I heard ya the first time.'

'You see a white station wagon drive past? How long ago?'

Joe stroked his chin. Manolis was already walking away when he heard Joe's long protracted drawl: 'Dunno . . .'

The response was not important: Manolis's course was already set.

He didn't even glance in his rear-view mirror. That was in his past now, in the lap of the gods.

He drove even more carelessly. With every rise in the road, every bend in the path, he refocused his eyes on the new horizon and imagined seeing the rear of a speeding white station wagon. And when it wasn't there, that only meant it would be there the next time he looked, so he'd better drive faster, harder, more daringly. The thought had occurred to him that they might have turned off the road altogether, gone bushbashing through the grassland and scrub, forged their own desperate route to freedom.

And then he saw it, just after the road's next rise. The wheels found the air, cleared the tarmac and returned to earth with a hefty, suspensionless thud. The chassis dropped, threatened to bottom out. The veins in Manolis's forearms thickened into tight cords as he struggled to retain control. Slamming his foot on the brake, he felt ligaments strain. He winced, sucking in hot air. The car pivoted, skidded. When it finally came to a standstill, it was at a ninety-degree angle to its original trajectory. He looked across his shoulder, out the driver's side window at the road ahead.

It was roos, dozens of roos, perhaps even hundreds — far too many to count. They blurred into each other, overflowed the road, spilled across the land. The asynchronous cud-chewing throughout the mob made them look like disinterested teenagers, rebellious, up to no good. They were assorted shapes and sizes, but all had the same look in their glassy black eyes. It was a look that reflected the depravity of their existence, the conditions they'd been subjected to and the treatment they'd received. Backed into a corner, abused, starved, they turned on each other, kicking and slashing and brawling for dominance within a hierarchy. And when they'd finished cannibalising each other, they turned their wrath on the nearest humans.

Re-engaging the accelerator, wheeling the car back onto its course, Manolis eased his way through the mob cautiously, almost deferentially. They were on his road, but his road was on their land. This level of respect heightened when he saw the likely reason behind their gathering: a trail of furry bodies, tails and paws and decapitated heads. The survivors sniffed at the bloodied chunks; a few lapped at the pools of blood before skipping away in revulsion.

Following the road, the carcasses, Manolis felt his mouth drain of all saliva and his stomach turn oily. He nudged the car forward gently, waiting for the living to move, lightly beeping his horn. A few of the more brazen, more combative specimens approached the car, reared back onto their tails and boxed with

328

their hind legs. The side panels were left with deep indentations, as if clubbed with a heavy implement. The lack of windscreen made Manolis momentarily fear for his safety, should one of the more belligerent boomers be bold enough to leap onto the car's bonnet; he would be powerless to defend against a forceful kick. Reluctantly, he reached for his gun.

On the road ahead he saw the thick tyre marks, and the darkening skid disappearing off into the surrounding scrub.

39

The wreck was close to inaccessible for the number of roos encircling it. At first Manolis tried to shoo them away, but he was forced to draw his weapon, raise it above his head and fire into the air like some traffic cop during a riot. The gun blew a hole in the sky, the shot resounding for several seconds. Startled, the animals bounded in every direction at once, some of them slamming into each other before finding an eventual path to freedom.

His gun still drawn, Manolis stepped cautiously towards the car with a great sense of unease. Sweat rained from his forehead; his fingers went numb. Not watching his footsteps and dragging his right foot, he rolled his left ankle on the uneven ground. Wincing, cursing, he staggered on. From the rear, the vehicle looked undamaged. The impact appeared to be front on, something as yet unknown, something beyond wildlife, which had left the occupants slumped in their seats. Or could it have been the mother of all roos? Manolis recalled Kerr's story about the local man kicked to death after a roo smashed through his windscreen and panicked in the unfamiliar, claustrophobic space.

Anticipating the passenger to be more likely armed than the driver, he approached the car's left side, finger on the trigger, watching for movement. Unperturbed by gunfire, outback crows circled overhead, raucous at full volume.

It was Vera in the passenger seat, her short, stocky

330

frame barely visible above the window line. She was at a sad, awkward angle, her head against the door, a punched hole in the windscreen the width of her broad, flat forehead. Coming closer, Manolis felt vomit rise in his throat. Blood was flowing profusely from a ragged, gaping wound that revealed her chalk-white skull and fleshy-pink brain. Her eyelids were closed. A grist of blowflies had already gathered, buzzing in and out of her open wound.

To her right, slouched across a bent steering wheel, was her husband of forty years. He was also unmoving, broken fragments of glass littering the dashboard onto which his arms now lay like two lumps of cut meat. The slivers caught the light, sparkled like diamonds. Manolis circled the front of the car watchfully, paying careful attention to the position of Rex's hands, cut and bleeding.

Facing the crumpled bonnet and concertinaed engine, hissing and leaking, Manolis finally saw what had stopped the station wagon's forward momentum: a boulder lying in wait amid a clump of long, concealing grass. Jagged and irregular in shape, it had likely been in that spot for thousands of years, continually and microscopically sculpted by scouring hot winds and rare drops of rain. The car had impacted head on, barely making a dent in the rock's surface but sending its occupants hurtling into the windscreen at deadly speed.

Christ, thought Manolis. They got away. I've failed.

Wiping his brow, he hung his head, sighed, felt the weight. He pocketed his weapon and stood before the wreck, eyed it with contempt. He imagined organising a tow truck, an ambulance. The coroner would be involved. Not that there was any rush. The only imperative for him now was to drive, again.

The case had slipped away, through Manolis's fingers. He had failed his duty to the dead. All that remained was to minimise the damage. A life still hung in the balance.

And yet, his anger persisted. He wanted to unload his revolver into the grille of the station wagon, blast it as if practising down at the firing range. But the forensics team would be all over the wreck and questions would be asked. It was a headache he didn't need, especially after the meticulous nature of the local investigation. He scuffed the earth with his boot, scattered dust, grimaced in pain. In the end, all he could do was raise his arm into the air and fire three pressure-outlet shots into the big blue ether.

The impact was made with the third charge, as its echo continued to sound.

Manolis was re-holstering his weapon, about to limp away, when he heard a noise. Turning, he eyed the wreck, its two quiet occupants.

'What the f . . .'

It was an arm; its position had changed. Hadn't it?

Manolis took a step, shielded his eyes from the glare, looked closer. The big black birds continued to loop overhead in threatening arcs.

Another step, a guarded hand on his revolver, finger twitchy. And then he saw it, for certain this time. Movement.

Cobb's former mayor reared up languidly like a corpse rising from the grave, bloodied head first, heavy like a kettlebell. He appeared to hover a moment, unsteady, before slumping back into his seat. He did not move again, as if that one simple corrective action had sapped his entire stock of energy.

But Manolis moved. Faster than ever, even with sore ankles, summoning superhuman strength and restorative ability.

Launching himself at the car door, he nearly yanked it off its hinges. Rex looked across at him, deathly white eyes filling with blood, turning pink. He did not flinch, try to escape or attempt to reach for an unseen weapon. Instead, his eyes and his whole face seemed to melt with welcome relief.

'Con,' he said. 'Con, ya bloody greaseball bastard. About time you turned up.'

Rex was concussed and had again mistaken Manolis for his dead father. Manolis paid little attention. At that moment he was more interested in saving Rex's life than hearing whatever ethnic epithets he had to share.

With great effort, Manolis guided Rex out of the cabin, helped him stand on jelly legs. The old man came groggily, deep-red blood oozing from an open head wound. His wife did not move; there was no bringing her back. Manolis checked his watch, noting the approximate time of death for future documentation.

He lifted Rex's arm, draped it across his shoulders for support, took his full weight. Together they hobbled to the car. Rex went voluntarily, without resistance, as if a friend, his designated driver, was escorting him home after a long night on the grog. Manolis eased him into the passenger seat, secured his seatbelt. Removing his shirt and rolling it into a makeshift bandage, he wrapped it carefully around Rex's head, stemmed the bleeding. He considered fixing handcuffs to Rex's wrists and reading him his rights, but decided that both acts would be futile.

Rex continued jabbering as they drove, the car briskly picking up speed.

'Con . . . Con,ya bastard . . . '

Manolis didn't know whether to respond to the confused babblings of an individual suffering a severe brain injury. He wanted to ask about Molly, to confirm Fyfe's story about how she was stoned. In the end, he stayed silent and drove faster.

The car was now travelling at drag-strip speed. Manolis squinted, eyes searing with the scouring wind. He kept one eye on the blurring road ahead and the other on Rex, eyelids heavy, head lolling, blood trickling. Keep him talking, Manolis told himself. Keep him awake. Keep the guilty hateful bastard alive.

'What's that, Rex, mate? Sorry I took so long. How are you feeling?'

His question went unanswered. Manolis looked across — Rex's eyes were closed, lapsed into unconsciousness. Manolis shook Rex's shoulder, returning his mind to his body, and repeated his query.

Another protracted pause filled the windswept cabin. Rex's breathing was laboured, shallow. When finally he responded, it was with eyes closed, in a barely audible whisper through bloodied lips and shattered teeth.

'Con . . . bastard . . . '

Manolis pressed his foot down harder. 'Rexy? Mate, you OK?' Rex was unresponsive, his breaths now depthless, lips turning blue. Manolis locked eyes on the road. And drove.

40

Hitting a reception hotspot near town, Manolis's phone buzzed to life with multiple messages. He didn't stop to check but knew who they'd be from.

The hospital appeared like a billabong in the dry, perilous outback. Manolis left skid marks in the emergency bay, showed his badge. Two teenage paramedics appeared, stubbed out their smokes, hiked up their baggy trousers and stretchered Rex inside. Manolis bent forward, hands on knees, and exhaled a tight lungful of brown air. Rex's injuries were extensive, his chances of survival slim, and even less behind the doors of Cobb Base Hospital.

Manolis saw Joe, back against a wall, smoking a tense cigarette with a faraway look in his eyes. The muscles in his legs convulsed to some hidden beat. They acknowledged each other with matching head flicks. It was a simple gesture that conveyed thanks and signified shared horrors of mercy dashes through blinding heat. Their missions were accomplished, at least for the time being.

Manolis walked over. 'Any news?' he said.

Joe took a vicious drag on his cigarette, the end glowing bright orange. He held the smoke deep inside him for some time before finally exhaling and shaking his head despondently.

Manolis returned to his vehicle, fell into the seat. Needing strength, he reached for his wallet.

'*Agori mou . . .*'

He stared at it a while, the tiny photo of a tiny face

inside the plastic sleeve, smiling, happy, wanting his dad. Young Christos was fast approaching his second birthday. Manolis had missed his first; he'd been working a case. It had been another nail in the marital coffin, and a major regret that he replayed in his mind every night. He hadn't been a good father. Too focused on his work, she'd said, too obsessed with the dead to care about the living. He hoped his son would one day forgive him. He hoped Emily would too.

Manolis had thought he was bulletproof, that divorce would never happen to him because he had borne witness to a long, successful marriage and somehow knew the secret. He didn't. His parents had argued, fought. They'd broken the odd dinner plate and door hinge. But they had never walked away. They knew what marriage meant, and that gnawed at Manolis like the blade of a dull knife.

His pocket rang. Straightening his back, he pulled out his phone.

'Finally,' Kerr said. 'Where are you?'

Manolis kept staring at the photo, scanning his mind for how to respond.

'I'm . . . in town.'

She paused, searching his voice. 'Are you alright?'

'One hundred per cent. Any update on Onions, Omari, his family?'

The reception dropped out; Manolis only caught half of what Kerr had said, asked her to repeat it. He heard the wind blowing down the phone line.

'No change, he's still in solitary. I haven't yet seen his wife and daughter; they're being processed now, admitted, which is taking some time. But you really need to come and end this.'

'On my way.'

336

Manolis turned the ignition and then the steering wheel in the direction of north. Driving to the detention centre, he felt an unfamiliar sense of freedom and relief. At last, this was something welcomed, a moment of joy and vindication. To Manolis, exonerating someone wrongly accused was almost as satisfying as convicting a criminal. And in this case it would be even more rewarding.

★ ★ ★

At the detention centre gates, Manolis was met by two guards who blocked out the sun. They were expressionless and armed, ready to rumble.

Kerr appeared. 'You made it,' she said, smiling.

Manolis examined her face all over. She was sweaty and creased, the dark lines in her skin reflecting an accumulated tension.

'You OK?' he asked.

'I'm fine. What happened, where's Sparrow?'

'Where's Onions?'

'He's coming now.'

'And Omari's family?'

'They're still inside.'

The two officers were led to the administration building where they sat and waited in the air-conditioned calm. Manolis asked for a cup of water, which he was given with great reluctance. He told Kerr about Rex and Vera, and Sparrow, of course. She was immediately distressed; she loved him like a little brother.

Onions arrived, tie straight, shirt immaculate.

'Sorry to keep you waiting, Detective. We've had a rather challenging morning with unexpected developments.'

'I heard,' Manolis said. 'I thought you said Omari made up a family to improve his chances of a protection visa?'

Onions's face flushed pink with embarrassment.

'Ah, so you do know. Yes, it turns out we were wrong. It happens from time to time — our intelligence isn't always accurate. In this case, it was the Greek authorities who made the error. You can see how it might happen, they're overrun with people and claims and are nowhere near as resourced as we are.'

Manolis needed to stay cool. This wasn't quite the stand-off with Fyfe or pursuit of Rex and Vera, but Onions was still a formidable individual within his kingdom. His time would come. Quietly, Manolis vowed to build his case, starting with Fyfe's testimony. But at that moment it was the asylum seeker's freedom Manolis had at the forefront of his mind.

'Well, that is unexpectedly good news,' he said. 'And I have some good news of my own: there's been a breakthrough in the Molly Abbott investigation. For the time being I can't say any more, but I can say this: Ahmed Omari had nothing to do with it. He's innocent and needs to be released from solitary ASAP. I believe Constable Kerr already informed you as such. No doubt Omari's family is desperate to see him after all this time, especially his young daughter.'

Onions looked at his staff, then back at Manolis. 'I understand that. But Omari is in the managed accommodation area for behavioural management. This area is for detainees who incite mass unrest or have undertaken real or threatened acts of self-harm. For people who are abusive, aggressive, antisocial or non-compliant. Omari spat at my guards, at my staff. That is intolerable behaviour. I assure you that we don't

338

like having to put anyone in there for any extended period of time. We take all other options first — it's a last resort. Ultimately, it's for their safety, and the safety of others, I can assure you. The government has a duty of care to protect asylum seekers from harm, and to prevent harm being caused by them too.'

Manolis deliberated, a long and restless pause. He resented hearing the same sermon Deacon had recited from the same operational bible. And there was an unsettling amount of 'assuring' going on. Finally, he asked, 'What's zipping?'

The detective's question seemed to come from nowhere. Onions' expression was blank. Kerr looked at Manolis with confusion.

'Sorry, what, zipping?' Onions asked.

'Yes,' Manolis said.

Another pause. 'Is that some kind of new drug?'

Manolis studied the manager, his face inscrutable.

'No,' Manolis said.

'Then I'm sorry, Detective. I haven't a clue what you're talking about.'

Manolis straightened his back and cleared his throat. 'It is my understanding that Omari spat at your guards after being assaulted during a strange underground practice called zipping, which he was subjected to due to his implication in the death of Molly Abbott. Because he is no longer a person of interest, I think it only fair that he be released from the managed accommodation area to see his family.'

The tone in his voice told Onions that something had changed. He swallowed.

'And then,' Manolis said, 'you also have some explaining to do . . . '

The two men stared at each other for some time.

'Of course, Detective. As I said, it's been a challenging morning. Right this way.'

They walked with purpose, and with Manolis now leading the way, bad ankles and all. Kerr followed, with Onions' lanky, praying-mantis frame loping a few metres behind. Two guards brought Ahmed's wife and daughter, their arrival now processed, their faces wet with joyful tears. Manolis greeted them warmly, the woman in a black hijab and the small girl in a grubby pink tracksuit. The child was malnourished, doll-like, a human whisper, but she couldn't stop smiling at the prospect of seeing her long-lost father.

Approaching the three shipping containers, Manolis felt his blood curdle. His breath quickened and the pulse ticked in his neck. The locks were unfastened, the chains released, the doors opened. Hard sunlight poured in, white dust billowed into the air.

Manolis was the first to enter. The guards stood back with Ahmed's family, waiting for him to emerge, to be reunited.

From the doorway, Ahmed looked like he was sleeping, head down, breathing deeply. His chair faced the furthest corner of the container. His spit hood was still firmly applied.

But then Manolis noticed that the detainee's hands were hanging by his sides, and the chair's wrist straps were unfastened.

And it was only when he approached the young asylum seeker that he realised that Ahmed wasn't sleeping, wasn't breathing deeply, and that part of his spit hood was stuck in his mouth and halfway down his throat.

He wasn't breathing at all.

41

Manolis clutched at his ribs, winced in pain. It especially hurt to climb stairs, which left him short of breath. But as the hospital lift was still stuck between floors, he had no choice.

With the local community keen for closure, Molly's funeral had been planned for some time and would now happen swiftly. The church ceremony was sparsely attended; word had spread of what had taken place. Principal Ian Searle delivered a short eulogy in the echoing nave of Saint Matthew's, repeating almost verbatim his witness testimony to police. The pine coffin was painted a bright sunshine yellow. Manolis was a pallbearer along with Searle and two detention-centre guards, their imposing bulk finally put to good use. Onions didn't attend, which Manolis noted. Joe Shrewsbury sat in the last pew and took regular swigs from a paper-bag bottle of whisky.

Molly was buried in the family plot in the adjoining cemetery, next to her parents Graham, the war hero and alderman, and Edith, the housewife. It was less than a hundred metres from where her life had ended ten days prior. There were no roses — Molly hated those. Wearing a corn-yellow tie loaned to him, Lee Francis Cook tossed a red gerbera into the grave instead. The guards shovelled dirt on top, tiny rocks raining on the coffin like hailstones.

Pushing through the heavy double doors, Manolis entered the intensive care unit. It looked more like an ordinary ward, such was the level of understaffing and lack of resources. Jaundiced yellow light pooled across the linoleum floor. Machines beeped mournfully, as if needing their own beeping machines. He had tried to visit earlier, but had not been allowed by staff due to the extent of the injuries.

He found a nurse, asked politely. Around her neck she had a surgical mask held in place with rubber bands, and wore smudged red lipstick. Coughing, she consulted the various scraps of paper in her pocket, and then pointed to a blue curtain hanging in the furthest corner.

Clutching the curtain's rumpled edge, Manolis braced himself for what was on the other side. He flung it open with a single, decisive motion.

Sparrow lay in traction, swollen eyes closed tight. The constable was breathing steadily, chest barely moving. A slow, digital beeping echoed from a nearby machine. His neck was fixed in a medieval brace.

Manolis stood beside the bed, folded his hands respectfully in front of his waist, and exhaled heavily. He looked down at Sparrow as a loving parent would look on a sick child. Feeling a presence, the young Aboriginal man stirred, flicked his eyes open. A slow but reassuring smile crawled across his blue lips.

'Serves you right for jumping from moving vehicles, Constable Smith,' Manolis said.

'Yair,' Sparrow croaked. 'But they were driving like bloody loonies. I felt safer taking my chances with the road instead of a tree or roo.'

Manolis wanted to tell him he was proven right. Instead, he suggested that Sparrow 'go buy a lottery ticket'.

'Prob'ly, good idea,' he said. 'Then I can retire early, and stop having all this bloody fun.'

'What did the docs say?'

'Just a few scratches. I'll be fine.'

Manolis rolled his eyes. He conveyed mild amusement but felt grave concern.

'I'll be fine,' Sparrow repeated.

Manolis touched Sparrow's arm, transferred warmth into his cold skin.

'I'm pleased, mate. Can I get you anything?'

Sparrow shook his head. 'Thanks for not letting me cark it. Yer blood's worth bottlin'.'

'Be seeing you.'

Sparrow gave an unconvincing thumbs-up, closed his eyes and slept.

Following the unmissable sound of torturous coughing, Manolis relocated the nurse, made a second enquiry. This time, he had to show his badge. The patient, he was told, was on heavy morphine.

Behind another blue curtain, a pair of bloodshot eyes stared at a hole in the ceiling. Manolis stood at the foot of the bed, his face hard-boiled.

'Rex, do you know where you are?'

The vacant red eyes drifted, met his gaze. Rex's head was bandaged like a clumsy turban, his wounds crusty with yellow pus and dried blood. Mournful streaks of silver ran down his face. Given the lack of hospital hygiene, Manolis was more concerned about the risk of infection than he was for Rex's injuries. Looking down, he noticed the hairless patch of skin on Rex's arm that he'd seen the day he arrived in Cobb. Rex had claimed it was due to a burn he'd got as a child. Manolis now realised it was where he had hung the gaffer tape during the stoning, before ripping it off.

'Rex,' Manolis said again. 'Where are you?'

Rex moistened dry lips, squinted. 'Con . . . Is that

you, mate?'

The bed's side rails were up. Manolis leaned in, cranked the handle and reluctantly raised Rex's head with three firm jolts.

The detective was dismayed. Despite days of recovery, the old man's brain was still scrambled. Manolis had prepared a list of charges including fraud, tampering with evidence, obstruction of justice and interfering with a corpse. He thought it still possible that Molly's death was murder, but decided not to pursue the charge because of the element of doubt. Not that there was any point placing Rex under arrest now. He would leave that to a later time, assuming Rex regained his faculties.

Manolis eyed the old man, searching for an approach. Molly's phone records had revealed the nuisance calls were from Rex, probably harassing his wayward daughter-in-law for helping a desperate brown man with his visa application. For an exiled politician plotting a triumphant return to power, that was unthinkable.

'Con? Is that you?'

Manolis was ready to turn, walk away. He was disappointed and dissatisfied. But then, he pulled up the plastic visitor's chair and sat. And for no reason other than his own amusement, he decided to play along.

'Yeah, yeah, mate. It's me, it's Con. Come to see how you're going. How you feeling?'

Without warning, Rex became agitated. He rocked from side to side and turned his neck in every direction. Manolis wondered whether it was the medication and considered summoning the nurse to administer a sedative. But Rex soon calmed and began babbling under the cloud of concussion.

'Have you killed him, Con? What have you done, have you killed Dingo?'

Manolis arched an eyebrow. Killed what? A dingo? Did he mean . . . Jimmy Dingo?

Speaking with no teeth, Rex was hard to understand.

'Stabbed him in the thigh? Oh God, Con . . . no.'

Manolis felt pinned to his chair, restrained by the chains of history. When finally he tried to speak, his voice was a dry whisper in his throat.

'Rex? The hell are you saying?'

The old man swallowed painfully, his mind apparently disappearing into hazy, grey thought. After a moment, a slow, gradual head shake emerged that filled Manolis with dread.

'No, mate, no. I don't understand and don't think I ever will. Even if your sister was pregnant, even if that's what they do in your bloody village. You didn't have to kill the poor bastard.'

Manolis stared at the floor in stunned silence. Over the past few days, Con had visited his son in increasingly detailed dreams, appearing as a young chef, a dying invalid, a gaunt spectre. Manolis wanted them to end.

The nurse had told him that Rex remembered nothing of the moments after the accident, the memories having already atomised in his mind. He had hit his head hard and would be experiencing the effects of delayed concussion for some time. But Manolis had also heard of people who had lost their short-term memory, and yet could remember things that had happened long ago.

Rex coughed, his lungs rattling. Manolis wanted to dismiss his words as gibberish, the output of a damaged brain. But terrible suspicions bloomed in his mind. And then the old man said something Manolis could not ignore.

'Go, Con, go before first light. Take your family and go. Leave the knife. I'll bury it where we said.'

'Where? Rex, where?'

Rex didn't respond. Manolis looked at him a long time, at pupils like drill bits.

What was he supposed to do now? He was haunted by people either dead or dying. Should he challenge his mother? It was futile; she would stay silent, out of respect for the dead. Was this the 'other stoning' from a long time ago that Ida had been referring to? It had to be; she must have confused the stabbing with a stoning. Both were ritualistic killings.

Manolis blinked hard. Could he still save this god-forsaken town . . . ?

Standing abruptly, Manolis dragged his chair across the lino with a grating drone. He leaned in close to Rex's face, tasted his morphine breath. They spoke a while longer in near whispers until Manolis swished the curtain.

'Rest up, old friend,' he said. 'It was good to see you.'

Without another word, Rex watched him leave.

★ ★ ★

Manolis drove to the station in Sparrow's Ford sedan, the passenger seat still stained dark with Rex's trauma blood. He found Kerr manning the front desk, looking bored, quietly writing reports. The sight of Manolis made her smile, adjust her ponytail. Approaching the counter he was cautious, almost self-conscious.

346

'They pick him up?' he asked, referring to correctional officers and her former boss.

'Yeah, the screws are transferring him now.'

'Good.' Manolis was satisfied. The thin blue line, while not entirely restored, had at least been outlined. Detective Inspector Porter had been very pleased to receive Manolis's recent phone call, and with the final outcome of the case. Those higher up were less impressed; a mess now needed to be cleaned up.

'What about Omari's widow and daughter?' Manolis asked.

'They're with a host family in a safe house.' Kerr gave him the address. 'Physically they're doing well, eating and drinking. But they're overcome with grief. The social workers visit each day. Fortunately, there's strong community support, they're rallying behind them.'

Manolis's eyes softened. 'I'll try to drop in on my way back to the city. And then do the same for Fyfe, deliver some flowers and chocolates.'

'No flies on you, eh, sport,' she said, folding her arms.

Manolis shrugged. 'I have my job, my family. And you do too.'

'But we need a new sergeant . . . ' Her words were earnest.

He came around the counter. She uncrossed her arms, let them fall by her sides. He extended his hand. She looked at it, at him, took it, shook. After a moment of awkwardness, they hugged. He smelt her shampoo, eucalyptus and tea-tree extract. He let go first. She held on a little longer.

He wanted to explain things. To talk about how returning home had made him fully appreciate his immigrant roots and wild refugee blood. To say how naïve he had been in not imagining how this case would challenge his values and beliefs. He felt angry and ashamed at what he had witnessed, as if he was unknowingly part of some perverse social experiment. He wanted to tell her about his son and wife and how much they meant to him.

But something stopped Manolis from saying anything, the words turning to dust in his throat.

'I reckon you'll do fine,' he said instead. 'You're ready, and I'll make sure that's very clear in my report.'

The hint of a smile appeared on her lips, her eyes half-closing.

'When this place wears you down,' he said, 'and it will, come visit.'

Kerr scanned his face for sincerity. He tried to make his eyes clear, calm, his forehead released of tension.

'Same for the city,' she replied, 'and you.'

'Don't worry, I'm not finished here yet.'

* * *

The detention centre was quiet; business as usual. Manolis summoned Onions from the front gate. He was again forced to sit and wait, watched like a bug under a magnifying glass by a trio of sunburnt guards who whispered and sneered. Deacon had a fresh black eye and mocked Manolis with his cut-down knife, holding it up and dangling it back and forth. The guards all had a good, hearty laugh. Manolis pitied them. These men were drunks, addicts, gamblers, perverts. They emerged from the fringes and ghettos, the slums and shadowlands. They had been raised by television and befriended by Catholic priests. They

348

spent hours in prison yards and before parole boards. And yet these were the same men who were now judging him. Manolis wanted to pulverise them with bare and bloodied fists, to string them up by their red and blue intestines.

He knew that Ahmed Omari's memory would haunt him like those of so many others he'd been unable to save. They all became ghosts who hovered above his bed when he slept, who crawled into his ear and appeared in his dreams, his nightmares. He was often trying to save them there too, his conscience conspiring to somehow place them in further jeopardy. And when he failed them a second time, he woke breathless and gasping for air.

Onions arrived, black-leather shoes polished to within an inch. He apologised for missing Molly's funeral, explained that he'd had other important business to attend to.

'It was unfortunate timing,' he said.

Manolis approached the facility manager, stood in his personal space, their chests threatening to touch. The sum total of his message was three words, delivered with quiet and clinical precision.

'Expect an investigation.'

Onions stared back coldly and breathed hot air from his nostrils.

★ ★ ★

Manolis returned to his car, reached into his pocket and retrieved his tobacco and papers. He eyed them a moment, then screwed them into a tight ball and hurled them to the floor.

Reaching into his other pocket, he found his phone.

One bar of reception. It was enough.

'Hello? Hello, Em . . . ? Hi. Sorry it's been a few weeks, and thanks for answering.'

They spoke a while. When Manolis finally hung up, he'd organised a weekend playdate at a suburban park, and had soft tears in his eyes.

Down the road, he stopped at the Cobb Friendly Grocer, helped himself to a shopping trolley with a wonky wheel. He traversed the aisles, picking up bottles of tepid mineral water, expired blocks of dark chocolate and a garden shovel from the same aisle as the rolls of gaffer tape. He paid an exorbitant outback sum and asked the pimple-faced attendant for directions.

Accelerating through town, Manolis passed groups of men swilling from bottles. Bins overflowed, loose newspapers blew, wandering the streets like stray dogs. He continued on through the settlement south of town, the one-room tenements, corrugated metal and wood scraps and earthen floors. He slowed at first but then picked up speed when the locals showered his vehicle with cans, bottles and rocks.

Reaching his destination, first by car, then on foot, Manolis cocked his elbow, drained half a water bottle with a sharp crack. The mineral belch that followed scattered the assembled kangaroos in all directions. At least his ribs were pain free, for which he was grateful. Dark clouds were massing, the first Manolis had seen since leaving the city. In the middle distance, a cloudburst dumped precious rain onto the parched land.

Bending his back, he broke the earth in the scrub with his blade and started digging.

Acknowledgements

Sincere thanks to Dexter Petley of Jericho Writers for astute editorial advice and patience; to Jonathan Myerson and Claire McGowan at City University, London for the opportunity; to Katharina Bielenberg and Barry Scott for incredible publishing; to Kate Goldsworthy for unparalleled editing; to Zoë Waldie for insight and guidance; to Kathryn Heyman for wisdom and mentoring; to Jeanine Leane, Kerry Reed-Gilbert and the First Nations Australia Writers Network (FNAWN), and Sayed Hussainizada, Jerome Mukiza Rugaruza, the Asylum Seeker Resource Centre (ASRC) and Migrant and Refugee Settlement Services Australia (MARSS) for helpful comments; to Frances Fyfield and Dreda Say Mitchell of the Arvon Foundation for early instruction and encouragement; to Lee Gordon, Anthony Ferguson and Maurits Zwankhuizen for reading and feedback; to Martin Shaw for being an agent extraordinaire; and to my family for their enduring love, support and belief.